A
KIND
AND
SAVAGE
PLACE

A
KIND
AND
SAVAGE
PLACE

RICHARD HELMS

First published by Level Best Books/New Arc 2022

This novel is entirely a work of fiction. The names, characters and incidents portrayed in it are the work of the author's imagination. Any resemblance to actual persons, living or dead, events or localities is entirely coincidental.

Cover image courtesy of Menno Van Der Haven / Dreamstime.com

A small portion of this book was previously published under the title "Goodnight Saigon" in the anthology Only The Good Die Young, Crime Fiction Inspired by the Songs of Billy Joel, edited by Josh Pachter.

First edition

ISBN: 978-1-68512-077-1

Cover art by Level Best Designs

This book was professionally typeset on Reedsy.
Find out more at reedsy.com

For Elaine

Praise for A KIND AND SAVAGE PLACE

"Heart-breaking, unflinching, and evocative—Richard Helms' wide-screen coming of age historical novel creates a new Spoon River. The fabric of a small town and its residents is woven with hopes and fears, with love and bitterness, with the power of family and obligation, and with relentless and devastating change. Fans of Wiley Cash and William Kent Krueger will be especially drawn to this multi-generational clash of cultures—and the life-changing lessons, large and small, that must continue to be learned."—Hank Phillippi Ryan *USA Today* Bestselling Author

Chapter One

C lyde Dillard once witnessed a cat funeral.

It was a hot night. 1942. He slept in his bedroom on the ground floor of his parents' house in Prosperity, North Carolina. The house was divided into two wings, separated by a breezeway with jalousie windows that opened on sweltering summer nights so people could sip iced tea with lemonade and listen to *Lum and Abner* or *The Shadow* on the radio without melting into skin puddles on the flagstone floor.

Clyde lay on the sheets in his skivvies, the window open so the breeze could waft across his pudgy, sweaty body. Outside, the glow from a streetlamp splashed in every direction, creating ghostly shadows on the trees.

It was after three in the morning. Dozing fitfully, Clyde didn't hear the brief screech of brakes or the sudden death outside his window.

He awakened sometime later to a keening howl. He recalled the stories Aunt Kelly had told him of banshees, the ethereal beings who sat on a family's doorstep and heralded death inside. His heart skipped a beat as he imagined a banshee had come to visit their home, the moaning screech rising and falling over and over.

Shaking, he drew back the curtains and rubbed his eyes. There was no ghost, no howling specter. Instead, he saw a circle of cats crouched under the streetlight, outside the brilliantly lighted circle on the asphalt. In the center of the circle lay the motionless body of a tabby, its head at a precarious angle, its scruffy body sprawled carelessly. The circle of cats took turns eulogizing him in their mournful, howling cries, each feline lamenting the tabby's passing in turn.

As if on a signal, the circle of cats slowly dispersed. Each member of the funeral party slinked out of the spill until only a single, melancholy mourner was left. This last cat stretched, stuck its tail straight up, emitted a terrifying shriek, and—its piece spoken—stole into the darkness.

In the intervening years, Clyde hadn't seen another funeral, human or animal, and he'd never seen a creature die, save for the occasional fish he pulled from Six Mile Creek. Death largely spared his childhood.

When he was drafted into the army at the height of the Korean War, he imagined he might be sent directly to the Thirty-Eighth Parallel. The military had other plans for him. He whiled away his three-year stint in an office in Anchorage, reviewing and filing paperwork and developing a powerful devotion to alcohol that would stalk him like a jilted girlfriend for the balance of his life. When his parents died in the most unlikely of circumstances—their car stalled at a railroad crossing in Mica Wells as a Southern Railway freight train bore down on them at full steam—he was unable to get back to North Carolina before the funeral.

Having inherited the house free and clear, he naturally gravitated back to Prosperity upon his discharge and, in 1953, at the age of twenty-two, he settled into day-to-day life as a clerk in the local hardware store. He resigned himself to a life of obscure but dedicated work without ever contributing a thing of consequence to the world, after which he expected to be utterly forgotten.

Nothing in his life prepared him for what happened in 1954.

Chapter Two

A rlo Pyle imagined himself an enlightened man. He believed he was open to most ideas, as long as they weren't communist or fascist. He'd left his wife and daughters behind to fight Hitler and his jackbooted thugs all over Europe and had no desire to allow those ideas to infiltrate *his* country. Otherwise, he perceived himself open to change. In truth, the southern roots of unreconstructed racism dug deep into his skull and wrapped themselves around his brain like tendrils of razor wire.

After returning from Europe, Arlo bought an auto shop in Prosperity. He was good with his hands, understood engine mechanics, and enjoyed jaw sessions with the various friends who'd drop in from time to time when business was slow. Word of his craftmanship spread. By the early 1950s people from as far away as the county seat in Morgan would bring their cars to Prosperity for Arlo's meticulous attention.

In late winter of 1953, a Negro teenager named Everett Howard walked into the garage and waited patiently against a wall as Arlo adjusted the timing on a Hudson Hornet. It was common for curious kids from the town to drop in and watch. There weren't five television sets in all of Prosperity. Hanging out in Arlo's shop was worlds cheaper than taking the bus to Morgan for the picture show.

"Something I can do for you, Ev?" Arlo asked when he finally looked up.

"Yes, sir," Ev said, almost a whisper, afraid to make direct eye contact. "I'm out of school. I'm not going back."

Prosperity had an elementary school, a junior high, and a high school for whites. Colored children went to a smaller, rougher, poorly heated school from kindergarten until they dropped out at the earliest legal age. The graduation rate at the colored school hovered around zero. Nobody expected Ev to stay in school. Everyone regarded him as a bit on the slow side. He could read most words, and his writing was legible, but his command of more complex subjects went lacking.

"I…" Ev's voice trailed off.

"Yes, Ev? What is it?"

Ev took a deep breath and blurted, "Would you give me a job?"

Arlo sighed. He pulled a couple of six-ounce bottles from the ice in the Coca-Cola chest, and handed one to Ev.

"Thank you kindly, Mr. Arlo."

"Do you know anything about cars?"

"A little, sir. I can change tires good. And I'm good at washin' them."

"You ever worked on an engine? How about putting new tires on a rim? You know how to work an Iron Jack?"

"I can learn, sir."

"C'mere.," Arlo grabbed a speed wrench from his tool chest and fitted it with a spark plug socket. He pulled a box from the shelf and handed both to Ev. "Change the spark plugs on this Hornet here."

As it happened, changing spark plugs was one of the things Ev understood. He laid the plugs side-by-side on the workbench, pulled the ignition wire from the front plug on the straight-six engine, unscrewed the old plug, and torqued the new plug in its place. He repeated this with all six plugs.

"Why'd you only unhook one wire at a time?" Arlo asked.

"Didn't want to get them confused, sir. If I put 'em back on the wrong plugs, the car won't run right."

"No, it won't. You know that much, I reckon. I'll be honest with you. Ain't much mechanical work around here for you. I could do with a fetcher and an all-around chore boy, though. You fetch parts, wash cars, change plugs when I ask, sweep the shop, pump gas, and keep the shelves stocked, and I reckon I can pay you seventy-five cents an hour. That's the minimum wage. I don't reckon you'll do better elsewhere with no high school and no training."

Ev Howard went to work as a fetcher for Arlo Pyle's auto shop. He picked up and delivered parts from warehouses all over Bliss County, or from whatever local junkyard would let a youngster of Ev's complexion rummage through the inventory unmonitored. Ev proved to be a reliable worker, adept at ferreting out obscure parts for older cars that found their way into Arlo's garage.

During Ev's second week at the garage, Arlo said, "Hey, Ev. You like to fish?"

"I do, sir," Ev told him. "I know a few nice places to catch brook trout on Six Mile Creek."

"You got a tackle box for your gear?"

"No, sir."

Arlo handed him a battered stamped steel toolbox he was replacing. When Ev opened it, a hinged shelf attached by rivets swung up to reveal additional storage below. The shelf was divided into compartments, the perfect size for hooks, spinners, weights, and bobs.

"I can have this?"

"Beats tossing it in the trash," Arlo said.

"It's a beauty." Ev admired the dented, shopworn box. "I don't know how to thank you."

"Tell you what. Bring me a couple of brook trout and we'll be jake."

Later that night, Ev arranged all his equipment in the compartments on the hinged pop-up shelf. He stowed a scaling knife and a fish line in the bottom, and scratched *E. Howard* into the enameled face of the tackle box with a nail, so nobody would mistake it for their own and walk away with it.

* * *

In 1954, about a year after Ev Howard came to work for him, five dollars went missing from Arlo Pyle's petty cash box.

Arlo found Tom Tackett at the brake lathe, shaving thousandths of an inch of steel from the inner surface of a brake drum. Threads of iridescent

5

metal spooled off the cutting head, pooling around Tackett's feet like fine tinsel.

Tackett was in his middle twenties, recently mustered out of the Army after the end of the Korean War. He'd allowed his hair to grow long, and he tortured it into a pompadour, laden with enough pomade to lubricate a battleship. He swept it in from both sides in the back, to form a ducktail Arlo found contemptible. It was a rebellious style, copied from Yankee street toughs and Hollywood hedonists, and had become a raging fashion over the last year after the release of *The Wild One* starring Marlon Brando. Arlo swore, if he ever managed to get Adele to squeeze out a son, he'd never allow him to have a ducktail.

"Tom?"

"Yeah, boss?" Tackett said, grinning. Both of his top front teeth were chipped, as if someone had broken off the inside corners of his incisors with a BB gun. Sometimes, the gap whistled when he talked.

"Did you take petty cash for anything? Pay a vendor?"

"No, boss. Why? Some money missing?"

"Five bucks. Can't recall using it myself."

"I saw Ev come out of your office this morning."

"I can't imagine Ev would steal from me."

"Cain't never tell with them kind. My daddy used to say all they want is tight pussy, loose shoes, and a warm place to shit."

"That's enough," Arlo warned. "I won't have that talk in this garage. I'm a Christian man, river-dipped and born again. You keep a decent tongue in your head when you're under my roof."

"Sure thing, boss. Don't mean I didn't see him."

Arlo returned to his office and recounted the money in the petty cash box. It still came up five dollars short.

His only suspect was Ev Howard. He had no hard evidence, other than the word of Tom Tackett. Tackett was openly prejudiced, but Arlo didn't believe he'd falsely accuse another man—of any color—of a crime like theft.

The idea the young man he'd given an opportunity might steal from him grew inside his head like a carbuncle, until he could stand it no longer.

* * *

Ev had taken Arlo's truck to Morgan to pick up a load of alternators from a storehouse. It was early April, but Bliss County was under a heatwave. Sweat ran down his face and chest like rivulets of thawed runoff on a stone mountain cliff. He'd removed his smart gray and white pinstriped shirt while he loaded the truck, to prevent soiling it. He was proud of the shirt. On one breast was an embroidered Pyle Garage emblem. On the other was a patch with his name. Arlo had given him five of them, one for each day of the week. They were a recognition of the trust Arlo placed in him. The shirts hadn't been cheap. If Arlo paid for them, it meant he trusted Ev and expected him to stay around for a while. Ev was determined to take good care of his work shirts.

As he drove out of Morgan, Ev watched the landscape transform from office buildings, shopping centers, banks, and grocery stores into fertile, rolling farmland. He pulled the truck into a parking space next to the garage. Tom Tackett leaned against the building, smoking a cigarette, his arms stained to the elbow with grime.

"Hoo-boy, you in the shit now," Tackett said, smirking. He jerked his head in the direction of Arlo's office.

Arlo walked out of his office and crooked a finger at him.

"Give me a minute, Ev?" His face was dark and hard. Ev couldn't recall when Arlo had looked as stern.

"Yes, sir." He followed Arlo into the office. Arlo sat behind his desk. Ev had never asked to sit in one of the office seats, and he wasn't about to presume the privilege now.

"Got some money missing from the petty cash box," Arlo said. "You wouldn't know anything about it, would you?"

"No, sir."

"Tom told me he saw you in my office this morning, and there's five dollars missing now. You want to tell me why you were in my office?"

"I was emptying the trash, like I do every day. I don't want to talk bad about Mr. Tackett, but I don't think he likes me. I think he'd prefer to see

7

me fired."

"I know he would," Arlo said. "Between you and me, Tom's lied to me once or twice. But lying ain't stealing. This is a serious thing, this missing money. I want to believe you, but I'm going to ask you to turn out your pockets."

Ev complied without hesitation. The search yielded seventy-eight cents and a worn bone-handled pocketknife. Arlo examined the pitiable contents of Ev's pockets again before he spoke.

"I'm gonna give you the benefit of the doubt, Ev, because you've done good work, and as far as I know you've never lied to me. Hell, I don't know if you're smart enough to lie. What do you think?"

"I done told a whopper or two in my time, Mr. Pyle, but never to you. I promise."

"I'll take you at your word," Arlo said. "Get back to work."

Despite his reassurances to Ev, Arlo remained unconvinced. He truly wished to believe in the boy, but the missing cash had planted the seeds of doubt deeply in his mind.

Chapter Three

The smaller agricultural towns in northern Bliss County were clustered like grapes around the Morgan Highway, with boundaries more fluid than concrete. Prosperity was a farming community, as were most of the small towns that included Mica Wells, Tulip Springs, and Wolfville, names held over from Revolutionary War times. The land in Prosperity had been cultivated by families named Wheeler, Poole, Tackett, Burch, Craighead, Pressley, Broome, Mosack, and Newton for over two hundred years. Many farmhouses were in Prosperity but connected to land in Mica Wells. During a wedding inside one Primitive Baptist Church, the bride would stand before the preacher in Tulip Springs and the groom in Wolfville. A hike from the center of one town to the other would scarcely raise a sweat.

In Mica Wells, an enterprising young man named Rennie Poole converted an old hay storage barn into a bluegrass music hall. He laid a plank floor, covered it with peanut shells, and installed surplus gym bleachers along one long wall of the barn for seating. A kerosene heating system blasted hot, oily air in the winter. In the summer, he handed out funeral home fans at the door.

Poole, who owned the feed and seed in Morgan on which the farmers of Prosperity depended, called it the Mica Wells Bluegrass Barn. He puffed out his chest and proclaimed he was giving back to the fine people in Bliss County, who'd bestowed him with such admirable business success. He conveniently neglected to mention the decent profit the Bluegrass Barn made itself each week.

People had a choice on Saturday nights. They could relax on their porches, listening to the Grand Ol' Opry on a static-filled AM signal from WSM in Nashville, enduring the constant crackles and pops from thunderstorms hundreds of miles away. Or they could head to Mica Wells and catch some live bluegrass and country, played by some of the biggest names in the Carolinas.

On a warm Saturday night in early May 1954, Coral Pyle arrived at the Bluegrass Barn with several of her friends. She'd be seventeen in a couple of weeks. She was only an inch or so over five feet, with wavy blonde hair she pulled back in a ponytail, eyes the color of a robin's egg, and a reputation for trouble. The baby of Arlo and Adele's family, she'd gotten away with murder almost since birth.

Arlo and Adele had brought four daughters into the world before Arlo ventured off to Europe to vanquish the Hun. After the rampant angst of the first baby, the more relaxed approach to Daughter Number Two, and almost *laissez-faire* childrearing with the third girl, Coral's upbringing had been left largely to herself, with her parents' indulgence. Coral was the prettiest of the bunch, and the liveliest. She could sing better, dance better, and had more friends. Everyone loved Coral.

Two of the daughters had married and moved away as quickly as they could. Only the third daughter, Grace, remained in Prosperity to languish in the reflected glow of her younger sister. Grace was pretty enough, and smart enough, but she was no Coral. Everyone said so.

Sometimes they said it to her face.

Several of Coral's friends had decided to come together and asked Coral to join them. It took her about ten seconds to overcome Adele's objections, so she arrived at the Barn before her parents and Grace.

The first person she saw as she climbed from her friend Stacey's car was Jude Pressley. He'd parked his rodded Willys Overland coupe in the gravel lot three cars down and was chatting with his buddies Owen Wheeler and Billy Mosack. All of them wore Prosperity High letter jackets. Jude glanced across the cars at Coral and gave her a small wave. An electric jolt arced across her chest.

Jude graduated from Prosperity High the previous year after leading the football team to three county championships and scoring thirteen school records. Pictures of Jude at quarterback and Owen Wheeler and Billy Mosack filling out the backfield had been enshrined in the trophy case at the high school under a plaque proclaiming them *The Trinity*. Coral wasn't interested in Owen or Billy. Her sister Grace had gone to a couple of school dances with Jude the previous year, and Coral had crushed on him ever since. He was tall and athletic, with jet black wavy hair and sky-blue eyes, and his crooked smile gave her strange sensations she could neither control nor completely understand.

Owen Wheeler apparently told a joke because all three of them guffawed. Billy Mosack grabbed Owen's letter jacket and dragged him toward the entrance of the Barn. Jude Pressley stayed behind.

"Hi, Coral. You're not with your family tonight?" he asked, after greeting the other girls.

"They're coming. I rode with Stacey and the girls. I like your car."

Jude glanced back at his Willys. He'd bought it for a hundred bucks, money he'd earned hoisting fifty-pound bags at Rennie Poole's Feed and Seed during the summer, and had given it a flashy new Earl Scheib paint job. It was electric red, like nail polish, and glistened undercoat after coat of hand-rubbed carnauba wax.

"Maybe I'll give you a ride sometime," he said.

"I'll hold you to it. You headed inside? Billy and Owen already went in."

* * *

Arlo and Adele Pyle arrived a couple of minutes after the girls and Jude entered the barn. By the time Grace and her parents made their way inside, the teenagers were clustered on the top tier of the bleachers at the far corner.

"You think she'll be okay in that crowd?" Adele asked.

"I think she'd be okay in *any* crowd," Arlo said. "At least, this way, we can keep an eye on her. She can't take off without us knowing."

Albert Allen and his Smoky Mountain Boys opened their set with *Mule*

11

Skinner Blues. When Albert Allen showed up, Rennie Poole never worried about keeping the crowd until the end of the night. They always closed the third set with a seven-minute rendition of *Orange Blossom Special* that started slow and gradually built to a crescendo of foot-stomping, clog-dancing, and horsehairs flying off the fiddle bow. Nobody dared leave before Allen's fiddler played those first *wah-wah plink-plink* notes.

Nobody except the teenagers. After the first set, they bypassed the refreshments to congregate in the parking lot. Many nights, it wasn't uncommon to find the second set strike up with several automobiles in the gravel lot still rocking on their springs. Many of Bliss County's youngest citizens owed their existence to the Mica Wells Bluegrass Barn.

At the first intermission, Coral found The Trinity standing next to Jude's Willys, passing a pint bottle back and forth. Coral put on her most petulant face and waggled a finger at Jude.

"Does your dad know what you're doing out here?" she asked in jest.

He handed her the bottle. "Does yours?"

She took a swig, made an obligatory face, and handed the bottle back.

"I'm bored," she said. "They won't play *Orange Blossom Special* for at least another hour and a half."

"Wanna take a ride?" Jude asked.

* * *

"I installed triple Strombergs and had the head milled," Jude explained as he drove a dark stretch of Harley Stukes Road. Fog had descended, and the headlights formed two yellowish cones in the mist. "Guy in Morgan did the button-and-tuck."

Coral wished he'd talk more about her. "I'm surprised you didn't go to college. You could have gotten a football scholarship."

"My grades could've been better. A couple of smaller schools gave me a look, but nothing came of it. Anyway, what would college do for me? I'm not planning to be a lawyer or a brain surgeon. Fact is, I don't know what I'm gonna do."

He turned off Harley Stukes Road onto a rutted oiled lane Coral recognized. Her heart sped up as the car bounced over the path until it broke through to a field lit barely by moonlight. This was The Bluffs. Coral saw a staked chicken wire fence posted with warning signs. Beyond the fence was a sheer drop-off into a wide segment of Six Mile Creek. Two other cars were already parked near the barrier. Jude steered toward the other end and turned off the engine.

"What is this?" Coral demanded. "The old *out of gas* routine?"

"No, this is the *hereafter* routine."

"What?"

"If you're not here after what I'm here after, you're gonna be here after I'm gone."

She slapped his arm playfully and giggled.

"That one was old when my parents were teenagers!"

"You think they came up here?"

"I know they did. I heard my mom tell Mrs. Freeman she and Daddy used to come up here once or twice a week. She laughed about it! You wanna know something?"

"What?"

"I think they made my oldest sister Emily here. I found my parents' wedding certificate. My sister was born only seven months after they got married." She turned on the radio and searched for a channel. "I had the biggest crush on you when I was a kid."

"You're still a kid. What are you, a tenth-grader?"

"I'm a junior. I'll be seventeen in a couple of weeks."

She found a station playing Doris Day's *Secret Love*. He placed his right arm around her shoulder and pulled her toward him. "So, I was your secret love?"

"Had to be secret. You were dating my sister, after all."

He leaned in and kissed her. To his surprise, she opened her lips, and her tongue darted into his mouth. He pulled away, smiling. "Nothing happened between us," he said, as he gazed into her eyes. "We went out two times, and I barely got a goodnight kiss."

"I know," she said before she kissed him again. "Poor Grace."

Within minutes the windows of the Willys fogged, little rivulets of condensation coursing down the glass. Jude managed to undo the back of her dress and pull it off her shoulders and around her waist. He stroked at one of her breasts through the thick cotton brassiere.

"You can go under," she said. "It's okay."

He slipped one hand under her bra and caressed her nipple. He was delighted to find her full and soft and responsive to his touch, but the angle was awkward.

"Oh, hell," she said as she pulled away. She fumbled behind her and undid the bra, allowing it to fall to the seat. He stared at her, his eyes big.

"Better?" she said.

"It sure is." He pulled her to him. They kissed for a few more minutes, as he explored her breasts and back with his hands. She fondled him through his pants as she gave herself up to her pleasure. He slipped a hand under her skirt and tugged at her panties. Her pleasure changed to panic. She kissed him one more time and pulled away.

"Not yet," she said, placing her hand over his, the one under her skirt. "I won't wind up like my mother."

"Oh," he said, sitting back against the bench seat. "I see."

"Don't sulk," she said. "We can still have fun. Mom told me about... stuff."

She backed up to the passenger door and gestured for him to face her. His boxer shorts tented with his erection. She grasped at the waistband, pulled them down, and stroked him slowly and deliberately. He groaned and swallowed hard once or twice.

"Wow," he said.

"I ain't even started yet." She began to lick and kiss him. She could feel him swell under her fingers and lips, as she slid him into her mouth. Less than two minutes later, it was over, and he lay back against the driver's door, panting and huffing.

"Your... mother... taught you... *that?*"

"Sure. Her mother taught her. Mom said she'd be saddled with ten kids if she hadn't learned how. Women have done it for centuries to avoid children.

Mom said every new generation thinks it invented sex. I think she may be an unusual woman."

"I'll say." Jude pulled up his pants. "I guess we should head back. It's late."

"Don't you tell anyone." She grabbed her bra from the floorboard and put it on. "I don't want people thinking I'm some sort of slut. Nobody can know what happened tonight."

"No. Never! I wouldn't tell. I like you, Coral. You're...special. I'd like to see you again."

"Oh, I bet you would." She pulled the bodice of her dress up and finished dressing.

"I mean it."

She turned her back to him. He stared at her.

"Zip me up?" she asked, exasperated. The magic was draining quickly from the evening.

They drove back to the road, and in ten minutes they were in the gravel lot at the Bluegrass Barn. They could hear the thump of music inside.

"Oh, hell!" she said. "How are we going to get back to our seats? My parents are sitting right by the door."

He stepped outside and crossed around to her door. "Come with me," he said.

He led her to the other end of the barn, where they found a back door. "It's locked," he explained. "But only on the outside. In a minute or so, someone will come out. People come and go all night long."

On cue, the door creaked open, and a man walked out. He barely glanced at the teens as Jude held the door for her.

"You go in first and have a seat with the gang," he said. "I'll follow in about five minutes. It'll look like you just went to the bathroom." He pointed toward the ladies' room.

The hallway was dimly lit, and nobody could see them from the main room. She stole a quick look to be certain and kissed him hard on the lips.

"Our secret," she said. "And I'm gonna hold you to a date next weekend."

Chapter Four

L ife at Arlo Pyle's garage didn't improve for Ev Howard.

After a run to Morgan for auto parts, he poured back three glasses of sweet iced tea with his lunch. By the time he returned to the garage, his bladder was bulging. He parked the truck and walked inside quickly, straight to the restroom at the back, unintentionally slamming the door in his haste.

Hubert Pressley, Jude's father, chatted with Tom Tackett. Hubert was Rennie Poole's store manager at the Morgan Feed and Seed. Like Jude, he was tall and dark, but years of fried food and other indulgences had settled in his gut, which lopped over his belt. His double chin wobbled when he talked.

"Huh," Hubert said. "What do you make of that?"

"What?"

"You let that boy use the same bathroom as you? Ain't you scared of catchin' some weird nigger disease?"

Tackett pierced a quart can of oil with a stamped metal spout. "Not until now."

"That's the same washroom your customers use."

"It is," Tackett said.

"Don't seem right. Do you know what I heard on the radio on the way over? The Supreme Court up in Washington says we have to allow the nigger kids in our schools."

"That a fact?"

"Supreme Court says we can't do nothin' about it. Now you let some coon use your bathroom. Before you know it, there won't be a decent place for a white man to take a shit."

Tackett tossed the empty oil can into the waste barrel and straightened up.

"Now you mention it, it don't seem right."

"Don't know what the world is coming to."

"Arlo good as caught that boy stealing from him a few weeks back, and he didn't do nothin' about it," Tom said.

"Don't like it. Don't like it a bit," Pressley fumed.

Ev opened the washroom door and headed toward the truck.

"You got a lot of balls, using the white toilet," Pressley said. Ev faced him, careful not to make too much eye contact.

"Sir? Mr. Pyle told me I could. I got his permission."

"Maybe I ought to have a talk with Mr. Pyle. I'd hate for his business to go south on account of being too friendly with your kind."

"No, sir," Ev said, still confused as to Hubert Pressley's point. "If you don't mind, I need to get back to work."

* * *

At the end of the day, Arlo called Ev into his office.

"Ev, I had a conversation with Hubert Pressley this afternoon. Hubert says you were rude to him. Says he criticized you and you bucked up to him."

"I don't remember the conversation that way at all, Mr. Pyle. Mr. Pressley was upset because I used the bathroom at the back of the shop, like you told me I could. I don't know why he got riled. You said I could go there."

Arlo leaned back in his chair and rubbed his jowls with a calloused hand. He pursed his lips and blew out a resigned blast of air.

"Hubert Pressley has a boulder where his brain should be, but he also has important friends. We live in a tough world. It's double-tough for your people. I'm afraid I'm about to make it tougher. Before you go, hose down the old outhouse back of the garage. I'm gonna ask you to use it from now on."

Ev knew better than to argue, or even to ask why. His new accommodations would not be the first outhouse he'd used in his life when there was a perfectly good toilet with running water only yards away.

The outhouse was a mean, rough structure, a hundred years old, with rotting cypress walls, a door creaking on rusty hinges, and a peaked tin roof that guaranteed sweltering temperatures in the summer months and bone-chilling cold in winter. The seat, with its single hole, was as old as the structure itself, weather-worn, and splintered. The only light came from the gaps in the walls and a colloquial crescent moon carved into the door. When Ev opened the door, he was greeted with an electric buzzing sound. Three hornets flew out.

He returned to the garage and knocked on Arlo's door jamb. Arlo looked up from some invoices on his desk.

"Yes, Ev?"

"Beg your pardon, Mr. Pyle, but I was cleaning the outhouse..."

"Yes?"

"It ain't a fit place for an animal, let alone a man. There's hundreds of wasps in there, and the place will flat blow up if someone touches a match to it."

"I'm sorry I don't have a better option for you," Arlo said.

"Would you mind if I fix it up? It wouldn't take more than some boards and nails, and maybe some copper flashing. I reckon I could do it in a day."

It was the most pathetic thing Arlo Pyle had heard in recent memory, Ev asking for permission to window-dress his little corner of a Hell he never should have inhabited. He pulled the petty cash box from underneath the register, extracted a bill, and handed it to Ev.

"I won't ask you to build your own shithouse outa your pocket," he said. "Ten dollars should cover all your materials. Also, fixing up the shitter is part of your job description now. You can tend to it when you don't have other duties. I'm sure sorry about this, Ev. You don't deserve what's happening to you, but discouraging customers never comes to a good end."

"Yes, sir," Ev said. "If you don't mind, I can take the truck to Morgan and get the wood and nails and copper tomorrow."

"The hell with copper. You get a square of asphalt shingles. We'll give your outhouse a proper roof." Arlo took another five out of the petty cash. "Here's another five for the shingles. You need more, you come to me."

* * *

With fifteen dollars' worth of Carolina yellow pine, nails, a square of shingles, and a gallon of fire-engine red paint, Ev Howard constructed an excretory palace the likes of which Bliss County had never beheld.

Little of the rotting cypress exterior could be saved, but the frame was solid white oak, fumed to a deep golden bronze by a century of privy ammonia, and would last another hundred years. The rafters were a different story. They were cheap pine. Decades of heat and humidity had pitted and decayed them until they sagged precariously. Ev had to figure out how to rebuild them by copying the angles onto a large sheet of corrugated cardboard as a template.

He installed a small window high on the left side to let in light. It was the perfect size to illuminate the inside and still preserve his privacy. He built a small flower box on each side, in which he planted the cheapest seeds he could find in the garden section of the Piggly Wiggly.

It was topped off by an asphalt shingle roof, like a house.

After he brushed on the last ounce of paint, he stepped back and admired his handiwork. It was a masterpiece of an outhouse, a triumph to be proud of. Inside the door, he painstakingly painted the legend: *This Outhouse Bilt By Everett Howard May 1954.*

* * *

Late that night, Tom Tackett nailed a crudely wrought plank over the door, hastily lettered with paint-dripping words:

COLOREDS ONLY

Chapter Five

For her seventeenth birthday, Jude Pressley gave Coral Pyle a locket on a thin gold-filled chain. He purchased it while on a trip to Morgan with Owen Wheeler.

When Owen had asked why, Jude said, "In case I meet someone special. I think it's classy."

He'd cut his picture from a yearbook in the Prosperity High School library and had pasted it into the recess in the locket. When Coral opened it, she threw her arms around him and kissed him as if he were departing on a suicide mission.

Jude was anxious to drive to The Bluff, but Coral had other ideas. "I'm tired of sneaking out of the Bluegrass Barn. I'm seventeen. I want to go on a real date."

"We could go to the picture show in Morgan," he offered. "They're playing a western with Gary Cooper and Burt Lancaster."

"A movie would be nice." She fingered the locket. "It can't run too late. I want time to thank you properly for my birthday present."

Jude pulled out his wallet and counted his bills. His forehead furrowed as he did the math.

"What is it, darling?" Coral loved to imitate the sophisticated people she saw on the movie screen.

"After I bought the pendant, and filled the tank in the car, I'm a little... well... short for the movies."

"You can't afford ice cream afterward either, I suppose?"

He dug a toe into the ground. "No. I can't."

"Hmm..." she said, drawing out his discomfort. She enjoyed teasing him. The first night they were together, in his Willys coupe at The Bluff, they had been frenetic. The clock was ticking, and she had to get back before her parents noticed her missing. Their later trips there had given them more time to explore and play, and she'd found new delight in extending his anticipation. It made her feel powerful. "I see the problem. Whatever can we do about it?"

"I could borrow five bucks from Owen or Billy. I can pay them back when I get my check at the feed and seed next Friday."

"I have a better idea. I know where there's some money, and we won't have to pay it back. Drive over to my dad's garage."

* * *

"What in hell is that?" Jude said, pointing at the tiny red shack as they pulled into the lot next to the garage.

"An outhouse," she said. "One of dad's employees built it. Negro boy named Ev."

"The sign says *Coloreds Only*. Kind of uppity of him, claiming it for himself."

"He built it because your dad pitched a hissy over Ev using the same washroom as white folks."

"Oh," Jude said. "Sounds like Dad."

"Let's go inside. I have a key."

She unlocked a door and flipped a light switch. A bare bulb set into the ceiling glowed and cast eerie shadows around the work area.

She led him to the alcove office at the rear, unlocked the door, and pulled him inside the pitch-dark room. She kissed him passionately, the way she'd seen Rita Hayworth do in a movie in Morgan a few weeks back.

"You're getting me all worked up," Jude said as he broke off the kiss. "You keep this up, we'll never get to the movies."

"Patience," she said. She turned on a desk lamp. "Daddy always keeps forty or fifty bucks in here. I took five dollars a few weeks back. He never

21

said anything about it. And what the hell? His money eventually becomes my money. It's all in the family."

She pulled a five from the petty cash box and started to put it back in the drawer. She stopped and drew out another five.

"A little extra," she said. "You never know what might come up."

* * *

Instead of the western Jude expected, the theater played a romance about American girls looking for love in Rome. Jude found it mostly boring, though a couple of the girls were cute. He glanced over at Coral several times, to find her staring raptly at the screen, as if whatever was happening up there was of earth-shaking consequence. He hoped the movie would put her in the mood.

"So," she said as they left the night lights of Morgan in the rearview mirror. "Are you taking me home?"

"Do you want to go home?"

"Hell no. It's early yet."

"We could drive up to The Bluffs."

She sighed. Heavily.

"I don't like it so much up there anymore. Last week, while I was…you know…"

"Blowing me?"

She slapped his arm. "Don't be crass. I looked up and there was this guy walking right past the car, headed to the woods. If the windows hadn't been so fogged, he could've looked right in on us. I want a private place to play."

"I think I know the spot."

"Really? Where?"

"Your dad's garage. It was plenty private there."

"Ew. No!"

"I'm kidding. I know another place. It's private, and with the full moon tonight I bet we could find it even without flashlights. We'll need the blanket from the trunk."

He turned onto the Old Village Road, which ran into a shallow valley. After rolling across a bridge fording Six Mile Creek, he turned again onto a rutted oiled dirt road. They wended through several stands of oaks and poplars. He stopped at a rotting wooden gate. A sign read *POSTED: NO* and something garbled and smeared with time and the elements.

"This farm belonged to Henry Lincoln," Jude said. "He died last year. I suppose his estate owns it, but nobody is checking around, at least until someone buys it. Owen and I hiked up Six Mile Creek a few summers back and found a neat spot. I'll show you."

Jude retrieved a heavy woolen blanket and a couple of flashlights from the floor of the rumble seat. He hoisted the folded blanket over his shoulder and handed one of the lights to Coral. Jude left the gate open and illuminated a trail carpeted with a bed of pine needles.

Coral heard water splashing ahead.

"Six Mile Creek?" she whispered.

"Yeah," he said. "Why are you whispering?"

"I don't think we're supposed to be here. What if someone hears us?"

"The house is two hills over and it's empty. Old Village Road is half a mile away. The next farm is two miles up the road. Relax."

Six Mile Creek varied in width as it traversed the heart of northern Bliss County. In some parts of Prosperity, it was no more than ten feet across. In others, it grew to fifty feet wide, the bed lined with water-eroded stones, and the water flowed without sediment, as clear as glass. Brook trout and bream basked in shallow pools, eager to strike at any shiny object that broke the surface. Jude led the way as they hiked several hundred feet through a pine-strewn forest. The soil grew sandy in the alluvial plain of the creek.

The needle-covered path dropped at a steep angle through the trees. Ahead, Coral saw glints of moonlight reflect off rivulets of water flowing over stones. The trees disappeared, and the earth beneath their shoes grew dense. The canopy of limbs and leaves and needles vanished, replaced by a torrent of stars projected from a sky so dark she imagined she could cup a million brilliant pinpoints in her palm. She swept the area with her flashlight. They were on an immense flat rock slab a hundred feet long.

23

It melded with a cliff rising seventy feet above her head. The slab jutted halfway out into Six Mile Creek, creating narrows that funneled the water into a rapidly flowing cascade emptying over a six-foot waterfall, where it flowed into a still, flat pool.

"My God," she gasped. "I've never seen anything like it."

Jude pulled her to him. "This is our secret place. The only other person who knows about it is Owen. I reckon old man Lincoln did since he put up the gate to keep people out, but he's long gone." He panned across the creek and the trees and the cliffs with his flashlight. "You wanted private."

She illuminated the sheer rock face behind them. "It's beautiful."

He pulled the blanket from his shoulder and unfolded it. She helped him spread it on the rock ledge, smooth as tile from eons of weathering.

"We could come here during the day when I'm not working this summer," he said. "The pool is great for swimming. The rocks and the shade keep it cool all the way to August." He rolled up one end of the blanket to make a bolster pillow. She knelt, and he lay next to her.

"A secret place," she said. "For us and us alone."

"You won't tell anyone about it?"

"Who needs crowds?"

"I have something else to show you." He dug into his pocket and pulled out a small round hinged plastic container, about the size of a silver dollar. He handed it to her.

"I got it at a colored pharmacy in Morgan, to make sure I didn't run into anyone I knew."

He shined the flashlight on the object. She read the molded label on the top of the container. *Duke Prophylactics. Manufactured by the Circle Rubber Corp., Newark, NJ.*

"You said you weren't gonna end up like your mother," Jude said. "I figured, if we used one of these, you wouldn't have to worry about it."

"I see…" she said.

"It's to go over my… you know. My thing. When I gush, it holds it all in. You can't get pregnant."

The idea thrilled her. She would not have dared to tell him, but a year earlier she'd enjoyed a brief, intense romance with a classmate, during which she'd lost control and allowed him to enter her. In less than a minute, it was over. She'd sweated out the next two weeks, frightened to death he might have impregnated her. When her period arrived, she cried herself to sleep and swore the next man to squirt his seed inside her would be her husband. Every time she and Jude were together, she wished she could enjoy him with abandon, but her fear of premature maternity hung over her like a lurking vulture.

The Circle Rubber Corporation of Newark provided a convenient solution to her predicament. She'd heard about rubbers but had never seen one up close. Her father, who was never happier than when children were around, never would have purchased any.

"No pressure," he reassured her. "I wanted you to know it's here, if you want to."

In her romantic, barely seventeen-year-old mind, his thoughtfulness and consideration for her needs overwhelmed her. Any man who put such great effort into providing for her safety must be a keeper. Tears formed at the corners of her eyes. She turned off her flashlight, so he couldn't see.

She lay on the blanket and pulled him to her.

Chapter Six

Arlo Pyle didn't discover the missing money until the following Wednesday. An automotive belt vendor dropped by the garage. Arlo needed a few items, no more than ten dollars' worth. Instead of writing a check, he offered to give the man cash.

He knew something was amiss as soon as he opened the petty cash box. He always kept the money, about fifty dollars, in two tens, four fives, and ten ones. He'd replenished the cash box at the end of the last week and hadn't touched it since. Yet two of the five-dollar bills were missing.

The money must have been taken when he was out to lunch, he reasoned. Every day, from noon to one, he walked to a nearby diner. He always took off at noon, and he always returned at the top of the next hour. His predictability, he surmised, had been his undoing. Someone who knew the times of his comings and goings waited for him to go to lunch and raided the cash box.

That suggested an employee—either Tom Tackett or Ev Howard—had stolen the money. Both options troubled him. Tackett was an able mechanic, but he was crude, perpetually angry, and occasionally devious. Being a liar didn't make him a thief, though.

Ev was accused once already of stealing from the cash box, but Arlo found it difficult to indict the young man. Ev was deliberate and motivated, but he'd always seemed a little *slow*, and not at all underhanded. Also, he'd always treated Arlo with respect and even a small degree of reverence.

Arlo had no desire to indict either of his employees. Yet the money was missing. There was no doubt. Twice in two months. Something had to be done.

Tackett was under a Ford truck in the garage, changing out a muffler. Ev washed a DeSoto Deluxe sedan out back. Arlo strolled into the garage.

"Tom?"

"Yeah?" Tom said, from under the car.

"Any vendors come by while I was out to lunch the last couple of days?"

"Not as I recall, boss. Only one I've seen was the belts guy. Why?"

"There's some money missing from the petty cash. About ten bucks. Any idea what happened to it?"

Tom rolled the creeper out from under the car. His face was smeared with road grime.

"Again? You think I took it?"

"I'm not accusing anyone. Right now, I'm trying to figure out what's what."

"Check with Ev. I don't know nothin' about it."

Arlo found Ev meticulously coiling the rubber hose after finishing the wash job. Sweat rolled off his face and shoulders and soaked his undershirt. Water droplets from the mist hung in his wiry hair and glinted like Christmas tree lights.

"Got another job for me, Mr. Pyle?" he asked.

"There's ten bucks missing from the petty cash, Ev," he said. "Any idea where it went?"

"No, sir. After what happened last time, I don't get nowhere near your office, unless you're in it. I don't want to give you cause not to trust me."

"I appreciate your effort. Were there any customers at the shop while I was out to lunch over the last couple of days?"

"I think a woman came in with a flat tire on Monday."

"Was she alone?"

"Had a kid in the car with her. Looked five or six maybe. Been a slow couple of days, sir."

"I hate to do this, Ev, but I have to ask you to turn out your pockets again."

"Did you make Tackett pull out his pockets?"

"I will, if it comes to it."

Tom Tackett watched the exchange through the doorway. Knowing he hadn't taken any money from the box, Tackett had no interest in giving Ev the benefit of the doubt. He harbored little regard for coloreds in the first place. Having Ev around the shop aggravated his hatred and made him fantasize ways of ridding himself of his vexation.

When Ev had gone out to wash the car, he'd taken off his Pyle Garage shirt to keep it from getting soiled. It hung on a rack inside the back door.

Tackett had twelve dollars in his pocket. It would cost most of his walking-around money, but in the long run it could be worth it. He folded two five-dollar bills and slipped them into the breast pocket of Ev's shirt.

Ev pulled everything from his pockets and laid it out on top of a weather-beaten equipment bin. It made a pitiable pile, with no money except for a quarter and several dimes.

"This is everything?" Arlo asked.

"All I brought with me today."

"Where's your shop shirt?"

"Hanging inside the door."

Arlo gestured for Ev to follow him inside. As soon as Arlo picked Ev's shirt from the rack, he could see the bulge in the breast pocket. He drew out two five-dollar bills. Ev's eyes grew wide.

"I told you the truth, Mr. Pyle. I got no idea where that money come from. Honest. I would never steal from you. It's wrong."

"Like I always said," Tackett remarked from the corner. "Cain't never trust a nigger."

"Knock it off," Arlo warned. "Ev. I'll give you one last chance. You explain where this money came from, and if it's legit we're good. Maybe you put it in your pocket this morning and forgot about it."

"No, sir! It's true, I got paid last Friday, but all my money is at home, safe and sound. I never seen that money, and I sure didn't put it in my shirt pocket."

"Step into my office."

Ev followed Arlo to the back, and Arlo closed the office door. The last thing Ev saw before the door slammed shut was an expression of triumph on Tom Tackett's grimy face.

Arlo pulled the cash box from his desk. "You worked nine hours Monday and Tuesday, and you put in three today. Twenty-one hours, at seventy-five cents an hour, comes to a little under sixteen dollars. You already got yourself ten you didn't deserve." Arlo extracted a five and a one from the box. "Here's six dollars, your pay up to right now, including the missing ten dollars. I want you gone, Ev."

"You're... you're firing me, Mr. Pyle?"

"I got no choice. You've lost my trust."

"What about Tackett? You done told me already he's lied to you!"

"But he never stole, as far as I know."

"Neither did I!" Ev protested, his eyes tearing up.

"The money says otherwise. I'm sorry, Ev, but you can't be around here no more. You can keep the shirts."

Still confused, Ev Howard took the money, tears stinging in his eyes almost as much as the rebuke from the man he'd come to admire, and he left without another word.

* * *

Dinner at the Pyle house that evening was a sullen affair. Arlo came to the table looking as if he was headed to a funeral.

"Bad day, sweetie?" Adele, asked, as she plated chicken-fried cubed steak with milk gravy, mashed potatoes, and green beans.

"Not the best."

"Well, cheer up. Week's more'n half over." She smiled at him sweetly and pulled a cake pan of cornbread from the oven.

"What happened, Daddy?" Coral asked.

"Had to let one of my men go today. Ev Howard."

"The Negro boy who built the outhouse?"

"I feel really bad about it. He was a good kid, for his kind. Hard worker. I trusted him."

"Then why'd you fire him?"

"Caught him stealing. A few weeks ago, five dollars went missing from

29

the petty cash. I gave him the benefit of the doubt, even though Tom Tackett saw him in my office. Today, there was ten dollars missing. I found it on Ev. He didn't leave me any choice. I had to turn him out."

"Ten dollars?" Coral asked.

"Yep."

"From petty cash," she said.

"Seems a shame to toss away a dependable job for so little money," Adele said.

"Sure does," Coral said thoughtfully. "I guess you didn't have any other choice."

"Doesn't seem so," Arlo said. "Pass the cornbread, please?"

Coral didn't say a word. She could see the malice and grief in her father's eyes, and she feared if she told the truth, he might direct it toward her.

Chapter Seven

Ev Howard sat on his front porch and weighed his options. He was still confused. What happened at the garage didn't make sense.

As soon as he returned to his small, three-room frame house, he went directly to the dresser in his bedroom to check his money. It was right where he left it. Every dollar was accounted for. Yet ten dollars had found their way into his shirt pocket.

The disappointment on Arlo's face rocked Ev more than getting fired. Over the months he worked at the garage, he'd never known a moment when Arlo had treated him unfairly, or with the slightest hint of prejudice. Ev respected Arlo, and never would have thought of disappointing his former boss.

He wasn't in bad shape. He had a hundred dollars saved. He'd inherited the house, free and clear, from the grandmother who'd raised him. For the cost of the annual property taxes, which came to only ten or twelve dollars, he'd have a roof over his head for as long as he cared to stay.

It wasn't a palace, but it was watertight, and it stopped the wind and cold in the winter. He'd planted a vegetable garden in mid-May, with rows of tomatoes and cucumbers and peppers and even a few heads of lettuce. There was a fine stand of snap beans which he'd can when they were ripe, so he could eat them through the winter if need be.

As for protein, he wouldn't starve soon. He knew a great place to catch brook trout on Six Mile Creek. A couple of fish could feed him for four days, and he'd caught as many as ten in a few hours before.

He rocked on the front porch and watched the sun descend into the trees across the street. He was going to be all right. Losing his job was a setback, but he'd find another.

He only wished he could get the image of Arlo's disappointment out of his head.

* * *

Jude Pressley was mowing the front lawn on a hot day for early June. Pushing the reel-style unpowered mower around the yard had soaked him with sweat. He looked forward to grabbing a shower, wolfing his dinner, and meeting Coral at the high school for a drive out to their secret spot.

They had managed to keep their affair secret. Even Owen Wheeler and Billy Mosack—whom Jude trusted more than anyone—knew nothing about Coral. They had to be careful. If Arlo even suspected what his baby daughter was doing, there was no predicting how he might react.

A black Chevrolet turned off the street into his driveway. Jude soaked a rag in the spigot at the side of the house and wiped his face with it as a tall, rugged man stepped out of the Chevrolet.

"Coach McCandless!" Jude dropped the rag to greet the man. "What are you doing here?"

Pete McCandless, the head coach at Ryland College, took his hand. "Checking up on you. Wanted to see if you were feeling healthy."

"I'm fine. Why?"

"Your father told me you had taken ill last year. He intimated it was chronic."

Jude shook his head. "I haven't had so much as a cold in years."

An expression of concern crossed the coach's face. "Oh. I see. Mind if we sit for a minute?"

They sat on the front porch as Coach McCandless struggled to find the right words.

"Jude, sometimes parents harbor unrealistic expectations for their children. You're one of the best quarterbacks your high school has ever seen."

"Set thirteen records."

"I know. Very impressive. However, in the vast sea of high school quarterbacks, I'd rank you somewhere in the bottom third."

A wave of anger rose in Jude's chest. Even in the oppressive Carolina sun, he could feel his cheeks and ears redden. "Really?"

"High in the bottom third, maybe at the top, but in the bottom third nonetheless. Those guys in the top third? They're going to places like UCLA and Notre Dame and Alabama. They were snapped up almost before they got to high school. The middle third? They're headed for the smaller state universities. Then there's your third. They wind up at the small private schools, the church colleges, teaching colleges. Places like Ryland. How many offers did you get last year?"

Jude leaned forward and hung his head. A few droplets of sweat fell off his hair, onto the painted wood floor. "None."

"You'd have gotten four, if your father had permitted it. I knew three other colleges who approached him with letters of intent. He told them all the same thing. You were sick."

"Why would he do that?"

"Because he loves you, and he wants great things for you. I think your father was holding out for a better offer. It wouldn't be the first time. I took him at his word, and I passed on you."

"What a dirty deal," Jude said. He stood, walked to the edge of the porch, and spat into the azaleas.

"There's more. Coaches talk to one another. Once word got around, the coaches at any of the larger colleges who might have taken an interest in you to fill their depth charts were scared off. Your dad—with the best of intentions—pissed in the well."

Jude turned around. A lone tear carved its way through the caked sweat and dirt on his cheek. "So I'm screwed?"

"Luckily, no. The boy we signed last year got hurt toward the end of the season, and it doesn't look like he's coming back. We have a slot open on the bench."

"The bench?"

"You're a year out of high school, son. You haven't played a second of organized ball in a year and a half. We'd want you to ease in, while we get a chance to see how much of your skills you've retained."

"Gosh," Jude said. "It's a generous offer, considering how my dad shined you on."

"It's not the first time. I'm glad I decided to drop by. I meant what I said. In your league, you were hot. You could be as hot in ours. There are benefits to being a big fish in a little pond. I'm prepared to offer you a scholarship if you'll come play for us. Full ride, tuition, room, board, books, the works. I think you'll find our boosters are enthusiastic about their players, too. You won't have to worry about walking-around money. This could be a real opportunity for you."

Coral flashed into Jude's mind. Ryland was seven hours away by bus.

"I might need to think on it," he said.

"You have other offers?"

"Hell... I mean, heck no, Coach."

"Why don't I meet with you and your father this weekend? Bring some papers along for you to sign?"

McCandless was right. Jude had nothing holding him back except Coral. Perhaps they could sweat the distance for a year, until she finished high school, and perhaps he could convince her to come to Ryland, too. In his adolescent brain, the existence of an improbable solution made it a certainty. Jude allowed himself to relax.

"Sure, Coach. I appreciate the opportunity."

They shook on it. Before he stepped from the porch, McCandless said, "Don't be hard on your father. I know you're disappointed, but he had the best of intentions. Everything's worked out in the end, right?"

* * *

The first thing Rennie Poole did after building his house on Wiley Crook Road in Prosperity was add a pleasure dome out back that would make Kublai Khan envious. The exterior looked like an ordinary barn. It was closed in, weather-tight, heated in winter by a wood stove and a huge stone fireplace and cooled in summer by two new window air conditioning units. Every window had screens to keep out the mosquitoes and horseflies in the spring and fall. The floor was heart-pine, sanded and polished to a gleam, with Persian rugs scattered about to keep a chill from creeping in. In one corner, clustered around a stone fireplace, he'd placed chairs rough-hewn from local yellow pine trees and shellacked to a golden sheen.

At the far end was a mahogany bar, complete with a refrigerator full of Pabst and Rolling Rock. In the center of the barn was the most expensive and elaborate pool table Rennie could find.

Rennie Poole was a self-made man, and proud of it. Like most people in Prosperity, he'd been born into a farm family. Unlike most of them, he'd escaped, at least partially. In his opinion, the vagaries of weather and the vicissitudes of infestations left each harvest an untenable roll of the dice. Regardless of the bounty or paucity of each growing season, the man who sold seeds and plows and rakes and hoes and overalls would never go out of business. His enterprises had made him enviably wealthy in his early forties. He enjoyed surrounding himself with the trappings of success.

The barn was more than a rural pleasure palace. It was also the headquarters of the local klavern of the Ku Klux Klan. Rennie Poole served as Grand Dragon.

Fifteen men met in the barn that evening. Nobody wore hoods or robes. Most of the men had come directly from their dinner tables. Rennie drank Kentucky whiskey. Most of the men opted for beer. Tom Tackett had won three straight games of eight-ball. Tackett caught Poole eyeing him from the bar. If the Grand Dragon decided to take the next challenge, Tackett would find a creative way to lose convincingly. It was bad form to beat Rennie Poole in his own den.

"You boys shoulda seen it," Tackett said as he lined up his next shot. "The look on that thievin' nigger boy's face was priceless. *I don' know where dat money done come from, Missa Pyle!* I was like to bust a gut. I tell you, boys, that was sweeter than sex, and I been with a coupla ten-dollar whores..."

Clyde Dillard separated from the crowd and retreated to the fireplace. Isolating from the others in the room relaxed him. He wasn't entirely certain why he accepted every invitation Hubert Pressley issued to attend the meetings. He wasn't a Klansman. He had no intention of joining, and he was unsure whether he liked the idea of being associated with those who had.

A shy, homely sort, Clyde knew his social calendar was largely blank space. He worked at the hardware store from open to close and went straight home to eat and indulge in his one great luxury and his one consuming vice.

Since leaving the military and returning to Prosperity to work in the hardware, he'd managed to cadge away a little from each paycheck. Over time, he had accumulated a handsome amount of cash, which he splurged on an RCA Master 21 television set. It was the largest screen at the store, a full twenty-one inches on the diagonal. If he sat close enough, it was almost like going to the movies, but Clyde was careful not to sit too close. He'd read the radiation from a television tube could fry your man parts if you got too near it, and your children would be born with three eyes, two noses, twelve fingers on each hand, and the brain of a salamander.

He needn't have worried. His last date had been in high school, an unfortunate and humiliating memory. At the urging of his buddies in the Army, he had hired a prostitute or two. He hadn't enjoyed the first one much, since it was his first time—for almost everything—and he had no idea what to expect. The second was more fun, but he'd been discharged shortly after. He'd heard about hot pillow joints in Pooler, the metropolis over in Parker County, but driving an hour into the big city for the sole purpose of getting his ashes hauled felt mildly perverted.

At the ripe age of twenty-three, Clyde Dillard's career as a lover was practically stillborn. On a great day, he was passably plain, with a large nose, recessed chin, jug ears, thinning hair, and a concave chest. Social engagement was a minefield. People weren't drawn to him. He wasn't witty. Making conversation was difficult. He figured, perhaps someday, when he became desperate enough, he might find a homely spinster with a pleasant personality and settle for what he could get.

Yet he desired to be with people. Men, he'd discovered, bonded with him, perhaps because he didn't threaten them. He had an unpleasant image in his head of himself as a terrier being led on a leash by Hubert Pressley. The image came, unbidden and unwelcome, every time Pressley laid a hand on his shoulder and pulled him around as he worked the room. Rennie and Pressley were born politicians. Pressley was a man of means, the manager of Rennie's store in Morgan, and the future co-owner of Poole's Feed and Seed in Mica Wells. Pressley's train was going places. He'd suggested there might be a seat on it for Clyde.

So, at Hubert's urging, Clyde attended Rennie Poole's klavern meetings. It was mostly a lot of farmers and merchants drinking and playing pool and telling dirty jokes, but Rennie was sure to take ten minutes out of every session to rant about his complaint of the week—Jews, Negroes, Catholics, miscegenation, desegregation, and the general overall decline of once-glorious Dixie.

Rennie Poole was a fireplug. Considerably under six feet tall, his closest friends suspected he accentuated his height using elevator shoes he'd ordered from an ad in the Saturday Evening Post. He was a square little man—square body, square head, large square hands—with shoulders almost two and a half feet across, thick biceps and forearms from years of hoisting fifty-pound bags of seed, a strong dimpled chin, a sharp, straight nose, and thin lips. His eyes dared you to look away once they riveted on you.

He pulled a wooden milk crate in front of the bar and—with a little help from Hubert Pressley—stood on it without spilling a drop of his Tennessee whisky. He passed the glass to Pressley and clapped his hands to get everyone's attention. The din of conversation dropped to a low murmur. Most of the men shuffled toward the bar. Clyde Dillard remained in his chair by the fireplace.

"Gentlemen!" Rennie called out. "I'm delighted to see so many people at our little social club this month. Everyone got enough to drink?" The crowd cheered back. Some held longneck bottles in the air. "Gentlemen, the Jewnited States Supreme Court has demanded we allow the coloreds to attend white schools. The traditions of our forefathers seem to mean nothing anymore. Black people—impertinent, ungrateful, lazy, greedy people whom our ancestors rightly owned—have demanded a piece of the action. They forget their place. Didn't our faithful Knight Hubert Pressley see a colored boy using the white people's shitter over at Pyle's Garage?"

"I did!" Hubert proclaimed. "In front of God and everybody."

"It's a symptom," Rennie continued as the noise abated. "I won't lie to you, my brothers. We are in dangerous times. This country was built on the backs of decent, God-fearing white men. Our blood was spilled on the flowers of Bunker Hill and Antietam and Bull Run and the Bulge. Our ancestors carved out of this wretched wilderness a society unlike any other in history—the greatest nation on the face of God's Green Earth. Every great human achievement was attained by a white man. We are culturally and biologically and intellectually superior! Now, nine old, unelected, unaccountable men in Washington have determined we are to be best served by mongrelization. Make no mistake, dear friends, if you let those black children darken the doors of our schools, there will be hell to pay."

Rennie paused for a moment as the room erupted again and held up his hands to bring them back as he returned his voice to a normal volume and put on his most sincere tone.

"I don't claim to know the answer to our predicament. I'm no sage. Like you, I make my living from the soil. We all do, one way or another, right? I'm just an old country boy, but it appears to me several things are true. The coloreds want more than they're due. They are multiplying, my friends, faster than horny jackrabbits. They intend to overwhelm us with their numbers. I predict a time, before we all go to our eternal rewards, when your wives and mothers won't be able to walk into a grocery store, a pharmacy, a movie house, or a public park without being accosted by a sex-crazed African buck. People who used to know their place are encroaching on our domain. Will we allow it, my brothers?"

"No!" they all shouted.

"All right!" Poole shouted, a huge grin on his face. He was on a roll, and he knew it, but Poole also knew when to pull the plug. He lowered his voice again and abandoned the tactic of fiery rhetoric. He'd planted all the seeds required for one evening. He merely needed to sit back and give them an opportunity to germinate.

"My friends, I won't bore you further with my rants and rages. I know we are in total agreement. I trust, when the moment to act comes, you will recognize it and join me in protecting our rights as free white Americans. I merely wished to welcome you to my home, and to let you know—you are not alone. You are not abandoned. There are thousands of people across this great country who think exactly as we do. We are rebuilding a great movement, my friends, and you will be a fundamental part of it. You boys go ahead and play and drink. Hubert and I will bring the desserts to the bar in a few minutes."

Chapter Eight

Ev Howard spent the morning hoofing the sidewalks of Morgan, looking for Help Wanted signs. He filled out an application at the Piggly Wiggly in the center of town, though the manager assured him there weren't any openings immediately. The manager at the Chick 'N' Shake, a local drive-in, regarded him stonily and made it clear he didn't allow any coloreds to work the front of the store, though there might be a night janitor opportunity soon. The story was the same everywhere. *Nothing now. Maybe later.*

Frustrated, Ev stopped at a barbecue joint in Garveyville, a black neighborhood in a valley between the center of Morgan and the railroad tracks. The shack specialized in pulled pork, roasted low and slow in a converted fifty-five-gallon drum smoker and served with mounds of creamy coleslaw, baked beans mixed with more brown sugar than conscience dictated, collard greens, and hushpuppies—a buck a plate and a dime for a bottomless glass of iced tea with fresh lemonade. He'd gone there because it was run by a black man, to serve the black community that lived around it. Ev didn't have to worry about accusing eyes or the outright denial of service he'd sometimes encountered at the lunch counters in downtown Morgan.

It was the middle of the afternoon. The lunch crowd had dwindled to Ev and a couple of other diners. The manager dropped by to chat.

"Sure is good," Ev told him. "Wish we had a decent barbecue joint in Prosperity."

"That's where you live?" the man asked.

"Little one-bedroom place my grandmother left. Only problem is, there aren't a lot of jobs in Prosperity. I worked at a car repair place until a few days ago."

"What happened?"

"Boss thought I stole from him, but I never took a dime. Swear to God."

"White man?"

"Yeah, but he's always been fair to me before."

"That's the way they are. Turn on you in a second if they believe you've stepped an inch out of line. You're looking for a job?"

"Been pounding the pavement all morning and into the afternoon."

"I hear tell the Southern Railway people are hiring porters over at the depot. Might want to look there."

"I'm obliged. Think I might get a refill on this iced tea?"

* * *

All his life, Owen Wheeler had been Number Two.

Jude Pressley was always a little more handsome, a little more athletic, a little more popular, and Owen spent most of his life in the shadow. Owen was tall, but still stood an inch shorter than Jude's six feet and heavy change. Unlike Jude, he was anything but dark, with sandy hair that turned near-white as he worked the farm under the summer sun, and sea-green eyes and lightly freckled skin. Jude was the epitome of *tall, dark, and handsome.* He was the romantic idol, the star, the center of attention. Owen was a halfback. On the field, he stood behind Jude, where it seemed he'd spent most of his life, dutifully ran the handoffs and took the punishment of the defensive line and the tackles, and he went long to receive Jude's perfectly flung spirals. Jude basked in glory. Owen nursed bruises.

He sat in a cushioned wicker sofa on the gallery of his parents' farmhouse. He loved the deep, shady front porch. His father had installed electric ceiling fans to keep the air moving on steamy Carolina summer days.

The farm had been in his family since before the American Revolution. Owen's farthest-back immigrant ancestor arrived only a few years after the

Mayflower, as an indentured laborer for a Virginia planter. He stepped off the boat in Accomack with a cloth case containing everything he'd brought from the old country to build a new life. In time, he'd flourished, and when the British king handed out land grants in the newly settled Carolinas, he'd arranged to obtain two hundred acres.

The most recent house had stood for over thirty years. Owen's grand-father had ordered it from the Sears catalog. It was a classic Craftsman home, with a gambrel roof, lots of windows, and the expansive shady front porch. It arrived on a single boxcar at the Morgan train station in 1921, pallets of boards and bricks and sacks of mortar and windows and doors and hardware, a jigsaw puzzle house Owen's grandfather and his neighbors loaded onto wagons and panel trucks and transported to its final location.

Owen loved the house. It was his favorite spot in the world, along with the rolling, fecund hills and fields of the Carolina Piedmont surrounding it. He couldn't imagine how a person could leave a farm behind and pursue some other line of work. He loved the smell of the soil after it was tilled, and the way the fields transformed from brown to green almost overnight, and the crispness of harvest season. He'd inherited a special gift for making things grow. It had never occurred to him he might ever be anything other than the next generation to maintain the legacy of the Wheeler farm in Prosperity.

And now, a bolt from the blue.

"Let's see Jude top this," Owen muttered to himself as he re-read the letter that had arrived in the noon mail. The words were short, succinct, and direct.

Greetings, from the President of the United States! You are hereby directed...

Jude Pressley's Willys turned off the Morgan Highway onto the quarter-mile rutted gravel drive leading up to the front porch. He hopped out almost before the engine was still.

"Owen!" he yelled, holding up a sheaf of papers. "Wait until you see this!"

He took the steps two at a time and handed the papers to his friend. Owen glanced over them.

"What is it?" he asked.

"It's a Letter of Intent. Ryland College offered me a full ride to play football!"

"You're going to college?"

"They want me to be their quarterback. I mean, I know it's not a prestige school, but their schedule is solid—Tusculum, Newberry, Carson-Newman, other little schools with stout football rosters. And I can get a degree!"

"Gonna be lonely around here the next couple of years," Owen said, as he handed his own letter to Jude.

"I don't get it," Jude said, after reading it over. "You've been drafted? Why are they drafting guys if we aren't fighting a war?"

"Beats me."

"Can't you get out of it?"

"Don't know that I prefer to," Owen said. "It might not be so bad. Nobody's shooting at us right now. Maybe I'll get a posting someplace interesting, like Germany. It would be an opportunity to see the world on someone else's dime. My dad's healthy. The farm is doing okay. I suppose I could run off and see the world for a couple of years. It might work out."

"Did you tell Billy yet?"

"Haven't even told my folks. The letter came this afternoon. This is a hell of a thing."

"It is." Jude collapsed into a chair facing the loveseat. "It's a hell of a thing."

Chapter Nine

Coral was determined she wouldn't spend a blistering, windless Saturday afternoon on the front porch driving off flies with a funeral home fan. According to *Reader's Digest*, over one million air conditioners had been sold in the previous year. Why couldn't at least one of them have found its way to her home?

She told her mother she was going for a drive, to get some air moving around her. She took the second car to the Lincoln farm. The short hike through the woods, so dark and foreboding the first night she'd come, now seemed like a pleasant familiar stroll.

She hadn't packed her swimsuit. Her mother would have noticed, either from the bulge in her pocketbook or when it showed up in the wash later. Besides, there was no need. While she'd been apprehensive the first time or two Jude had brought her to The Ledge, she'd come to realize it was as private as her own bathroom at home. Perhaps more so since her bathroom at home was shared by four people.

The night Jude had given her the locket and had produced his package of Duke's condoms had changed her life. She believed she had become a woman that night. Everything had changed. She remembered the weight of him above her in the utter darkness of their retreat, a little pressure, and then a sensation the like of which she had known only once before. She had been careful to wince and give out a little cry of pain as he entered her, as she did not want him to know she was not a virgin. Jude was inexperienced and a little clumsy, but he grasped the fundamentals quickly, and by the second and third time they had made love he had become more self-assured and assertive. Each time was easier for her than the one before. She found that she not only enjoyed sex but wanted to get better at it to please him.

That was the problem. Even in the culturally advanced world of 1954, there were few places to obtain accurate, dependable information about lovemaking. There were those scandalous Kinsey studies, of course, but try finding one of *those* in provincial Prosperity, North Carolina. She'd checked, however surreptitiously, at the library, but there was no listing for Kinsey in the card catalog. Even if there had been, she was not sure she would have dared to get within three stacks of its shelf. Certainly, the library would have material that salacious kept under some sort of armed guard and, even if it weren't monitored, no teenaged girl of any standing in Prosperity would dare be seen perusing it.

She couldn't rely on her girlfriends at school. As soon as she asked a question, they would descend on her like interrogating harpies, demanding to know with whom she was perpetrating the dirty deed.

And God forbid she should approach her mother. It was one thing for Mom to tell her how to avoid unwanted pregnancies by pleasing a boy in other ways. It was quite another for Coral to approach her for advice on maximizing pleasure once she'd sold the farm.

She had seen some of the magazines that had accumulated over the years in her father's garage, and one or two of them had been embarrassingly graphic. She never understood why her father had not tossed them out, but there they were. Most of them had only girlie pinup pictures, but a few revealed full nudity. There was the one magazine she had found, cheaply printed, illiterately written, and unpleasant to touch, but it had contained many photos of men and women doing *it*. The positions looked awkward, and the people didn't appear to be enjoying themselves. They looked hurried and earnest and workmanlike. One could not fault their athleticism, but they did not appear joyful.

She rolled out the blanket she had secreted in the trunk and spread it on The Ledge. She reached up, undid the knot on her sundress, and allowed it to drop to her feet. Her underwear quickly followed, and she stepped to the pool and slipped underneath the water.

She loved water flowing across her skin, uninterrupted by textiles. It was sensuous and luxurious, in a way she had never experienced in a bathtub. She could float out to the middle of the pool, exhale a little, and her entire body would slip under the surface, suspended weightlessly. When she and Jude swam at night, if she concentrated in the pitch darkness and stared straight up into the heavens, she could imagine she was adrift in space, lost among the stars, a speck of dust in the immensity of the universe.

Of course, this was impossible in the middle of an afternoon in June, but it was godawful hot, and the water was cool. She floated and relaxed, and allowed the heat to be drawn out of her and dissipate in the liquid. As she was buoyed in the water, her mind emptied, and calm rolled over her like a warming fog.

* * *

Clyde Dillard's store had stocked a new selection of Garcia Mitchell fishing rods and reels, and Clyde used his employee discount to snatch one up. It was a beauty, with the new cap reel instead of the old spinner style he'd always used. The rod was fiberglass, with a stout cork handle wound in silky red string. Clyde imagined how many brook trout he could land with such a rig.

He packed a ham sandwich and a bottle of Coke for lunch, assembled his tackle, and set off on the hike toward Six Mile Creek, the sun beating on his battered fishing hat and making his scalp sweat underneath, soaking his thinning hair. He didn't care. He wasn't working, and he was going to have a hell of a meal after he cleaned the fish. No fish camp within fifty miles could match Clyde Dillard's fried trout dinner. His only regret was, absent the most mind-boggling of miracles, he'd again enjoy it in solitude.

"Oh, well," he muttered. "More for me."

He meant more than just dinner. Next to the slaw in the refrigerator were two cartons of wide-neck Rolling Rock beer. Clyde intended to decimate most of their number over dinner and afterward. Jackie Gleason was on at eight o'clock. *The Honeymooners* was a lot funnier after Clyde dropped six or seven dead soldiers into the trash. If he was still conscious after Gleason, there was either the Saturday Night Fights on ABC or *The Jimmy Durante Show* over on NBC. Surely, with such a panoply of entertainment options, nobody could honestly claim boredom on a Saturday evening.

One thing was certain. Long before the local channels played the national anthem and switched to the test signal for the night, Clyde would be passed out on the couch, dreaming beer-drenched fantasies of South Seas paradises populated by naked native girls.

He made his first cast into a quieter part of the creek. The easy part of the day began. He secured the rod in the crook of his arm and sat back until something hit, and ate his lunch slowly. On such an afternoon, he couldn't see the profit in rushing anything. He concentrated on recalling Gleason's show from the previous week. He was able to remember a couple of jokes, and he chuckled at them, and Clyde was happy.

The sandwich digesting and the bottle drained, Clyde turned his attention back to fishing. The float lay motionless on the surface of the pool's still waters. Deciding he wouldn't bag any trout there today, he reeled in the line and headed downstream toward another pool he remembered from when he was a kid.

He was almost there, concentrating on the roots breaking the surface of the sandy soil on the narrow, poorly maintained path along the creek bank, when he looked up, and his heart skipped a beat.

Someone was in the pool. In all the years he'd come to this spot to fish, he'd never seen another person. Yet, there was no mistaking it. It appeared to be a woman.

And she was naked.

"Whoa," he said before he could stifle it.

* * *

Coral's head snapped around, splashing a rooster comb of water from her hair.

She was certain she'd heard a voice. She arced her body to submerge it, her feet barely brushing the slimy smooth cold stone bed of the pond, and she craned her neck to look for any intruders. Her heart hammered inside her chest. She was naked and alone, defenseless against anyone who might happen upon her. She had been foolish to come out by herself. She considered calling out, to ask if someone was there, but it would only give her away. She slowly floated to a boulder that provided some scant cover and waited.

After a couple of minutes, she relaxed. She convinced herself she only heard a bird, or perhaps a tree branch falling. She had allowed her imagination to run away with her, and now she was embarrassed at her stupidity. In any case, she didn't feel like hanging around anymore.

* * *

As soon as he said, "*Whoa*," Clyde knew he should have held his tongue. The woman's head popped out of the water and frantically whipped around as she looked for the source of the sound. He was too well-concealed for her to spy.

Save for the prostitutes who'd bounced his bedsprings in Alaska, Clyde had never seen a grown woman naked. He'd seen plenty of pictures, for sure, but not in real life. He was aware of his excitement and arousal, even as the sharp buzz in the back of his head suggested what he was doing was wrong. The idea confused him. He'd happened upon the woman in the creek. He hadn't plotted to disturb her privacy. He'd done nothing illegal or immoral. At the worst, he was guilty of bad manners for continuing to look. And, if anything, the entire situation was *her* fault. What kind of decent person ran around buck nekkid in the middle of the afternoon?

She stuck her head up again and looked around. Then she did the most remarkable thing. She stepped out of the water, walked across the rocky bank of the creek, and wrapped herself in a blanket. While she'd been every bit as naked in the pool, his view had been mostly obscured by the water. Now, iridescent as the sunlight glinted off her dripping body, her entire form was revealed to him. She was beautiful, her skin nearly flawless. Her breasts were firm, her behind rounded, her legs trim and muscular.

She dropped the blanket and faced him, and he feared his heart might stop. He couldn't make out her face, but he could see everything else in Technicolor clarity as she bent to pick up her underclothes. Within a minute, she dressed, rolled up the blanket, and hiked up the hill.

Chapter Ten

Coral watched Jude explore the bank of Six Mile Creek opposite The Ledge. He looked around the base of trees and in the crevasses between boulders for any sign suggesting a person had been there. He policed the area for fifty yards in each direction before he forded the creek and returned to where she sat, her knees drawn up and her arms wrapped around her legs. She wore a sleeveless broadcloth shirt, a pair of white shorts, and an expression of concern.

"Can't find anything," he reported. "Whatever you heard out here, it wasn't a person. Might have been a crow, or maybe a couple of deer."

"I suppose you're right."

"I've been here bunches of times, and I've never seen another human. We could be the last two people on Earth, for all the company we're gonna get out here."

"If you're sure…"

"If I weren't I wouldn't do this." He dropped his pants and stepped out of them, and then peeled his shirt off over his head. He tossed his boxers into the pile and headed for the pool. "I'm hot. Going in for a swim."

Jude said earlier he had big news, but since he picked her up at the library, he'd remained quiet and reserved. They'd only been together for a month, however surreptitiously, but she believed she could read his expressions. Something was on his mind.

She stripped and joined him in the pool. She was careful to remove the necklace and locket. They weren't waterproof, and Jude's picture was paper. He'd trespassed and vandalized to obtain it from the school library, rather than mutilate his own high school yearbook. She didn't want his efforts to go to waste because she was careless with her jewelry.

The heatwave continued unabated. Thunderstorms were forecast later in the day, but for the moment the sun was bright, and the sky was a deep Carolina blue. She glanced cautiously toward the other bank, to reassure herself they weren't being observed. Each time she saw nothing made her feel better.

After cooling in the pool, they returned to the blanket and allowed the sun to dry their bodies. She became drowsy until his hand caressed her belly. As he moved it and explored, her heart quickened. She rolled over and embraced him, pressing her mouth against his. Coral hadn't touched his body in almost five days, and she almost couldn't contain her hunger for him. Their initial adolescent fumbling gave way to passion, and they grappled on their coarse blanket on The Ledge.

"You have a Duke?" she asked. Their pet name for the condoms.

"One left."

"Give it to me."

She opened the round plastic box and extracted the rubber. Placing it on him, she unrolled it with her lips as he groaned in pleasure and appreciation. But she wasn't done yet. Instead of waiting for him to climb onto her, she grasped his shoulders, straddled him, and guided him inside of her. She rode him on The Ledge until he exploded inside her, and she rolled off and lay on her back next to him, huffing and gasping, the sweat from their skin mingling as their arms encircled each other and their fingers intertwined.

"Jesus," he said. "Where'd you learn that?"

"I have my ways," she said, gulping for air.

"You... uh... did you? You know?"

She turned her head to face him. "Oh, fuck yeah. Twice. Couldn't you tell?"

He sat upright. "Why, Miss Coral, how you talk."

"I figure, if I'm gonna do it, I might as well be able to say it. Not in public, obviously. A girl has to maintain her reputation."

They lay on The Ledge and held one another, until Jude said, "Have you given any thought to what you're doing after graduation?"

"Sweetie, I haven't given much thought to what I'm doing *tonight.*"

He propped up on one elbow. He traced random designs in the drying perspiration on her stomach as he spoke.

"Think you might go to college?"

"I suppose. My grades are good enough. Why?"

"Where do you reckon you'd go? You want to be at a big school or a little one?"

She shut her eyes to block out the glare from the sun. "I've lived in a little place all my life. Big school might be a nice change, for at least a while. Why?"

"The reason I couldn't come here with you yesterday. Dad and I met with Coach McCandless from Ryland College. He offered me a scholarship. All expenses paid."

She opened her eyes and sat up. "To play football?"

"Yeah!" he said, still a little amazed at it himself. "They need a quarterback. I figured I'd go off and play my first year. After you graduate next May, you can come to Ryland, and we can be together there."

Her face darkened. "You've already agreed?"

"Well, sure. I signed the letter of intent yesterday. Football practice starts in five weeks. I'll leave for Ryland the first of August."

"And you didn't discuss it with me first?" she said angrily. "God *damn* it, Jude! You said I was important to you."

"You are."

"Not enough to consult before you go making life-altering decisions. The least you could have done was tell me about it."

She was crying, which was the last thing she wanted him to see. She knew her face went blotchy and ugly when she cried. She turned away from him. He placed his hand on her shoulder, partly to comfort her, and partly to keep her from walking away.

"Please be happy for me," he said. "It'll break my heart if you aren't. An opportunity like this comes along once in a lifetime."

"An opportunity for *you*, sure." She refused to yield to his pull against her shoulder. "But what about me? What do I do for the next year? Senior prom is coming up. Are you taking a bus all the way from Ryland to escort me? I don't think you give one fucking damn what *I* want."

"It's not like I'm going to the moon."

"Might as well be," she argued. She rose to her feet. "I'm hot and bothered and worked up. Gonna go cool off."

"Me, too."

"Stay. I haven't decided I want you near me yet."

She stomped toward the pool, the tears still brimming in her eyes. She felt betrayed and abandoned. At barely seventeen, she didn't have the emotional skills to cope with her disappointment.

Her blurred vision prevented her from seeing the slick patch of lichen on the stone surface near the water. As she stepped on it, her foot slipped out from under her. She pivoted, trying to regain her balance, and her other foot found the patch and also slipped. As she fell heavily, the left side of her head bounced off the rock. She saw a starburst of blinding red light, and pain lanced through her skull.

* * *

Jude began running the instant Coral lost her footing. He was ten feet away when she stood, wobbling on her feet. The left side of her head was bloody, her hair matted. She looked at him strangely.

"Ju—?" she croaked, as if calling to him, but never finished the word. Her eyes rolled up in their sockets, and she collapsed again. The back of her skull hit another rock outcropping. She crumpled to the ground and lay motionless.

Jude knelt at her side immediately. Blood gushed from the wound at the back of her head when he tried to cradle it. Her eyes were open, both fully dilated. One skewed off to the right. She wasn't breathing, and when Jude palpated the arteries in her neck, he couldn't find a pulse.

"No!" he screamed. "Oh, God! Please, no! Oh, *Jesus!*"

His impulse was to run to his car and try to find the police or an ambulance, but they would never arrive in time. He was only nineteen, and he had no idea what to do. Slowly, as he sobbed next to her body, the grim truth wended its way into the part of his brain that was still rational.

In an instant, Coral had died.

There was no escaping it. She was irrevocably, irretrievably gone. He had to go to the police, even if she couldn't survive.

And tell them what? He'd been screwing Arlo Pyle's daughter for over a month? They had carried on a secret love affair? He could imagine the outcome. Arlo might kill him. Even if he survived, there would be scandal. He could kiss his scholarship goodbye.

They had been scrupulously secretive. Despite the fact Coral had expected him to brag about their sex life to his buddies Owen Wheeler and Billy Mosack, he hadn't mentioned a word to anyone. He knew she hadn't dared to tell her friends because she'd told him so.

There was nothing he could do for Coral, but he wasn't obligated to dump his entire future down the drain. Her demise didn't have to mean the death of his dreams. If he walked away from The Ledge, nobody would ever know he'd been there. He could move on with his life without fear of destroying everything he'd ever hoped for.

How long did a body take to decompose to the bones? With time, her bones themselves might be reclaimed by the creek. She'd be the talk of the town for a while after disappearing. Over months and years, she'd be slowly forgotten. In a decade, folks would say, "Remember that girl who went missing in 1954? Whatever happened to her?"

Or she might be discovered in a day or so, lying naked next to the still waters of the pool, her clothes carefully left behind. Everyone would suspect the truth. She came out to escape the heat of the afternoon, decided to go for a swim, and fell. A tragic accident. There was no reason for Jude to be part of the story, or to catch any of its shrapnel.

He'd know. He recognized and accepted immediately the price he'd pay. If he had any hope of salvaging his dreams, it would come at the cost of her accusing face in his head for the rest of his life. There was no other way, he concluded, tears streaming down his face and merging with the river of mucus from his nose. To save himself, he had to abandon Coral. Walking back to his car and leaving her behind was the down payment on his lodgings in Hell. He'd make the mortgage payments every night for the rest of his life, but—at the very least—he'd *have* a life.

He dressed quickly and rolled the blanket, never seeing the glint of gold as Coral's locket fell to the ground near her discarded clothes. Something about walking away felt like a betrayal, and when he turned toward the path back to his car his feet wouldn't move. Instead, he sat back down and held Coral's cooling hand and wiped away tears, trying to unravel the knot of emotions inside his head, until the sun settled behind the trees on the other side of Six Mile Creek.

As darkness descended, he kissed her one last time, and trudged up the hill to his car

* * *

That night, as Arlo fretted at home waiting for his daughter who had missed supper, and as Jude Pressley rocked back and forth hugging his knees and weeping on the twin bed in his room, and as Everett Howard slumped in a chaise on his front porch and tried to understand with his limited ability why a man who had treated him with respect had suddenly turned on him, and as Clyde Dillard watched Ed Sullivan and drank himself into a stupor, it began to rain.

Huge thunderheads grew over Bliss County. Lightning arced across the sky twenty times a minute. Water poured as if to wash every trace of sin and iniquity from the countryside. Six Mile Creek swelled and nearly crested its banks. The pool where Jude had left Coral's body rose two feet, and the entire creek became a torrent that swept everything downstream, including Coral herself. Her clothes were washed into the cataract, borne miles away, never to be found. The locket, which Jude failed to see as he made his escape, wedged in a chink in a boulder near the water's edge.

As the waters rose, Coral's already bloating body drifted toward the Old Village Road.

Chapter Eleven

Ev Howard woke on Monday morning feeling inexplicably happy. The rest of the world sat in traffic on the way to their nine-to-five, but Ev didn't have to worry about them. He had no job, but there were a few bucks in his pocket, and he felt no desire to hit the bricks again to look for new work. Instead, he went fishing. If he could land a decent trout or bass, he wouldn't have to spend money for dinner.

The bridge over Six Mile Creek on the Old Village Road had been built with pedestrians in mind. Beyond the guardrail on each side of the road was a narrow concrete path for people who chose to wear out shoe leather instead of rubber tires, and a second guardrail to keep them from falling into the waters of the creek thirty feet below. Ev waved at a couple of cars as they whizzed past him, and he opened the battered and rusted tackle box. He tied a hook to the string he'd knotted onto the end of an eight-foot bamboo pole. In a baby food jar at his feet were nightcrawlers he'd harvested from the mud in his garden after they were drawn to the surface by the thunderstorm. In his simple way, Ev apologized to the first worm he pulled from the jar as he speared it on the hook and thanked it for the role it would play in filling his belly. He swung the pole out over the creek.

And he saw the body.

The floodwaters hadn't been kind to Coral Pyle. She'd been dashed against tree stumps and tumbled mercilessly over the rocky creek bed. Her naked corpse came to rest against one of the steel supports holding up the bridge abutment, where it lay twisted and battered. Despite nature's abuse, her face was still recognizable, and it terrified Ev Howard. He wasn't terribly bright, but he knew nothing good could come of him being associated with the dead girl lying below the bridge.

He ran. He ditched his bamboo pole over the side of the bridge and didn't even bother to grab his battered tackle box.

He recognized his error halfway home, but he dared not return to the bridge to retrieve the box. If the body was already found by some other poor soul, he was damned one way or the other. He packed some meager belongings into a canvas duffle and set out on foot to find a place where nobody'd ever heard of him.

* * *

Coral's body was discovered by a boy who had also come to the bridge to fish. The youngster ran to the nearest house and telephoned the Sheriff's Department. Prosperity didn't have its own police station. All Bliss County law enforcement outside the Morgan city limits was in the charge of the sheriff.

Arlo and Adele Pyle had been panic-stricken all morning. Coral hadn't returned home the previous night. Her bed hadn't been slept in, and all her clothes were in place. After checking with her friends by telephone without success, Arlo had called the Sheriff's Department. The desk clerk there tried to reassure him, reminding him teenagers don't always think clearly about what they're doing. He told Arlo to call back in a couple of hours if Coral didn't show up.

Deputy Brian Mattox examined the body wedged between two rocks under the Old Village Road bridge. After reporting to his superiors over the car radio, he was informed of the missing person report. Putting two and two together, he fetched Arlo and brought him to the scene, which now swarmed with police cars and an ambulance. Adele begged to go with them, but Arlo told her to stay home, reasoning that, if it was Coral, it would be unbearable for her to see their daughter battered and pummeled by water and rocks.

It took him only a second to identify the body by the purple blotch on her shoulder. He collapsed to the concrete and wept as he leaned against the bridge abutment.

"How do I tell Adele?" he sobbed. "How am I gonna tell her mother?"

Mattox drove him home and accompanied Arlo inside to break the news. The house was set back from the road almost two hundred feet, but any passersby could have easily heard Adele's scream.

* * *

Within an hour of the discovery of Coral's body, the telephone party lines across the entire town were filled with people—housewives, businessmen, teachers, teenagers—fighting to talk over one another as they speculated on what had happened to the girl.

Rennie Poole quickly arrived at Arlo's house with Hubert Pressley in tow. Rennie never balked at an opportunity to publicly demonstrate his caring social engagement. They found Arlo on his couch, a half-empty bottle of cheap whiskey on the coffee table, a glass sweating out onto a coaster. He'd cried nonstop since hitting the bottle. He drank and drank, but nothing drove out the image of his sweet baby daughter, bloated and discolored, her empty, milky eyes staring unfocused at a cloudless sky.

"Where's Adele?" Rennie took the glass from Arlo's hand.

"Bedroom," he said. "Took a coupla Seconals. She's asleep."

"Grace?"

"On a graduation trip to Myrtle Beach with friends. I called her. She's coming back tomorrow."

"What happened, Arlo?" Rennie asked.

"Don't know," Arlo's voice was slurred by whiskey and tears. "She's dead. That's all. Somebody done killed my baby." Saying it brought on another round of sobs.

"Maybe it was an accident," Hubert offered.

Arlo said, "I don't know nothing yet, boys. You got here quick."

"We were drawn to a friend in need," Rennie said. "Is there anything we can do? Anything at all? Get you something from the grocery?"

"Can't think," Arlo said. "Don't know which end is up."

Deputy Mattox rapped on the screen door. "Mr. Pyle? Is it okay to come in?"

Rennie Poole gestured for the deputy to enter.

"What?" Arlo said, his voice heavily affected by the booze.

"Do you recognize this tackle box?" Mattox asked.

Arlo looked at the box, blinked a couple of times, and nodded. "I give it to Ev Howard. Colored boy. Worked for me. Maybe a year ago. Maybe longer."

"The one I saw using the white folks' toilet," Hubert said.

"And Ev Howard worked for you? Until when?" Mattox asked.

"Coupla weeks ago. I fired him for stealing," Arlo said. "What's this all about?"

"Yeah," Rennie added. "Does Ev Howard have something to do with Arlo's daughter?"

"Don't know," Mattox said. "We found this tackle box on the bridge. Might be a coincidence. First time I was there, I assumed it belonged to the kid who found her."

Rennie stepped closer to Mattox. "Arlo fired this boy Howard and his daughter got killed in the span of a few days. Don't sound like any coincidence to me. Looks like revenge, pure and simple."

Something seemed to click behind Arlo's eyes. He looked up at the deputy. "Did Ev Howard kill my baby?"

"We don't know. Can you tell me where Howard lives? I can drive over and inquire as to how his tackle box wound up at the scene of a murder."

"Murder?" Rennie asked. "So that's definite?"

"It's not official until the coroner in Morgan issues a ruling, but the doctor who examined her at the creek says it don't look like any accidental drowning. I don't want to upset you, Mr. Pyle, but it looks like someone stove in her head with a pipe or a baseball bat or something. Maybe a big rock. They're doing an autopsy now. We should know for certain by nightfall."

* * *

Mattox returned less than a half-hour later. Arlo was passed out on the sofa, snoring loudly. Rennie Poole and Hubert Pressley watched over him to ensure he didn't die from alcohol poisoning.

"Kid bugged out," Mattox reported as he walked in the door. "The front door was open, and I saw... um, indications of a hasty departure. Looks like this Howard boy's gone rabbit on us."

"You need help looking for him?" Rennie asked. "I can have fifty men here in an hour."

"We aren't to that point yet. I'll take this tackle box into Morgan and sign it in as evidence at the Sheriff's Department, see if we can pull some prints off it. The autopsy should be complete in a few hours." He pointed toward Arlo, curled up on the sofa. "You might want to cut him off. He won't be any use to us if he vanishes into the bottom of a bottle."

Rennie Poole collared Mattox. "What in hell is wrong with you?"

"Beg pardon, Mr. Poole, but you need to let go of my shirt."

"You *know* this Howard boy killed Coral. Why are you dancing around it? You gonna let this nigger slip through your fingers while you follow procedure?"

"I've seen more than one man get off because some deputy fucked up the chain of evidence or jumped to a wrong conclusion. If this Howard boy killed Coral, I'll volunteer to walk to Central Prison in Raleigh and pull the lever on Old Sparky myself, fry his ass proper. Until we're certain, he's only a material witness. Once I get to Morgan, I'll put out an all-points bulletin. Ever' deputy in three counties will be on the lookout for him, and all the local police officers, too. No offense, Mr. Poole, but the best thing you can do right now is take care of Arlo. He don't look like he's handling this at all."

"What in hell do you expect. He just lost his baby daughter. You listen to me. I got a lot of pull with the sheriff. I can make your way up the ladder in the department easy, if you know what I mean."

"I'd advise you to stop there."

"Soon's you have anything definite, you let me know. I want to hear it first. You give me the word, and I'll have men beating the bushes. We'll find Ev Howard, and we'll see to it he gets what's comin' to him."

* * *

Owen Wheeler and Billy Mosack drove to Jude's house, where they found him sitting on the front porch, staring at the highway.

"C'mon," Owen said. "We're headed to the hardware."

"My dad's already there," Jude said. "He and Mr. Poole took off a while back."

"Hop in the back of the truck," Owen said. "Don't want to miss this one."

At first, Jude waved them off. He had no desire to be anyplace where people were talking about Coral. His friends were relentless, though, and he finally climbed into the back of Owen's truck with all the enthusiasm of stepping into a tumbrel bound for the guillotine.

As the day wore on with no word from Morgan, men had congregated at the hardware store, the center of cracker-barrel politics in Prosperity for decades. Whenever anything of importance occurred in town, the men all knew where to go to discuss it. Clyde Dillard anticipated the avalanche and had iced a couple of cases of Coke and restocked the fried apple pies in the case at the front of the store.

Arlo Pyle sat in a chair in the corner, bent over, cradling his pounding head in his hands. Visitors stepped forward to offer words of consolation. Arlo never raised his head. The gravel and shell parking lot overflowed with cars and pickup trucks from all over town.

Rennie Poole held court. He was in his element, now—the rabble-rouser, the carnival barker, the tent preacher, the hootchie-kootch shill, the racing tout. When it came to bending groups of people to his will, he naturally took center stage. It wasn't necessary for him to say with authority that Ev Howard was the murderer. He knew every man in the room, and their sentiments. His intimation that Howard was responsible for Coral Pyle's death had been heard and interpreted as established fact.

"Where is this Howard boy now?" one man demanded.

"On the run," Rennie answered, striving to hammer as much subtext into the statement as possible. "Deputy Mattox went to Howard's house and found it stripped to the wallpaper. Now, I'm just an ol' country boy, but I know how to add one plus one, and I know every one of you here do as well—"

He stopped as Brian Mattox stepped into the room. Mattox removed his campaign cover and crooked a finger at Arlo. Robotically, Arlo stood and trudged to the door.

"Excuse me," Rennie said. "I need to tend to Arlo. You boys wait. Could be news."

Mattox led Arlo to his cruiser, where he spoke softly to the stricken father. Arlo covered his eyes with his hands and sank to his knees, wailing in sorrow. Rennie crossed the lot at a dead run and helped Mattox pull Arlo to his feet.

Arlo grasped Rennie's head with both hands, his eyes wide, and spittle flew from his lips as he cried, "She was raped! That goddamned nigger done gone and raped my baby before he killed her!"

Chapter Twelve

"What?" Rennie said.

Arlo was too stricken to speak. Mattox answered for him. "The autopsy results are in. She died of blunt force trauma to the head. It also revealed she... you know. Before she died. There was evidence of recent...sexual congress."

Arlo wailed again. The crowd inside the hardware store was already mulling over their options. With Rennie Poole occupied outside, Hubert Pressley took control.

"You heard him, men!" he shouted. "Not only did Ev Howard kill Coral Pyle, but he... ah... *insinuated* himself upon her beforehand. This is a symptom, my friends, a symptom of a growing cancer in our great republic! People call for civil rights, but how can you ever grant such rights to those who are not civil? Are we to stand by and watch our wives, sisters, daughters, and mothers violated by people with no more morality than a rock, and cast aside like so much garbage?"

The men in the store yelled, "No!"

"Do you trust the Sheriff's Department to find this horrendous killer?"

"No!" several more joined in.

"Can we wait for the *authorities* to mete out justice for Coral Pyle?"

Now everyone joined in, save for Jude Pressley, who had removed himself to a far corner of the store. He sat silent, horrified.

Rennie Poole and Deputy Mattox walked Arlo through the door as Hubert finished his sneering reference to *authorities*. Mattox stepped forward.

"Listen to me!" he yelled. Everyone turned in his direction. "What you're talking about is wrong. The evidence we have right now is circumstantial. All we know is Coral Pyle and Ev Howard's tackle box were found at the same location. Who knows how long the box had been there? Arlo himself said Howard was a simple boy. Maybe he left the box long before Coral died."

"So why'd he run away?" Tom Tackett yelled, and the crowd erupted again.

"We don't know he did," Mattox argued. "He was fired a couple of weeks ago. Maybe he's off in Morgan or in Pooler, looking for work."

"And maybe he's on the run because he raped and killed Coral to get back at Arlo for firing him!" Tackett yelled.

The mob's sentiments leaned in Tackett's direction. A panicked look crossed Mattox's face. Rennie gripped his shoulder, jerked his head in the direction of the door, and Mattox followed him outside.

"They're going to do something terrible," Mattox said.

"Even if they are, you can't stop them now. You have to ask yourself how you respond."

Mattox turned to him straight-on. "What are you talking about?"

"Be reasonable, Brian. As I see it, you have three choices. You can call in reinforcements from the Sheriff's Department in Morgan. That'll give you—what?—five or six more men? To do what? All we're suggesting here is you allow us to help find this Howard boy."

"And when you do?"

"Hell, Brian, he might be a hundred miles away by now. Your second choice is join in with those men and help us get justice for Coral."

"I won't. It's wrong."

"Option three is turn a blind eye. You and I both know the sheriff. He's got no foundation, no core set of beliefs dictating his acts. And he drinks."

"Mr. Poole..."

"Hell, everyone knows it. The sheriff is simply not a man to be trusted in a crisis. All handshake and no backbone. He'd sell one of his balls for a vote and the other for a bottle of hootch. Character tells, and his tells a lousy story. We should look to the future, consider who we want leading the department into the second half of the century. Could be a bright, conscientious, talented young man like yourself."

"What are you saying?"

"Go do your job. Use every resource at your disposal to locate Ev Howard and bring him before a judge. We might keep an eye out 'round Prosperity. If we see the boy, maybe we can give you a call."

"Or take matters into your own hands."

"And," Rennie continued, "should you decide to make a run at the sheriff's office, I'd strongly encourage you to pay me a visit at the Feed and Seed for a campaign contribution. You look like a young man with promise."

Mattox walked across the gravel and shell lot, stopping at the edge of the highway. He stared across it for a long time. He shook his head a couple of times, spat into the weeds, and walked back to his cruiser.

"I'm headed to Morgan. You keep your boys in order, Mr. Poole. I mean it. If you locate Howard, I expect a phone call."

Rennie returned to the hardware and addressed the crowd. "Deputy Mattox has decided to pursue this investigation from Morgan. My suggestion is we do what we can here in Prosperity to help him out. I'll pay one hundred dollars cash to any man who brings Ev Howard in. Hubert, Clyde, you boys come with me. Everyone else, team up!"

The men fanned out looking for Ev Howard. Clyde Dillard, who'd never killed a single living creature larger than a brook trout, grabbed a twenty-two rifle from the hardware store sales rack and stuffed a handful of cartridges in his pocket, more to fit in than with any intent of inflicting harm. He was a good-hearted man and wanted to do what he could for Arlo Pyle. He was also excited Rennie Poole asked him to search with him and Hubert Pressley. Being important and wanted was an unusual but welcome sensation.

The Trinity—Jude Pressley, Owen Wheeler, and Billy Mosack—climbed into Owen's dilapidated Ford farm pickup. Crammed shoulder-to-shoulder in the cab, they struck out over the winding country roads between Prosperity and Mica Wells in search of the presumed murderer. Billy had a Colt Police revolver his father had left behind before being killed at Anzio, and Owen Wheeler brought along a double-barrel shotgun he used to shoot copperheads on the farm. Jude sat next to the passenger window and stared at the passing countryside, unarmed, afraid to say a word.

They scanned the world illuminated by the headlights, searching for any stray movement, any lone pedestrian walking the road's overgrown, weed-choked shoulder, anything at all that didn't belong. Owen had a radio in the truck, and they listened to the local station in Morgan for any news alerts indicating Howard's apprehension by the sheriff. All they heard was music.

* * *

Ev Howard sat in the train station in Tulip Springs, waiting for a Southern Railway express to Columbia, when he heard a report on the radio naming him as a suspect in the murder of Coral Pyle. He walked, as calmly as possible, out the door and hid in a scrapyard until dark. It gave him time to think about his situation.

Perhaps he should go back to Prosperity and explain what happened, what a horrible coincidence everything had been. He was simply in the wrong place at the wrong time. He knew Mr. Pyle to be a decent man. If he could get Mr. Pyle to believe him, he'd be halfway home. Ev saw the world in concrete terms, divided irretrievably into good and evil. Surely, the people he'd known all his life in Prosperity were decent and charitable. They would listen to him. They'd realize he'd done nothing wrong.

Or they wouldn't, and he had no idea what would happen. Arrest? Imprisonment? What if he couldn't prove he was innocent? He was a black man in a white man's world. They made all the rules. He'd tried to follow them, as best he could. Now, their rules could destroy his life.

He was terribly confused. Three or four times he turned back toward the railroad tracks, determined to steal aboard a car and disappear.

His profound sense of responsibility and his belief in the best in people overcame him at last, and he turned again toward Prosperity. He'd tell them his story. They would believe him.

* * *

They caught him at an intersection. Howard was deep in thought and he forgot to check the highway in all directions before crossing. His timing couldn't have been worse. He immediately froze in a glare of headlights as Owen Wheeler rounded a bend, slammed on the brakes and skidded to a stop inches from him. All three young men were out of the cab in seconds.

"Ev Howard?" Billy yelled.

Ev turned and ran into the cornfield beyond the roadside ditch. Owen and Billy sprung from the truck. Ev was fast, but he was pursued by Prosperity High's all-time fastest running back. He didn't get fifty feet before Owen tackled him. Ev screamed and struggled as Owen and Billy lifted him over the tailgate of the truck and dumped him in the bed.

"You and Billy get in the back with him," Owen ordered. "Jude, take my shotgun. Hold it on him every second." He thrust the shotgun into Jude's trembling hands. They ordered Ev into the front left corner of the bed and covered him with their weapons from two angles. Rennie Poole had told them to come directly to Arlo's garage if they found Howard. Owen pointed the truck toward Prosperity.

"We're gonna be heroes, boys!" he shouted out the window. "Gonna get a nice reward from Mr. Poole. Maybe get our pictures in the paper when we turn this boy over to the sheriff. How do you like them apples?"

Billy responded with a war whoop. Jude remained silent, unable to take his eyes from Ev Howard's terrified face.

At Arlo's garage, many of the search parties had returned already, tired and frustrated at their inability to find the killer. Rennie Poole was back with Hubert Pressley, Clyde Dillard, and several cases of beer. Clyde, widely known to drink far more than he should, shied away from the crowd as they popped open bottles. He stayed in the shadows of the garage, watching fearfully as the men became drunker and angrier.

By the time Owen pulled into the lot with Jude and Billy holding Ev Howard at gunpoint in the truck bed, the mob's sentiment had devolved from justice to revenge. Howard found himself surrounded by armed men, most of their faces twisted in anger and disgust.

"Take him in the back," Hubert told his son. "Set him in the corner and guard him with the shotgun. If he tries to run, stop him any way you have to." Jude went pale as his father gave him the order. Apparently, Hubert didn't think he got the message. "You have to blow this fuckin' nigger into the middle of next week, you got my permission. You hear?"

Jude nodded, his eyes wide with fear. Hubert returned to the crowd.

"You heard him," Jude stammered. "Please. Get in the corner."

Tears rolled down Ev's cheeks. He wiped his nose with his forearm. "I didn't do nothing," he said quietly, peering up at Jude.

"I know," Jude whispered. "Jesus, I know."

* * *

With Ev Howard securely under guard in Arlo's office, Rennie Poole stepped into the bed of Owen Wheeler's pickup and addressed the crowd.

"We got him, boys! That murdering sack of shit is ours!" The crowd held up their bottles and weapons and cheered. "If we had left this matter to the sheriff, this bastard Howard would still be walking around, free to terrorize any white woman in the county! But we stopped him!"

Another huge cheer rose in the parking lot.

"Job ain't done yet. What do you suppose is going to happen if we deliver this murdering nigger to Morgan? I'll tell you, dear friends. I know the sheriff. I've known him for over a decade, and when it comes to real justice, he is no better than a communist or a Yankee. If we deliver Howard into the sheriff's care it might be months, or even years, before the case goes to trial, and some Jew lawyer might get the boy off on a technicality!"

The crowd—farmers, welders, day laborers, mechanics, gas jockeys, short-order cooks, shopkeeps, and machinists, many of whom had no more than seven or eight years of school—reacted to the dog whistles in Rennie's speech and immediately screamed their contempt. Rennie, an expert fisherman, gave them some line. Then he cut them off again by raising his hands and prepared to land them in the boat.

"We know, my friends! There can be no doubt Ev Howard raped and killed Coral Pyle. Now, I'm just an old country boy, but I know what the

Good Book says. An eye for an eye, and a tooth for a tooth! I ain't gonna abide any Jew lawyer letting this boy slip the noose!"

The infuriated crowd chanted, "String him up! String him up! String him up!"

Inside the garage, Jude listened, and he knew it would be only seconds before the mob descended on them. He stared at Ev, cowering in the corner.

"Go," he said.

Ev stopped weeping and stared at him. "What?"

"Get. Go out the back way. I'll sprawl on the floor like you attacked me. You get out, and you run like your life depends on it, you hear?"

"Why you doin' this?"

"Just do as I say. Knock me over and run, boy!"

Before Ev could run, Arlo Pyle, still unsteady on his feet from grief and alcohol, dropped back into the garage. He arrived just as Jude fell to the floor and Ev stepped over his body. Arlo grabbed Ev by the shirt collar and flung him back into the corner.

"I don't understand," he slurred. "I tried to be kind to you. In return, you stole from me. When I fired you, you went and got your revenge by murdering my beautiful daughter. I did right by you, didn't I?"

Tears streaming down his cheeks, and snot bubbling in his nostrils, Howard protested, wailing, "Mister Pyle, I didn't do nothing! I went fishing and I saw the body in the creek, and I ran away because I was scared to death. I beg you, sir. Listen to me. I didn't do it!"

Pyle stepped away. "You're on your own, boy. You brought it on yourself."

Arlo took the shotgun from Jude and trained it on Howard, who cowered in terror.

"No, please, Mr. Pyle! Don't do it!" Ev cried out.

"Ain't gonna be me," Pyle said. "We'll leave it to the good people of the community. Get up, boy. Court's in session."

He handed the shotgun to Jude, grabbed a jerry can of gasoline, and walked out the back door, directly to Ev's outhouse. He doused the tiny shed with every drop of gas in the can, stood back, lit an entire pack of Pyle Garage paper matches, and flung them. The outhouse erupted in flames. Jude could feel the heat from the doorway and squinted at the sudden blinding brilliance of the fire. The crowd in front of the garage saw the glow, and then smoke and flames, and cheered in victory. Arlo watched it burn, then took the shotgun from Jude and led Ev at gunpoint to the parking lot.

Jude stayed behind and vomited into a trash barrel.

* * *

"We know what to do!" Rennie Poole yelled outside. He turned to Clyde Dillard. "Clyde, go to your store and fetch us about fifty feet of good, stout rope."

"What?" Dillard said. "Rope? What for?"

"You can't be that stupid," Poole said. "We're gonna make this right... tonight!"

The mob cheered Poole's declaration, but Owen Wheeler stepped into the spill of light from the shadows.

"Wait," Wheeler said. "We brought this boy back here to deliver to the sheriff. What you're talking about ain't no better than what he did to Coral."

"He's right," Billy Mosack yelled. "We don't want any part of a lynching."

"You're young," Poole said. "Not much older than this murdering nigger, so I'm gonna forgive your disrespect. You take my advice, and you hang back while we men do what needs to be done. Clyde, go get the rope."

Clyde glanced from Owen to Poole, his eyes begging for some way out of the situation. He rooted in place, hoping divine intervention would solve the dilemma for him. Something hard and cold pressed into his lower spine, and a hand clasped his shoulder. He heard Hubert Pressley's voice in his ear.

"You've been in the Army, Clyde. You know what a forty-five will do to flesh and innards. Now, are you gonna get the rope or what?"

Clyde Dillard might have been terrified, or enraged, or even ashamed that events had conspired to place him in his predicament. Instead, he was relieved. The pistol pressed against his backbone absolved him of responsibility in the matter. If he complied at gunpoint, nobody would blame him in the least later, either in a court of law or in the Great Accounting in the afterlife.

He allowed himself to be pushed along the sidewalk to his hardware store, where Hubert picked out the stoutest length of rope he could find.

The mob bound Ev Howard's hands and feet with jute twine. It bit into his skin like razor wire. They stuffed a greasy rag into his mouth to stifle his screams and tossed him into the back of Owen's pickup. Rennie ordered Owen to sit with another man from the mob in the back of the truck, holding guns on Howard in case he decided to attempt an escape from his horrible fate. Owen protested again but, in the end, he climbed into the truck bed, took the gun, and trained it on Ev Howard's chest. Ev's eyes were bloodshot with terror. A cascade of tears rolled down his face and soaked his shirt collar. Twin streams of snot ran over the foul rag that gagged him.

"I'm sorry, boy," Owen whispered. "I tried."

A caravan of ten cars and pickup trucks followed them deep into Bliss County, down a dirt road. They pulled the vehicles into a circle at a clearing with a huge black walnut tree in the center, their headlights facing into the center of the circle, casting eerie shadows on the hardwood forest surrounding the clearing.

The men in the mob hoisted Ev from the back of the pickup. The boy twisted and bucked trying to escape, his eyes bugging with fear. Veins popped on his throat and forehead like vine tendrils as he struggled furiously against the twine slicing through the skin of his wrists and ankles. Blood flowed from the wounds in rivulets, staining the cuffs of his shirt, and dripping onto his threadbare cotton socks.

The rest took only a few seconds. Rennie Poole slung the rope, onto which he had fashioned a skillfully practiced noose, over a limb of the black walnut tree about twelve feet off the ground, securing it to the tree's base. Without the benefit of a scaffold or a gibbet, they dropped the noose over Ev Howard's head and stood him in the back of the pickup. Arlo Pyle himself took over the controls of the pickup and drove it about six feet—all that was necessary to drop Ev Howard from the tailgate.

The older men cheered and hooted and howled as Howard flailed and twisted at the end of the rope in a futile effort to free himself from the noose. His head seemed to inflate and turn eggplant purple as he struggled. It took no more than a minute for his body to go slack. When he did, the crowd screamed again in triumph.

Clyde, Billy, and Owen didn't join in the celebration. They huddled in the bed of a truck, too frightened to say a word, as Ev Howard swung back and forth like the pendulum on a grandfather clock, and the rednecks who had taken his life passed bottles and fired weapons into the air and congratulated one another on their heroism.

Jude sat in the front seat, turned the radio up as loud as he could to drown out the cheers of the crowd, and he wept openly over the shame he'd carry to his grave.

The circle of cars and their pooled headlights and the screams of the mob reminded Clyde Dillard of something in his past, but he couldn't put his finger on what it was.

Chapter Thirteen

The fan in Jude's bedroom window failed to provide the least relief from the stifling heat. His bedsheets were sodden with sweat, his pillow with tears.

In thirty-six hours, he'd watched two people die. Jude had engaged in intricate mental calculus and cowardly concluded his future was more important than the life of an innocent black youth and the dignity of the girl he had claimed to love with all his heart. Abandoning Coral was bad enough, but she was already dead. If he had acted like a man, taken her home, and explained to her parents how she'd passed, Ev Howard would be alive. The tears and the psychic anguish returned. He had to do something, find some shred of decency to assuage the devils that danced inside his head.

Jude rose, dressed hurriedly, and backed the Willys out of the driveway in neutral, allowing it to roll downhill several hundred feet before popping the clutch to bring the engine to life. He drove through the gloom, his windows wide open, the radio blaring. The wind whipped around his head, smelling like new-mown grass which yielded to diesel as he left the highway onto an oiled dirt road.

Ev was gone. The rope was gone. There was no sign anyone had visited the site, save for a lone, darkened pickup truck with two other youths sitting in the cargo bed.

"Owen. Billy," Jude said as he approached the truck.

Owen said, "Couldn't sleep either?"

"Couldn't get the image of that boy dangling from a tree out of my head."

A bucket filled with ice and beer sat beside Owen. He handed a bottle to

Jude, who popped the cap on the edge of the tailgate. Foam rose from the long neck and ran across his hand. He ignored it.

"Liberated the beers from Arlo's garage," Owen said. "There was plenty left over."

"Got a shovel in the truck," Billy said. "Figured we'd come out and cut the boy down, give him a decent burial. Someone beat us to it."

"Any idea who?" Jude took a long pull from the bottle.

"Hot money says Rennie Poole had something to do with it," Owen said.

"Covering his ass," Billy added.

"I reckon," Jude said. "Got a shovel in my trunk, too."

"What the fuck happened?" Owen tossed an empty bottle deep into the darkness. A second later, they heard the tinkle of glass breaking on a rock. "How'd it all roll so sideways?"

"We were taking that boy to the sheriff," Billy said. "Right? That's what you thought?"

"Should have," Owen said. "Taking Howard to Arlo's Garage, we parked a bullet between his eyes."

"I reckon you two boys are getting out of here in the nick of time," Billy said, holding up his bottle in salute. "Must be nice to get as far away from this clusterfuck as possible."

"You told him?" Jude asked Owen.

"Yeah. It came up."

"Nice of you to trot off and leave me stranded," Billy said, but they could hear the good wishes in it. "Think Coach McCandless could use a halfback?"

"I can ask," Jude said.

"Don't bother. If he wasn't interested last year, he sure won't be now. I was jerkin' you off, you goofball."

Jude forced a smile. "Sorry. Guess nothing's funny tonight."

They drank and listened to the night sounds in the woods until Owen spoke.

"Everything's changed, boys. Nothing's ever gonna be the same again."

Chapter Fourteen

Owen was inducted in July. Jude left for Ryland College a week later. Students weren't allowed cars on campus, so he entrusted his treasured Willys to Billy Mosack for safekeeping. The second week in August, Billy drove it to the garage and asked Arlo for a job. Arlo agreed immediately. Neither of them ever mentioned it, but they both knew it was the least Arlo could do for one of the men who caught his daughter's killer.

By the summer of 1956, Owen and Jude were getting on with lives far away, and Billy was stuck in tiny Prosperity, setting distributor points and blowing out clogged fuel lines.

It wasn't so bad, being out of their shadow. There was no doubt he and his friends were close, but for some reason, Billy always came third. Whenever they were together in the same car, Billy took the back seat. If they met a trio of promising girls at a dance, Billy would be hustled off to the one with a great personality.

Things were different with Jude and Owen gone. Billy might have been the shadow member of The Trinity, but now he was the only one left in town. When he walked into the Prosperity High School grandstand for Friday night football games, he was mobbed by kids who hadn't even been students when he graduated. Billy liked the newfound attention and admiration, but he was still dissatisfied. He yearned for excitement and adventure. He wanted to be more than the high school jock who had peaked at eighteen.

* * *

A pickup truck pulling a car on a trailer dropped off the highway into Arlo's Garage. A tall, lanky man with a graying flattop haircut and a protruding Adam's apple climbed from the truck and stretched, arching his back and twisting his shoulders.

"Long drive?" Billy asked.

"All the way from Weaverville. Didn't even stop to piss." He talked in a flat midwestern drawl that sounded a little like Henry Fonda in *My Darling Clementine*. Billy checked the car on the trailer. It had started life as a 1936 Ford three-window business coupe. The front and rear fenders were gone, as was the front bodywork surrounding the engine, save for the hood and grill. The doors were welded shut. The windshield had been replaced with chicken wire. The rear window was missing. A hefty steel rollbar had been installed rear of the bench seat, with bars extending backward at a downward angle. Someone had painted an elaborate number *75* on the door, and the words *Holden Radio Service* behind it.

"Nice hot rod," Billy said.

"Son," the man said, "this here is a modified. It's a race car."

"Figured that out when I saw the number. Are you Holden?"

The man glanced back at it and laughed. "Holden's a sponsor. Name's Harold Bloomquist, but most people call me Hop. I think I got a water pump problem on the truck. Squeals like a shortchanged whore. When I stopped for lunch yesterday, I noticed water running underneath."

"Bad pump seal, and your bearing's shot. Happens all the time. You're in luck. Got a pump on the shelf in the back. I can replace it in an hour or so. Pull your truck into the bay. I'll get right on it. Surprised you didn't figure it out yourself." Billy lifted the truck hood.

"I'm no wrench monkey. I only drive the damn thing. My mechanic jumped ship in Weaverville. Hundred-lapper. Finished sixth. Got seventy bucks and a steak dinner voucher. The steak gave me the shits. You got a place to eat around here?"

* * *

Billy finished the water pump and slammed the hood on the truck. Hop Bloomquist was still at lunch, so Billy took a few moments to examine the modified. It was a beast, painted bright red with yellow numbers and lettering. The inside was spartan, the dash a mass of empty holes where knobs and buttons had been. The steering wheel was wound in a spiral of cord sealed with wrap after wrap of black electrical tape. The bench seat was filthy. Clods of dirt littered the floorboard. A military surplus fighter pilot harness in the front seat held the driver in place.

"She's a beaut, ain't she? It's fast, all right," Hop said as he returned from lunch.

"Sixth place fast."

"Pay a thousand to win, and you're gonna draw the best shoes from all over the south. Ever'one who finished in front of me was a track champion."

"You're not?"

"Never stayed in one place long enough."

As Billy prepared the bill, Hop stared out the window at his race car.

"They opened a new track just the other side of the South Carolina line," he said.

"Uh huh."

"Three-eighths mile. High-banked clay. Thought I'd try it out tomorrow night."

"Hope you win," Billy said, handing the bill to him. Hop passed him a couple of tens.

"Like I said, my mechanic took a flyer in Weaverville. Got tired of the road. You ever worked on a flathead?"

"Sure," Billy said. "Plenty of times. Sweet little motor."

"Don't suppose you'd be interested in coming to South Carolina tomorrow night, lend me a hand as chief mechanic?"

"What's it pay?"

"Dollar-three-eighty." Hop spat a brown gob of tobacco juice into the dust. "Hell, son, I don't know. Depends on what we win. I'll give you a third. Most boys would jump at the chance just to be around it."

Billy chuckled. "Mr. Bloomquist, I am in, under, and around cars every blessed day. Going to a race track on the weekend sounds like a busman's holiday. If there's a buck in it, though, I'm in. For a third."

* * *

As they rolled the modified off the trailer the next evening at the ostentatiously named Upstate Speedway, Billy was surprised to see how low it sat on the ground. The roof only stood as high as the middle of his chest.

"You cut the springs," he observed.

"Sure. Everyone does," Hop told him. "You'll find a lot of modifications made to this car. Why we call them modifieds. Look, you're new to all this, so I'll explain. We're running a heat and feature system for qualifying. Everyone who shows up gets to run the forty-lap feature event. We're gonna run a coupla five-lap heat races to set starting positions. Winner of the first heat starts first in the feature. Winner of the second heat starts second, and so on. Get it?"

Hap donned a Corker pudding basin motorcycle helmet and a pair of goggles and climbed into the modified. The unmuffled exhaust blew clouds of dust around. Without a word, Hop put the car in gear and pulled onto the track.

Billy had never been to a race and was shocked when the cars turned into a corner and suddenly lurched sideways, drifting ass-out through the turn while the driver frantically sawed the steering wheel to maintain control. From the pits, it seemed as if the cars flew past at breakneck speed.

He climbed into the bed of the pickup to get a better view, in time to see Hop glide into turn three. The rear end came around, and the car spun nose-first into the loosely packed mound of dirt on the inner berm of the corner. He tried to back up, but his tires whirled impotently in the mud. The flagman put out a red flag, stopping practice, and Hop pulled himself gingerly from the car. Billy could see the grimace on his face as he cradled his right hand in the crook of his left arm.

The tow truck deposited both the modified and Hop at their pit spot, and Hop pointed at the car. "No real damage. Take the car to the hose station and clean it up."

* * *

"Guy in the ambulance says it's broken." Hop held a towel full of ice on his rapidly swelling right wrist. "A lesson for you, boy. If you're ever in a spin, and you're about to hit something, for Christ's sake take your fuckin' hands off the wheel. When the front tire hit the berm, it spun the steering wheel. The spoke grabbed my wrist."

He held up the motorcycle helmet. "You think this will fit you?"

Chapter Fifteen

Hop spat into the dust. "Drove a hundred fifty miles to get here, had to pay for a new water pump, and paid five bucks for registration. Don't feel like leaving empty-handed. They pay thirty dollars for last place, enough to compensate me for my gas and registration, and leave a little left over for food and to get this wrist in a cast. All you have to do is go out, drive around at whatever speed you're comfortable, and make it to the feature."

"That's all," Billy said sarcastically. "Are you nuts?"

Hop smiled. "Naw. That's just a rumor my ex-wife spreads around."

"I've never driven a race car in my life!"

"Hell, boy, every guy out there was a dirt virgin once. Tonight's your turn."

Billy shook his head, kicked at a clod of clay, and looked at the modified. The idea was enticing. Like every other kid in Prosperity, he'd grown up with a love of cars. And, like most of his teenaged peers, he'd indulged in his share of back road antics in his youth. He'd driven a car or truck since he was fourteen. What was racing except driving?

"What if I crack it up?" he asked.

"My loss. I'm betting you'll be fine. Once you're out there, you'll see. It really isn't all that hard."

* * *

Billy dropped the car into gear and pulled onto the track for the first time. Immediately, gouts of clay flew up from the front tires. A clod of it stuck in the chicken wire directly in front of his face. He drove a couple of laps slowly on the inside of the track to get a feel for the handling.

Nothing terrible happened, so he grabbed a higher gear and punched the gas. His eardrums rattled. The rear end of the car broke loose and swerved to the right. Instinctively, he lifted the accelerator and turned the wheel to the right to correct. The car stabilized, and his heart rate zoomed. He pressed the pedal again as he dove into the first corner, tapped the brake, and steered for the inside. Immediately, the rear end swung around, and he found himself sliding sideways. The car arced higher and higher in the corner and rolled over the crest backward into the parking lot. He jammed the brake, dropped it into first, and drove around the outside of turns one and two to the backstretch, where he was able to reenter the racing surface. He drove straight to the pit, where he found Hop waiting.

"Why'd you come in?" Hop shouted over the engine.

"I almost wrecked it!"

Hop gestured for him to cut the engine.

"Look, kid," he said. "That's nothing. Ten or twelve guys are gonna jump the cushion before we get out of here tonight. It's part of it. Lemme give you a quick lesson. First, you got a shit-ton of horsepower under your foot. I want you to imagine you got an egg between your foot and the pedal, and that egg is all you got for breakfast tomorrow. Step on the pedal soft, so you don't break the egg. Got it?"

"Okay."

"Next thing, you're entering the corner too hot. You get—say—halfway between the flag man and turn one, get out of the gas. Aim the car at the inside of the corner and wait for the rear end to break. Don't force it to break—it'll do fine on its own. When the car takes a set, you get on the gas and correct the slide with the wheel. Do it right, and you'll be full-throttle pulling out of the corner to the next straight. You'll get it in no time. Remember, turn the wheel as little as you have to, and don't force the car—float it."

"Yes, sir," Billy said.

"Now get back out there and cut me ten or twenty laps."

* * *

Billy gridded third in the five-car field in his heat race. He'd been alone on track during the short practice. The idea of taking off from a flying start with four other cars bunched around him was unnerving.

The cars lined up at the exit of the pits. The flagman gave a signal, and all five engines roared to life. Billy's heart pounded in his chest. He was lightheaded. His stomach clenched.

When Billy looked back on the next several minutes later in his life, all he could recall was a blur of sensations. It seemed as if all his nerve endings were on high alert. The starter dropped the green flag, and the field pounded into the first corner. The first and second place drivers hooked bumpers, disappeared over the edge of the banked turn, and Billy found himself leading the heat.

The next five laps were an exercise in precision, as he focused on power-sliding through the corners. He was so intent on keeping his lead, he forgot to think about the egg and backing off before the corner and all the other stuff Hop told him. He was simply...*doing* it. Before he knew it, he saw the man on the flag stand wave a white banner. He had no idea what it meant, so he kept going until the man showed him a checkered flag the next time around. He'd won his first race. It had taken less than three minutes from flag to flag.

"Shit hot!" Hop shouted when Billy parked the car. "You're a natural, kid!"

Billy's ears rang from the noise inside the car. He cupped his ear. "What?"

"You picked it up in no time flat."

"It was fun," Billy climbed from the car. "Like...like I was out there. Not me and the car. Just...*me*. Like the car and me were attached. Is that supposed to happen?"

Hop took the helmet from him and tossed it into the car. "Son, that's what they call being a race driver."

* * *

The feature race could have gone better. Based on his win in the second heat, Billy slotted on the outside of the front row. The modifieds would run forty laps. Billy drove as hard as he could, but in the end, he finished third.

"Damned decent!" Hop congratulated him as Billy climbed from the car back in the pits. "Third in your first feature race ever, and a heat win. Don't get me wrong. You ain't no Jimmy Bryan or nothin'. I mean, you were running against a bunch of Carolina shit-kickers, but tonight, you were nearly King Shitkicker. You might have a knack for this, kid!"

"It was fun!" Billy yelled back, unaware he was shouting over the ringing in his ears. "You do this every week?"

"From April until October on the Dixie Circuit, sometimes two or three nights a week. Some winters I head south and run the Grapefruit Circuit in Florida. Watching you out there gives me an idea. There's a race in Concord next weekend, pays five hundred to win. I won't be able to drive with this wrist for at least a month, maybe longer. Think you might be interested in tagging along and driving this beast for a few weeks?"

Billy didn't have to think for a second. "Sure!"

Hop handed Billy a fistful of five-dollar bills.

"Third place paid a hundred dollars," Hop said. "This is your half."

"You said I'd get a third."

"When you were going to be a wrench monkey, sure. Drivers get more."

"When you were driver, you were going to take two thirds. Maybe I should get more than half."

"Car owner's share," Hop said, smiling. "But you're right to haggle. Always demand more than you think the owner will pay. Let's hose down this hoss and find a nice steak house for dinner."

* * *

Billy finished second at Concord and earned a whopping hundred-fifty dollars for his efforts as his share. The next week, at the Peach Bowl Raceway in Georgia, he scored his first win and took home three hundred dollars. In only three weekends, he'd earned more than he could in three months working for Arlo Pyle.

On the Monday morning following the Peach Bowl win, Billy handed in his notice at the garage. He'd found what he wanted to do with his life.

Chapter Sixteen

When the owner of Prosperity Hardware barely survived a heart attack in 1957, he decided the moment had come to tap the brakes and appreciate the time he had remaining. As soon as Clyde Dillard learned of his boss's intent to sell the store and move to Florida to live out his remaining years in warmth and sunshine, he called Hubert Pressley.

"Prosperity needs the hardware," Hubert told him. "Mayor Poole is having a social over to his lodge this Tuesday night. Why don't you come along, and I'll hook you up with some people who will be delighted to invest. How much does Earl want for the store?"

Clyde told him.

"Can you lay your hands on—say—three thousand?"

"I got some savings. I inherited my house, free and clear. I reckon I can borrow on it to make up the rest."

"You go to the Farmer's Bank in Morgan. Tell them I sent you. You'll get your loan. You come to Rennie's place on Tuesday, and I'll introduce you to some people who will provide the rest."

Clyde went to bed that night and tossed and turned for hours, going over all the details. Even the six-pack of Rolling Rock he'd pounded back earlier in the evening didn't lull him to sleep, as he imagined the grand opening of Dillard Hardware. He could see the sign above the door in his imagination. It gave him a tremendous thrill. He was about to become a man of substance. People would respect him now, by golly.

* * *

Hubert Pressley invited Rennie Poole to dinner that night. Over their meal, Hubert described Clyde Dillard's plans. Rennie nodded as he buttered a baking powder biscuit.

"It's good," he said. "I gotta tell you, Hubert, I had a lot of sleepless nights after that unpleasantness in 1954. Thought perhaps we might have gone too far stringing that boy up the way we did. Things have turned out better than I hoped. After I won the mayor's race last year, I thought we'd put the entire mess behind us, but it never hurts to keep people in your debt. They're more likely to hold their tongues that way."

Four of the men clustered around the black walnut tree from which Ev Howard swung had died. Only ten or so were left. Rennie had placed Hubert in charge of keeping them in line. He thought it a good policy to keep the whole thing under wraps until every participant either forgot about it or had too much to lose if they divulged their role. Rennie Poole was anxious to help Clyde buy the store, because he was also buying the pathetic little man's silence.

* * *

Clyde Dillard awoke on Saturday morning with his usual pounding hangover headache. He poured several glasses of water down his throat, along with a couple of Goody's powders, and gathered his fishing gear for a Saturday sojourn to Six Mile Creek.

He was about to become an important man in Prosperity. The idea thrilled him. He found his usual spot, tossed the line out into a pool, and waited. Three years ago, he'd seen the naked woman floating there. Clyde had almost convinced himself he'd hallucinated the entire thing. Even so, he'd revisited the site on many occasions in hopes of catching a glimpse of her again.

As soon as he was in view of the rock face, he saw it was empty. Something did catch his eye, though. The sun was at precisely the correct angle to glint off a small, highly reflective object caught underneath a boulder near the edge of the water.

He waded across the creek and picked up the object—a locket attached to a thin gold chain. He opened the locket but the picture inside had deteriorated over years of repeated rainstorms and scorching summer heat. He could discern the outline of a face but none of the features. He stuffed the necklace into his pocket.

Who knew? His prospective status as a man of means in Prosperity could make him more attractive to women. If he were able to corral a girlfriend in the future, the locket would make a lovely and convenient present.

Chapter Seventeen

The couple in the hotel room across the alley were screwing again. They had the windows open, and they weren't being at all coy about it. Owen Wheeler sat in the window of his Saigon hotel room, barefoot in a pair of chinos and a tank shirt, and blew cigarette smoke into the night as he listened.

If any place in the universe genuinely resembles Hell, Owen thought, *it must be South Vietnam.*

Reenlisting, it turned out, had been a bad idea. After a tour in Germany, he should have taken his discharge papers and humped it home as fast as he could. Instead, lured by a reenlistment bonus and the prospect of a few more years of attentive *frauleins*, he signed the papers to re-up almost without thinking. A month later, he received his billeting orders. Vietnam. Part of a new program intended to help the South Vietnamese Army train to deal with insurgents who had pestered the country for over a decade. When he received his orders, Owen took ten minutes to find the place on a globe. He scoured his memory, searching for any insult or offense he might have committed to be sent to this trivia question country in the butt crack of Indochina.

The moans and creaks of the bed springs increased in volume. *They must be newlyweds,* he mused, as the ash of his cigarette lengthened. *Or maybe they're trying to set some sort of record.*

Owen didn't wait for them to finish. He pulled on a lightweight cotton shirt and some shoes and made his way to the lobby. He dropped a dollar on the concierge, more money than the young man had seen all week.

"Anywhere to place a bet around here?" he asked in the paltry French the Army had taught him.

"Sure thing," the youth said, in heavily accented English. "You want, I take."

"Just tell me where," Owen said. "And if there's a password."

* * *

Among the first acts Ngo Dinh Diem took as Prime Minister of South Vietnam in 1954 was to close the Binh Xuyen casinos. This proved an unpopular measure, and by 1958 gambling houses began to reopen with a somewhat lower profile than before. Owen found himself in one of them, accessed through the back of a pho house.

He wandered over to a *pai gow* table manned by a bald, one-eyed dealer. Owen could have spent most of the evening there for the equivalent of U.S. taxi fare. He played listlessly, never betting more than the table minimum, fully aware that—being gangsters—the Binh Xuyen organization was under absolutely no obligation to run a fair table.

He had been at the table for almost an hour when a man in uniform sidled onto the chair beside him. Wheeler glanced at him and did a double-take.

"Colonel Thanh!" he said. Thanh was the last person Wheeler expected to find in a semi-legitimate Saigon casino, especially wearing ARVN fatigues and the three-flower insignia.

Thanh appeared half-snockered. He turned toward Wheeler and squinted a little.

"Yes?" he said. "You look familiar. Wait. Wheeler, right? Specialist Wheeler? I saw you only a couple of days ago, at the American emplacement in—"

"That's right, sir."

"Yes," Thanh said. He drew it out. "I recall now. Nasty business, that. Where are you from, Wheeler?"

"North Carolina. A small town called Prosperity. I'm sure you've never heard of it."

"Don't be so certain. I spent time in the states. Went to college there."

"Where?"

"Hofstra University. Long Island."

"New York."

"Go Flying Dutchmen. I lived off-campus with three other guys. Place called Hempstead. Bet you never heard of Hempstead."

"I guess we're even," Wheeler said.

Owen realized he and Thanh were almost the same age. He'd been fooled by the rank before, but as a slightly inebriated Thanh reminisced about his frat days on Long Island, his features softened, shed the mask of war, and revealed a youthful face. Owen could imagine Thanh yukking it up at a kegger with a bunch of sophomores, dressed in a Hawaiian shirt and chinos and Bass Weejuns, not a care in the world. A guy like that, Owen wouldn't mind hanging out with.

None of that really mattered, though. Owen had already decided to kill Colonel Thanh.

* * *

The first man Owen met upon walking off the plane on his first arrival in Vietnam was Bud Abraham, a tall, slender black man who escorted him to the divisional barracks. A seasoned veteran, Bud had survived five Long Range Recon Patrols—*lurps* for short. A lurp might take four days, during which the patrol's only link to the relative safety of their base was their radioman. The mission was to prepare and advise Vietnamese soldiers to defend their own country from the PLAF insurgents, but once the black flag rose and bullets flew, every man in a uniform was fair game. Bud had already seen several patrol buddies go home in bags with stenciled numbers.

Owen had never fired a weapon in anger. He was petrified. He wasn't the only one. A guy five bunks down whispered prayers for an hour each night before falling into fitful sleep—impassioned pleas to allow him to survive just one more lurp. Owen caught another kid crying in the shower, scouring at his skin trying to remove other people's blood long since rinsed down the drain.

After four lurps of his own, Owen was still alive and becoming familiar with the routine. It didn't make things easier.

As Owen cleaned his M14 rifle, Bud Abraham poked his head around the corner.

"Got a briefing," he said. He didn't need to say more.

They were headed back to the jungle.

* * *

A DeHavilland Beaver dropped them in a clearing outside a no-name ville deep in the jungle. It was a pleasant enough place, with huts and water buffalo and the ubiquitous rice paddy. The people stared at them as they hopped to the ground and the Beaver turned, taxied for a couple hundred feet, and rose again in the sky.

Owen and Bud were led by a first lieutenant named Riley, who had recently graduated from the University of Michigan with a degree in English Literature. In the Army's obtuse calculus, this perfectly suited him for combat command.

They were to take five green ARVN recruits, most of them Montagnards conscripted from the Vietnamese highlands, in a large circle through the jungle, eventually arriving back at the ville. Along the way, the Americans would demonstrate warcraft and survival skills, so when the real thing came along the ARVN pukes would be marginally less likely to be slaughtered.

The first thing Owen had to do was teach the ARVN boys to pack their gear. Packing was always a trade-off. If you couldn't grab vital equipment from a poorly packed ruck when things went south, you died. They could pack food, or they could pack ammunition. Take too little of either, you died. There were dozens of ways to die on a lurp, and it was Owen's and Bud's job to teach the conscripts how to avoid every one of them.

Riley took the lead, with Bud carrying the radio in the rear. Owen and the ARVN conscripts spread out in the middle. The entire countryside conspired to impede them. Vines grew across every path, ready to snare a man's foot and send him sprawling. Holes might be covered with fallen leaves, waiting patiently to break an ankle. Tripping over rocks was commonplace. The typical four-day lurp was a constant battle with terrain, mosquitoes, wild animals, fungus, poisonous plants, and—if you were truly unfortunate—stray Viet Cong patrols.

Making a fire was forbidden. They might as well have shot flares to indicate their position. Instead, they ate cold food from tins retrieved from their rucks and drank sparingly.

"Tents are for pussies," Bud informed the recruits. "On a patrol you make yourself as comfortable as you can against a tree or a rock, keep your weapon and ruck immediately available, and grab whatever shut-eye you can between watches and nightmares."

He didn't mention tigers.

They lost a man the first night. Around one in the morning, while the camp slept except for an ARVN guy who was supposed to keep watch, one of the conscripts slipped out of the tiny clearing to relieve himself. He didn't hear the *chuff* off to his right or see the yellow eyes following his movements through the trees. He didn't hear the padded footfalls tracking him.

His screams woke the camp, followed by a horrifying roar and the sound of thrashing in the jungle. One of the ARVN soldiers grabbed his carbine and ran in the direction of the sound to help his comrade. Bud seized him by the ankle and dragged him back.

"Don't bother," he said, solemnly. "Dude's dead already. You can't blame the tiger. He only wants to eat like the rest of us."

After sunup, they divided the dead man's rations and ammo, buried the rest of his ruck, and continued humping through the jungle.

The patrol trekked almost twelve miles the second day, sweat rolling off their bodies and soaking their fatigues. The rucks on their backs grew heavier and more oppressive with each step. They made camp near sundown in a small clearing on the edge of the jungle, the farthest point they would reach from the village where they had begun. Exhausted, they wolfed some rations and collapsed against trees to rest before beginning the circular trek back to the ville at daybreak.

Two hours later, the sound of the ARVN lookout firing on full automatic into the jungle rattled them awake. Bud leapt to his feet and grabbed the carbine from him.

"What the fuck!" he shouted.

The soldier trembled as he pointed into the undergrowth and shouted, "*Con hổ!*"

"*Tiger*," Riley interpreted.

"Stupid fuck!" Bud shouted at him. "Why don't you just radio the VC and give them our position?"

The man might have replied if a bullet hadn't screamed in from the jungle and spattered his brain over the campsite, accented by the delayed sonic whipcrack of a rifle in the brush.

"Incoming!" Riley cried. Everyone in the camp hit the dirt and grabbed for their weapons. Two more muted slaps broke the jungle silence as bullets flew over their heads.

"Radio Base," Riley ordered. "Give our position and tell them we're under fire. We need a gunship and exfil here, pronto!"

As Bud checked the map and tried to raise the base, Riley turned to Owen. "How many you think are out there?"

"Beats me, Loot. Might be a single sniper. Could be a whole fuckin' platoon."

"We're sure as shit sitting ducks in this clearing. Let's get into the brush." They fanned out in a loose semicircle, facing the direction from which the shots had come.

"Any luck?" Riley rasped to Bud.

"They're on the way. Twenty minutes out. We pop flares and smoke when they get here."

"Let's see what we're up against," Riley said. "Everyone fire a short burst in that direction."

Their rifles spat out a quick volley, and Riley held up his hand to signal cease fire. Five distinct flashes blazed in different locations, seventy yards away. The returning bullets shredded fan leaves over their heads.

"Think I shit my pants, Loot," Owen said.

Riley smiled grimly. "Good. I wasn't the only one. They have our location now. Best if we keep moving. Stay together, though."

He raised a hand and gestured to the ARVN conscripts to rotate to the right, deeper into the jungle. In the faint moonlight, Owen could see their terrified faces. One of them dropped his rifle, held up his hands, and shouted in Vietnamese. He ran into the jungle in the direction of the firing and was cut down.

"So negotiation is off the table," Bud said calmly. He drew a bead, squeezed off a two-shot burst in the direction of the flash, and was rewarded by a truncated scream in the distance.

"Think there are four more," Riley said. "Unless they have a sniper posted nearby."

"If they did, we'd already be fertilizer," Bud said. "Support's fifteen minutes out."

"Keep moving," Riley ordered. "But stay in the vicinity of the clearing. It's the only place the Beaver can land. Bud, tell the jet pilot to light up everything ain't within thirty yards of the clearing."

Bud Abraham was conveying the information when he took a round several seconds later. One of the VC soldiers swept the area with a Type 56, spraying where Riley's team had traversed seconds before. Bud, bringing up the rear with the radio set, was shot as the clip ran dry. The bullet entered his abdomen on the right side, exited his back, and lodged in his ruck. He collapsed onto his stomach.

"Hit!" he yelled. Owen looked back, saw his friend stricken, and crawled on his belly to him. Riley and the ARVN Rangers returned fire while Owen dug through Bud's ruck for something to stanch the bleeding.

A VC soldier sprang from the underbrush ten yards from Bud and Owen, his rifle raised to fire. On adrenaline-pumped reflex, Owen swung his M14 around and shot the man high in the chest, just under the collarbone. He crumpled to the ground, screaming in pain. Riley jumped onto him and ripped the rifle from his hands.

"Jesus," Riley muttered as he looked at the man's face. "This kid can't be older than fourteen."

The drone of the Beaver rotary engine rose in the distance, along with the high-pitched roar of F-86 Sabres.

"Get to the clearing!" Riley shouted. "There might be more in the jungle, and the fast movers will be here before our ride. We don't want to be in the weeds when they get here." He pointed toward the Viet Cong insurgent Owen had shot. "I'll help Bud. You drag this asshole, Wheeler. Intelligence might be able to get something useful out of him."

* * *

Bud Abraham was lucky. The bullet passed through without badly injuring any other vital organs. He'd caught the magic BB, the one that would send him home with no permanent impairment.

"You'll be back in Georgia in a couple of weeks," Owen told him. "You saved us all, getting the Beaver to pick us up. Shame you passed out. You should have seen it, man. The fast movers swooped in over the trees, fifty calibers blazing, phosphorous tracers lighting up the sky. The jungle looked like a cornfield back home when the harvester hits it. Never saw the like of it in my life."

A nurse stopped by Bud's bed and checked his vital signs. She was cute. In another situation, Owen might have asked her out, but he was exhausted and looked eight kinds of ugly. He needed a shower. He could smell his own stink. It wasn't a great time to hit on her.

The nurse smiled at him and turned to leave, but another nurse stopped her.

"We're almost out of B-positive," the older nurse said to the cute one. "Why don't you ask around, see if anyone can donate?"

Seeing the opportunity to score some points with the nurse, Owen stood and interrupted them as politely as he could.

"I'm B-positive," he said.

"I don't think so," the cute nurse told him. "You're exhausted. After three days of rations and bad water, you're probably dehydrated."

"Could use a bath and a meal I don't have to break into with a can opener, but I feel strong, and I'm ready to help."

The two nurses looked at one another, and the older one said, "Any other time, I'd turn you down, but a patient in surgery needs B-positive badly. Come on."

Owen smiled at the younger, cute nurse as the older one led him out of the recovery tent. She smiled back. Maybe he had a shot after all.

"Who's in surgery?" he asked, passing the time as she prepared to insert the IV to draw his blood.

"That Vietnamese kid you brought in from the jungle. You'll feel a little pinch..."

* * *

Riley stuck his head around the corner. He looked worried. "Wheeler. Got a minute?"

Owen followed the lieutenant to a hut where Riley shared a hot desk with four other officers. An ARVN colonel—Owen could tell by the three blossoms on the officer's olive drab blouse collar—stood and greeted them.

"This is the man?" the colonel asked.

"Specialist Wheeler," Riley told him. "He helped me bring the boy back."

"I am Colonel Thanh," he said, shaking Owen's hand. The colonel's English was faultless. "I would like to thank you, not only for helping Lieutenant Riley retrieve a valuable asset, but also for keeping him alive for interrogation. I am informed you gave your own blood to save his life."

"To tell you the truth, sir, I did it to impress a nurse."

A quizzical look crossed Thanh's face. Then he smiled. "Whatever your motivation, the South Vietnamese Army is grateful for your assistance. We extracted a great deal of information from the traitorous scum you delivered, information which may prove beneficial in breaking the back of the PLAF insurgency. Now, if you will excuse me, I have unpleasant business to which I must attend." He turned to Riley. "We have obtained everything necessary from this prisoner. I have two sergeants retrieving him now. I accept transfer to our custody. Thank you again, Lieutenant."

"Anytime," Riley said. Owen could hear the lack of enthusiasm in the lieutenant's voice as Colonel Thanh made his exit.

"What's going on?" Owen asked.

"You heard him. He's taking the prisoner."

"Where?"

Riley stepped over to the window. "He isn't taking him anywhere, Wheeler. He's just *taking* him. The Geneva Conventions don't cover treason. Justice for traitors in this country is firm and quick. The boy was tried and convicted the instant he put on those black pajamas."

Owen watched two ARVN sergeants drag the wounded kid across the compound, his bare toes dragging in the dirt. The gauze bandage over his surgery incision was splotched with fresh wet blood. The boy's skin shone pale in the razor-sharp sunlight. His hair hung like sodden twine on his forehead. His eyes drooped as the pain-killing drugs in his system stupefied him. Owen wondered whether he knew what was happening.

"We can't let them do this, sir," Owen said. "This is wrong."

"We're visitors, here by invitation." Riley's voice was mournful. "We can't interfere."

The ARVN sergeants caught up with Colonel Thanh. They propped the kid against a tree. Thanh walked up to the kid, drew his pistol, and—without a second's hesitation—parked a bullet between his eyes. The boy's body slumped to the ground, and Thanh squeezed two more rounds into the back of his head.

Owen watched through tears as blood—so recently *his* blood—pooled in the dust at the base of the tree. Thanh barked an order to the sergeants and walked away. The sergeants each grabbed an ankle and dragged the body face-down to be disposed of.

"This isn't our war," Riley said, still without turning around. There was a catch in his voice.

"Kind of feels like it is, sir."

"You've been through a lot," Riley said. "I'm authorizing a five-day pass. Go into Saigon. Drink a case of beer. Get your ashes hauled. Say goodbye to Bud before you go. He'll be halfway stateside when you get back."

* * *

At the bar, as Thanh prattled on about his college days on Long Island, Owen formed a plan to kill the colonel.

He wasn't completely certain why the colonel would die, beyond the fact that killing the VC kid had rendered Owen's sanguine sacrifice a complete waste. Perhaps it was the way Thanh had summarily shot him without a single outward indication of pity or remorse. Owen wondered how many children Thanh had executed since the beginning of the conflict with the insurgents. Perhaps Owen had grown to hate everything about this godforsaken jungle hellhole, and Thanh was just the unlucky bastard who was going to carry the weight for it.

Perhaps Vietnam had driven Owen a little crazy.

Whatever the reason, Thanh was going to die. The only remaining question was *how*. Infantrymen weren't typically issued sidearms, and even if he had one Owen wouldn't have carried it on leave. Besides, guns were messy and loud. Shooting Thanh would draw far too much attention in the packed Saigon streets.

"Did you go to college?" Thanh asked, shaking Owen out of his reverie.

"No," he said, quietly. "Drafted a year after high school."

"Tough break," Thanh said. "Perhaps when you return home."

"Maybe," Owen said. "Who knows?"

Thanh gazed at him curiously. "Is something wrong?" he asked. "You look...troubled. Is this about the kid the other day?"

"What about him?" Owen asked.

The bartender sliced limes and lemons with a six-inch knife several feet away. Owen watched him and remembered his basic training and the admonition of one of the drill sergeants. *"There is no body cavity or major organ that cannot be reached by a five-inch blade and a good stout arm."*

The bartender's knife gave him an inch to spare.

Thanh's glass was almost empty. Owen suddenly saw his immediate future in Technicolor clarity. He pointed to the glass.

"Let me get the next round," he said.

"Thanks," Thanh said. "I'll be right back. Have to drain the moat." He slapped Owen's arm with inebriated collegiality and headed toward the men's room.

Owen felt the sting of the slap sink into his skin like acid. He ordered a couple of drafts. While the bartender drew them, Owen placed his arm over the untended knife, slid it across the bar, and secreted it the front pocket of his chinos. He pulled out his shirttail to cover the wooden hilt.

The plan crystallized in his mind. They'd drink a little more, and Owen would suggest they take a trip down the street to a brothel for some friendly and cheap companionship. Once alone outside the back door, in the alley, Owen would place an arm around Thanh's shoulder, a comradely gesture, and—after checking to make sure nobody was watching—he'd plunge the blade into Thanh's stomach. He fantasized about Thanh's eyes growing wide with pain and terror, and the confused look that would cross his face.

"Yeah," Owen would say. *"This is about the kid the other day."* Then he'd twist the knife and rip it across the man's aorta. By the time anyone found the fallen colonel, Owen would be back in his hotel room. Just another robbery gone south on the mean streets of Saigon.

After draining their schooners of beer, Owen made his play. Thanh bought in immediately, delighted to share an adventure with his new American buddy. Owen's heart pounded and an adrenalin roar in his ears, like ocean waves, drowned out the din of the casino as they approached the door to the alley. Their progress was impeded by two ARVN MPs who walked through it. One of them pointed in his direction.

A freezing cascade of panic rose in Owen's chest. Was it possible they knew his plan? That was irrational, he reasoned. The Vietnamese weren't psychic.

The taller of the two MPs stood in front of them, while the smaller one hung back to keep an eye on the room. The tall MP barked something to Thanh in Vietnamese. Thanh became drunkenly indignant, and while Owen couldn't translate it directly, he recognized the tone of an order when he heard it. The MP was unimpressed and insistent. He took Thanh by the arm, squeezing so tightly that Thanh winced. Thanh turned to him.

"These men are arresting me!" he shouted. "They say I have conspired with the Viet Cong!"

Owen looked on, confused. Thanh? A turncoat? It didn't make sense.

"Tell them!" Thanh pleaded. "Tell them you know me. Tell them you saw me execute that traitorous VC scum only a few days ago!"

Owen relived the mental image of the boy lying at Thanh's feet, their mixed blood soaking into the dirt, and he smiled.

"Sounds like a personal problem to me," he said, as Thanh's eyes widened. "And, as much as I'd like to help, the United States Army is not allowed to interfere in the military dealings of South Vietnam. Hope you work it out."

He pushed past the MPs into the alley and dumped the knife in the first trash heap he found.

* * *

Owen reported to Lieutenant Riley's office as soon as he returned to the encampment. He found Riley at his desk, reading over a dispatch. When Owen walked in, Riley placed the sheet on the desktop.

"Thanh's been arrested," Riley said.

"I was there. Ran into him in a casino in Saigon. We had a drink or two before they arrested him."

"I see. You know I speak Vietnamese?"

"Yes."

"Thanh didn't. He made a mistake, letting me watch the interrogation of that kid you saved. I...heard things. He didn't kill the kid because of the insurgency. The kid recognized him. Knew about him. Thanh killed the kid to shut him up."

"You could have stopped it!" Owen protested.

"I could have. But then what? He's a colonel in another army. I had no hold on him. After I sent you to Saigon, I contacted his superiors. They took over from there. Tell me. How did he look when they arrested him?"

"Scared shitless," Owen said. "And guilty as hell."

Riley nodded, and Owen thought he saw the hint of smile form at the corners of his mouth. "Good," he said. "I called you in here for this. Apparently, whatever fuckery got your ass sent here is wiped clean. You have new orders." He handed Owen the dispatch he was reading when Owen entered the office. "You're reassigned. Tokyo. You leave on the next transport out, at fourteen hundred hours. Better start packing. All I can say is, you're one lucky son of a bitch. First night in the Ginza, toss one back for me, okay?"

Chapter Eighteen

Owen Wheeler punched out of the Army as quickly as he could in 1961 and devoted himself to bringing in the largest, most profitable crop the Wheeler farm could produce. They raised corn and soybeans and tobacco in the spring and planted collards and spinach in the fall. Amos Wheeler was happy for the help. Most farm families popped out a baseball team of children to ensure plenty of hands. Amos and Mary Wheeler had only managed to produce a single son. Amos was gratified, because it meant the farm would remain in the Wheeler family for at least one more generation.

While Amos Wheeler had staunchly refused to join Rennie's klavern, Rennie had not rejected the Wheeler family, and had come through during hard times with the sort of loans and favors that made them only slightly less dependent on Poole than Tennessee Ernie Ford was on *de company sto'*. The family obligation would pass on to Owen, who recognized he'd someday be burdened with his father's debt to the feed and seed king.

When Rennie Poole won the Prosperity mayoral race in 1956 in a landslide, nobody was surprised, given that the town was made up of farmers like the Wheelers who all owed Rennie for one favor or another over the years. He'd called in a lot of chits to reach the mayor's office and had maintained a stranglehold on it ever since through cajolery, intimidation, and outright bribes.

"That's the way Rennie operates," Amos Wheeler had cautioned his son. "He always thinks about the long game. A favor offered today might not make a huge dent in world affairs, but he knows, somewhere down the road, the debt can be called in at the best possible time—for him."

Whenever Owen watched Rennie play the room, glad-handing and back-patting, a fake smile seared onto his face, Owen was reminded of what his father had told him.

"Always keep an eye on Rennie," his dad had said. "Watch both of his hands at all times. Rennie Poole is a scared little man who fears death. He lies in bed at night, quaking at the prospect of dying and being forgotten as if he'd never been born. He manipulates those he can't buy, by invoking their deepest fears and portraying himself as the savior. He reviles anyone who disagrees with him and will shame them into submission with their darkest secrets, and he sees his own weakness in the face of everyone he meets and accuses of his own faults. He knows the great lie, repeated often enough, becomes the truth. Never trust that man."

* * *

Mary Wheeler had felt poorly for several weeks in May of 1962. There was nothing specific she could point to, no constant or debilitating pain, but she seemed to slowly deflate between Easter and Memorial Day. Her energy flagged. Some mornings, she could barely raise herself from her bed before sunrise. The color retreated from her cheeks, the skin on her hands turned to crepe paper, pulsating blue veins in her hands as visible as if she were covered in translucent glass. Her hair became dry and lifeless.

She finally gave in to Amos's insistence that she see a doctor. By the time the specialists determined the cause of her symptoms, cancer had spread like kudzu through her body. She evaporated over the summer and disappeared entirely in September.

Amos Wheeler lasted almost a year after his wife died. A heatwave had beaten the crops into stumps. On the hottest day of 1963, Amos dragged in from ten hours' work, opened a frosty bottle of ginger ale, and sat on the deep, shady front porch under a ceiling fan spinning so frantically it whined like a hive of yellow jackets. Owen found him an hour later, the condensation from the bottle pooled on the glass tabletop, his father's fully dilated eyes focused on a point at the opposite end of the universe.

* * *

Almost like the ironic hero in an O. Henry parable, Amos Wheeler saved the farm by dying. The proceeds of his sizable life insurance policy were more than enough to compensate for the lost crops of 1963, and even provided enough to pay off the Wheeler debt at Rennie Poole's Feed and Seed.

Rennie was behind the counter the day Owen walked in with the check in the breast pocket of his work shirt. The mayor hustled around the counter and immediately grasped Owen's hand in his most political grip.

"Owen," he cooed. "Once again, please allow me to express my sincerest condolences on the loss of your father. Amos and I never entirely saw eye to eye, but he was a good, decent man."

"Yes," Owen said. He drew the check from his pocket. "I believe this covers our entire account with your store."

Rennie looked puzzled for an instant but recovered quickly when he saw the amount on the check. "I can't say for certain," he replied. "I'd have to look at the books. I take it this is from a life insurance payment?"

Owen nodded.

"Are you completely certain you want to use that money to settle your account here? There are so many improvements you could make to the farm with it instead."

"As much as you want to keep the Wheeler family beholden to you," Owen said. "the work that needs doing on the farm can be achieved with sweat and elbow grease. Don't need a lot of money for that. I might attend the Town Council meetings a little more frequently as well. Someone should be there whose rights to self-expression aren't squelched by their debt to its mayor."

"I would never..." Rennie started.

"Don't finish that sentence," Owen said. "I'd hate you to get bound up in your own words. My father thought you were a tumor on this town. I'm inclined to agree. If you'd just make out a receipt for the check, we'll be good."

Owen's hands shook as he parked his truck in front of the Wheeler farmhouse and stepped up to the deep covered front porch. He walked inside and headed straight for the kitchen sink, under which he stored several bottles of liquor. He selected one, poured an inch of amber liquid into a wide glass, and pounded it back. Since his return from Vietnam, he'd discovered the only way to quiet the shakes was a few ounces of the fruits of fermentation.

Chapter Nineteen

The traveling NASCAR circus tented for the Memorial Day weekend of 1962 at Charlotte Motor Speedway, the mile-and-a-half high-banked asphalt track Curtis Turner had carved out of a thousand acres of farmland in Cabarrus County two years earlier. It was the morning of the World 600, the longest NASCAR Grand National race of the year.

Billy and Hop lounged on nylon-webbed garden chaises inside the shady, voluminous rear of the panel truck they used to haul the race car. Their years together had been prosperous. Hop, as team owner, wore a houndstooth jacket, a white shirt and a bolo tie, and a cream Stetson. Billy wore his fireproof driving uniform, zipped open to the waist. Outside the truck, a team of five mechanics scrambled around Billy's car, prepping it for the race while Hop and Billy lounged in the truck and collected the credit. The radio played a broadcast from Indianapolis, where another race of some significance would run on the same day.

"Ever seen an Indy 500?" Billy asked.

"Sure," Hop said. "Been to a couple of them. It's a hell of a race. We should run it."

"We run Charlotte on Memorial Day. Can't be in two places at once."

"You aren't married to NASCAR. You want to go to Indy, we can go to Indy. Even Fireball Roberts couldn't just show up there with his helmet in his hand and get a ride, though. Nobody north of the Mason Dixon ever heard of Billy Mosack. We'd have to move to Indiana or Ohio and start running sprint cars, build you a reputation among the open-wheel set."

Sprint cars were the ultimate beasts of short-track motorsports. They weighed a thousand pounds dripping wet and sported engines with ungodly horsepower. Like the modified he'd driven, they had no fenders, but they also had no roof and no roll cage to protect the driver, who sat tall in the cockpit, shoulders, and head above the coachwork, sawing at a school bus steering wheel as the car plowed sideways through the corners, the spinning rear tires flinging rooster-tails of dirt skyward. Sprint cars were fury unleashed on a half-mile of packed clay, easily the scariest racing cars in the world. In America, racing for real money and prestige meant Indianapolis. To get there, you had to drive sprints.

"They take their racing seriously in the Midwest," Hop continued. "It would be an adjustment, for sure, but you have the best reflexes I've seen in years, kid, and you got wrists like cast-iron vises."

"You think I could drive one of those sprint cars?"

"I think you could drive the box it came in."

"I'll think on it," Billy said. "Gonna grab a burger. Want one?"

"I'm good. Don't eat too much. Don't want to puke all over yourself in the middle of the race."

* * *

A cinderblock diner stood in the middle of the speedway infield. The open windows allowed the aroma of hot grease and grilled meat and onions—the lifeblood of the racing fraternity—to waft through the area, drawing drivers and crew to some of the most dubious food on the face of the planet.

Billy found Wendell Scott standing outside the diner door.

Scott, a World War Two veteran of Patton's tank corps and a regular on the Dixie Circuit, had constantly found his path to racing success impeded by the accident of his birth as a black man.

Billy had first met Wendell at a race in Danville, Scott's hometown, where the Negro driver flat skunked the field and finished the race in a different time zone. It had taken ten years of false promises, blatant obstruction, and quiet, dedicated driving, but Wendell had finally won respect at his hometown track. Outside a twenty-mile radius of Danville, Scott was still a black man trying to compete in a sport populated otherwise by white faces. Wendell did every stitch of work on his own race car in addition to driving it. He pulled more from shoddy equipment than any other wrench or shoe Billy had seen.

"Wendell." Billy extended his hand. A slight, shy man, Wendell took it gently. His hands were rough as a rasp and stained with grease and oil.

"Mr. Mosack," Wendell said.

"Billy. Any man who beats me on the track calls me by my Christian name. Grabbing a burger. Want to join me?"

Wendell stared at the dirt under his feet with watery blue eyes. "Well, I don't know."

"C'mon. It's on me," Billy said.

It was common knowledge that Wendell spent more on the upkeep of his car than he did on himself. A driver who commonly left the track with less money than when he had arrived, he had been known to skip meals for an entire weekend to make the race. He was humble, but also dedicated to racing. He had come to depend upon the kindness of his fellow racers, if only to survive to the next weekend and the next speedway.

"I can pay my own way," he said. "Mr. Howard, the new promoter, paid me some appearance money. Not sure I want to eat in there. The boy behind the counter don't like me."

"You're a NASCAR race driver," Billy said. "You care what some soda jerk who works here two weekends a year thinks?"

"I think he spit in my food yesterday. I care about spit in my food."

"Come with me."

Wendell followed him into the diner. Billy drew the attention of the cook behind the counter.

"Two cheeseburgers, all the way, and fries. Want a Pepsi, Wendell?"

"Sounds good."

"Two Pepsis."

He paid for the order and leaned forward, as if to tell the cook a secret. Instead, he whispered, "You spit in this man's food and I'll come across that counter and hold your face against the flat top until it sizzles. Any questions?"

The cook drew back as if he had been shot. He shook his head furiously and set about preparing the order. Even so, Billy watched him carefully until he delivered their meals. When they sat at a booth, Wendell slid five quarters across the pine tabletop.

"I pay my way," he said.

"I won't insult you by refusing it." Billy pocketed the money.

"You're a good man."

"I'm King Shitkicker from a wide place in the road in North Carolina, and a few years back I might have spit in your food myself. But that was then. Things change, right?"

"Sure," Wendell said, his eyes betraying his insincerity.

"Not fast enough for you, I reckon."

"It's taking its time." Wendell munched on a fry. "Beats the hell out of working the mill, though. Working the mill's as bad as being in prison. Practically the same damn thing. You go in the mill in the mornin' and can't leave until they unlock the doors. The company store has a lien on your soul. I reckon, living hand to mouth with a race car, at least I'm my own warden."

"Where I come from, only Negroes I ever saw worked in the farm fields. Didn't have any of your people in our school. I do remember one, though. Reckon I'll go to my grave before I forget his face."

"Who's that?"

Billy shook his head. "It's not important. Can't change what's happened in the past, can we?"

"No. I suppose not. Need to ask a favor. Broke a distributor shaft in practice this morning. Don't have a spare. You got a Ford distributor on your truck?"

That explained Wendell's hangdog expression when Billy met him at the door to the diner. He wondered how many other drivers Wendell had buttonholed without success before he had come along.

"We'll set you up," Billy said. "Eat your food. Thinking of getting a slice of apple pie. Want one?"

* * *

Nelson Stacy won the race, after almost five grueling hours. Billy Mosack struggled most of the day to stay in the top ten. Stacy took home over twenty-five thousand dollars. Tenth place paid a grand, plus another five hundred under the table from the promoter for showing up, called *appearance money* in the sport, and a few hundred in contingency money from companies that placed stickers on every car in the field. A couple grand for a weekend's work, even split with Hop, still beat all hell out of truing brake drums back at Arlo's garage. Fact was, they could race two or three times a week, and both Hop and Billy had earned a great deal of money a thousand dollars a pop.

The speedway promoter hosted a post-race reception for the drivers and car owners at the swanky White House Hotel in Charlotte. Billy headed straight for the bar, while Hop—whose primary job was scaring up sponsorship money to keep the team rolling—excused himself to work the room. Billy noted that Wendell, who had finished near the bottom of the field after crashing, was nowhere to be seen. The only black people in the White House Hotel wore red uniforms and lugged baggage for guests.

An hour later, Billy had spoken to everyone he cared to. He placed his glass on a wait tray and was preparing to leave when Hop appeared out of the crowd and grasped his arm.

"Want to introduce you to someone." He dragged Billy through the crowd to a table where two people sat. The first was a tall, rugged-featured man with pewter hair, dressed in an open-neck sports shirt and an Italian blazer, smoking a genuine Havana Robusto.

"This is Carling Underwood," Hop told Billy. "Mr. Underwood, Billy Mosack."

The two shook hands, and Underwood said, "Have you met Chloe Beck?"

The woman next to him was stunning, her raven hair piled high and lacquered to a glossy sheen, crowned with a plastic tiara. She was still in her glittery Victory Circle dress, complete with the banner proclaiming *Miss 600* crossing her gravity-defying breasts like a bandolero.

Billy took Chloe's hand. Chloe reminded Billy of a hundred Hollywood starlets. Her eyes were captivating—a deep, translucent aquamarine that stood out starkly from her otherwise dark features.

"No," Billy said. "Nice to meet you."

"You're a driver?" Chloe asked. "This is all new to me. Until I won the contest last week, I'd never even seen a race."

"Did you enjoy it?" Billy asked. "I was in car seventy-five."

"The red and yellow car! It's so cute!"

"I never heard anyone call a Grand National car cute," Billy said, and Hop and Underwood joined in when he laughed.

Hop said, "Mr. Underwood's from Indianapolis."

"What sort of business are you in there?" Billy asked.

"Grains. I'm a grain wholesaler. Biggest in the state."

"He's also a huge race fan," Hop said. "Has his own stable of sprint cars. Lee Wallard drove for him, and so did Parnelli."

Underwood took a sip of his drink and said, "I enjoyed watching you today, Billy. You picked up a lot of positions after a tough start. Impressive. Where'd you finish again?"

"Tenth."

"Were you disappointed?"

"I was delighted. We had a fifteenth-place car. I beat the spread."

Underwood chuckled. Billy glanced at Chloe. She smiled at him, and his heart quickened.

"Billy and I were talking about sprint cars and Indianapolis only this morning," Hop said. "We're thinking about moving north, barnstorming the AAA tracks. Maybe take a stab at Indy."

"Really?" Underwood said. "You've driven a lot of dirt cars, Billy?"

"He was Dixie Circuit champion in modifieds," Hop said. "They're practically just sprint cars with roofs."

"This is a coincidence. I have an empty seat in one of my sprinters. I also signed a contract last week with Kurtis-Kraft to build a couple of roadsters for Indy next year. "

Hop said, "We discussed selling our NASCAR operation and moving north, maybe buy a couple of sprint cars and a roadster for the Brickyard. Of course, we could also invest in a going operation, if there's a seat there for my boy Billy."

Underwood measured Billy with his eyes, then he drained his glass.

"Why not? Guy who won the Dixie Circuit championship should adapt readily to an open-cockpit car. There's a hundred miler at the state fairgrounds in Du Quoin in three weeks. Let's put Billy in my sprinter and see how he fares."

"I'll do right by you, Mr. Underwood," Billy said.

"Call me Carl."

"How about a refill, Carl?" Hop asked.

"Wouldn't turn it down."

"Chloe?" Billy asked. "Can I bring you a drink?"

"Seven and Seven," she said, her eyes iridescent. "I'll go with you."

He took her hand as she stood with difficulty, her body constricted by the gold dress that hugged her like paint. She kept her hand in his as they crossed the ballroom to the bar. Just before they got there, she grabbed his arm and pulled him out a side door into a service hallway.

"Got a cigarette?" she asked.

"You don't have any?"

She held her hands out to her side and gestured at the dress that revealed every curve in her body.

"Yeah. I see your problem." Billy handed her a Marlboro and lighted it with his Zippo, then lighted one for himself. She exhaled a cloud of blue smoke.

"Oh, thank God. That's better than coming. I've wanted a smoke all day long."

"You're not allowed to smoke?"

"Not when I'm in public wearing the getup. Destroys the whole virginal illusion. I was right. I had you pegged as a Marlboro guy. Burly man like you. You look kinda like that cowboy in the commercials. We better get back inside. Don't want to keep Daddy Carl waiting."

They ordered the drinks and returned to the table. The men talked for another half-hour, hatching plans for Billy's move from NASCAR to the AAA and plotting his sprint car debut at Du Quoin. Billy kept an eye on Chloe, who must have been bored to death but never broke character as the doting sycophant.

They parted with a handshake agreement and an appointment to meet in Indianapolis a week later. Underwood took Chloe's arm and led her to the elevators.

"You want her?" Hop asked as Billy watched them leave.

"Can she be had?"

"Take a number. She's a self-serve buffet, boy. The Automat of Love. You can't be first, and you won't be last, but ain't nothing stopping you from being next."

* * *

After six hundred miles of hardscrabble racing in blistering temperatures, Billy should have been exhausted. He dropped into bed around ten, but sleep wouldn't come. After an hour, he dressed and took the elevator to the bar. While the party upstairs had featured an open bar, North Carolina didn't have liquor by the drink for sale, so the bar only served beer and wine.

Chloe Beck sat in a booth nursing a glass of wine. Billy had the bartender draw him a schooner of Rolling Rock, and he slid into the booth facing her. An ashtray between them was half-full of lipstick-smeared butts.

"Got a cigarette?" she asked. "The bartender is sick of me bumming off him."

Billy pulled a hard pack of Marlboros from his pocket and slid it across the table. She slipped one between her lips as he struck a flame on the Zippo.

"You're not..." He snapped the Zippo closed and pointed upstairs.

"Good God, no. Daddy Carl's fun, and he likes to spread his cash around, but he is not in it for the long haul. He's a gentleman, mostly, even if he never heard the phrase *ladies first*. How about you, Ace? Can't sleep?"

"It's Billy."

"I remember. Can't sleep, Billy?"

"Big day." He sipped at the beer. "So, you and Carling aren't…"

"Shacking up? No. I'm trying to decide whether I should blush."

"Logical assumption. Handsome rich man. Beautiful woman."

"You think I'm beautiful? I've waited half my life for some man to tell me that." She smiled slyly.

"Yeah. I get it. Have a nice night." He slid out and took his beer to the second booth down from her. He searched his jacket for a cigarette before he remembered he'd left them on her table. At least he still had his Zippo. He took a swallow of beer, leaned his head against the Naugahyde padded back of the booth, and closed his eyes.

The sound of a pack of cigarettes falling on the tabletop roused him. Chloe slid into the booth across the table.

"You give up way too easy, Ace," she said.

"Where I'm from, it's impolite to impose yourself on a woman once she's given the signal to back off."

"Where's that?"

"Here in North Carolina. Not too far from here. Place you never heard of called Prosperity."

"Small town boy. Of course, most of the racers I've encountered are. Don't find a lot of them who grew up in New York City. Not sure why. Seems like driving a New York taxi would be great training."

Her eyes were glazed.

"You're on something," he said.

"Sure. What about it? They don't do stuff back in Posterity?"

"Prosperity. Sure they do. It's like anywhere else."

"You still live there?"

"Hell no. Got the fuck out as soon as I could and never looked back."

They both laughed. He pulled a Marlboro from the pack and lighted it.

"You should pay them a visit. You're a big-time racing driver. Just cadged yourself a ride in the Indy 500 next year if you don't get killed between now and then. Time to rub their noses in it."

"You'd do that?"

"In a second."

He blew a few smoke rings, just to show off. "Maybe someday. I want to be a lot richer and bunch more famous. Got a couple of buddies to impress."

"Farm boys?"

"One of them. The other's in the NFL."

"What's that?"

He cocked his head. She smiled back. *Yeah*, he thought. *She knows.* "We were the offensive backfield of our high school football team. Conference champions. Our quarterback set thirteen records."

"He'd be the guy in the NFL."

"Yeah. They called us The Trinity. It was always the three of us, and I was always the holy fucking ghost. I'll go back to Prosperity when I'm Number One."

"You got a little inferiority complex going there, Ace. Something I heard on TV," she said. "These football buddies from back home are dancing in your head and calling the tune. You let 'em in. You can toss 'em back out."

"Easy to say."

"Scrape 'em off. Don't measure your worth against their yardstick. Set your own standard."

"Maybe you're right." He drained his schooner.

"Before you came in, I was thinking of calling a cab. The speedway's been great to me, but not enough to put me up in this place. Should I call a cab, Ace?"

"What's the other option?"

"If you're going to mope around the bar all night, I could take your room."

"Sorry. Headed up in a few minutes."

"Even better."

He palmed the cigarettes and slipped them back into his shirt pocket. "I'm not into sloppy seconds."

"Oh, you don't have to worry about that, Sugar. Daddy Carl likes his vice versa, if you know what I mean. His love bus don't stop at the Y."

"Are you speaking English?"

"Your future car owner likes things a specific way. I can show you, if you like, but I suspect you require a certain disposition to enjoy it. Let's put it this way. Nothing gets sloppy. It's a half-hour cab ride to my apartment, and Chloe's pooped. What do you say?"

Chapter Twenty

By 1963, Jude Pressley should have been on top of the world. Coach McCandless had proven fallible at best when it came to predicting his potential. Jude's performance had led tiny Ryland College to three straight championships in a small, easily ignored conference. It would have been four if a wiry ex-soccer player from Yugoslavia hadn't shanked a field goal attempt with seconds to go in the final game of Jude's freshman year.

Somehow, Jude drew the attention of several National Football League teams. When the time came for the 1958 college draft, the Chicago Cardinals called his name almost as an afterthought deep in the twenty-sixth round. He warmed the bench as third-string quarterback for two years before he was traded to San Francisco, where he still rode the pine, but he did get some snaps anytime the starter pulled a muscle and the second-stringer had the clap. He'd even started two pre-season games. The money was stout, he had a great apartment on Russian Hill, his bank account strained at the seams, and he was largely uninjured, his face unmarked by gridiron violence.

Then came November twenty-second.

It was cold and dreary. Jude arrived at the stadium to hop the team bus to the airport for their flight to Green Bay, only to find his team members standing around shell-shocked. J.D. Smith, a Negro running back, sat on the ground crying.

"What?" Jude said as he looked around the room.

They told him. Dallas. A motorcade. Shots. A dead president. Camelot in ruins.

The flight was quieter than after any loss. Nobody wanted to talk. When they arrived in Milwaukee and boarded the bus to Green Bay, the airport was like a tomb. People stared into space. The news had left most people in a tearful stupor. Nobody knew what to expect. With the Cold War, the recent Cuban Missile Crisis, and the burgeoning war in Southeast Asia, the future was anything but certain.

By gameday, a few of the Forty-Niners were enraged. They wanted to strike out in some way, against somebody, but had no clue who to blame. An hour and a half before the game, every eye in the locker room was riveted to a television mounted on the wall, as Kennedy's accused killer shambled down a hallway in Dallas, a police officer on each arm. They witnessed the unthinkable tableau as a man in an overcoat and hat stepped forward, broke through the crowd, and shot Oswald live on television. By the time the game was supposed to start, everyone had learned the awful truth. Oswald had been murdered. Any chance of learning who had authorized Kennedy's assassination likely had died with him.

Jude saw worry on the faces of the fans. Some, undoubtedly, believed this would be the last football game they would ever attend. With their youthful, energetic president lying on an embalmer's slab in Washington, there was reason to fear the Soviets would take advantage of America's momentary confusion and launch an attack to settle the Cold War once and for all.

The Negro players on the team, led by J.D. Smith, were particularly disillusioned. Under Kennedy, they had seen incremental advances in civil rights. Now, with that cracker high school teacher from Texas in the White House, nobody knew what to expect. Their champion in the white community was lost.

Nothing made sense anymore.

Jude hadn't put great effort into building close relations with his Negro teammates. He liked them well enough, but whenever he was asked to join in their postgame celebrations, he'd begged off, complaining of fatigue or poor sleep the night before.

The fact was, being around them made him uncomfortable. He could start a conversation with J.D., for instance, but within a couple of minutes, Smith's face would contort in his imagination, and slowly transform into Ev Howard. The memory of Ev swinging from the black walnut tree in Prosperity lanced at his brain. Every time the mental image manifested, he panicked and felt trapped. The price of keeping his secret had been dear. Ev Howard lived in his head now, his accusing voice condemning every step Jude took. Being around the black teammates only cranked up the volume.

The Forty-Niners' play on the field was as lackluster as the enthusiasm in the stands. They trailed Green Bay almost from the start. Coach Hickey tried to rally his athletes, but it was no use. To a man, they all wished to be somewhere—*anywhere*—else.

In the third quarter, quarterback Brodie rolled his right ankle while being sacked. He came up limping, and Hickey called a timeout to get him off the field for a few minutes' rest and a consultation with the trainer.

Hickey called Jude's number.

The first play was a handoff to J.D. Smith. The back gained a yard and a half before being drilled and planted on the turf. The second play, a short screen pass, went wide. On the third snap, Jude sent the wide receivers downfield. He trusted his line, dropped back, and waited to see which of the receivers wasn't double-teamed.

He didn't see Green Bay's tackle dust off the lineman assigned to guard him. He only saw the blur to his left, and he dropped back a little farther to buy a half-second to decide, before rocketing the ball.

They hit him like a freight train an instant after he flung it. One tackle launched at his knees, rolling him off balance. The other hit him high, driving him forward.

His right knee went first. There was a grisly audible *pop*, and a rolling wave of fire climbed up his thigh and grew into a basketball-sized sphere of agony in his midsection that stole the light from his eyes. The second hit twisted him in place, his legs wrapped up, and his vertebrae banged together like castanets as he fell to the ground screaming.

It only took half a second to end his professional football career. He lay on the field, staring at a frying pan sky, every nerve in his body blazing in

119

agony. He tried to rise from the frigid turf, but his leg refused to work, and his spine protested so vehemently he thought he might faint.

They lifted him screaming onto a stretcher and carried him to the locker room, where a doctor waited. One of the bearers gave him the bad news. He'd connected with his receiver, but the play had ended two yards short of the first down. San Francisco was forced to punt.

"Three and out," Jude said, grimacing as the doctor examined him. "Three and fucking out to pasture."

Five weeks later, he arrived at the stadium on crutches for a team meeting, his leg still encased in plaster from hip to ankle. As he hobbled to the front door, an assistant quarterback coach intercepted him.

"Coach Hickey would like to see you," he said. "And, sorry Jude, but bring your playbook."

Chapter Twenty-One

Rennie had kept his promise. When Deputy Brian Mattox decided—with Rennie's encouragement—to run for sheriff in 1956, Rennie saw to it his election was a runaway success. On balance, Mattox had been a good sheriff, though he frequently turned a blind eye to events that reflected poorly on his benefactor Poole. Sometimes, he carried out Rennie's dirty deeds, such as teaching Owen Wheeler the meaning of humility.

A week after paying his debts at Rennie's Feed and Seed—and promising to take up his late father's role as the perpetual burr under Rennie Poole's saddle in Prosperity—Owen was on a trip to Morgan when red flashing lights illuminated his rearview mirror. A deputy named Stilson extricated himself from the cruiser and tightrope-walked the white line at the edge of the Morgan Highway to reach the driver-side window.

"License and registration," he ordered perfunctorily. Stilson took his time examining the documents, and for an instant, Owen wondered whether the deputy could read.

"Got a broken taillight," the deputy said. "Gonna write you up for improper equipment."

"What?" Owen said. He hopped from the cab of the truck and walked around to the rear. "That wasn't broken yesterday. I'd swear to it."

"It's broke now," Stilson said, writing on the ticket pad. "Get it fixed and show the repair receipt to the judge, and he'll drop the citation."

Owen was stopped three times in the next two weeks, always by Deputy Larry Stilson and always in roughly the same one-mile stretch of the Morgan

121

Highway. Each time, Stilson cited him for some missing or broken part on the truck—always a part Owen could have sworn was fine the day before. He was never charged with anything that would leave a criminal record, because the point wasn't to break him with fines. Anything official would leave a paper trail, and every citation was dismissed in less than a minute at traffic court in Morgan, though usually only after waiting two or three hours to have his case called. Owen saw through the game almost from the start. Rennie was dispatching his personal thug brigade to send him a message.

The pressure from Rennie Poole and Sheriff Mattox only made Owen dig in deeper. He attended every Town Council meeting without fail. He spent hours reading local ordinances and council propositions, so he could speak intelligently about them when his turn at the public comment lectern came. The harder Rennie tried to drive him into the dirt, the more resilient Owen became, and the more determined he was to block Rennie at every opportunity.

To maintain his independence from Rennie's colloquial cabal, Owen was certain to keep his accounts with the Feed and Seed up-to-date. After each harvest, he zeroed out his balance. While he knew Rennie was irritated at losing any financial hold he might have on Owen, the mayor always accepted the payment graciously, as he did in October 1965 when Owen made his autumn visit.

"I wish every customer was as prompt with their payments as you, Owen," Rennie said as he wrote out a receipt.

"I bet you do," Owen replied.

"You have no idea. Sometimes I think issuing credit was the dumbest business move I ever made. Do you know there are some people in this county who still owe on credit I gave 'em five years ago?"

"And I'm sure you meticulously calculate the interest each month. Apparently, you've forgotten that I paid off a ten-year debt to you just a couple of years back."

"You'll have to allow me to return the favor. I'm having a little get-together at my home next weekend. You're invited."

Owen folded the receipt and slipped it into this overalls pocket. "Don't reckon I'll be able to make it. Plan to be busy."

"Doing what?"

"I'll think of something. Hanging out in your little Klangri-La with a bunch of guys in hoods isn't my idea of an entertaining evening."

"Never could figure out you Wheeler boys. A friend offers a gesture of neighborly courtesy, and you bite his fingers off. Come on by. The Klan days in Prosperity are in the past. We're just a social club these days. Just a bunch of good ol' boys tossing back a few and telling tall tales. We live in a different world now, son. It's the middle of the 1960s."

"You may not wear the robes anymore, but your soul is still branded with the blood drop cross," Owen said. "I'll take a pass, Rennie."

Chapter Twenty-Two

The world had changed since Jude's injury in Green Bay. He'd been a retired football pro for almost as long as he had been an active one. A lot could happen in only four years. He missed a great deal of it, floating in a drug-and-alcohol-induced haze. Getting booted from the game hadn't done away with the chronic pain.

He didn't have to worry about money. His frugality over the years he played professional ball had paid off. He maintained a healthy bank account. Some might even call it robust. Handled with care, it could last him years, perhaps decades. The Russian Hill apartment was the first thing to go. Instead, he'd leased a flat in a duplex on the other side of the city, on Cole Street in a mildly depressed section called The Haight. With a little work, and a lot of painkillers, he'd painted the place, furnished it comfortably, and found it met his needs without overtaxing his bankbook.

He worked when the inclination struck him and his knee allowed, waiting tables or tending bar. Most people, after they got a couple of drinks in them, were fascinated by the tale of his sports career. Some offered to buy him drinks. Jude never refused their generosity.

His tiny neighborhood changed dramatically in the summer of 1967. San Francisco had always been a mecca for nonconformists. The beatniks took over North Beach a decade earlier, bringing with them cool jazz and coffee houses and inscrutable poetry. The burgeoning homosexual community south of Market Street in the Castro district was one of the worst kept secrets in the city.

And now, hippies in The Haight.

At first, the strange young people were like an alien species flooding into his neighborhood. In Prosperity, they would be cast aside, or arrested as vagrants, or even attacked as some sort of threat. Jude had always found the beats pretentious, as boring and colloquial as they claimed the rest of society to be. The hippies were different. They appeared to genuinely believe in a new idea—casting aside the trappings of quiet desperation, as Thoreau had written, and embracing a simpler, communal existence. The core of the hippie movement was built on sharing rather than acquisition. For a man who had grown up in the buckle of the Bible belt—and under the incessantly avaricious shadow of Rennie Poole—the movement offered a fresh and enticing new lifestyle.

The drugs were better, too. Morphine and codeine only put him to sleep and constipated him. He'd been too timid to try heroin. The hippies brought weed and acid to The Haight. Marijuana, he'd found, mediated his chronic pain and allowed him to function, after a fashion. LSD was… well, LSD. Something completely different.

Jude had no interest in it until the previous winter, when some ex-professor from Harvard named Leary had appeared at a huge gathering of the tribes in Golden Gate Park.

It was a pleasant January day. Jude was bored out of his skull, and his knee was acting up, so he decided to take a short walk into the park, the eastern boundaries of which were only three blocks from his apartment. Crowds of younger kids walked past him as he limped along, headed toward the Polo Fields.

In his narcotic haze, Jude had ignored announcements of the gathering, and he was astounded to discover it had attracted over a hundred thousand people. Drawn by the novelty, he settled in next to a group of kids wearing hand-woven shawls and suede boots, the ostensible uniform of The Haight. One of them handed him a lighted joint. Jude took a drag and passed it to the next person. The kid who had handed him the joint smiled.

"Cool, dude." He turned to the girl on his other side, kissed her, and fondled her breast.

"Right on," Jude said, perfunctorily, and turned his attention to the stage where a local band called The Grateful Dead jammed. Every minute or so, it seemed as if another joint made the rounds. Jude's knee stopped throbbing. He allowed himself to fall into the music, bobbing his head along with the beat.

A short, stocky man with wavy long hair and a thick drooping mustache stepped through the crowd, handing out tablets. He wore a tan leather jacket with a dirty fringe. Jude recalled him working the sound equipment for The Grateful Dead.

"What is it?" Jude asked as the guy pressed a tablet into his hand.

"White Lightning."

"Son, this ain't like any white lightning they used to make back home," Jude told him. "Comes in big glass jugs there."

The man laughed. "It's LSD man. Acid. I make it myself."

"You some kind of chemist?"

"I'm all sorts of shit, man. Owsley Stanley. Folks call me Bear." He extended his hand. Jude grasped it.

"Jude Pressley."

"The football player?"

"A few years back."

"Groovy!" Stanley dropped another tablet into Jude's palm. "Hope you enjoy it." He moved on to the next cluster of kids lounging on the lawn. Jude examined the tablets. They didn't look like much.

"What the hell?" Jude popped the first tablet into his mouth.

Ram Dass, a former Harvard professor, took to the stage with Timothy Leary to talk about the benefits of psychedelics. As he melted into the landscape, Jude had to agree. Maybe these crazy kids were onto something.

"Tune in, turn on, and drop out!" Leary cried from the stage. The words, amplified by the enormous speakers, reverberated through the park. Jude thought he could see the sound waves pulsating in the air.

"Right on," Jude muttered. Leary was chanting the watchword to Jude's life. There was no greater dropout. He'd quit the town of his birth, the career he loved, and—for much of the last four years—his membership in humanity. He had been on the downhill slide for years, and the laws of inertia suggested he was unlikely to change.

But, he mused, *at least I'm not in denial about it. That should count for something.*

He didn't recognize it at the time, but the Human Be-In of January 1967 was when Jude Pressley joined the hippie ranks.

In San Francisco, his life perspective changed. Fueled by weed and acid, he was drawn into existentially profound conversations with people he met in the park. Where he'd feigned interest while tending bar before to get better tips, now he found himself listening to his customers, not critically or impatiently, but with interest and concern. He connected with them in a way he hadn't before.

Intrigued by the philosophies of his hippie friends, he began to read. Drawn in by the works of Ferlinghetti, cummings, and a new guy in town named Brautigan, he spent time at City Lights Bookstore, and even volunteered to work there in exchange for a break on prices. The drugs might have expanded his mind, but he still had to furnish the fresh space.

He stopped visiting the barber, and he let his beard grow. In less than half a year, Jude Pressley fully and pleasantly assimilated into the new culture of Haight-Ashbury.

* * *

Summer of love, my ass, Jude thought, as he lounged on a tattered wool blanket on the eastern edge of Golden Gate Park and waited for the orange barrel acid to kick in. *I haven't gotten laid in days.*

It was a sunny day. Jude sprawled on the moth-eaten blanket, naked from the waist up, the June sun warming his body as he waited for the acid to kick. LSD had been declared illegal in California a year earlier, and of course, grass had been illegal for decades, but nobody in The Haight seemed to care much about laws when it came to drugs.

A young girl who was probably nineteen but looked forty dropped to her knees next to him on the blanket. He'd seen her in the neighborhood before, panhandling for spare change or hanging out with friends. She wore a stained white shirt, a crocheted vest, gingham miniskirt, and soft leather pioneer boots.

"Hey, man," she said.

"Hey."

"I'll blow you for five bucks."

Jude could feel the electric buzz in the back of his head that portended getting off, and for an instant, he wasn't certain he'd heard her correctly.

"What?"

"I'm hungry. I want to eat. I don't have any money." She seemed to be listing all the deficits in her life. "I'll give you a blowjob if you'll pay for some food."

Jude dug into his pocket and came up with a five.

"Skip the blowjob. Go eat."

"You don't like me?"

"I like you fine. Go. Eat." He closed his eye again.

She returned sometime later. Might have been an hour. Maybe a month. He was tripping like crazy, and she knelt next to him again. She didn't touch him, and she didn't try to talk to him. Instead, she hummed, softly and sweetly, as she stared at his face. He vaguely recognized the tune as a hymn he'd heard in church when he was a child. In his psychedelic brain, the humming sounded like a muted saxophone.

"You could be my daddy," she said, after a few minutes.

"I might be," he said. "What was your mother's name?"

"I mean my daddy here. In San Francisco. You could take care of me."

"Sweetie, I can barely take care of myself."

He opened his eyes. Her face was a contorted grotesque. Her smile was broad and wide, and her brilliant white teeth glittered with points of light. Her eyes were deep blue, the bluest Jude had ever seen, with pinpoint pupils, which meant she was doing heroin. Everyone in The Haight bore the physical stain of their addictions in their eyes.

Her eyes closed, and she swayed in rhythm as she hummed the ancient spiritual. She worked on variations of some random tune she allowed to evolve inside her head. Jude was vaguely aware she had slid beside him and lay on her side watching the rise and fall of his chest.

"I love you," she said. The words vibrated and pulsed inside his head.

"Sure you do." He rolled over to make space for her on the blanket.

* * *

The girl followed him home as twilight fell on Golden Gate Park. He was careful not to encourage her. That wasn't the way things were done in The Haight. If she followed him home of her own free will, that was her trip.

As they approached Jude's apartment on Cole Street, a man sat on the steps of a building two doors down, playing a resonator guitar. He was short and slight, with a mop of jet black hair that fell over his forehead in sweaty ringlets. He was working on a twelve-bar improvisation, sliding the neck of a tallboy up and down the fretboard, and not doing badly. The heavy sweet scent of ganja mixed with sandalwood hung in the air. The guitar player nodded in his direction. Jude waved back. The girl nestled in behind Jude, on the next higher step, and watched over his shoulder. After a few minutes, the man with the guitar and the jitterbug eyes walked over to them and held out his hand.

"Charlie."

"Jude. I don't know her name."

"Lucy," the girl whispered.

"Cool," Charlie said. "Moved here from Berkeley a few weeks back."

"What was wrong with Berkeley?" Jude asked.

"Nothing. Liked it fine. My old lady said the scene in The Haight was more eclectic, whatever that means."

"Pardon me if I don't seem to focus. Doing some orange barrel," Jude said. "Don't know about her. I think she's a junkie. We met at the park." Lucy didn't say anything, but she appeared to shrink a little behind him. "Gonna grab something to eat, and maybe put on some music and crash."

"I'm hungry," Lucy complained.

"What did you eat with the money I gave you?" Jude asked. Lucy's eyes had already told him the answer. "Come on. If I give you more money, you'll park it in your arm. You hungry, Charlie? Want to get some food?"

* * *

"Who were you before you came to San Francisco?" Charlie asked, between bites of shao mai dipped in gyoza sauce.

"What makes you think I'm not someone now?" Jude asked.

"You're tripping in Golden Gate Park on a Tuesday afternoon. You're either independently wealthy, or on the skids from something better. Don't mind telling you I got out of prison recently. I ain't proud, man. Nobody got a deed on my soul. I was on McNeil Island, up in Washington. Got out three months ago. Whaddaya think about that?"

"What for?" Lucy asked.

"Piddling shit. Passing a federal check I stole out of some broad's mailbox. They took it personal. I been locked up, one way or another, for half my life."

"Half your life?" Jude asked. "How's that work?"

"A lot of it was in juvie. I had kind of a tough childhood. That bother you, Slick?" he asked Jude.

"None of my business. Where'd you learn to play the blues?"

"McNeil Island. Wanta hear something awesome? I got taught by Alvin Karpis. How about that?"

"Who's Alvin Karpis?" Lucy asked, pausing from gnawing on a rib.

"A gangster," Jude said, without looking up from his plate.

"They called him Creepy," Charlie said. "Don't know why. He was always nice to me. What about you, Slick? What sort of road brought you to this party?"

"Football," Jude said. "I was a reserve quarterback for the Forty-Niners, and the Cardinals before that."

"Johnny Football!" Charlie exclaimed.

"Really?" Lucy asked. "You were a pro?"

"They paid me. Pretty well, actually. Didn't get a lot of playing time. Only took thirty or forty game snaps in my entire career. I don't talk about it much anymore."

"I bet I watched you play on the television in prison," Charlie said.

"You'd probably lose that bet, unless they focused on the bench and caught me picking my nose."

"So, why'd you quit?"

"Got hurt. Couldn't play anymore."

"Oh, yeah," Charlie said. "That's why the limp."

"Can't dance, can't play football," Jude said, picking up a rib. "It's not a thing. I was never a big deal anyway. Played at a tiny high school in a tiny town and went to play for a tiny college in a tiny conference. In the NFL record books, they'll stick my stats in the fine print. I just play it day to day these days. This is bumming the shit out of me. Let's talk about something else. What are you gonna do now you're out of prison?"

"Gonna be a star, man. Guy in prison gave me the names of some people he knew in Hollywood, and Creepy's gonna help me make some connections in Vegas."

"Good luck with that. I'm tired. Think I'll head on home and crash."

Lucy snaked her hand around his arm. "I got nowhere to sleep tonight. Can I come with you?"

"Sure. Whatever. See you, Charlie. Keep practicing. Maybe you'll make it big someday."

"Oh, ever'body gonna know my name, Slick. Thanks for the eats."

Chapter Twenty-Three

San Francisco might have languished in the rock-and-drug haze of the Summer of Love, but for most of the country, 1967 was The Long Hot Summer.

Between June and September, no fewer than one-hundred-fifty-nine race riots broke out across the United States. Something about the hot months provoked the most violent passions in people. The incessant, oppressive, overwhelming heat soaked into every pore. You could bathe twenty times a day and still walk around with a thin sheen of sweat. Minor squabbles became knife fights. Long-simmering disagreements devolved into blood feuds.

The torch was lit. As if handed from one runner to another, the riots spread across the country, carried on the shoulders of millions of people who believed their dark faces made them invisible to the powerful, and who demanded a slice of the pie. They exorcised demons that had ridden on their ancestors' backs across stormy seas in fetid quarters too small to sit upright. They demanded justice for hundreds of years of backbreaking labor, bent at the waist for hours on end in blistering temperatures. They had waited patiently since Reconstruction for full acceptance and enfranchisement, only to be denied again and again, and in the summer of 1967 they abandoned patience and restraint and due process and stood up to the social system that had oppressed them for centuries.

Bliss County—where, only a few years before, the county's stalwarts had cheered as Ev Howard swayed at the end of a bristly hemp rope—wasn't immune.

Clyde Dillard's hardware remained the rallying point for the men in Prosperity during any emergency. In the Long Hot Summer of 1967, the mounting riots in cities and towns across the country alarmed many of the town's white citizens, and Rennie Poole had declared they would meet at the hardware on a Wednesday night in July to discuss options.

Hubert Pressley, as always, stood at Rennie's side. It seemed every five years added another chin under his pudgy lips. Rennie looked much as he had back in 1954, save for his slightly longer hair. It now barely danced across the tops of his ears and curled against his neck in back, a political concession to the new liberality in the country which Rennie detested but eagerly exploited.

Owen Wheeler, enjoying his position outside the Rennie Poole machine, leaned a ladderback chair against the wall and waited for the mayor's bombast. He didn't have to wait long. Owen didn't trust Rennie Poole, but he did respect the power the man wielded like an eight-pound sledgehammer. Especially now.

Mayor Rennie Poole had decided to run for Congress.

"Dear friends," Rennie stood on the same apple crate he'd used on the night he goaded Prosperity's men into hanging Ev Howard, "I don't have to tell you we live in dangerous times. We have all seen the riots on our television sets, entire city blocks burning on the six o'clock news, and I know every one of you has asked the same question. Will the peace of our quiet, agricultural community be shattered by shouts of anger and flames of dissent? I love my Negro friends, but I also remind myself that *they* are not the problem. They are law-abiding citizens who know their place and are content with the way things have been in this country for over two hundred years. It is the malcontents of whom I speak this evening—the violent and angry contingent who ask for more than they're due. They take what they want and leave behind a smoking, burned-out husk. We must remember the words of the heathen leader of the black Nation of Islam, the man who called himself Malcolm X, who said the black man in America must step forward and grab power by any means necessary." He paused and allowed the last sentence to sink in. *"By... any... means... necessary.* Listen to those words, my friends."

Owen allowed his chair to return to all four legs, as loudly as possible. The men in the hardware store turned in his direction.

"You forgot to mention Malcolm X's house had been firebombed two nights before he made that speech, Mr. Mayor," Owen said.

"By his own people no doubt, the same ones who murdered him," Rennie parried. "We are not talking about decent God-fearing people, the kind, patient, cooperative Negroes who mostly represent their race in Bliss County. We must be prepared, my friends..."

Owen felt a hand on his shoulder and found Sheriff Mattox glowering at him. Mattox had left his Bliss County sheriff's uniform at home, choosing instead to show up in khaki trousers and a Ban-Lon collarless shirt, but he still carried his authority like a tinpot stormtrooper. He jerked his head toward the door. The message was unmistakable. Owen followed him into the parking lot.

A dozen years sitting behind a desk in Morgan had thickened Mattox. The dark circles under his eyes testified to both the rigors of his elective position and the demands put on him by Rennie Poole. Mattox stopped next to Owen's truck and lit a cigarette. He blew a cloud of smoke into the air over his head, opened the driver's side door, and jabbed at Owen's chest with his middle finger.

"You want to cool it," he said. "It's not a good idea to challenge the mayor. He might think you're ungrateful for the favors he's done for you."

"He did my father favors. I inherited the debt. You're out of uniform, Brian. You want to think twice before poking me with your finger again."

"Decorated war hero or not, you're back home now. Farms are dangerous places. If you're on the right side of things, you might find deputies and firemen and ambulances get there a little quicker. Rock the boat, they could take their time."

"You're threatening me?" Owen clenched his right fist.

"Naw." Mattox flicked the cigarette out into the street. It streamed a shower of bright orange and golden cinders as it struck the pavement. "You can walk back inside and take your seat and keep your fucking mouth shut, or you can climb in your car and go home. Your dad irritated Rennie more than a hemorrhoid, and I reckon you're his son. You can think whatever you want, harbor whatever opinions you want, long as you keep 'em to yourself."

Owen fingered Mattox's white Ban-Lon shirt. "Nice. Part of the Klan's summer collection?"

Mattox's eyes lit with anger. He stepped back.

"Don't suppose they make them in men's sizes?" Owen pressed. He tensed his body and prepared for whatever was about to come.

A battered 1940s farm truck careened into the hardware parking lot and stopped with a screech of tortured tires. Jess Varley, a farmer from the far side of Prosperity, hopped out.

"Sheriff!" Varley shouted as Mattox squared off with Owen Wheeler. "Thank God you're here! There's a riot in Morgan!"

Chapter Twenty-Four

Like many of the disturbances in the Long Hot Summer of 1967, the Morgan riot sprang from a confrontation between a Negro youth and a police officer.

At nineteen, Angeloe Teeter was as pleased as he could be with himself. He'd worked part-time jobs for three years, saving every penny, and had amassed almost three thousand dollars. His dream machine—a new Mustang—was priced within his means if he could get the dealer to knock a hundred or so off the list.

Angeloe stood only five and a half feet tall and might have weighed a hundred twenty-five pounds after Thanksgiving dinner. Expecting resistance, he dressed in his best shirt, a white button-down broadcloth, and the pinstriped wool trousers from his only suit.

The dealer was suspicious at first. Angeloe had to show the money before he was allowed a test drive. He wasn't embarrassed. He'd spent his entire life in Garveyville, the black neighborhood in Morgan, and was used to the suspicions of white people. He felt the clicks of door locks whenever he walked through the grocery store parking lot. He'd seen the segregated bathrooms and the sequestered areas of restaurants. He'd sipped from rusted water fountains labeled *Colored Only*.

When he was ten, his father and mother had driven to Atlanta to visit relatives. They stopped in a small town in Georgia because the main street was blocked for a parade. They sat a hundred feet back from the barricaded intersection. Crowds of people stood five deep, waving flags and banners. The women held handkerchiefs aloft and waved them like doves' wings.

There was the smell of popcorn and hot grease and onions and spices in the air. A slightly offkey band played *Dixie* in the distance. Angeloe's father stepped out, looked, and climbed hurriedly back into the car.

"We'll find another way." He pulled a U-turn to head back out of town.

"What?" Angeloe's mother had asked.

"Klan," he said, without elaborating.

Through the back window of his father's sedan, Angeloe spied a phalanx of peaked white hoods march by the crowd.

"What's Klan?" he asked.

"Men with snakes coiled in their heads," his father said. "Sick men. Men who hate ever'thing that ain't them. They the kind of people think it fun to dip a cherry bomb in rubber cement and roll it in BBs, light it off and roll it into a crowd of our people. We want nothing to do with them, son. You see Klan, you get!"

"James," his mother said, in a voice she used when he needed to be reined in. She cupped his arm lightly.

"Boy's got to learn," his father said. "Got to know how things are."

Cowed by his father's anger and fear, Angeloe had been afraid to ask any more, and his father didn't volunteer more until three years later. The boy gawking through the back window at a receding Ku Klux Klan Easter parade had become a gangling, skinny teen. He was spending more time with friends from school and from the neighborhood than he was at home, and his mother worried constantly about him.

Angeloe sat on the front stoop, whittling on a boxwood stick with a penknife, when his father handed him a cold bottle of ginger ale and sat next to him.

"It's time for us to talk," James said.

"'Bout what?"

"Things you need to know. Might be you already know some of this, but you're still a kid, and your momma worries about you. As far as you can see, in both directions, how many white people live there?"

"No white people live in Garveyville, Daddy."

"That's right, son. They don't. 'Cause they scared. Was a time they owned us. They could buy and sell us, like cattle or swine. They could kill a black man, and nobody would do nothin' to them. They fought a great war about it, and they lost. That loss stings, Angeloe. It's like every white baby born in Bliss County come into the world with poison ivy under their skin, itching to get even for a war that was lost before their great-granddaddy was born. They can't let it go. They fear we are going to rise up and take from them what we earned."

"What?" Angeloe asked.

"A seat at the table. All your life, you gonna face this. White men have run the table all my life. They don't want to give up an inch of it if they can help it. You buck up at a white man, even joking, and you might get your skull caved in or worse. Maybe the reason there ain't a white family living as far as you can see up one side of the road and the other, is because we're safer this way. Less chance to get caught up in something."

"What are you saying?"

"Things are better now than when I was a boy. They'll be better for your children. But, for now, this is the way it lays, boy. When you deal with white folk, be polite. Don't fuss. Don't cuss. Don't look 'em direct in the eye, 'cause they see it as a challenge. Dress right and remember to say please and thank you and sir and ma'am. You treat every white person you meet with the same respect you give your momma. Trouble comes enough for our people. You don't want to invite it."

Angeloe parked the Mustang at the dealership and told the salesman he'd like to make a deal. The salesman gave Angeloe a bill of sale and the papers to take to the license bureau, and Angeloe wheeled out onto Eisenhower Boulevard in a car with only six miles on the odometer. He cranked down the windows, found Chatty Hattie's show on the radio, and cruised to tunes by Peaches and Herb, and Tammi Terrell, and Otis Redding.

After two or three trips up and down Eisenhower, Angeloe stopped for a burger and a Coke at the Chick-N-Shake, where kids from his high school hung out. He pulled off the highway into the parking lot. A carhop appeared at his window and took his order. Angeloe didn't want to eat in his new car, so he stepped out and sat at one of the picnic tables on the concrete pad between the lot and the restaurant. It gave him an opportunity to admire the Mustang.

A cherry-red '65 Chevelle rumbled into the lot. Angeloe recognized it immediately. Sonny Hoskins had lettered in three sports at Morgan High but had been passed over by every college in the state due to *character issues*, which was one way of saying Sonny woke up each morning determined to find how many feet of a two-by-four he could jam up someone's ass. The *someone* in question was irrelevant. Anyone would scratch the itch.

Angeloe wasn't concerned. Inexplicably, Sonny had always been decent toward him. Always slight in stature, Angeloe had never tried out for any of the high school sports. He presented no threat to Sonny Hoskins' fragile self-esteem. Sonny had never done anything to Angeloe, even if there was plenty of evidence of offenses against others.

Sonny parked the Chevelle on the right side of Angeloe's Mustang. He and his buddy Jake Hood stepped out. Even though he was more than a year out of high school, and despite the sweltering July heat, Sonny still wore his letter jacket as a talisman representing the greatest glory he'd ever know.

Sonny eyed the Mustang and held his door carefully and respectfully away from the gleaming new sheet metal, at the same time he tilted the driver seat forward so his girlfriend Shelley Anne Bobsey could get out. Shelley Anne had been the Bliss County Corn Queen at the Harvest Festival the year before, and was rumored to do borderline supernatural things with her mouth. Distracted, still talking to another girl in the back seat as she stepped out, she pushed the door so hard it bounced off the passenger door of the Mustang.

Angeloe heard the sickening sound of metal banging and scraping and was on his feet in an instant. He dashed around the front of his car as Sonny slammed the Chevelle door. He saw the ding from ten feet away.

"Damn!" he said. "I just bought this car today, Sonny!"

"Angeloe? This is *your* car?" Sonny went from recognition to incredulity in the blink of an eye.

"Look what you did!" Angeloe pointed out the ding.

"Pop it right out, buff it, you're good. Sorry, dude. Lemme buy you a

Coke."

"Ain't no Coke gonna fix this, Sonny! This car is brand new. Only fifteen miles on it. Look at this!"

He ran his hand over the sheet metal and felt the indentation and the paint chip with his palm. It looked as if someone had bounced a BB off it with an air rifle.

"Don't know what you want me to do," Sonny said. "I said I was sorry. Tell you what. Let me get your food. And I know a guy who can fix your door. He owes me a favor. Gimme a couple of days, and he'll make it showroom cherry. You'll never know it was dinged. I owe you that much."

A blue and white '57 Bel Aire pulled into the lot and parked three spaces from Angeloe's Mustang. Angeloe recognized the three youths in it from his street in Garveyville. The driver leaned on the car, his elbows and forearms resting on the roof.

"Hey, Angeloe, everything cool?"

Angeloe waved him off. "It's all right."

They were still talking animatedly when Morgan Patrolman D. B. Edge showed up, the bubble-gum machine on the roof of his car spinning and dashing oscillating scarlet beams on the entire lot. Edge had worn a badge and a gun for almost thirty years. He was long and lean, his face sun-etched into a map of crags and canyons. His eyes had been bleached gray by years of sun streaming through the windshield as he patrolled every hardtop highway, gravel path, and oiled dirt road in Bliss County. He was nicknamed Boss Nigger-Knocker on the Morgan force, and he was one of Rennie Poole's oldest and closest pals from their old days in hoods and robes. Of all the possible cops who could have driven into the lot, D. B. Edge was the least providential for Angeloe Teeter.

He stepped from the cruiser but left the flasher on. Resting his right hand on the butt of his service revolver, he held out his left hand like the cutting edge of a plow.

"Want you people to separate," he said.

Almost reflexively, Angeloe adopted the submissive posture his father had taught him. He dropped his gaze to the asphalt, and stepped back up onto the concrete, away from Sonny. Sonny and his crew remained by the side of his Chevelle.

"What's goin' on here? Sonny? This boy getting into it with you?"

"No," Sonny said, relaxed as he could be as he leaned against his car. "There ain't no fight, D.B.."

"'Cause, when I drove up, it looked to me like you was buckin' up on one another."

"It ain't like that," Angeloe said, and instantly regretted it. Edge gestured for Sonny and his gang to stay put and turned his attention to Angeloe.

"Mebbe you want to tell me how it *is*?"

Water collected at the corner of Angeloe's eyes, and his stomach hurt. "This is my car, sir. I bought it today, not three hours ago. I came here to get something to eat, and Sonny parked next to me, and when he opened the door it hit my car. It's brand new."

"*Your* car?" Edge asked. "You sure you didn't borrow it? Maybe took it out on a test drive and decided you wanted to act like a swinging dick in front of the white girls here, make like you owned it? Don't reckon you stole this car, now, did you?"

"No, sir. It's mine. I paid cash for it."

Edge stepped forward again until he loomed over Angeloe like a vulture waiting for a wounded squirrel to die.

"Your name, boy."

"Angeloe Teeter."

"Where you live?"

"On Hope Street, other side of the railyards," Angeloe said, and remembered to add, "...sir."

"And this here car is yours? You paid cash for it? Fancy hot little sports car like this?"

"Got the papers in the glove compartment."

Edge showed no interest in checking the glove compartment. "Car like this must run almost three thousand dollars."

"I paid twenty-seven for it. They give me a discount."

"Where would a boy from Garveyville get his hands on three grand?"

"Worked for it, sir. Saved it over three years."

"An industrious nigger," Edge said. "Well, I have seen it all."

He glanced at Sonny Hoskins and his crew. They all chuckled nervously.

"Gimme your paperwork," Edge told Angeloe, who eased by the police officer to get to the passenger door. He grabbed the handle and, being unfamiliar with the lightness of the doors, and with adrenaline squirting through his veins, he pulled it open too quickly, bouncing it off Sonny's knee. Sonny yelped and hopped on one foot, cradling his shin in his hands.

Edge was all over Angeloe in a second. He grabbed him by the collar of his white Oxford cloth shirt and bent him over the Mustang's roof. Because Angeloe was short, the roofline hit him at mid-chest, and the impact drove all the air from his lungs. Stars danced before his eyes as he slumped to the pavement. The edges of his vision crinkled like wadded tin foil.

The three black youths streamed out of the Bel Aire. From their perspective, a peckerwood cop had jacked up one of their neighbors for no reason. Sonny stopped hobbling and bent over to help Angeloe, but the black kids saw a known white bully joining the cop in a beat-down of one of their own. They ran around the front of the car to take up Angeloe's defense.

Jake Hood drew a length of motorcycle chain from under the front seat and swung it back and forth to scare them off.

"The fuck, man?" one of the black youths said. Edge looked up from Angeloe to see three black faces standing over him.

Instinctively, he drew his gun. His finger jerked, and the revolver went off, striking Angeloe in the leg. Angeloe stared at the hole that materialized in his best wool trousers, and a dark, glistening patch of wetness that spread to the size of a pancake in seconds.

"Oh God! Oh Jesus! I got shot!"

Everyone froze. Edge took the opportunity to crabwalk back to his cruiser, slam and lock the doors, and call for backup.

All three of the black youths bent over Angeloe to see if they could help, which Jake Hood saw as his opportunity. He waded in, swinging the chain at any dark-skinned head he could find. Angeloe tried to stand. Jake wrapped the chain around his skull. One of the youths from the Bel Aire took a swing and hit Sonny. Sonny pushed him away, right into Shelley Anne, and the two of them collided and fell to the sidewalk with the colored youth on top of her.

"Goddamn it!" she wailed. "Get this nigger rapist off me! He's bleeding all over my dress!"

Angeloe crawled along the asphalt beside his car and winced as Jake's motorcycle chain shattered the side mirror, spraying shards of glass in every direction. Some of it fell in Angeloe's hair. He bled from his leg and from a long, greasy laceration in his scalp. Blood ran down the right side of his face.

The scream of sirens filled the air as two more police cruisers skidded into the lot. As soon as Angeloe crawled to the rear of his car, two strong hands grabbed his shirt, yanking him upward. D.B. Edge bent Angeloe over the back of the car, bloodying the rear glass, and tried to cuff him. Angeloe turned his head to the officer. "I been shot, sir. I need a doctor. I need a hospital!"

Edge's elbow slammed into his mouth. Three teeth skittered across the deck lid of his new car. Angeloe tasted something metallic and wet, as blood streamed from his lips and smeared in the shape of a burgundy rose on the bodywork.

Angeloe was stuffed into the back of Edge's car. He watched helplessly as the police officers waded into the crowd of brown and white, swinging billy clubs and truncheons and shotgun butts, cracking skulls and laying people out on the asphalt. He saw one officer break out the rear glass of his Mustang with a nightstick before he passed out.

* * *

When Angeloe's father and mother arrived at the hospital, they found him snoring softly, still under anesthesia from surgery to remove the bullet, a bandage circling his head to protect the seventeen stitches required to close the laceration left by Jake Hood's bicycle chain, and his right handcuffed to the steel frame of the hospital bed.

By an hour after sundown, word spread through Garveyville. Frustrations and anger had bubbled and seethed under the surface for months as they had watched other cities across the country boil and burn. The fury broke through their constraints and overflowed in tears and shouts for justice.

The march started before anyone knew whether Angeloe Teeter was alive or dead. Small groups gathered in front yards and on covered galleries through the evening as the sun fell and dew condensed on the grass and lightning bugs flitted from magnolia to azalea. A pregnant moon rose over the trees, the one they call the Thunder Moon because it always appears in the hottest days of summer.

Attracted by their mutual gravity, the circles of people coalesced into a crowd. Bolstered by group pressure, the calls for vengeance grew louder and more confident. Men and women who had cowed in the face of the police in the past now marched toward the police station in Morgan to demand an explanation. Others in Garveyville joined in. Angeloe Teeter's beating and shooting was only a fever spike in the chronic infection that had eaten away at Garveyville's body for as long as anyone breathing could remember.

In the distance, thunderheads rose like heavenly anvils. Streaky scars of chain lightning arced back and forth. Faint rumbles of distant thunder rolled over the rooftops, but the people of Garveyville marched on, bound for the courthouse a mile away.

By the time they found their way to Polk Boulevard, they were over five hundred strong. Somewhere in the middle of the mob, a woman sang:

...We shall overcome

We shall overcome one day...

The people around her picked up the chorus. Hundreds of voices echoed off the downtown buildings. Their steps fell into time with the meter of the song as they marched on, their songs growing in volume and vigor, their confidence bolstered by their numbers.

The courthouse was ringed by police officers. They stood, like obsidian statues, silent, motionless, waiting. Morgan's police chief, Luther Rhodes, stood outside the phalanx, watching as the crowd advanced. His armpits were stained dark with anxiety sweat. He held up his hands, and they stopped singing.

"I'm gonna ask you folks to return to your homes," he shouted, without explanation.

Thomas Blevins stepped to the head of the crowd. Blevins was tall, rail-thin, and bald. He might have been seventy or even older. There wasn't a person on Hope Street who remembered him as a boy, but Blevins had been instigating for as long as anyone could recall.

"A Morgan policeman injured a colored boy today," he said. "Shot him and beat him about the head. The boy's mother is fit to be tied. We don't know yet whether this boy is gonna live or die. We have come for an explanation."

"I understand your concern," Rhodes said. "The boy you mentioned assaulted a white boy in the parking lot at the Chick-N-Shake. Some argument about cars. The colored youth resisted arrest. His injuries, regrettable as they are, were incurred as a consequence of his resistance. His injuries are on him, Mr. Blevins."

"I don't suppose the officer was D.B. Edge?" Blevins asked.

"I'm not going to discuss any specific policeman on this—"

"'Cause Edge been nigger-knockin' folks from Garveyville since six days before baseball. You tell me D.B. shot this boy and beat him into pudding, and I'm gonna question his explanation of how it went down."

"Department policy is to never discuss internal police affairs or personnel matters with the public. I'm sure you can understand the reason—"

Blevins turned and faced the crowd. "Edge done it!" he shouted.

From somewhere on the outer fringes of the gathering, a rock sailed through the air and slammed into the foot of one of the riot policemen. He howled and fell to the ground, holding his ankle and foot as if they might fall off. His side of the cordon immediately pushed into the crowd, brandishing baseball-bat-sized riot sticks, trying to drive them back.

The other policemen stared at them, and back at Chief Rhodes, as if asking what they were supposed to do. Most of them had spent years handing out speeding tickets and parking tickets and Policemen's Ball tickets. Few of them had military experience, and almost none of them had ever been trained to cope with a mob of riled-up Negroes.

Someone lobbed an empty soda bottle. It shattered at Rhodes' feet. Rhodes danced a strange little jig as he tried to get away from the flying glass. Projectiles rained on the police encircling the courthouse. Blevins had lost control of the situation. He joined the police in trying to hold the pack back from the courthouse.

A block away, there was the crash of plate glass shattering and collapsing in shards on the sidewalk. Looting had begun, as hooligans took advantage of the burgeoning riot to line their pockets. Chief Rhodes grabbed Blevins' sleeve and turned him around. "You've done it now!" he shouted to the frightened man. "They're gonna take this town down to the studs."

"This wasn't…" Blevins couldn't find the words. "We only wanted to know why—"

Three of the protestors grabbed him away from Rhodes and pushed him up the street. Rhodes gave the signal, and the formation swung around to corral the crowd inside the town square. As he gave the orders, Rhodes doubted they would do any good.

* * *

"I have to get back to Morgan," Sheriff Mattox said when Jess Varley told him about the riot.

Rennie Poole grabbed the sheriff's arm. "We need protection in Prosperity," he rasped.

"The trouble is in Morgan," Mattox told him. "I'm gonna have to call in off-duty deputies as it is to support Chief Rhodes."

"You know damn well the deputies are the only law in the county outside the Morgan city limits," Rennie argued. He backed Mattox into a quiet corner of the store. He lowered his voice. "Be smart, Brian. You pull every deputy into Morgan to deal with a mob of uppity niggers, and you'll leave the entire rest of the county defenseless."

"We'll deal with that when it comes," Mattox said. "If we don't stop this mob in Morgan, it won't matter much."

"You need to remember who got you your big gold badge. I'm not asking, Sheriff. I'm callin' in a favor."

Mattox rubbed his jaw. "One deputy. One car. He can patrol between Prosperity and Mica Wells."

"I was hoping for more. Three deputies, maybe."

"Can't spare 'em, Mr. Poole. I need everyone I can get in Morgan."

"Gimme Larry Stilson, then. I know I can trust him."

Mattox shook his head. "Stilson. That S.O.B. you can have any day." He turned his back and walked out to the parking lot and his cruiser.

* * *

Owen pulled into the Piggly Wiggly parking lot a quarter before ten. He blinked in the harsh fluorescent light as he walked through the open door. A bored teenaged girl stood alone at the register, studying something fascinating in the chipped polish on one of her fingernails. She didn't look up at Owen. "Closing in ten minutes."

"I'll be quick," Owen said.

He dashed through the aisles, picking up staples and eggs and bread and milk. He grabbed a six-pack of Rolling Rock and another of sixteen-ounce Cokes.

He didn't notice the rotating lights in the parking lot until he checked out. A sheriff deputy's car sat diagonally across a couple of parking spaces, pinning in a mid-forties Studebaker that looked as if it had been attacked by sheet-metal moths. Deputy Stilson was out of this car, his gun drawn. A black man wearing overalls and a short-sleeved checkered shirt stood by the trunk, his trembling hands in the air.

"Caleb?" Owen called. He placed the groceries in his truck and walked toward the deputy. "Caleb Lightsey?"

The black man looked at Owen. "Mr. Wheeler. Thank Jesus it's you. This deputy has gone crazy!"

"What's the matter?" Owen asked Stilson.

"Mr. Wheeler, go back to your car. I am holding this man on suspicion."

"Suspicion of what?"

"Sir," the deputy said again. "This is a police matter. Doesn't concern you. Please return to your car and leave."

"The man you're scaring half to death is Caleb Lightsey. He works for me. He's a farmhand. I reckon this does concern me, Stilson."

"I caught this man loitering about in the parking lot. I looked in his backseat, and there are bricks in there. A bunch of 'em."

Owen looked inside the car and turned to Caleb. "You still driving around with those bricks I gave you last week?"

"I haven't had time to unload them," Caleb said.

"I had some old bricks stacked in the barn," Owen said. "Caleb's wife wanted to put them around her flower bed. I told him he could have them. What in the hell did you think Caleb was going to do with the bricks, Deputy?"

"You been to Morgan tonight?" Stilson said, without lowering his revolver. "The whole downtown looks like someone sprayed it with gasoline and struck a match. There's broken store windows on every corner. Word has it the niggers from Garveyville done gone on a rampage, same way they did in Atlanta and up in Newark."

"Enough of that language, Deputy. Remember you're in uniform and on duty. What's all the ruckus in Morgan got to do with Caleb?"

"Sheriff Mattox assigned me to patrol between here and Mica Wells. Mayor Poole specifically told me to keep an eye out for any nig—" he stopped and cleared his throat. "—any Negroes who might be up to some mischief in Prosperity."

"Since when does Mayor Poole give orders to sheriff's deputies?" Owen asked.

"Don't know and don't care. I have my orders. I was driving by, and I saw this…this man standing around in the parking lot next to his car like he was waiting for the Piggly Wiggly to close for the night. I figured he planned a little mayhem. I got out and that's when I saw the bricks."

"Put your gun away before someone gets hurt. Caleb's wife mops the aisles in the store after closing. He ain't here to bust out any store windows. He just wants to pick up his wife and go home. Unless you want me to file a complaint with Sheriff Mattox, you'll put your gun away and stop acting like a horse's ass."

"You got no cause to talk to me that way," Stilson said, more hurt in his voice than anger. He holstered his revolver, without apology. "I'm a duly sworn officer of the law carrying out my orders."

"Orders you got from Rennie Poole, who has no legitimate authority at the Sheriff's Department. Mrs. Lightsey will finish up her cleaning in a little bit. Why don't you move along, get on with your important patrol duties, so we can let Caleb's stomach settle?"

"You wouldn't be so cocksure if you saw what happened in Morgan tonight," Stilson returned to his sheriff's cruiser, apparently having fired his last salvo.

* * *

As the storm clouds rose over Bliss County later in the evening, Owen sat in the wicker loveseat on his front porch and watched lightning lance across the sky. He was halfway through his third beer when a pair of car headlights turned off the highway into his drive. Mayor Poole's Cadillac parked in the gravel circle in front of the house.

Rennie pulled himself from the car and stood at the base of the steps leading up to Owen's porch.

"Nightcap?" Owen pointed toward a bucket filled with ice and bottles, sweating a puddle on the porch floor.

"Don't mind if I do." He climbed the four steps, grabbed a bottle from the bucket, and popped the cap with a church-key. He settled into the loveseat perpendicular to Owen's chair. "I been driving all over town tonight, haven't had so much as a Co-Cola. I hear you harassed Deputy Stilson at the Piggly Wiggly."

"Nope," Owen said. "I corrected him. He was about to ventilate one of my farmhands."

"Why would he do that?"

"The man's a Negro. You declared open season on them."

"The niggers in Morgan dealt the play. My job is to protect the citizens of Prosperity."

"I'll thank you not to use words like that on my property. Remember whose beer you're drinking."

"So like your father."

"Leave my father out of this. You're talking to me."

"Amos was a good man, even if we frequently butted heads. He wasn't around when we caught the fella who raped and killed Arlo's daughter, though. What was his name again?"

"Ev Howard, but you know already."

"Sure I do. Yep, wasn't hide or hair of your dad around. But you were there, weren't you? As I recall, you and your football buddies brought the boy in."

"Which do you reckon gives you the most satisfaction, Rennie? Sticking the knife in, or twisting it? Whatever happened to Ev Howard rests on your head and Hubert Pressley's. You and Hubert were looking for an opportunity."

"You need a wife," Poole said. "Someone to take your mind off my business. I do hope you won't get any nasty splinters dropping off your cross. But drop you will because fuck with me and you're gonna need the wood."

Rennie walked back to his car and chucked the beer bottle into the darkness. Owen winced when he heard it shatter against the stone barbecue grill. Rennie opened the car door but didn't get inside. He leaned across the roof and pointed a gun finger at Owen.

"One thing, though." The glad-handing bonhomie left his face. For an instant, Owen could see flames and boiling brimstone behind the mayor's eyes. "Don't get in my way again, farm boy. There are a hundred ways I can run your place into the ground. Every seed, every farm implement, every hoe, every shovel, every boot, and pair of overalls you own—don't forget—they once belonged to me. There's a pipeline from my stores to your fields. I can shut it off any time I please. I reckon there's room enough in this county for the both of us, as long as you stay on your hundred acres or so of it and allow me the rest. Overstep your meager boundaries, and I'll squash you like a bug."

* * *

Angeloe Teeter left the hospital the next afternoon. The bullet wound in his leg would mend in time, the edges bonding and growing like a flat mushroom, leaving a keloid scar the size of a silver dollar. The lacerations on his head would heal, but for the rest of his life, he'd have hairless patches in his scalp in the rough outline of a motorcycle chain. The missing teeth would be replaced with a bridge, but that would cost more money than either Angeloe or his father had at the moment.

They drove to the Chick-N-Shake. Windows in the restaurant, crazed and shattered by flying rocks during the riot, were covered with sheets of plywood. A sign on the door said *Closed Until Further Notice*.

The Mustang was there. Three of the tires were flattened. The windshield was spider-webbed with cracks. Somebody had pounded on the fenders with an iron pipe, leaving dents the size of a basketball. The asphalt around the perimeter of the car was littered with flakes of paint. Gallons of rainwater had saturated the interior. Someone had used the open window as a privy.

Angeloe saw hundreds of fifty-pound bags of fertilizer he'd hefted and stored and retrieved in the warehouse at Rennie Poole's Feed and Seed. He saw thousands of hours he'd spent mowing lawns, delivering papers, washing cars, and painting houses. He saw the jacket of his only suit hanging forlornly in his closet at home, never to be paired with the ruined trousers again, and he remembered how proud he'd been when he wore the suit to church the first Sunday after he got it for his eighteenth birthday. He saw the hours he'd planned for this car, deciding which color to buy, and which options he could afford.

He saw a wreck that wasn't yet insured.

It could be repaired. In the hands of a skilled mechanic and a top-shelf body man, it could be returned nearly to showroom condition—but at what cost? Angeloe had spent every cent he had to buy the car.

Even if it could be repaired, every time he climbed behind the wheel he'd see some cracker's needle-dick hanging through the passenger window, pissing onto the upholstery. He'd see Jake Hood's motorcycle chain smash the side mirror. He'd feel D.B. Edge's bullet rip into his leg, and the man's calloused hands bounce him off the rear deck lid. He'd see his teeth skitter across the new paint. No matter how primped and polished a repairman might make the car, it would never again be pristine. Angeloe would know his dream had been ravaged and humiliated and desecrated by people whose moral oceans scarcely dampened the dust.

He'd see the truth. In 1967, in Bliss County, a black man was only allowed to dream and achieve what the white man permitted.

"I want to go to school," Angeloe said quietly through his tears. "I want to see to it people like D. B. Edge never wear a badge again."

Chapter Twenty-Five

The explosion of the six a.m. aerial bomb reverberated off the retaining walls and grandstands at the Indianapolis Motor Speedway, flushing wildfowl from the infield golf course. A tradition born in the earliest days of The Greatest Spectacle in Racing, the bomb's repercussions rattled the aluminum sides of Billy Mosack's motorhome parked outside Gasoline Alley.

Billy woke, as he did most mornings, cursing the day he'd met Hop Bloomquist. Getting out of bed should have been a relatively simple matter if Billy hadn't been held together by a miscellaneous collection of screws, plates, and rods. Simple acts, such as beginning the day, had to be planned carefully and executed with all the precision of a military invasion. He regretted ever allowing Hop to talk him into driving open-wheel cars. He growled a profanity and lay in the narrow camper bed trying to think of a good reason to roll over and go back to sleep.

Failing that, he rolled to his left, to present his backside to the wall. He put his weight on his good elbow, the one which hadn't been shattered in the flip at Springfield. This took considerable pressure off the compressed fourth lumbar vertebra—a souvenir of the ass-on visit with Trenton's first turn wall—that he'd promised for years to have examined by an orthopedic surgeon. Working on little more than willpower, ignoring the agony in his back, he raised himself on his elbow. This took two minutes, most of it spent in teeth-gnashing anticipation and several trial runs.

Suspended precariously between sitting and lying, Billy executed a tricky half roll to bring his left leg under his right. This was the point of no return,

153

as he pushed up on the good elbow again. He gasped audibly at another back spasm in the sacral region, which he owed to a pig of a sprint car he'd reluctantly agreed to drive at Langhorne. He sat upright at the edge of the bed, took a deep breath, and hauled himself to his feet.

In the bathroom mirror, Billy examined the disaster wrought from the Olympian physique of his high school football days. Twin scars, earned in a double femoral fracture at Corona Speedway in California, traced parallel white lines on his thighs, where the right one intersected with the sagittal scar left by his broken kneecap after a pissing match between a stuck throttle and the physical limits of traction at Riverside.

The burr holes in his skull hadn't disappeared overnight. He still couldn't remember the quadruple barrel roll at Milwaukee. He'd seen film of it, though, and was grateful for amnesia.

Even the brilliant smile beaming back at him in the mirror was store-bought. His upper incisors remained embedded somewhere in the third turn at Terre Haute, where he'd deposited them during the first of many sprint car flips before he'd learned to hunker down in the cockpit when the wheels left the ground.

Despite all the knocks and fractures and hospital bills, Billy was one of the lucky ones. He was a star in a sport that revoked the breathing licenses of dozens of drivers each season. He drove a hundred fifty nights a year, bouncing from quarter-mile dirt bullrings to asphalt superspeedways, and he made bank on most of them. He was famous and rich, and he had a gorgeous wife. He'd paid the freight with muscle, bone, and sinew, but he had to admit he'd do it all over again.

All of which, he surmised, meant he must be more than a little crazy.

The steaming shower shook out the creaks and rattles and Billy slid into slacks and a sport shirt. He torched another Marlboro. He had to stoke up early. Smoking wasn't permitted in Gasoline Alley.

The door to the motorhome opened. Chloe Mosack stepped in.

"About time you woke up," she said. "Banacek's been looking for you. I told him you went outside the track for some roach coach vendor food on Sixteenth Street."

He'd heard the whispers along Gasoline Alley. Chloe *was* stunning, but she possessed one great handicap. As Hop had tried to warn Billy before they married, Chloe had been born with the profound incapacity to keep her knees together. Billy was well-aware he wasn't the only driver in the garage who'd enjoyed her attentions, even after they married. He harbored no illusions about Chloe's character. He knew the ring on her finger wasn't a corral, and her attention span was limited. At least there was nothing she could bring home that couldn't be cured with a shot of penicillin.

Well, he mused, *almost nothing. Thank God for The Pill.*

Hop Bloomquist was long gone. He'd walked out shortly after Billy and Chloe married. Hop had heard the same rumors about Chloe, and had tried to advise Billy, who mistook it for jealousy or—worse—an attempt to sow discord so Hop could swoop in and claim her for himself. The blowout that followed in the garage area was legendary among the racing fraternity.

Billy regretted the way things ended, especially when Hop was found in a motel in Biloxi a year later, three days after he'd died of a stroke, an ignominious and undignified death. Billy had seen to it he was given a top-shelf funeral. Despite his many injuries and the rancor that had marked their separation, Billy knew Hop was responsible for every bit of the wealth and fame he enjoyed.

"I need another couple hours sleep," he complained. "Could have gotten it if the Speedway didn't reenact the Battle of fucking Guadalcanal every morning at six. I hear the bomb and get instant morning wood. What do you want for breakfast?"

Chloe stood. "Before or after?"

"Before or after what? The showdown with Banacek?"

"Screw Banacek," She unbuttoned her blouse. "Tell me more about this morning wood."

* * *

Billy walked into the garage where his team owner, an Aussie named Tony Banacek, oversaw the reconstruction of his car. Six crewmen swarmed over the chassis, attaching suspension parts as quickly as they could.

"How long before they get this pig back together?" Billy asked.

"Be done in an hour," Banacek said, without looking up.

"Will it turn this time? Farm plows back in Prosperity cornered better."

"It'll turn, but only if you quit interrupting and let them finish. Go grab a bite. Come back in an hour. It'll be ready before qualifying starts. Don't worry."

"Oh," Billy said, "I'm worried. After last weekend, I'm worried plenty."

It was Bubble Day at Indy, the last day of qualifying for the 1968 Indy 500. He had to make the race today or give it up and come back next year. Thirty-three cars had qualified already, a full field. He'd have to go faster than someone who was already in the field, preferably a lot faster. The slowest car so far had run the four-lap qualifier at a little over one-hundred-sixty-one miles per hour. The best Billy had mustered so far was one-sixty and change. He and twenty-seven other drivers were still outside looking in.

"I'll be back in an hour," he said. "Ready to shake her down."

* * *

The crew met his deadline. When Billy returned to the garage a little after ten in the morning, the car was ready. It sat on the floor, belly pan only two inches above the concrete. It was a three-year-old Halibrand Shrike, one of the first generation rear-engine cars to challenge the legendary bricks. It was hopelessly outclassed by Colin Chapman's Lotus cars and Andy Granatelli's revolutionary turbine machines, but it still looked fast standing still, and just starting in the 500 guaranteed a handsome payday.

Billy wrestled into his flameproof coveralls and shoehorned—painfully—into the car. It was tight, especially for a former football halfback. There was barely room for his elbows inside the constricted body of the car. The seat and belts squeezed him as if looking for juice. It was a hot day, with the promise of thunderstorms. The air was dense. A bead of sweat rolled between his eyebrows and down the bridge of his nose, absorbed by the plaid bandana he wore to prevent sandblasting his lower face at speeds up to two hundred miles per hour.

Despite the cramped discomfort, he was at home, semi-reclined in the upholstered fiberglass seat. Before him, through the spokes of the leather-wrapped steering wheel, the information cluster kept him apprised of the car's vital signs. Nowhere was he more comfortable, more attuned to every nuance of existence around him.

It was his sixth try at the fabled Memorial Day Classic. He'd qualified every year he'd entered. He either found the speed today, or he'd go home. Nothing could hurt more than not driving in The Show.

He took it easy for the first several laps, feeling out the changes Tony's crew had made. With each successive trip around the two-and-a-half-mile course, he increased the speed incrementally. There was no point in scorching the asphalt right off the bat.

As he opened the throttle, the cars ahead appeared to move backward toward him. He overtook other drivers, passing backmarkers in twos and threes on each of the long straights, and in the short chutes between the corners at each end of the Yard. The suspension barely flexed as Billy willed the car below the white line separating the groove from the track apron, and his fingers, as sensitive as any surgeon's, felt the barely perceptible transition over the paint through the wheel. In turn three, a lightly banked ninety-degree bend, he allowed the rear of the car to drift toward the outside wall and delighted as it snapped back into line just in time to begin another drift into four. Tony Banacek's boys had brought the car to life. Billy felt like he could drive it with his fingertips.

As the Shrike screamed down the three-quarter-mile front stretch, Banacek held out a blackboard sign at the concrete wall separating the track from the pits. At speed, Billy had scant time for reading, so the message was succinct: *164+*. It was all Billy needed to know. He had the speed to make the field, and then some. With luck, he'd start the race somewhere in the seventh row.

This was ecstasy. No meal, sunset, or woman had ever filled him with such pure unadulterated pleasure as the feeling of mastery, control, and power he enjoyed behind the wheel. Every broken bone, every concussion, every end-over-end flip had been worth it for one more shot at a Brickyard win. He couldn't help but smile under the bandana. He was in his element. He was home.

His reverie was interrupted by catastrophe.

A gut-wrenching metallic '*whirrr*' sound and a sharp vibration rattled the rear of his car as he neared the end of the front straight, followed by a sharp bang as the right rear wheel took leave of its hub. The bearing hanger dug into the asphalt, pitching the car directly into the outside concrete retaining wall, instantly shattering both of Billy's legs—again. In clarity only attainable in nightmares, Billy watched the shocked and horrified faces of the spectators in Section E of the grandstand as his rocketing juggernaut rolled, flipped, and vaulted into the safety fence, exploding as a stanchion lanced the fuel cell, spraying dozens of spectators with invisible flaming methanol.

The car landed hard in the middle of Turn One, ripping off the left side wheels. It rotated again on the naked rear suspension and slid on its left side toward the wall.

As soon as the car landed and he saw the wall, Billy knew what was coming. He couldn't help himself. He dared to look up. There was no point in ducking, not at this speed or at this angle. His last thought before impact was that he'd had one hell of a ride. He was going out richer and more famous than either Jude or Owen.

He was finally Number One.

He slammed into the wall, rollbar-first, still traveling over a hundred miles per hour, and everything went dark and silent and cold, forever.

Chapter Twenty-Six

Lucy came. Lucy went. Sometimes, she was gone for days at a time. Occasionally weeks. When she returned—dirty, strung out, diseased—Jude took her in and cared for her. He knew some of her sojourns went no farther than Charlie's apartment two doors east. Charlie was adept at scoring almost anything, including the heroin Lucy devoured more frequently than food.

From the beginning, Charlie had attempted to seduce her away. Jude hadn't discouraged him. Lucy was free to make her own decisions. What he resented was the obligation he felt to clean up the refuse Charlie sent back to him.

As Jude relaxed in the park, reading, Charlie walked up and dropped into a crouch next to him. "I'm having some people over tonight. Got a buttload of hash. Coupla real musicians, jazz guys, gonna drop by and jam. Want to join us?" Charlie asked.

"Why?"

"Trying to be polite, man."

Jude raised himself on his elbows. "You want to be polite, keep your hands off Lucy. I'm tired of scrubbing you out of her soul every time she comes home."

"Home? You think your pad is home for her? I love Juicy Lucy, man, but her address changes more often than the Nam body count. Your place is just another crash for her. Leave Lucy out of this. She's already in extra innings. I been wanting to talk with you for a while. I got some big plans. Me and some of my friends have a chance to move to Los Angeles. Big

159

ol' movie ranch outside the city. Turn it into a real commune, live off the land, get back to the garden and shit. Live like the original humans before technology came along and fucked everything up. This world is about to burn, and only the people who prepare are gonna come out the other end. You see what's goin' on all over the country. The black brothers have had enough. Lemme tell you, son, I been in prison for the better part of my life, and you do not want to fool with a bunch of brothers once they get angry and organized. They will fuck you the fuck up."

"You think there's going to be a race war," Jude said.

"Dude, it's started already. Look at Buffalo and Detroit and Atlanta. Look at the murders in Alabama and Mississippi. Half the fuckin' south is burning. White men and black men are at each other's throats. You don't know a thing about it."

An image of Ev Howard's bloated face above a roughshod noose popped into Jude's head, and he dismissed with a shudder as quickly as possible. "Don't I?" he asked, more to himself.

Charlie looked past him, toward Cole Street. Lucy strolled clumsily along the sidewalk. She saw Jude and Charlie, and waved listlessly, but made no move toward them.

"Well, whaddayaknow?" Charlie said. "Looks like your stray pet is *home* again. Give her a bath and bring her over tonight."

* * *

Jude helped Lucy out of the shower and wrapped her shivering, emaciated body inside a soft blanket. She'd lost almost twenty pounds in the last year. He held her close as she trembled underneath the blanket, to keep her from chattering her teeth into dust. Slowly, her body relaxed, and her breathing slowed.

Over the next days, she alternated between sleep and torment. Jude did what he could, but mostly he watched her suffer. He could walk over to Charlie's pad and score enough junk to take away all her pain, but the heroin was slowly killing her. The last time she'd walked out the door, headed God

160

knows where, he'd told himself—if she came back—he wasn't scoring for her again. Lucy wanted to quit. She'd said so many times. She couldn't shake her addiction alone. She'd gotten clean four times already. Each time, within weeks, she was back on the spike.

"This time," Jude said, as he stroked her hair, listening to her light, raspy snore. "This time, we get you off for good, and once you're clean we'll get you out of this city. We'll go somewhere up in the mountains, someplace where they don't have any junk, and you'll stay clean this time."

Lucy disappeared three days later. Jude made a food run to the co-op on the corner two blocks from their apartment. He was drawn into a conversation with the kid behind the counter, and before he knew it two hours had gone by. He hustled back to his apartment, to find she'd left a note pinned to his pillow.

Not strong enough. L.

* * *

Jude sat on his steps with a cup of coffee. He'd decided Lucy would return when she was ready, and this time they'd leave right away. No more drying out in the check-out aisle of the largest open-air pharmacy on the west coast. He planned on reading the Sunday newspaper, and then he'd hike to the park to look for her again.

Two uniformed policemen walked up. Jude wasn't worried. He hadn't done anything.

"Something I can do for you, officers?"

The taller one spoke first. "We're here about a young woman named Lucy Bodette."

"Did you find her?"

"What do you mean?"

"She skipped about a week ago. She was trying to shake a bad heroin habit. I think she fell off the wagon."

"I think she fell off the planet," the shorter cop said. The taller one held up a hand to silence him.

"Sorry for my partner. So, you haven't seen Miss Bodette in a week?"

"No. You guys are scaring me. What's happened?"

"What is your relationship with the young woman?" the shorter one asked.

"Casual. She's a friend. She crashes at my apartment from time to time. She comes and goes. Could you answer my question?"

The shorter cop scowled. "You damned hippies have screwed this city in one hole and out the other. What kind of animals are you? Where's your commitment to one another?"

Jude set the cup down. "Officer, I think you're about to step over a line."

The short cop moved toward Jude, but the taller one restrained him. "Take it easy, Ed. Lemme handle this." He sat on the stoop next to Jude.

"What's your name, son?"

"Jude Pressley."

"Got some identification?"

Jude handed over his driver's license. The tall officer turned to his partner.

"You know who we got here?" he said. "This guy was a backup quarterback for the Forty-Niners."

"Judging by his hair, I'd have guessed he was head cheerleader."

"That was you, right?" the tall one asked Jude.

"I rode the pine a few years. Got a few snaps in."

"I saw your last game. I could hear your knee pop over the television."

Jude pointed to the long vertical scar on his knee. "Still have a limp. What about Lucy?"

The tall cop took his hat off and placed it on his knee.

"I'm sorry to be the one to tell you, but we found Lucy Bodette dead this morning. In an alley several streets over. She had an envelope in her bag with this address on it."

Jude drooped his head sadly, but without tears.

"I had a feeling when she didn't come back after a few days. I guess it was only a matter of time. I don't know a lot about her, guys. I don't even know where her parents live. She never stayed in one place long enough to get mail."

CHAPTER TWENTY-SIX

"Does she have any belongings in your apartment?"

"A few clothes. I could put them in a paper bag if you like."

"Donate 'em," the short cop said. "Take 'em to the hippie flea market. I hear they need more fleas."

"Ed," the tall cop cautioned again. "It was obvious she died of an overdose. It looks as if she... ah... sold herself to get the stuff."

"She's done it before. First time we met, she offered to blow me for drug money."

"Fuckin' animals," Ed muttered.

"If you find any information on her parents, could you bring it to the local precinct?" the other asked. "Be a shame for this girl to wind up in a Potter's Field."

"I'll see what I can find. She took everything but a few clothes with her. If you can't find her folks, I'll pay for her burial."

After the officers left, Jude walked two doors down. He banged on Charlie's door. The little man opened it almost immediately. Jude shoved him inside and slammed the door, grabbed Charlie by the collar, and backhanded him across the face.

"The fuck, dude!" Charlie exclaimed, his eyes glazed.

"Lucy came here last week, trying to dry out, and you loaded her up with junk again."

"She needed her medicine."

Jude drove a fist up into Charlie's midsection, doubling him over. Charlie sat on the floor retching for breath. Jude kicked him in the kidneys, and Charlie rolled into a protective ball on the floor. Jude grabbed him under the arms, dragged him to his feet, and shoved him against the wall. He pressed Charlie's neck against the wall with his forearm.

"She's dead, you psycho bastard. She died in an alley with her pants around her ankles and a spike in her arm."

"Hey," Charlie said, as if getting jacked up against a wall happened every day. "It's her trip. She had a need, and I fulfilled it. I didn't give her the junk what killed her. She was goin' tits-up sooner or later anyway."

"Say that again."

"Scrape her off, man. Her hourglass ran out of sand months ago. Didn't matter who gave her the horse. Lemme go, dude. Let's talk this out. My offer stands. Come to Los Angeles with us. This city's as dead as Lucy. We can make something really beautiful on the ranch."

Jude threw him onto the flimsy kitchen table. The legs collapsed, and Charlie fell to the floor on top of it.

"You're a fucking virus," Jude said. "I wanted you to know. I hoped you'd take some responsibility for what happened. She was trying to stop, but the pain got to her, and you allowed it to control her. I can only think of one way to make you understand. Get ready for pain, Charlie, because I'm gonna kick the living shit out of you."

* * *

Jude dipped his right hand in a bowl of ice water. His barked knuckles ached and stung. He comforted himself with the knowledge there wasn't a bucket of ice water large enough to soothe Charlie's pain.

His hand went numb, and his fingers were rigid with cold. He pulled them from the ice and wrapped his hand in a clean dish towel. He lit a joint and stared out the window for a few minutes.

He'd picked up a black-and-white portable television second hand. It only had a twelve-inch screen, so he kept it on a scarred and battered coffee table two feet from the pile of pillows he called his sofa. He plopped onto the cushions and switched on the set. The first face he saw was the dour, somber Chris Schenkel, a stalwart on ABC's Wide World of Sports. Jude caught him in midsentence.

"...of today's tragic crash here at the Brickyard which took the life of standout driver Billy Mosack and injured twelve spectators. We would like to remind you the film we are about to show is graphic..."

As soon as he heard his buddy's name, Jude sat upright. He watched the loop of film over and over, hoping each time it would end differently. Through hazy shimmers of the methanol fireball, he watched Billy's car careen wildly into Turn One, catapulting wheels in every direction, tumble side over side, and smash into the wall helmet-first. The car exploded on contact with the concrete, bits of red fiberglass and metal and engine parts and Billy parts littering the track. Mercifully, the car remained on its side, Billy's remains trapped inside the cockpit, hidden from the cold gaze of the television cameras. Track workers spread canvas tarpaulins over the car before pulling it from the wall. A dark smear ran along the concrete. Even on the hazy twelve-inch black and white screen, it didn't look like oil or fuel or coolant.

Jude knew Billy had become a racing driver, but he had almost no interest in motorsports beyond the hot rod Willys he'd left in Billy's care. He had almost no interest in anything, really. His last five years, during which Billy had become famous, had been consumed with painkillers and hallucinogens and sex and rock and roll. He'd taken each day as it came, with no promise of more to follow, and no concerns with anything beyond the end of his nose. Except for Lucy, he'd invested himself in nothing since moving to The Haight.

Billy's fatal journey into the wall at Indy felt like a wake-up call.

Lucy was dead. His last binding tie to San Francisco was severed. It had been nine months since the Diggers marched an empty coffin through The Haight, proclaiming the Death of the Hippie. The neighborhood was no longer paradise.

The party was over. Time to go home.

Chapter Twenty-Seven

Nobody in Prosperity had heard a word from Jude Pressley since the end of his football career. Three weeks before Billy's fatal crash, while passing the time of day, his mother Sally Mosack had asked Hubert Pressley if he'd received any word of Jude. Hubert shook his head sadly, all three auxiliary chins wobbling. He'd heard nothing in almost two years. Jude might still be in San Francisco, but he didn't know for certain.

Now, a day before the funeral, Jude stood at Sally Mosack's door. He seemed quieter, less cocky, and he certainly looked different. He wore threadbare jeans and sandals, and a chambray work shirt. His shaggy coal-black hair fell below his shoulder blades, pulled back with a rubber band. Wisps escaped and fell across his cheek. His thick beard hid his strong chin and full lips. His eyes were sunken and dull.

She grasped him by the arms. "I never imagined you would come. Have you been home yet?"

"My plane got in only a couple of hours ago. I came straight here."

"Perhaps you should have seen your dad first. He misses you." She didn't see any expression of remorse on his face, which seemed curious. "Well, let's get you some food," she said, to break the silence. "Folks have been dropping fried chicken and hams and potato salads by the house for three days. We're going to have a wake here after the funeral tomorrow. I hope they'll take care of most of it. I know I'll never work my way through ever'thing."

"Let me get it," he said. "You've been through a lot. I can manage."

He fixed his plate, and another for her. She watched him the entire time, trying to see the teenage Jude Pressley, but the youth had disappeared. The man rummaging through her kitchen was a foreigner. They ate slowly and deliberately, and mostly in silence. Sally asked him what he'd done since leaving football, and all he said was, "Not much of anything." It seemed queer to her, since every man she'd ever met had done *something*.

"Are you here to stay?" she asked.

"Jury's still out. Is Owen Wheeler around?"

"Oh, yes. His parents died, you know."

"Yes."

"He manages the farm by himself. He's doing a good job."

"Owen was born to be a farmer. My father. How... how is he?"

"He misses you."

"The man my father misses drove off a cliff a long time ago. He longs for a memory that only exists inside his own head. But I don't want to be rude. You've seen him more than I have. Is he healthy?"

"He's put on a few pounds since you..." she couldn't find the correct word. *Left* didn't seem correct in some way. *Disappeared* seemed a little rude.

"He's still wrapped around Rennie Poole like a Virginia creeper?"

"I don't know what you mean. He runs Mayor Poole's stores. You know Mr. Poole is running for Congress?"

"It doesn't surprise me. I am sorry about what happened to Billy. I wouldn't be here otherwise. He was always a good friend. I think I neglected him, and I'm sorry. I'm uncomfortable asking you about this."

"What?"

"I don't want to seem rude, or insensitive. Before I left for college..."

She clapped her hands together. "Your car!"

"I know it's been fourteen years—"

"It's here," she said. "In the old barn out back. I'm sorry, but it might have been neglected. Billy left town in 1957, and hardly ever came back. He and his wife lived in Indianapolis, you know."

"I saw her on television. She's beautiful."

"She's a tramp if you ask me. I'm afraid Billy didn't put much upkeep into the car after he left. It's been sitting in the barn for over a decade. I'll show you."

He followed her out the back door. Sally slid open the barn door, which creaked on an aged, rusting track. Over the years, the siding on the barn had shrunk, allowing streaks of light to crisscross the dirt floor from the chinks in the walls. A hulking mass sat in the middle of the barn, covered with a large canvas tarp. Jude pulled the tarp away. Three mice scurried from under the chassis.

"Good sign," Sally said. "No snakes."

He rolled off the damp, mildewed tarp, stepped back, placed his hands on his hips, and sighed.

His hot rod was a mess. The tires had deflated years earlier and had sat on rotting flat spots ever since. The windows were intact and closed, which had limited some of the possible damage by elements. When Jude opened the door, which protested with a loud, dry, metallic creak, a musty sour odor rolled over them. Hundreds of dark, solid pellets the size of BBs covered the seats. The upholstery had been gnawed into ribbons, the stuffing in the seats pulled to make nests.

He smiled at her, in a strange, otherworldly way.

"It could be worse," Jude said at last. "A lot of work, I suppose. I had hoped I'd be able to drive it right away. I only have the rental car. Best laid plans, right? It's nothing. You have enough to worry about without having me pile more on you. I'll move it after the funeral. If I try to fix it here, the mice will keep moving back in."

He walked her across the yard to the back door. When they entered the kitchen, the water was running in the sink, and a young woman wearing an apron around her waist bent over it, scrubbing the plates they had left on the table. From behind, Jude could see her long, straight black hair and breathtaking legs.

"Chloe!" Sally called out when she saw the woman. "You shouldn't be doing dishes. I'll take care of it."

The woman turned around.

"Got a new boyfriend?" Chloe asked, as she visually measured Jude. "He's a big one, Mother Mosack." Her voice was throaty, like a longtime smoker.

"Jude, my daughter-in-law, Chloe. Billy's widow. This is one of Billy's friends from high school. Jude Pressley."

"The football player," Chloe said.

"A long time ago," Jude said.

"Oh, I know. Billy told me all about you. We were watching the game on TV the day you got hurt. Was the desert island you were stranded on a hot place? Or have you been living among the apes in Africa? Only explanation I can find for the whole castaway look."

"Chloe!" Sally said.

"It's not rude, Mother Mosack. I like it. Very mod. Totally with it."

Sally shook her head. "I don't understand half of what Chloe says."

"It's all right," Jude said. "They're compliments. I should go, before the whole town knows I'm here except my father. I'd hate for him to hear it on the party line."

"There's no party line anymore, Slick," Chloe said. "Twentieth-century civilization has come to Prosperity. Is that your car in the drive? I have you blocked in. I'll walk you out."

Jude took Sally's hand. "I appreciate the food. I was terribly sorry to hear about Billy. Same to you, Chloe. I know you had a horrible shock."

When they were out of earshot Chloe said, "I don't think my mother-in-law likes me."

"She thinks you're a tramp," Jude said.

"Why would you tell me something like that?"

"I took a lot of shots to the head playing football. I also do a lot of drugs. Sometimes I forget to filter my words."

He held her car door open. She rested her arm on top of the window.

"Hell, I already know what she thinks of me," Chloe glanced back at the house. "And she's not half wrong. You hanging around after the funeral?"

"Don't know. Depends."

"On what?"

"How I sleep. Visions come to me in my dreams, and they poke at my soul with pikes. Some of my nightmare demons have the faces of people in this town."

She cocked her head. "Far out. You are nothing like Billy described you. You got some with you?"

"What?"

"You said you do a lot of drugs. Got any?"

"Nice meeting you, Chloe. I suppose I'll see you at the funeral tomorrow. If you don't mind me saying it, I thought you'd be more distraught. I admire the way you're bearing up. I mean it. Please accept my condolences again. If you'll excuse me, I need to see my dad."

* * *

Jude found Hubert Pressley at the Mica Wells Feed and Seed.

"Jude?" Hubert could barely recognize his son beneath the shaggy hair and beard as he walked through the door. "Is that you, son?"

"I'm here for Billy's funeral, Dad."

Hubert beamed and wrapped Jude in a bear hug. Jude endured it, looking uncomfortable. "I reckon it's a blessing your mama can't see you looking the way you do, but by God it's good to have you here! Let's get something to eat, catch up on stuff."

"I already ate. I dropped by Sally Mosack's place. She had a lot of food. My plane got in this morning. I'm kind of tired. I wanted to see you before I go anywhere else."

"You still have your house key? You can go home and take a nap. We'll do dinner later."

"Let's keep the option open. I can bunk with Owen. But home's fine, too. I have a key if I need it."

"You... you don't want to stay at home?" Hubert asked.

"No, Dad. Home's fine. Owen's is fine. They're both fine."

"I don't understand, son. You're different. You've changed."

"Yeah," Jude said. "I guess I have. You look... prosperous. I like the store. Don't get me wrong, Dad. It isn't that I don't want to go home. I don't know what I want yet. If I don't see you at home tonight, I'll see you at the funeral tomorrow."

CHAPTER TWENTY-SEVEN

He walked out to the parking lot. Hubert followed him.

"Is this about turning away those college offers? Is that why you've shut me down?" he shouted at Jude's back.

Jude took off his shades and looked his father in the eye. "I think you give yourself too much credit. You always feel blameworthy around me. Maybe it's because you had to be both parents after Mom died. Maybe you've spent your entire adult life under Rennie Poole's thumb. Left to make your own decisions, your lack of practice betrays you. I'm not being eloquent. I've said these same things to myself for years."

"You're talking in riddles, Jude boy. I'm getting dizzy off your words."

"I know. Don't let it rattle you, Dad. If you love the rainbow, you gotta embrace the rain. I'll talk to you tomorrow if I don't come home tonight."

* * *

Owen Wheeler returned from Morgan and found Jude Pressley sitting on his front porch. A six-pack of Budweiser rested on the table next to him, minus the bottle from which Jude was sipping.

"As I live and breathe, it's the ghost of Jude Pressley," Owen said. He walked up the steps and stood over Jude. "You're in my seat, spook."

Jude stood and wrapped his arms around Owen. They hugged like long-lost brothers. Jude handed Owen a beer.

"Billy," Jude toasted. Owen clinked Jude's longneck.

"You see the wreck?" Owen asked.

"Only a hundred times. Can't get away from it on TV this week. Hell, Billy's been on the tube more than Vietnam since last Sunday. Lousy way to go."

"I don't know. He probably never felt a thing. Like flipping a light switch. So, you want to tell me where the fuck you've been the last five years? And what's with the hippie getup?"

"Same answer for both questions. I'm a gen-u-wine Summer of Fucking Love San Francisco hippie. See the flowers in my hair?"

Owen leaned over and sniffed. "Don't smell so bad."

"Jesus. Don't you have hippies in Bliss County?"

"Sure. Saw a couple of Rennie's redneck brownshirts kick the shit out of one outside the draft board in Morgan a couple weeks back. They heard he tried to register as a conscientious objector and decided to test how conscientious he was. Word is he's a stand-up pacifist, and he'll be able to eat solid food in a couple of weeks. He's also 4-F now, so it kind of worked for him."

"Sounds like you approve."

"Maybe I do, a little. I got my call, and I went. It sucked ass, but I went. While you and your hippie buddies have been marching in the streets, guys have been fighting and dying over a shithole you wouldn't buy for pocket change. There's nothing honorable up for grabs in Southeast Asia, but when Uncle Sugar calls, I feel like we're obligated to answer."

"Glad you made it back, brother."

They clinked bottles again. Jude pulled a joint from his shirt pocket. He lighted it, sucked a cloud of smoke, the ember glowing orange, and passed it to Owen.

"Been a while," Owen said, as he exhaled and passed it back. "Haven't had a taste since Nam."

"The shithole."

"Yep. Jesus, did we screw the pooch there. Body counts every night on the evening news." He took a third hit. "This is good shit, man. Smoke all you want. Keeps the mosquitoes down."

They drank and toked and watched the stars for a few minutes. "Sorry I didn't get back for your folks' funerals," Jude said.

"You were all the way across the country. You had games. I appreciated the cards and the flowers."

"I met Billy's widow today. Dropped by his mom's place to check on my car. Chloe was there."

"Is she as pretty in person as she is on TV?"

"She's stunning. It's strange, though. It's like...it's like somebody stretched skin over a stainless-steel skull. There's something really hard and impenetrable beneath her surface. I think she measures the ocean of her soul in thimbles."

"All you San Francisco hippies sit around talking like poets?"

Jude chuckled. Then his face clouded. "I want you to be serious for a minute. I've been thinking about this for fourteen years, and now Billy's gone. I can only think of one person to ask."

"If you're getting all serious," Owen said. "pass another beer this way."

He grabbed another bottle and waited.

"Do you dream?" Jude asked.

"Everyone dreams."

"What do you dream about?"

"Are you looking for something specific here?"

"I want to know if it's only me. If I'm right, you know what I mean."

"I don't want to talk about this," Owen said. "Best thing is to let the past go."

"You dream about him, don't you?"

"Only a man with no conscience wouldn't. You have dreams, Jude?"

"All the time."

"Let's leave it there. No point in rehashing it. You want to stay for dinner?"

"I'd like to stay… or a while." Jude upended his bottle and drained it. "The Summer of Fucking Love was the party before the hangover. For a brief time, it was righteous. Now, it's like everywhere else. The police told me a young girl who sometimes shacked up with me was dead. I nearly killed a guy who gave her heroin. I watched Billy die twenty-three times in one afternoon on the Wide Fuckin' World of Sports. The world became unhinged. The last thing Lucy said to me was in a note. *'Not strong enough,'* she said. Not *'Goodbye'*, or *'Thanks for all the times you held my hair while I puked in your crapper'*, or even *'Drop dead.'* She said, *'Not strong enough.'* What the fuck did that mean? She wasn't strong enough to resist her opioid demons? Or I wasn't strong enough to protect her from them?"

"Jesus, you can shit on a buzz," Owen said. "Come inside. I'll find us something to eat. Bring the beer."

"Here's the thing," Jude said, as Owen pulled a couple of pork chops from the refrigerator. "In my dreams, I see… you know… him. The guy we say we aren't going to talk about—"

"Yeah, yeah. I know what *him* means."

"When I see him, I also see Lucy. And they're both looking at me the same way, as if it was all my fault."

Owen seasoned the pork chops on a plate. He placed the saltshaker on the counter.

"And I see a fourteen-year-old Vietnamese kid. Let's leave it there. You aren't alone. We each carry a horror movie inside our head. Congratulations. You're normal. And how in hell could you be responsible for Ev Howard? That boy ripped up his birth certificate when he killed Coral Pyle. Sure, we delivered him to Rennie, but we didn't know they were gonna string him up."

"We didn't stop it."

"And we can't change it. You have a suit for the funeral?"

"Why?"

"Because you look like the kind of guy who doesn't. I can fix you up."

"Fix me up. That's what I need. That's what I was trying to say, Owen. I need something to hold onto right now. I sort of lost my connection to humanity. There is nothing of substance in my life. I need to find something to keep my head from running away with itself. Maybe I could stay here and help on the farm."

"I already have all the hands I can afford."

"I don't need money. I mean, I'm not immensely wealthy, but I don't have to work if I don't want to. I'll do whatever jobs you want to toss at me. Maybe a month or two bent over in the sun will help me find myself."

Owen dropped a cast-iron frying pan on the gas stove and dumped in a spoonful of bacon grease. "Sure. I could use the help. You can take the upstairs bedroom. I put a bath up there two years ago. It'll be like a private apartment. I have one condition."

"What?"

"Quit bugging me about Ev Howard. The past is best forgotten."

Chapter Twenty-Eight

As Jude dressed for the funeral, the telephone rang.

"Rennie Poole," Owen said, after hanging up. "He wants us to be the honorary pallbearers."

"I don't know what that is," Jude replied.

"We walk in front of the coffin as they carry it to the graveyard from the sanctuary. Rennie said it would be great symbolism, the surviving members of The Trinity bearing their fallen fellow into Valhalla or some Viking bullshit."

"Symbolism?"

"The TV cameras. Rennie's running for Congress."

"Fuck him. I'm not Rennie's dancing monkey."

"You might want to think twice. We... we haven't talked about how things are in Prosperity these days. I didn't want to rile you."

"I don't understand."

"You missed Rennie's Willie Stark routine during the Morgan riot last year. He had some sheriff's deputy named Stilson rousting colored people all over Prosperity and Mica Wells. I challenged the kid, and Rennie threatened to drive my farm under. It was a power play. Everything he does is about consolidating power. Rennie's entire world is separated into two camps—with him or ag'in' him. He punishes the people who oppose him. This shouldn't be a surprise for you. Your dad goes where Rennie goes and does what Rennie tells him to do. Brian Mattox is sheriff now. Rennie has a lien on Mattox's skin. Got him elected three times. Until we get our own police force, the Sheriff's Department is the law in Prosperity, and Rennie controls the sheriff. He has his own private fucking army."

"Jesus," Jude whispered. "Things have changed."

"It all turned on that night back in 1954. When Rennie and your dad took charge and got all their Klan buddies worked up, a light went on over Rennie's head. If the lynching had never happened, Rennie would still be pulling his pud over in Morgan, cackling about how he cheated some farmer out of a couple of bucks at the Feed and Seed. Ev Howard made Rennie Poole. Town turned a bad corner the night Howard died."

Jude didn't say much on the trip to the church. He rolled what Owen had told him over and over in his head, and he came to the same conclusion he usually did. He wasn't the hero in his own story. He was river flotsam, pulled along by a current he could neither see nor fight. He hadn't been drifting for the last five years. He'd been caught in an eddy, and now the stream had picked him up again, as it had Coral's body, and was dashing him against the karmic rocks he'd always known he deserved.

"They went with the closed casket," Owen explained as he and Jude walked up the front steps of the Ebenezer Baptist Church. He leveled his hand horizontally across his collarbones. "Nothing much left from here up, I hear."

The church was crowded. News vans parked in the lot next to the mourners' cars. Cameramen erected tripods on the lawn between the parking lot and the church entrance and loaded film into their cameras to record the pageant.

Sally wore a long black dress with black hose and shoes, and a wide hat with a dark veil. Chloe's widow-weeds were more provocative. Her black dress fell only to the top of her knees, adhering to her buttocks like vinyl. The seam in her charcoal stockings bisected her calves like a scalpel. She wore a pillbox hat and no veil, but she'd donned black gloves and two-inch black heels. Jude couldn't discern whether she was in mourning or auditioning for Holly Golightly.

Owen nudged him. "That's Chloe? She's a knockout."

"I think she knows."

As honorary pallbearers, Jude and Owen sat on the front row to the left of the aisle. Sally and Chloe sat to the right, escorted by their respective chaperones, Rennie and Hubert. The church was full. Billy had left town over a decade earlier. Jude didn't see many of their high school classmates. The people assembled in the musty church sanctuary seemed more curious than grief-stricken.

The organ fell silent as the doors to the church closed. Sunlight streamed through stained-glass windows depicting various miracles of the Apostles. A two-story cross made of mahogany loomed over the chancel at the front of the sanctuary. A pastor in his middle thirties ascended the three steps to stand in a walnut pulpit, from which he looked upon the congregants.

"Dear friends," he intoned. "We are gathered today to celebrate the life of a fellow traveler in Christ, Mr. William August Mosack."

Owen turned to Jude and silently mouthed *August?* Jude shrugged. He watched Chloe, who held a handkerchief to her mouth and nose, her shoulders twitching.

"A native of Prosperity, and a standout athlete, William elected to travel the highways from coast to coast, putting his life at risk every week for the entertainment of others. His devoted and loving widow, Chloe, is with us today to remember his life, brief as it might have been, and its impact on people far-flung from our tiny town."

Jude glanced at Chloe again, and her shoulders seemed to rock. On her other side, he saw Sally steal a quick, disapproving look at her. Jude leaned over to Owen.

"What's with her?"

Owen leaned forward and looked past him at Chloe. "I can't tell."

"But, through all his wanderings," the preacher continued, "William kept a small piece of Prosperity in his heart, along with the values and the morals instilled in him during his youth worshipping inside these very walls. One can only hope, in the violently tragic final instant of his life, which we all have seen many times, he found a sense of peace knowing he'd be transported instantaneously into the presence of our Lord and Savior—"

Chloe lurched forward, her shoulders simultaneously hunching and shaking. She covered her face with the handkerchief, and a huffing, choking sound emerged from behind it.

"Jesus," Jude whispered, "She's *laughing.*"

* * *

With Billy permanently consigned to the earth, many of the mourners and simply curious moved to Sally Mosack's house for the wake. Someone had set up a bar with soft drinks and iced tea and lemonade and a cooler full of ice, but no liquor or beer since Sally maintained a Baptist home. The counters full of food looked like a cafeteria.

Sally and Chloe emerged from their separate rooms after changing out of their mourning clothes. Sally had elected to stay in something muted and dark and plain. Chloe had donned a flowered sundress that left her arms bare. Several of the church women were appalled. The idea of a widow in Prosperity putting herself on display was scandalous and unthinkable, especially if the dirt was still settling on her late husband's coffin.

"You didn't come home last night," Hubert said, clutching Jude's shoulder.

"I stayed with Owen. I'm going to live there for a while. I'm putting in some work on his farm while I figure out what I'm going to do."

"What you're going to do? You didn't come back to stay?"

"I'll decide after Owen's crops come in. I hope to fix up my old Willys out in the barn. Come autumn, where I go is anybody's guess."

"This isn't the place or the time," his father said, "but I'd like to talk with you. I know something that might help make up your mind."

"I'm not going anywhere for a couple of months. I'm out of practice thinking any further ahead. Was Chloe Mosack crying or laughing at the funeral? I couldn't tell from where I was sitting."

Rennie Poole stepped up and interrupted them. "Hubert, can you gather everyone in the back yard in about ten minutes? I want to say a few words."

"Sure thing," Hubert said. "We'll talk later, son."

"Oh, we will!" Rennie said. "Did you tell him?"

"Tell me what?" Jude said.

"No," Hubert said. "I'd rather wait until after the wake." He checked his watch before walking away.

"What's he talking about?" Jude asked.

"Your father's right. This isn't the time. Don't worry. You're gonna like it."

He waltzed away, negotiating the crowd in the living room like oil sliding across the surface of a still pond.

It was exactly like the old days, a mirror of the last time he'd lived in Prosperity. Rennie and Hubert were hatching plans, expecting everyone else to fall in line. His stomach soured. He poured his tea into the kitchen sink, as his father herded people outside. Jude joined the throng trying to wedge through the back door. Rennie stood between Sally and Chloe. Jude noticed news cameras had been set up to record the gathering.

Once the yard was full, Rennie held up his hands to quiet everyone.

"Ladies and gentlemen. It warms my heart to see so many people turn out this afternoon to honor the memory of our fallen neighbor, Billy Mosack. Billy brought great honor and recognition to this town, but was taken from us long before his time. I would like to offer our deepest condolences to his mother Sally, and his widow, Chloe Mosack, and I would ask that we all take a moment of silence to remember Billy in our own fashion."

He bowed his head, and the crowd—except for Jude—joined in. Chloe glanced at him, and back at the ground.

"Amen!" Rennie proclaimed. "I have an important announcement. The Town Council has approved a major construction project at the high school. Over the summer, we will demolish the old football stadium and its rickety grandstands. In its place, we will erect a new, modern football facility, to be named the Billy Mosack Memorial Stadium."

Sally raised her hands to her mouth in shock, clasped them as if in prayer, and beat her chest, smiling upward. Chloe shook her head and smiled. The crowd erupted in applause.

Jude saw a blatant attempt to score political points over Billy's body, with the cameras recording. He searched the crowd for his father and found him whipping one corner of the group of mourners into a lather of applause and whistles and catcalls. He circled the perimeter of the crowd, toward the barn.

Inside, away from the heat of the day, the interior lighted only by the sunlight streaming in through the cracks in the siding, Jude sat on a bench and stared at the faded hulk of his old Willys heap. The barn smelled of ammonia and decay and neglect, the most honest thing he'd encountered since his return to Prosperity. He hung his borrowed jacket on the edge of a horse stall and rolled up his shirtsleeves. The Willys' hood creaked as he lifted it. He started to stick his hand in to test the throttle linkage but stopped when he saw the chaotic network of webbing glistening in the shafts of light streaming through the walls. The engine compartment of the Willys looked like a black widow convention.

"You sure must love this car," Chloe said, standing in the doorway, the crystal sunlight casting her long shadow across the barn floor. The rays rendered the thin fabric of her sundress translucent, providing Jude an arousing magic lantern show. He could smell her perfume on the breeze that wafted through the open door.

"I had some good times in it. You had difficulty maintaining your composure at the service. I can tell losing Billy has been a trial for you."

"You want to say that again? You seem to want to make a point."

"You were laughing."

"Oh. Soon as the preacher opened his mouth, I could tell he didn't know the first thing about Billy. Billy never expected to be delivered into the presence of Jesus. Not the way he lived. The only god Billy worshipped has pictures of dead presidents on it. He'd be mortified to know he was covered with Prosperity dirt. Billy hated this town. Hell, if it had been left up to him, he'd have been cremated and his ashes mixed with the paint they use on the walls at Indy, the only place on the planet he truly loved. Then, some tinhorn preacher who never laid eyes on Billy had the balls to say all this stuff that wasn't true. I was waiting for Billy to jump out of the box and throttle him. I found it all too bizarre and absurd for tears. Thought I'd step inside out of the sun. After an hour in a crowd of people, my skin starts to crawl."

"I'm not sure you understand how things work in small southern towns."

"Really? Well, I declare. How on Earth might I know how to behave in a small southern town? Guess I flat wasted those sixteen years growing up in Hot Coffee, Mississippi."

"For real?"

"Went to St. Anne's Catholic School in Yazoo."

"Explains why Sally doesn't like you. She's a Southern Baptist. She's not fond of Papists."

"Don't care much for them myself, especially nuns. That's not the reason. I've learned a lot about wills this week. Want to know what happens to all your stuff when you die and don't leave a will behind?"

"Not having much stuff, I never gave it much thought."

"If you're married, it sure doesn't go to your mama."

"Oh," Jude said. He pulled a joint from his pocket and lighted it. After taking a hefty drag, he held it up to her. She sucked on it like she was siphoning gas.

"It's not a huge estate," she said, the blue smoke billowing around her face like blood in water. "Billy liked to live it up, so there might only be a hundred grand or so in cash. We rented our place in Indy, so there's no house to liquidate. He had a ten percent ownership in some chicken and waffle places in Atlanta, and a smaller share of some burger joints spread across the south. I guess I'm the part owner now, which means a small but dependable income long as they stay in business. There're some stocks and bonds and shit. He did manage to get life insurance, about fifty thousand. Damned if I know how. Race drivers aren't ideal insurance risks. So, there's some money. Couple hundred thousand, maybe. Mother Mosack is pissed I'm not laying a little taste off on her."

"Understandable. She's his mother, right?"

"Hey! I earned this, Buster. You know what it's like, being a race driver's wife? Especially one like Billy, who ran a hundred-fifty nights a year at shitty little dirt tracks and asphalt bullrings in addition to driving the Champ Car circuit? There are two types of racing wives. One sits at home, tends to kids, keeps the house tidy, and sweats out the hours until her b'wana comes home—with a trophy or in a box. When hubby does come home, they have nothing to talk about, no common frame of reference. So they put the squirts to bed and hit the sheets, and all she can smell as he plows into her is the faint traces of methanol and three different brands of perfume from the women he fucked while he was on the road. Nine months later she squats out another link in the chain tying her to her sick, transient marriage. Gimme another hit of that joint, Slick."

"My name's Jude."

"Sure, Slick. *Jude* it is." She blew out another cloud of smoke and handed the roach to him. "The other kind of wife gets dirty with it. She takes an active role in his racing. Maybe she's in charge of his PR schedule, or maybe she takes care of his gear, or coordinates reporter interviews. Maybe she sits in a fancy elevated tent at places like Indy, or in splintered bleachers crawling with chiggers and ticks at the bullrings, and she keeps lap records or runs a stopwatch, and tries not to piss herself every time her husband hooks the cushion and spins toward the wall. I'm gonna have to spend half my inheritance on chiropractors after years of sleeping on motor home mattresses thinner than a pack of cigarettes."

"Why did you stay married?"

"I loved the stupid son of a bitch. You didn't know him, not after he hit the big time. Seems like he spent half of each year on the road and the other half in a cast. He was broken in a dozen places. His body was a road atlas of scars. The first hour of every day, he walked like he'd been pieced together with mismatched parts. He needed me to keep all the plates spinning on all the sticks. We had a partnership. He was also handy in the rack, once he limbered up. We resonated with each other, until the moment I watched him die."

"I know," Jude said. "I saw it dozens of times on TV."

"Should have caught the live show. It was a screamer. So are you gonna kiss me or what? Because I've been here for ten minutes already, and people are gonna talk."

Jude took her hand and led her toward the barn door.

"No," he said. "Today is about Billy. I won't do that to a pal."

* * *

Only a few people remained. Jude prepared a plate of food and carried it into the living room to eat. His father rounded the corner and spied him.

Hubert settled into the sofa next to him. The frame groaned and sagged under the added weight. "It's quieter now. Maybe we can talk. I've missed you, son. I wanted to make sure you knew."

"I know. And maybe you're right. I guess I've been angry at you for a long time, for standing between me and the college offers."

"But you got in, only a year later. And you made it to the pro leagues. You started two preseason games. Do you have any idea how few people in this world can say they were the starting quarterback in an NFL game?"

"I'm sure there's a stat for it somewhere. The football days are over, Dad. I had my shot, and I blew it. Maybe if I'd been a little larger, a little faster, things might have been different. Coach McCandless was right. I was always a third-stringer except here in Prosperity."

"So, what are your plans, son?"

"In a few months, I might be back in San Francisco, or maybe I'll take off for the Caribbean. The nice thing about being in the present is the million and one futures I can choose from."

"Let me offer you one."

"What?"

"A future. Coach Lafferty at the high school is retiring next month. How would you like to be Prosperity High's next football coach?"

Jude had iced tea halfway to his mouth but stopped and placed it back on a coaster.

"You're serious?"

"Why not? How many teams in Bliss County can claim a former pro quarterback as their coach? I can see the headlines now. *Hometown Football Hero Returns to Lead Prosperity to a Championship.*"

"Was this your idea, or Rennie's?"

"Does it matter?"

"Yeah, it does. You were a good father, but if you had one failing it was measuring yourself against Rennie's shadow. If I had one wish for my life, you and Rennie never would have met."

"How can you say that? Rennie's stores put the food on your table and the clothes on your back for eighteen years. I'm disappointed. You should be more grateful."

"It's not about material things, Dad. You let Rennie foreclose on your soul day and night. You let him rewrite your thinking. You let him walk around inside your head with his dirty feet."

"You don't know what we owe him, Jude."

"And he doesn't acknowledge what he owes you. How in hell could I coach football, anyway? I'd have to be on the faculty, and I don't have a teaching certificate. I was a college football player. I majored in physical education."

"We'll make you a gym teacher. Rennie knows which strings to pull to fast-track your certification. I can tell you, there are lot of boosters in this town who'd be willing to help you fill in the financial cracks, if you know what I mean. Football coach at Prosperity High takes home more than the principal. This could be the jumpstart your life needs. 'Course, you'd have to lose the beard and the rock and roll hair."

"Let me think about it," Jude said, as he drained the glass. "Excuse me, Dad."

The hallway bathroom was closed and locked. From his childhood, Jude remembered Sally had another lavatory off her bedroom. He knocked lightly on the bedroom door, barely a rap, and toed the door open. The room looked empty, save for some purses and suit jackets piled on the bed. Jude stepped inside and headed for the bathroom but froze when he heard a noise.

In a cheval mirror angled perfectly toward the bathroom door, Rennie Poole sat on the toilet lid, his pants around his ankles. A woman kneeled in front of him, the flawless skin and curve of her back naked from the waist up. Even at the awkward angle, Jude could see the flowered sundress puddling around the woman's waist. Her head, framed with anthracite hair, bobbed as Rennie urged her on, saying, "That's it, girl. Don't stop. Don't stop. Goddamn but you make an old country boy feel young again."

Rennie's face turned redder and redder, until Jude could watch no longer, and he snuck back out of the bedroom. The hall bath had opened. When he finished, he returned to the sofa, where his father still sat.

"When do you need to know?" Jude asked.

Chapter Twenty-Nine

In July, after a particularly hot and dusty afternoon in the cornfield, Jude and Owen sat on the porch and knocked back a couple of longnecks. The ceiling fans spun furiously to ward off mosquitoes as they enjoyed the transition to the cool evening.

"Who bought the Lincoln farm?" Jude asked.

"Nobody," Owen said. "Bank still owns it. There's a big *For Sale* sign out front, on the Morgan Highway. Place is starting to look ratty."

"Think they'd be willing to subdivide, maybe piece off an acre or two for a home site?"

"You putting down roots?"

"Can't stay in your upstairs bedroom for the rest of my life. Need a place to lie my head."

The next day, Jude contacted the agent listed on the miniature billboard posted at the Lincoln farm. The agent consulted with the bank. They were all too happy to break the property up, with one caveat. The land was zoned for agricultural use. If Jude wanted to carve off a chunk and build a house, he'd have to get the lot rezoned.

"I'd rather have your luck than a license to steal," Owen said when Jude told him about the restriction.

"Not following."

"Zoning in Prosperity is determined by the Town Council."

"Not the County Commission in Morgan?"

"Nope. Being the son of a councilman, I reckon you can get the place rezoned with a phone call."

"I...I haven't talked with my father much since I took the job at the high school," Jude said. "We aren't on great terms."

"Sucks to be you. If you want that house, make things right with Daddy. Did you hear Chloe Mosack is moving to Prosperity? She let her place in Indianapolis go and is looking for a house here. Can't imagine why, but I suppose she has her reasons."

"Where did you hear this?"

"Ran into her and Rennie Poole at the lunch counter in the drugstore the other day. Maybe you and Chloe can split the Lincoln property—you build on one side, she can build on the other. That would be interesting. I believe she has an eye on you."

* * *

As he drove into Mica Wells, Jude's head filled with the indelible image of Rennie splayed on the toilet seat in Sally Mosack's private bathroom, his face like a ripe tomato, his breath coming in huffs as he urged Chloe on. He saw every inch of her back, and the gentle curve of her breasts as they disappeared between Rennie's prickly pear thighs.

He didn't know which audacity offended him greater—Chloe snorkeling some guy on the day of her husband's funeral, or that she'd chosen Rennie Poole. He sensed Chloe's moral compass had no due north. There was something fundamentally absent in her. She'd elevated opportunism to a fine art. She reminded him of a chameleon, unconsciously adapting to any situation. What profit she expected to find in Prosperity evaded him.

So why had his heart raced when Owen told him Chloe was returning?

He pulled into the gravel and shell parking lot at the Feed and Seed and found his father in the office.

"Jude!" Hubert said, as he stood and came around his desk to shake his son's hand. "I had no idea you were coming today. How are things going with Owen and the farm?"

"Great, Dad."

"You look good without the beard and all that hair. Filled out, too.

Working on Owen's farm this summer has been good for you. How are the plans for the football season going?"

"I've been working on some plays I learned in the pros. I had an open meeting at the high school last week with kids planning to try out, and I've been studying last year's depth charts. This senior quarterback, Bickford, looks okay on paper, but I haven't seen him throw a pass yet. There's another kid I like, a junior. I'd like to give him a shake. Name's Tony Morven."

"The colored boy?"

"Yes."

"I don't know, son. Prosperity High has never had a Negro quarterback. You might want to think about this."

"I agreed to be coach with the understanding I'd have complete control over the team."

"And you do. I only hope you're open to suggestions along the way."

"That's not why I'm here," Jude said. "I'm thinking of building a house. You know the Lincoln farm? The bank's willing to subdivide and sell me a couple of acres, only the land isn't zoned residential."

"I see," Hubert said, as he collapsed into his desk chair like a canvas feed sack full of water balloons.

"I wanted to ask if you—the Town Council—might be convinced to rezone it. I can have surveyors out there next week to provide the exact property boundaries."

"Any particular reason why you want this specific spot?"

"I like the area. It bounds on Six Mile Creek. The fishing is good." He conveniently avoided mentioning the path through the trees that ended on a stone ledge that extended into the creek.

"Okay. Tell you what. You get a plat drawing, and I'll bring it up in the next council meeting."

"Sure you don't want to consult with Rennie Poole first?"

"You have a curious way of asking for a favor, son."

"You're right," Jude said. "I apologize. I'll get you the particulars on the lot next week. I have to get back to the farm."

On the drive back to Owen's place, Jude couldn't suppress the sense of having dipped his toe into quicksand, only to find his entire foot sucked under before he could stop it.

* * *

When he got back to the farm Jude found a red Ford Fairlane fastback parked in the gravel circle in front of the porch steps. He glanced through the open windows and saw black leather bucket seats and a wooden dash. The paint was almost the exact same shade as his Willys, which sat in pieces in Arlo Pyle's garage being rebuilt.

Jude stepped up to the porch and opened the door. Chloe's voice echoed down the narrow hallway. He walked into the kitchen and found her standing with Owen at the counter. Owen had popped open a PBR for each of them. Two crumpled empties languished in the sink.

"Look who dropped by for a visit," Owen said.

"Well, hi there, Slick!" Chloe leaned in and kissed Jude on the cheek. He stepped back, a little embarrassed.

"Oh, honey, don't take it personal," Chloe quipped, as she rubbed at the smear of lipstick on his cheek with a paper towel. "I kiss damn near everybody."

"So I've heard," Jude said. Chloe stared at him curiously until Owen broke the tension.

"You didn't kiss me."

She grabbed Owen by the collar of his work shirt and drew him in, planting a wet one on his lips.

"There, Sugar. Makin' up for lost time. My, my," Chloe said as she surveyed them. "I do not know which one of you is better looking. Isn't that a line from some movie? Like hanging out with those cute boys on *Route 66*. You clean up good, Jude. I like the GI thing you got going with the hair. You look like a drill sergeant I knew once. I like you better without the beard. Maybe I'll tell you why someday."

"The Fairlane?" Jude said. "Yours?"

"I suppose it's mine now. The Ford people gave it to Billy when he was a factory driver. I got rid of almost everything else, but I needed some wheels. Want to take a ride?"

"Some other time. I have to work on the tryout rosters for the team."

He turned away, but Chloe grabbed his arm. "No, Sweetie. You can't go. We're gonna have a party. Grab a beer and cop a squat. You boys got any music lying around?"

Jude gazed into her eyes, the pupils large as shirt buttons. They seemed to vibrate in their sockets.

"You're on bennies," he said.

"Oh, Slick, what I'm on is so much better," she said, smiling. "What do you expect? It's a fifteen-hour drive from Indianapolis. Baby, you're lagging way behind. Get yourself a drink."

Jude popped the tab on the can of beer she handed him. "Owen, my dad said the council will approve the rezoning of the Lincoln parcel. Know any good architects in Morgan?"

"Nope," Owen said absently, his eyes fixed on Chloe's curves. "There's a carpenter over in Mica Wells who hangs out at Clyde Dillard's hardware store. Roger something-or-other. Bet he knows someone."

Chloe had spotted the record player in the corner, a twenty-year-old Philco tabletop model clad in genuine walnut and featuring a dual-dial AM/FM radio, its face resembling a car grill. She flipped through records on the rack underneath the table. Seconds later, the room filled with the voice of Connie Francis singing *Al Di La*.

"Gotta tell you, boys, I've seen hipper stacks of wax," she said. "I think you need some Beatles or some Stones. I might go record shopping this weekend and spice up your collection. What do you say, Coach? Want to put something spicy in your rack?"

"Where are you staying?" Jude asked.

"With my monster-in-law, for now. I don't think that's gonna work out. I have maybe a week before her welcome mat no longer applies to me. I'll find something before then."

"You plan to move here for good?" Owen asked.

"Hell of a lot cheaper. Taxes and rent are eating me up in Indiana. Cost of living is lower here. I'm a widow on a limited income."

"Maybe Rennie Poole can help," Jude said.

"I have no idea what you mean, Slick. I think there's a hole in this beer can. Everything ran out. Owen, Sugar, could you grab me another one?"

Jude took the opportunity to slip up the stairs to his room. Someone downstairs put on a Duane Eddy record, and he could hear Owen and Chloe dancing in the living room. The record ended, and for a blissful time there was no noise, until Jude noticed a rhythmic thump from Owen's bedroom. The thump was joined by a series of metallic squeaks, huffing grunts, an anxious giggle, and unintelligible but unmistakable moaned exclamations. The pace became more frenzied, the voices more animated, deities invoked loudly.

Jude was glad Owen was getting his ashes hauled. He'd had a considerable drought. It bothered him that he was doing it with Chloe. The mix of emotions confused him and made it difficult to concentrate on his work. He sensed Chloe's attentions came with an enviable price tag. There was something dangerous about her.

A sharp feminine cry penetrated his floor, followed by a masculine one, and seconds later things fell quiet.

His stomach grumbled. He'd forgotten to eat dinner. Assuming Chloe and Owen were sleeping, he stole to the kitchen to make a quick ham and cheese sandwich. As he spread mustard on the bread, he heard the near-silent pad of bare feet behind him. He turned as Chloe opened the refrigerator door, hiding all but her head and feet from him.

"What's the haps, Cap?" she said over the top of the door. "The beer made me thirsty. Getting a Coke. Goddamn, I could stand in front of this fridge for a half hour. Have you hillbillies heard about air conditioning?"

Jude turned back to the cutting board. "Want a sandwich?"

"Wondering if I worked up an appetite?"

"Being polite."

She waved the refrigerator door back and forth, as if fanning the cool air across her. "I had a big lunch, and I didn't eat it until late. I'm good. Think I'll go back in and crash. Hope we didn't keep you awake. Your roomie likes it boisterous. Are all you jocks like that?"

He heard the hiss and pop as she opened the Coke with a church-key, and the thudding clank as the refrigerator door latched back. He turned back to her.

She stood at the refrigerator, naked, one arm languidly draped over the rounded top of the door, the other holding the soda bottle. Her sable hair, which had been in a tight beehive, had fallen about her shoulders. A drop of condensation fell from the bottle and landed on her right nipple. She swiped at it absently with the inside of her wrist. She looked exactly the way he'd imagined—the curve of her hip, the slope of her breasts, the India ink tangle of curls. He tried to appear unfazed, but his surprised gasp betrayed him. She locked her eyes on his, with a ferocity that surprised him, and refused to look away. He raised one eyebrow. She glanced lower.

"Cool," she said "Sweet dreams, Slick. Enjoy your sandwich."

She padded into Owen's room, the perfect twin globes of her beauty queen ass jiggling with each step. He watched her all the way until she disappeared into the darkness and closed the door.

"Jesus," he said, shaking his head.

He took the sandwich and a soda to his room, where he locked the door and ate. After watching the wavering picture of the flickering black-and-white portable TV, he stripped to his shorts and hit the sheets with the windows wide open, the sheer curtains undulating in the gentle breeze like wisps of fog. Beyond the screen, lightning bugs flitted and courted. In the distance he heard the drone as cars plied the Morgan Highway. The ceiling fan creaked as it dried the sweat on his chest and legs.

Chapter Thirty

As his father had promised, the parcel carved from the Lincoln farm had been rezoned for residential housing, a three-acre section that straddled the oiled dirt lane running along Six Mile Creek and included a swinging gate marked *"Posted: No..."*

The house plan he chose was a Louisiana planter's cottage, with a deep, wide, covered gallery in front and a huge screened porch with a fireplace in back. Hot tubs were all the rage in Marin County, across the bridge from San Francisco. Jude had spent many pleasant hours soaking with friends, so he planned to install Bliss County's first wooden barrel hot tub on the screened porch. He also built a garage for the Willys coupe, which still languished at Arlo Pyle's shop. Tom Tackett had promised to have it ready by Labor Day, but his third wife had gone into labor two weeks early and delivered a son whom they'd christened Harvey, but whom Tom called Slim.

The first day of August, Jude returned from football practice and spent a quarter-hour dousing under a tepid shower to remove the dust and dried sweat. He tossed on a pair of cutoff jeans shorts and a pullover sport shirt and grabbed a beer from the refrigerator before walking barefoot to the front gallery. He saw Owen at the stone grill beside the house.

"Whatcha doing?" he asked.

"Changing the grate on the grill. Chloe's coming over tonight. Grilling steaks and roasting corn. You're invited. There's plenty in the fridge."

He hefted a new cast-iron grate onto the grill, pulled off his leather work gloves, and trotted up to the gallery, taking a seat perpendicular to Jude.

"What do you think about Chloe?" Owen asked.

"You two have spent a lot of time together. I'd be more interested in knowing what *you* think of her."

"I think she's terrific."

"Why?"

"I don't get you."

"If you mean she's terrific as in *'I'm so glad I'm getting to fire my milkshake cannon regularly'*, then yeah, I'm on board. Happy for you, brother. She obviously rocks the rack. I stuff cotton in my ears every time she stays over. But I don't know whether you know enough about her to say she's terrific in general."

"You're making fun of me," Owen said.

"I make fun of almost everything. Not this. Really, what do you know about her, besides the fact she can wake the dead with her thunderpussy? What's her favorite ice cream flavor? What's her favorite movie? Has she read any good books lately? Can she read? I love you, man, but I don't think you're seeing straight. I've met a lot of women like Chloe in my time. When I was with the Forty-Niners, we called them starfuckers."

"You're about to cross a line." The veins in Owen's neck stood out like baby snakes under the skin.

"Not as bad as the one you're about to cross. We've been buds since we were kids. You asked what I thought, so I'll tell you. When I picked up my car from Billy's mom, she and I had a talk."

"Sally hates Chloe because of the estate. She'd say anything."

"Would she say her son—our friend—was cuckolded repeatedly while they were married? Go to Indy. Walk around Gasoline Alley. Want to know who stuck it to Chloe? It's the guy wearing a helmet. Billy walked through the pits knowing half his competitors had pumped a load into his wife. You want a reservation in that section of Hell?"

"I was mistaken," Owen said, his voice like frozen steel. "Now that I think of it, I only have enough in the fridge for two."

Jude held up his hands and sighed. "It's groovy. I'm happy you're having a great time. Ride this one for the full eight seconds and bail. She's not the one, pal. I'm going to Morgan. Catch a movie. They're playing an Elvis flick.

Speedway. Hey, you and Chloe should check it out. See if she recognizes anyone. While I'm handing out advice, you'd do well to throttle back on the hooch. You're turning into a stereotype. I can tell what's next by the look in your eyes, so I'll make it easy for you. I can pack before Chloe gets here."

"Good idea," Owen said, the muscles in his jaw tight.

Jude stopped when he got to the stairs. "On the day they buried Billy, I saw Chloe give Rennie Poole a hummer. Next time she gargles your flopper, remember Rennie got there first. I'm not saying this to hurt you. I love you, dude, but right now you are getting carried out to sea and Flipper's nowhere in sight. I'll let you know if the movie's any good."

* * *

There was no football practice the next afternoon. Jude awoke alone in his childhood bedroom. It was disconcerting at first, until he regained his bearings.

Despite his business successes, Hubert had remained in the house he and Jude's mother had built thirty years earlier, before the war. Jude's mother had died suddenly when he was twelve years old. He had come home from school, and she had cut him a slice of chocolate cake and poured him an ice-cold glass of milk. She was making a leg of lamb, he recalled, and was cutting up onions and carrots on the counter and talking about the really amazing deal Mr. Worthy the butcher had given her.

Jude had a question for her. Years later, he had no idea what the question might have been, because in the next several seconds he had a lot more to worry about. He said, "Mom?" seriously enough to imply that he wanted to know something important. She turned, perhaps a little more quickly than usual. Her smile twisted into a scowl, her eyes rolled up in their sockets, and she fell directly to the floor. She clawed at the cutting board on the way down, scattering onions and carrots across the kitchen floor. The knife speared the linoleum floor and quivered.

Jude sat, watching. He didn't understand what was happening, and he waited for his mother to push up to her knees and get back on her feet.

Instead, she just lay there, her eyes open and staring at the toes of his shoes.

A massive cerebral hemorrhage, his father told him later. Nothing to be done about it. No way to know it was going to happen, and nothing to do once it did.

Jude recalled the way his father delivered the news. Direct, to the point, and matter-of-fact about it. Jude couldn't discern whether his father was grief-stricken, relieved, remorseful, or simply didn't give a damn. In later years, it occurred to him that his father might have been masking his true feelings in order to spare his son a share of his torment. In his attempt to normalize a tragic loss, he instead made—once again—the wrong decision with the best of intentions. It seemed that was Hubert Pressley's hallmark.

There was no practice that afternoon, and Jude's tenure as a farmer was apparently behind him. After breakfast, he pulled out the lawnmower and was working on the front yard, wearing only cutoff jeans and a pair of sneakers, the sweat rolling off him, when a scarlet Ford Fairlane pulled into the drive. The big-block engine pounded the ground like a piledriver.

Chloe climbed from the car. She scowled at him over the roof. She wore a red-checkered broadcloth shirt knotted under her breasts. Her white shorts clung to her like gray on a battleship. She didn't remove her red Lolita sunglasses.

"You got a problem with me?" she demanded.

He untied a rag from the handlebar on the mower and wiped at his face with it as he walked toward her. He stood at the passenger door. They addressed one another across the roof of the car.

"In general, or are we discussing something specific?"

"You know what I'm talking about. Owen said you told him my mother-in-law was badmouthing me."

"He and I had a long conversation. It ended badly."

"Exactly what did Sally tell you?"

"Owen didn't give you the play-by-play?"

"He was too angry. And upset. I don't believe you know how much he loves you. Do you care?"

"I cared enough to pass along a warning. Billy talked to his mother before he died. He told her how you'd turned your motorhome at the track into a carnal lending library."

"She's lying."

"I saw you blow Rennie at Billy's wake. You made a pass at me only an hour before, in the barn. Who's lying here? You should really talk about this with Owen. I'm just the fuckin' messenger."

Her face blanched. She held a hand up to her mouth.

"You... son of a bitch," she hissed. "You don't understand anything. You don't..." she covered her eyes with her hand. She stomped up the steps to the front porch, dropped into a mildewed white rocking chair, bent at the waist, and cradled her face in her hands.

Jude watched from the car.

"You want a drink or something?" he asked. "Got some fresh iced tea."

He returned with a glass of tea for each of them. She took it without looking at him and sipped.

"The world is not kind to a single young female with no education," she said. "You're either someone's secretary, someone's maid, or someone's whore, but things are changing, Slick. Have you read *The Feminine Mystique*?

"Is there a *Classic Comics* edition?"

"I fled Mississippi with a GED, twenty bucks in my purse, this rockin' body, and the fact I really, truly love a fun roll in the hay. Some guy picked me up in a bar in Atlanta, convinced me I had the face and body for beauty pageants. I learned about blowing the judges on my own. When I won the *Miss 600* title, I was thrown into a world I'd never seen before. There was money and power and adulation. Especially money. For a girl who grew up back in the trees, it was like Christmas morning every day. Your mayor is a tenacious man. He's small and cruel and bigoted, and he knows things. When I said I was thinking of moving to Prosperity, he pulled me aside and read my life history like he'd written it. He said nobody in this town would accept a racetrack slut, but for a favor, he'd keep our secret. That's what he called it. A *favor*."

"Rennie trades in them."

"I didn't know Billy had already talked with his mother about me. If I had…"

The tears started again.

"At least," she sniffled, "I know now where Rennie got his information. If she wasn't my mother-in-law, I'd kick that bitch's ass. I still may. I reckon I might as well pack my bags. Now that you told Owen about what I did with Rennie, Prosperity doesn't smell so good anymore. Thanks for the tea."

"Wait," Jude placed his glass on the table between them. "Swear to me, on whatever it is you hold sacred. You have no intention of hurting Owen."

"Hurt him? I love the sweet bastard. I've had dreams lately about being a farm wife, like June fucking Lockhart on *Lassie*. How do you rationalize something like that?"

Jude stared out into the yard as Chloe finished the glass.

"Don't worry about Rennie," he said. "I'll take him out of the picture. He won't blackmail you anymore."

"The hell he won't. He's going to be a congressman in a few months."

"My dad's tight with him. I'll find a way."

"Why would you do something like that for me?"

"I'm doing it for Owen. If you're lying and you wind up screwing up his head, I'll come for you. You need to come clean with him, tell him the same story you told me. Tell him you want to clear the air about your past and tell him how you're trying to change. If you volunteer the information, without him bringing it up, you'll at least sound sincere."

"You don't trust me?"

"I don't even know you. What I think doesn't matter anyway. You need to think about how you're going to make this right with Owen."

Chapter Thirty-One

While his primary duties revolved around the football team, Jude also had to carry three physical education periods each morning. In the afternoon he taught driver's education classes. His office was a picture-window fishbowl looking out at the boys' locker room in the gym.

Principal Thomas Black collared Jude in the school office the first day the Prosperity High faculty returned for the fall semester. "Jude, I want to introduce you to someone."

A woman in her early thirties stood next to him. She was petite and blonde, standing only as tall as Jude's chest. She had blue eyes and a pert, upturned nose. When she smiled, she revealed perfectly even teeth. "This is Grace Corey."

"Jude Pressley." He took her hand.

"Grace is a music teacher," Black explained. "Grace, Jude is our football coach. I believe you two have something in common."

"We sure do," Grace said.

When Jude heard her voice, he realized he knew her.

"Grace..." he said. "You're... you're Grace Pyle. Arlo's daughter."

"You didn't forget me after all these years." She turned to Principal Black. "Jude and I went out a few times when we were students at Prosperity. Though, I seem to recall he took someone else to the prom."

"Yes," Jude said, absently. "I... I suppose I should apologize."

"Don't know why. Kids do dumb things. We can't hold you responsible for stuff you did when you didn't know any better, right?"

"I suppose," was all he could say.

"All is not lost," Black said. "You two are the most junior faculty. Your job descriptions include chaperoning dances throughout the year, including the Welcome Dance later this week. Guess you'll get another shot at taking Grace to the prom, Jude."

"I think her husband might object," Jude joked. "You said your name is Corey now?"

An awkward expression crossed Black's face.

"It's all right," Grace told him. "Thanks for the introduction to an old friend."

Black excused himself.

"I'm widowed, Jude," she said. "Fucking Vietnam, right?"

"I'm sorry to hear it."

"It's been a few years. Gave me time to get my master's in music. And, here I am. Back in Prosperity."

"Both of us."

"You took a more interesting path. Bet you have a lot of stories."

"Maybe I can tell you later. I… I need to work on the class rosters. This teacher stuff is all new to me. I'm still figuring it out. It's great to see you again, Grace."

"Sure. It's nice seeing you."

"Yes," Jude said. "We'll talk soon."

He hustled toward the gym, his heart hammering inside his chest like a caged beast, his breath rapid, his head woozy. He stopped at a water fountain and gulped several mouthfuls to ward off the cottony dryness that left him nearly unable to speak. He finally made it back to his office, closed the blinds on his fishbowl window, collapsed into his office chair, and tried to slow his ragged, racing pulse.

He didn't recognize Grace immediately, because she'd changed. She'd been pretty enough in high school, but in the fourteen years since he'd last seen her—on the day of her sister's funeral—she'd transformed herself. Life had written on her face, revealing the beauty that had always been waiting to emerge.

Jude had never divulged his deepest secret to anyone. There was nobody on earth he could talk to about his profound guilt and how his cowardice had spurred the unnecessary murder of Ev Howard. Because he could never tell anyone about Coral, there was also nobody to whom he could reveal his greatest shame.

He could no longer remember Coral's face.

He could recall the curve of her body, the tanned legs, the compact bosom. He could hear her voice, and he could even find a snippet of a memory of her smell. He remembered sunlight glinting off the droplets of water in her hair. All of this came back to him readily, but the space between her chin and forehead was like flat, unworked clay.

He knew he could drop by the school library and check out her picture in the dusty high school yearbook in the stacks. He'd come close several times, but stopped, as if allowing himself to access her image might rip open a mental scar and spill out a humour so vile it would consume him.

Whether through some confluence of genetics, or his own wishful thinking, as soon as he knew Grace's name, he'd also recognized a single, irrevocable, immutable fact.

She had Coral's face.

* * *

"Can you believe they still do these things?" Grace said as she entered the gym on Jude's arm. "I figured sock hops would have disappeared by now."

"The 1960s are taking a while to get to Prosperity," he told her.

He looked around the room. Crepe paper garlands and streamers hung from the rafters and the basketball backboards. Posters hung along one end of the gym reading *Welcome Class Of 1971!* At one corner, a disk jockey wearing sparkling white jeans, a red satin shirt, a paisley silk ascot, and an open Nehru jacket stood behind twin turntables, spinning forty-fives. The snack bar in the gym lobby had opened for refreshments. Jude suspected the entire Welcome Dance was a ploy to build a cash reserve from the concession stand. Schools—especially money-starved rural schools—had to scrounge for every dime they could find.

Jude learned this the hard way when he discovered he might be forced to reuse the football uniforms from the previous season. Procuring new uniforms, it turned out, was Jude's job. During the summer, when he was toiling on Owen's farm, he should have been wooing local businesses for donations. Nobody had told him.

With the first game three weeks away, the clock had almost run out. After mulling over his options, he'd settled on two possibilities. The team could limp along with old uniforms, or he could swallow his pride and crawl to his father again for help. Going to his father meant going to Rennie Poole. Running for Congress, Rennie might pile up some political capital by coming through with a last-minute reprieve.

He'd casually mentioned the notion at dinner a week earlier with his father. Hubert had listened carefully, asked Jude to pass the biscuits and the butter, and said he'd discuss the problem with Rennie. Jude had spent most of that night lying awake in bed, debating how large a chunk of his soul he'd pinched off this time.

Grace squeezed his arm as they walked through the door, and he felt a jolt of adrenalin blossom in his chest. Each time he laid eyes on Grace, he found the resemblance to Coral—at least, his faulty memory of Coral—uncanny. Each time they shared lunch or met in the hallway, the impact was less jarring, but the cumulative effect on him was like a five-mile run. He was always left breathless and sweating.

Teenagers filtered into the gym. The disc jockey spun The Monkees' *I'm A Believer* on the turntable, and the opening organ notes blared through megaphone loudspeakers mounted at each corner of the space above the bleachers. The kids had clumped into groups, all at the periphery of the glossy basketball court, staring at one another like medieval enemy camps facing off across an empty valley, each waiting for the other to charge.

"What do you suppose our duties are?" Jude asked

"Same as when we were the students," she said. "Break up the clenches, make sure nobody spikes the punch, confiscate booze and weed to keep it for ourselves, and try to get everyone home before they're pregnant or catch the clap."

"So young, and yet so cynical."

"Not so young."

"I don't recall you being such a wild child in high school."

"Still waters. How many points for catching some kid smoking in the bathroom?"

They patrolled the gym for the first hour, after which two other teachers took over. It had been a particularly disappointing venture. Nothing salacious happened. On their last pass through the crowd, Grace and Jude ran into each other in the middle of the floor as the disc jockey spun up a forty-five of The Delfonics' *La La Means I Love You*. Grace grabbed Jude's sleeve before he could pass.

"Uh-uh, Coach. You owe me a dance. I think I can do this one without breaking a hip."

Jude glanced around, nervously. Even in his teen years, he hadn't been a skilled dancer. Reluctantly, he grasped her right hand and put his arm around her waist. The top of her head came to the middle of his chest. She gazed up at him as they swayed.

"You promised stories," she said, after an awkward half-minute of silence.

"What?"

"When we met again the other day. I said you must have a lot of stories. You said you'd save them for later. It's later."

"There really isn't much to tell. College football, pro football, career-ending injury, San Francisco hippie—"

"You weren't."

"Hair halfway down my back, beard, love beads, crash pad, the whole scene, man."

"Acid, communes, orgies…"

"All part of the benefits package."

"So, why'd you come home?"

"You knew Billy Mosack?"

"Sure. What happened was terrible."

"I came back for the funeral. But before… Let's say I had nothing left in

San Francisco. The whole scene there is kind of a drag lately. It was groovy for a while, but it wilted on the vine."

She lay her cheek on his chest. "I wouldn't have come back if my mother hadn't died. With my sisters married and moved away, I was the only one to help Daddy. I don't mind coming home so much, but I don't want people to think I couldn't hack it in the world."

"I don't have to worry about that. I proved I couldn't hack it. Did it on national television. I guess I always knew I'd come home someday. Reckon I'll be here for the foreseeable future. I'm building a house."

"You are?"

"Out at the old Lincoln farm. Subdivided a few acres beside Six Mile Creek."

"I worried about returning," she said, smiling up at him. "I figured maybe I'd used up the pool of bachelors here who might be interested. I'm not on some sort of manhunt, but I didn't sign on to enter a nunnery at thirty either. Once you bury a husband, though, people treat you differently. At least I didn't have a baby. Babies are bachelor repellant, and they keep repelling for eighteen years. It's bad enough being a widow in her middle thirties."

"You'll do fine. You look great," Jude said.

"Says the older man." She laughed. "I appreciate it. And I gotta tell you, Coach, that Louisville Slugger you've been banging against my tits the last couple of minutes has done wonders for my self-esteem."

"What?" Jude became aware of his arousal. He started to back away, but he didn't want the entire student body to learn more than they had expected about their new football coach. As if sensing his impulse, she pulled him back toward her. "Oh, Jesus," he said, looking around. "I really didn't...I mean, I wasn't trying to...you know..."

"Relax," she said. "I've seen one angry before, though I must say yours seems particularly hostile. Let's dance in the direction of the boys' locker room. Soon as we're clear, you can make a dash for your office and do... *whatever* with that."

"I'm not going to do anything with it!"

"I mean make it go away, Coach. Take a cold shower or something. Jesus, you're cute when you're mortified."

* * *

Jude sat in his office, too embarrassed to return to the gym. Maybe, if he stayed until they turned the lights out, Grace would have gone home and he wouldn't have to face her.

She'd been so familiar in his arms. She was the same height, the same shape, and the same build as his memory of Coral. He was still primally conditioned to respond in the most instinctive and reflexive way in her arms.

Eventually, he decided he was being silly. He straightened his jacket and tie and ventured back into the gym. He found Grace standing with another teacher. She saw him at the same instant and waved him over. He pointed at his chest. She waved even more urgently. He navigated his way around the crowd dancing in the middle of the floor.

"Your dad and Rennie Poole are here. They've been looking for you. Have a nice shower?" She grinned mischievously.

"We'll never speak of this again."

"The hell we won't. I'm gonna milk this for years. Wait. That didn't come out right. Go see your father. He looked ripe to pop. Damn!"

He found Hubert and Rennie talking with Principal Black in the lobby. Black looked happy, but perhaps a little intimidated by Rennie. Hubert spied Jude at almost the same instant and waved him over.

"Coach Pressley!" Rennie said, gripping Jude's hand. "Boy, it feels good to call you that! How's the team look this year?"

"Impressive," Jude said. "I can't promise a championship, but we'll hold our own."

"Good to hear, son." Rennie finally released Jude's hand. "Your dad and I would like to show you something."

He followed Rennie and Hubert to Rennie's gold Lincoln Town Car in the parking lot. Rennie opened the trunk. In the spill of the streetlight, Jude saw an opened box revealing a brand-new football uniform, complete with helmet and pads, in Prosperity's team colors.

"I made a couple of phone calls," Rennie said. "I have a commitment from four large businesses in Bliss County to provide full uniforms for every player this season, with no cash outlay by the school. All you have to do is put signs promoting their businesses around the outside fence of the new stadium."

"Easily done," Jude said immediately. "I appreciate it. Nobody told me I was responsible for doing this. I'll be on top of it next summer."

"Not a problem, son. Not a problem at all," Rennie said, patting him on the shoulder. "There is one other thing we need to discuss. I have heard disturbing talk here and there that you're considering putting Tony Morven in as starting quarterback this year."

"I don't know why that would be disturbing." Jude glanced angrily at his father.

"Ty Bickford has been waiting two years for that position."

"So I've heard."

"He had a good record last year."

"That's true. But Tony has a faster forty-yard dash, he's nimbler, he throws a frozen rope, and I like his work ethic better."

"I'm sure he's good," Rennie argued. "But Ty is a senior."

"Football is a meritocracy, Mayor. The best players get on the first team. You want to win games, don't you?"

Rennie sighed. "I have failed to make my point adequately. Please allow me another attempt. I'll be blunt. Tony Morven is colored. He's as black as the underside of a manhole cover. While you were off in San Francisco braiding flowers in your hair and chanting and avoiding baths, things were changing around Bliss County, and not for the better. The feds forced us to close the colored schools and fully integrate them into the white schools. There are a lot of people still sore about that. Now, you want to slap them across the face by starting a black quarterback? I've always admired you, son, but that shit won't flush. Half the money I raised for the uniforms came from the tractor supply store in Morgan—you know, the place that rents out the harvesters and cultivators each year to half the population of

CHAPTER THIRTY-ONE

Prosperity? You know who owns the tractor supply?"

"No," Jude said, a cannonball-sized lump forming in the pit of his stomach.

"Wes Bickford, Ty's uncle. Wes is excited about Ty playing out his last year of high school eligibility as the starting quarterback. I believe he has some informal wagers going with Morgan's civic leaders regarding just how many touchdowns Ty will score this year."

Jude stared at the beautiful green and silver uniform in the trunk of Rennie's car. He imagined his entire team wearing the same uniforms, running out to the gridiron from the field house. Then he saw Tony Morven's potential and Ty Bickford's laziness and sloppy play, and his skin itched.

Jude stepped back. "The uniforms aren't a gift, are they?"

"I never give shit away for free," Rennie said. "It's bad for business. You look like someone licked the red off your candy cane. Relax. You have Tony Morven for two more years. He's a fast little buck. Put him on punt returns and special teams, and make sure he memorizes the playbook. Who knows how attitudes will change around here after Ty graduates?"

"Dad," Jude said. "I'd like to talk to Mayor Poole alone."

"Anything you can say to me..." Rennie started.

"It's alone or nothing."

Hubert looked back and forth at Rennie and Jude, and finally pulled out a handkerchief and mopped at his brow. "It's a mite hot out tonight anyway. Think I'll go in and get a Coke. Want anything, Mr. Poole?"

"No, Hubert. You go ahead. I'll catch up."

Hubert walked out of the circle of light from the pole lamp and disappeared into the darkness. Inside the gym, the Supremes sang about hearing a symphony.

"Do they have to play that boogie music?" Rennie complained.

"Half the *Billboard* list is from Motown these days. I guess you'd prefer the Four Freshmen."

"What is it you want to say?" Rennie said. "It's obvious you've got something stuck in your craw, boy—"

Jude put one hand on Rennie's shoulder and brought his other fist up almost from the asphalt into Rennie's midsection. Air exploded from the mayor's mouth. His eyes bulged, and his face turned ghastly pale as he gasped and tried to force wind into his paralyzed lungs. Jude grabbed him under the arms and helped him sit on the curb. He sat next to him as Rennie choked and heaved.

"That isn't about the uniforms, Mayor. When I mentioned them to my dad, I knew whatever you did would come with a price tag. I saw you with Billy Mosack's widow at the wake. She told me later you threatened to spread her past around if she didn't drop to the tile and swallow your grease gun. I'll play Bickford. In return, you provide the uniforms, *and* you lay off Chloe. This is just a sample. If I hear anyone passing gossip about her sex history, I'm looking for you first and you'll get the whole package."

"What the fuck do you care?" he gulped. "What's this woman to you?"

"She was my friend's widow, and she's dating Owen Wheeler."

"So, she's hit the perfecta. Think there's a hat trick in her? Only one leg of The Trinity left, right? Or maybe she's already done you. Is that why you're so pissy? Did you get a little racetrack honey poontang yourself?"

"You're small and disgusting. You're a worm. What my father ever saw in you mystifies me. I grew up in Prosperity, though. I know how things work. You lay off Chloe, all the way, and provide the uniforms, and Bickford will start his senior year."

Slowly, clumsily, Rennie made his way to his feet. He straightened his tie, pulled down his jacket, and slicked back his pomaded hair with his fingers.

"Deal," he said, trying to retain some degree of dignity. "The punch was unnecessary. I'll square it someday. You can count on it. I give you credit for taking the shot. It's more than I imagined of you. That's not a compliment. Now, shall we return to the gym and announce the football team is getting new uniforms? I hear a couple of reporters might be hanging around waiting for a scoop."

Chapter Thirty-Two

I n 1950, an enterprising man named Alan Schafer recognized that tourists driving from North Carolina to Myrtle Beach might enjoy a nice rest stop halfway. He built a Mexican-themed gas station and beer hall at a wide spot in the highway in Dillon, South Carolina. He installed a hundred-foot-high sombrero-wearing mariachi out front, lit up in red and green neon. Over the years, he installed carnival rides, a go-kart track, a two-hundred-foot observation tower topped with a ludicrously enormous sombrero as the viewing deck, a miniature golf course, a reptile zoo, restaurants, hotel rooms, and multiple gift shops purveying ersatz Mexican sombreros and ponchos and huaraches manufactured in China. Signs for fifty miles in every direction, on every highway, advised motoring tourists of the delights awaiting them at the Alan Schafer's South of the Border.

The laws in Dillon regarding marriage were relatively relaxed. If you wanted to get married, you could apply for a license in minutes without a blood test and swear your vows after a twenty-four-hour waiting period. For a generous gratuity, the magistrate might issue the license and perform the service at the same time, post-dating his signature as if you had waited. Dillon became a homing beacon for star-crossed teens, impatient paramours, kissing cousins, and anyone who wanted their nuptials quick and dirty.

Weary of answering the late-night desperate knocks on his door by eloping teenagers, a probate judge in downtown Dillon erected a twenty-four-hour wedding chapel next to the courthouse. Nobody ever considered making a formal complaint about conflicts of interest. The wedding boom in Dillon provided plenty of lucrative fallout to go around.

In late October, Owen Wheeler drove Chloe Mosack across the South Carolina line to the tiny town of Dillon. After checking in at Pedro's Hotel, they drove straight to the courthouse to get a license. They gorged themselves on burritos and tacos and two pitchers of Corona Special at the Sombrero Restaurant, only steps from their hotel room, and they went to bed and annoyed their neighbors for a couple of hours before collapsing into deep post-coital slumber. They awoke the next morning—hungover, cotton-mouthed, chafed, and not particularly attractive—and grinned like lovesick schoolchildren, because this was their wedding day.

It was as squalid as a blessed event could be. At exactly one-thirty, twenty-four hours after they applied for the license, they reappeared, showered, combed, and somberly dressed—if slightly wobbly—at the magistrate's office. They retrieved the endorsed license and joined the line at the wedding chapel. They were lucky. It was a slow day. Only nine couples waited ahead of them. The woman at the front desk asked whether they would enjoy serving as witnesses while they waited. By the time their turn came before the officiant, Owen could recite the service by rote.

Wearing gaudy straw sombreros, they hopped in the Fairlane and drove two hours to Myrtle Beach, where Owen had reserved an oceanfront hotel room. Two days later, they dragged their sore, aching, sunburned, alcohol-sodden bodies back into the Fairlane and pointed it toward Prosperity. Four days away from a farm was a luxurious vacation. Owen had to get back to work.

* * *

Nobody learned about the marriage until the following Friday night. Prosperity was playing Morgan High School for Homecoming. A dance was scheduled afterward in the gym, at which the Homecoming Queen would be announced. Jude and Grace were again obligated to chaperone.

Owen and Chloe had attended all the home games since August. Jude had seen them huddling in the grandstand, and he'd waved at them once or twice, but otherwise, they hadn't spoken. Jude was surprised on the sidelines, only minutes before the game, when they appeared next to him.

"You should be playing Tony Morven," Owen said.

"*I* should be playing for Green Bay. Tony will get his chance. How're you doing, kid?"

He held out his hand. Owen took it, pulled him in, and gave him a big hug.

"Chloe told me what happened, how you got Rennie off her back. There's a rumor going around you cleaned that asshole's clock out back of the gym. Please tell me it's true."

"It isn't. The mayor and I came to an agreement. That's why Bickford is starting. Forgetting anything he knew about Chloe is part of his end. I might have punctuated the point with a love tap to the solar plexus, mostly for my own satisfaction."

"He won't let that slide, brother. Hope you got eyes on your six. Sometimes it's hard to see Rennie when he makes a run at you."

"I'll be fine as long as we have a winning season. So, we're jake?"

"Sure. You're the first to know." He held up Chloe's left hand. The light from the field lights twinkled off a diamond roughly the size of a grain of rice.

"Really?" Jude asked.

"Jude Pressley, I'd like to introduce you to Chloe Wheeler."

"You may kiss the bride," Chloe told him.

He leaned in and gave her a peck on the cheek. She pouted.

"We're keeping it quiet," Owen said. "We were concerned about making a big announcement. I mean, Billy died only five months ago. It's a little sudden."

"We need a celebration, though," Jude said. "I moved into my house last week. Why don't you and Chloe come out this Saturday? We'll grill some steaks and toss back some beers. It'll be a combination housewarming and wedding reception."

"Won't you feel like a third wheel?" Chloe asked.

"I know someone I can ask to balance things out. Congratulations, you two. Really. I have to get back to work, or those are the only congrats anyone is handing out tonight."

* * *

Ty Bickford rolled his ankle and pulled up lame after two possessions. Jude seized the opportunity to insert Tony Morven as quarterback. The junior lit up Morgan High for twenty-one unanswered points almost before they could blink.

In the fourth quarter, Prosperity led by fifteen with only a few seconds left. Jude spotted Rennie Poole in the grandstand. The congressional election was a week and a half away, and he was politicking like a demon. He'd buttonholed a couple of men and seemed to by laying out his platform point by point. Jude caught his eye, pointed at Tony Morven, held up two fingers, indicating the number on the second-string quarterback's jersey, and shot a thumbs-up. Rennie scowled and turned back to his captive audience.

That moment was as satisfying as winning the game.

* * *

"You remember Owen Wheeler?" Jude asked Grace as they observed students file into the gym for a victorious Homecoming Dance.

"Are you kidding? Everyone remembers Owen. He was one of The Trinity. Him and two other guys. Can't recall their names, but one of them is on the sign outside the new stadium."

"Okay. I deserved that. I lived at his place this past summer. We've stayed tight over the years. Did you ever meet Billy Mosack's wife?"

"I was out of town the week Billy died. I missed the funeral."

"Her name's Chloe. She met Owen at the funeral, and they hit it off."

"At the funeral?"

"Over time. Maybe a couple of months later."

"Oh, well, as long as she waited a decent interval."

"You don't approve."

"You never lost a husband, Jude. I don't want to talk about this right now. Keep an eye on Huggie Newton. I saw him pull a flask out of his jacket a few minutes ago. He's a sneaky little shit. We'll talk after the dance."

* * *

As the crowd thinned, Jude took the opportunity to step back to his office, where he dropped his jacket. In the locker room, he collected stray towels from the benches, tossing them into a canvas rolling bin. The custodian would wash and fold them, but Jude didn't think it was fair to ask him to collect also. He checked the showers to make sure the faucets were closed.

He jumped a little when Grace said, "So, this is where they keep all the naked men." She leaned against the tiled privacy partition separating the hallway from the locker room. Her pocketbook was slung on one shoulder. She carried her coat over her arm.

"One or two have passed through here."

"Smells like a locker room. You should do something about that. Hang up some of those pine tree air fresheners. Done soon?"

"Finishing up. Turning out the lights."

"How much gas do you have?"

"Full tank."

"Let's take a drive. We have things to discuss."

He scanned her face, looking for any clue. As always, she was inscrutable.

"I'll grab my jacket," he said.

Arlo's Garage had delivered the rejuvenated Willys just after Labor Day. It looked as immaculate as it had the day he finished it in high school.

"Your dad's shop did a great job on the car." He started the engine. The seats vibrated with the rumble of the hot cam and the new glass pack mufflers. "Took it almost down to the frame, but it's as clean as new. I put in a new radio. The old one didn't get FM."

"Drive," she said.

"Yes ma'am. Any place in particular?"

"I don't care. Take a header. Get us lost."

He pulled out of the school lot and turned onto Wiley Crook Road. As he cruised over the hilly country blacktops, stands of longleaf pine and poplar and oak and cherry flashing by in a dark blur, he searched the radio for a station.

"Leave it," she said.

"Have I said something to upset you?"

"It's not you."

They drove another mile, the twin headlights cutting through the darkness, their faces illuminated only by the orange glow of the instruments on the dash. No other cars shared the back-country road. They cruised through opaque open space as obscure as the void between galaxies.

"Being inducted into The Sudden Widows' Club is a crash course in bad decisions," she said.

"We're talking about Chloe?"

"You know any other new widows in town, Coach? I suppose being a race driver is a lot like being a soldier. You go in calculating the odds, but you never imagine the really big dice rolling against you. It's always the other guy who gets it. Each of us sees ourselves as the hero in our life story. Sometimes, we're the plucky sidekick. Sometimes we're collateral damage."

"Jesus," Jude said.

"Too deep?"

"I was thinking the same thing a few months ago."

She turned to him. "Really?"

"You're surprised? I just came off a five-year vacation from reality. You don't commit many heroic acts lounging on a blanket tripping your balls off in Golden Gate Park. You think Chloe is sleepwalking through this thing with Owen?"

"Doesn't sound like she's thought things through. This woman was married to one of Owen's closest friends five months ago. When you told me she'd taken up with Owen, weeks after Billy died, all the bad switches went off in my head. She's still grieving, but she doesn't know it."

"Oh, boy."

CHAPTER THIRTY-TWO

"What?"

"You're gonna hate this next part. They're married."

"Take the next right."

"That's the turnoff to The Bluffs."

"So?"

He glanced at her. She stared straight ahead, into the darkness.

He parked the car at The Bluffs a few minutes later. The scene was almost too familiar. The Willys. The Bluffs. The blonde in the passenger seat. He had known all along that the closer they got, sooner or later she might make a move. He'd already decided it would be up to her. He wasn't going to intentionally stoke his own guilt over Coral. If Grace decided to flood him with affection, Jude would have to decide whether to be swept away. It seemed the moment had come.

"Ah, Grace—"

"Married? They're *married*?"

"Um… yeah."

"When?"

"Last weekend. They drove to Dillon and did it there."

"In the shadow of the giant Pedro sign? Man, your buddy Owen is some yokel."

"He has a good heart."

"Hope it's insured."

"Yeah," he chuckled, but saw her face was serious again. "Oh. You… weren't joking."

"I don't see a future for this marriage."

"That's going to make this next part harder. I invited Owen and Chloe to the new house for a cookout this Saturday. I hoped you'd come, too."

"Like, as a date?"

"It's a free steak. All the beer you can drink. It's a celebration dinner. They aren't making a big deal about the wedding."

"Sure wouldn't want to make a big deal out of your own wedding. There's one light you want to keep under a bushel. Be honest, Coach. Do I need Listerine?"

"What?"

"Or are you one of those closet homos?"

"A closet... No!"

"Because it's fine with me if you are, but you really should keep the blinds on your office window closed. Don't want to lead yourself into temptation."

"Wait... what?"

"Jesus," she said. "You are so adorably dense."

She launched herself at him across the bench seat, planting her lips on his, her tongue probing him. The decision was made. He was swept downstream on the current of her. Eventually, she came up for air.

"High damn time," she said. "I've been meaning to do that for days."

"What?"

"You say *what* a lot. Don't tell me you haven't thought about it. I decided to get it out of the way. What do you think?"

"Is that a yes or a no on dinner?"

She smiled and leaned in toward him again.

"I'm weak. I can't resist a thick piece of meat. Sure. I'll be there. Are you going to kiss me again or something? It's getting chilly in here."

* * *

Chloe and Owen arrived on Saturday afternoon in the Fairlane. Neither had yet seen Jude's house.

"It's lovely," Chloe said as Owen helped her from the car. She accepted a kiss on the cheek from Jude. "And they built it so quickly. This isn't one of those new pre-fab homes, is it?"

"I had a great contractor," Jude said.

Grace stepped down the stairs to the driveway.

"I know you," Owen said. "You're Arlo Pyle's daughter. Grace."

"I'm surprised you remember," Grace said.

"Jude told you Chloe and I are married?"

"Congratulations. Why don't we all go to the back porch? There's a fire in the outside hearth, and we have some snacks out there. Jude's set up the grill."

"Am I wrong?" Owen asked Jude as they walked into the house. "Did you buy the land next to the spot we found on the creek?"

"The Ledge? Sure did. We can walk down in a bit if you like. I own it. My property line goes to the middle of Six Mile Creek."

"Why not now? Chloe, you should see this place."

"Maybe another time, Puddin'," Chloe said as she poured a generous glass of wine. "Mama's shoes aren't built for tramping around in the woods. Grace and I can amuse ourselves while you two reminisce."

* * *

"It's smaller than I remember," Owen said, as he and Jude walked on the rock shelf projecting out into the center of the creek. "Fishing still good?"

"I haven't tried yet. Busy season, coaching and all. Not really sure why I bought it at all."

He picked up a flat rock and skipped it across the pool, creating a series of concentric targets in the placid water.

"How does Grace like it?" Owen asked.

"Haven't shown it to her yet."

"Why not?"

Jude skipped another rock along the surface of the pool. "No reason, I suppose."

"Watch out for mermaids!" On the opposite bank, Clyde Dillard stood with a fancy fishing rig and a creel. He wore rubber waders over a pair of overalls and a red plaid flannel shirt.

"What's that, Clyde?" Jude called back.

"Mermaids! They're real. I seen 'em, right here in Six Mile Creek."

Owen shook his head. "I think you drank from the wrong bottle this morning!"

"I seen 'em, I tell you. Well, only one, but she was something! Blonde and blue-eyed and perky-titted, like some kinda fairy rising from the water. A goddamn mermaid!"

"When was this?" Owen sounded more amused than interested.

"A few years back. I keep coming here, gonna see another one someday, betcha. You keep an eye out. Watch out for the mermaid."

He waved and hiked downstream, toward the bridge over the Old Village Road.

"What do you make of that?" Owen asked.

"Clyde drinks," Jude said. He hoped Owen couldn't hear the fearful tremor in his voice.

Chapter Thirty-Three

Officer D. B. Edge walked into Belle's Breakfast Buffet in Morgan on a bright, sunny, Saturday morning in 1971. He piled his plate high with bacon, sausage, grits, eggs, biscuits with gravy, and stewed prunes to push it all through, and settled at his usual booth at the huge picture window. He arranged the silverware and his plate and the napkin and his cup of coffee and bowed his head to give thanks to the Almighty, who promptly smote him. Edge nosed over into his breakfast as his main cerebral artery burst. The autopsy said he was dead before his face hit the plate.

Garveyville threw a huge block party when the word got out. Angeloe Teeter wasn't there to join in the festivities, as he was busy graduating from Johnson C. Smith University in Charlotte, a semester early. He had majored in sociology, a hot field of study in the early 1970s as people tried to grapple with immense changes in the roles of women and minorities and understand the tumult of the previous decade and how it still reverberated like a gong. His minor was religion since he planned to become a preacher like Dr. King.

The prospect of social change lured Angeloe to Gary, Indiana in March of 1972 for the first National Black Political Convention.

Gary had been chosen for the convention because it boasted a strong, vibrant colored community, and had even elected a black mayor. The convention drew participants from all over the country. They represented fundamentalist Christian denominations, members of the Nation of Islam, militant soldiers of the Black Panther Movement, congressmen, and college professors. There were black nationalists, school integrationists, and ordinary people from major cities and small towns across America, brought together for the single purpose of enacting an agenda that would best serve the needs of all people, but especially the long-neglected needs of the black community.

Dr. King was gone, shot to death by a lowlife ex-pornographer at a hotel in Memphis, but there was no shortage of firebrands ready to take up his mantle. Angeloe was particularly interested in the rhetoric of a young preacher from South Carolina named Jesse Jackson. Only thirty years old, six years older than Angeloe, Reverend Jackson claimed King had died in his arms. In Angeloe's mind, that made Jackson heir apparent to King's legacy.

One of his professors at college had advised him toward modest expectations, but to make those expectations the focus of everything he did. "The secret of happiness," he'd said, "is learning to bloom where you're planted."

Angeloe was inspired. He recognized the same rule that had driven Rennie Poole for years. *All politics are local.*

The great civil rights leaders of the world might descend on a rural flyspeck like Morgan from time to time, and their impact was invariably electrifying. For every headline-grabbing general in the war for human and civil rights who flew in to give marching orders before winging away again to the next engagement, someone had to remain in the trenches, ready to go over the top into a hail of opposing fire and keep the battle engaged. What Garveyville lacked—what all of Bliss County lacked—was the spiritual commander who could keep the fires of equality burning long after the headliners were gone.

Angeloe thought he might be that person. He was called on a mission. He was small and wiry, but his devotion was strong. He might not tip the world, but he intended to make his tiny corner of it quake.

* * *

Rennie Poole was scheduled to appear at Prosperity High School to present congressional awards to specially selected students who had written essays on *What America Means to Me*. He didn't particularly care what the essays said. The entire enterprise was a put-on to provide him some camera time doing something other than stump speeches in a critical re-election campaign.

Rennie had recognized early on he could be successful in rural Bliss County on the whites-only vote, but it never hurt to buy a little insurance. He'd ensured at least half the essay contest winners were black, and he'd instructed the cameraman filming the proceedings to record him handing awards to *those* students. He was extremely careful to quash any suggestions he hadn't always been as open-minded. People who spread such rumors in Bliss County often discovered their lives changed, and not for the better.

Owen Wheeler was a particular annoyance. Rennie reviewed his life from time to time, mostly as an exercise in keeping score. He occasionally tried to recall any instance in which he might have treated Owen's father unfavorably. Amos Wheeler had been as racist as any other white farmer of his time, and he'd have benefitted from Rennie's klavern had he ever bothered to join. Despite repeated invitations and cajoling, Amos had stood firm. Even after Rennie dissolved the klavern—out of political expedience—and doffed his robe and hood, Amos found him detestable, and by extension, any organization Rennie Poole ran must be rotten to the core.

Poole had entertained greater hopes for Owen, especially after he and his high school buddies delivered Ev Howard to him, but had discovered he was equally incapable of controlling Amos's boy. Jude had sealed one avenue with their bargain in the high school parking lot, allowing Owen Wheeler to set himself up in opposition to Rennie. Increasingly, over the years, Owen had challenged him at town meetings. He showed up at each council session prepared to argue against any initiative Rennie had passed down the line. Some people chuckled. Owen was known to drink heavily. People sitting nearby were swathed in alcohol fumes during his diatribes before the Council.

When he'd decided to run for Congress, Rennie wasn't yet ready to release his hold on Prosperity. He'd talked Hubert Pressley into running for mayor. Hubert was a shoo-in. If Rennie lost his congressional election, which was improbable, he could still retain control over Prosperity through Hubert, and over the rest of agricultural Bliss County through his business empire. Affable, agreeable, not exceedingly bright Hubert Pressley would do whatever Rennie directed.

With Hubert as mayor, and most of the Town Council in Prosperity also hand-picked by Congressman Poole, the pillars of power in the tiny crossroads had consolidated by 1972 precisely as Rennie had anticipated.

One other change had taken place. Rennie decided his given nickname no longer fit the image of a legislator of national prominence. He'd reverted to the actual name on his birth certificate—Reynolds. Everyone across the county still called him Rennie, and he granted the privilege freely, except when attending a public event, when he insisted on being referred to formally.

The awards ceremony took place on the football field, the only place on campus large enough to hold the entire student population. A lectern and a semicircle of chairs had been arranged in the center of the field. At Principal Black's request, Jude was part of the ceremony. He and Hubert waited in chairs behind the lectern, along with the winning students.

"Where is he?" Jude demanded. His father shook his head.

"Said he'd be here right at ten. Let's wait five more minutes. If he doesn't show, we'll—"

He was interrupted by a roar and the rhythmic thump of rotor blades as a helicopter popped up over the woods behind the visitors' grandstand, swept in over the school and stopped, hovering in midair directly over the football field near the end zone. It descended gracefully and settled onto the turf. Rennie Poole hopped out and ran across the field, waving at the cheering crowd with both hands. In the main grandstand, two local television news crews sprang to life to film the spectacle.

Jude scowled. "Has to make an entrance."

Rennie, without acknowledging either Jude or Hubert, stepped to the microphone and directly addressed the crowd.

"Sorry I'm a few minutes late, folks! I had a pressing engagement in

Pooler. I am pleased and proud to represent our congressional district, and especially my hometown of Prosperity! We can all be proud of the citizens our community is producing, as evidenced by the essays my office received in response to this contest. It is my great privilege and honor to award these wonderful young people, the future of our great nation, and to recognize their deep and abiding love for and faith in our country."

A smattering of applause rippled through the students in the grandstand. Lunchtime loomed, and they were restless and irritable. Few of them cared about Rennie Poole or the nerds on the field getting medals. More of them were intrigued by the helicopter.

Rennie introduced Hubert to the crowd, some of whom were aware he was mayor. Most were unimpressed. The congressman said, "And, I want to take a moment to congratulate the mayor's son, our own football coach Jude Pressley, on his state championship this past season!"

The students erupted. They could easily relate to Prosperity football. Jude stood and waved to the throng but didn't approach the lectern. Rennie waved at him once or twice to come forward, but Jude took his seat again. Unfazed, Rennie continued, handing out the medals and plaques to each of the six students, taking every opportunity to mug for the cameras as he did.

As Principal Black dismissed the students, Hubert put a hand on Jude's shoulder.

"Hey, son. Got any Pepto in your office?" His face was dotted with sweat, and his cheeks were ruddy.

"Sure," Jude said. "Bottle of it in the cabinet next to my desk. I'll walk you over."

Rennie stopped them. "Thanks for vamping for me, Hubert. I hoped to get away from Pooler sooner."

"Don't look now," Jude said. "I think your pressing engagement left lipstick on your collar."

"Really? She did?" Rennie asked, before realizing what he was saying. "Well, shit. Gotta keep the constituents happy, you know. Jude, I'd like to talk to you for a few minutes, if you don't mind."

"We're headed to my office," Jude said.

223

"Alone," Rennie said.

Jude thought it over. "Okay. Here's my office key, Dad."

Hubert held the key up, winked at them, and lumbered away.

"Good man, your dad," Rennie said.

"What do you want?"

"Have I said something to offend?"

"Breathing your air is offensive, Congressman. You only want to powwow when you need something. Don't mistake anything I say for constructive criticism. We aren't buddies."

"That's the problem," Rennie said. "Buddies, that is. I need you to have a word with your buddy Owen. He's getting in the way of a lot of important initiatives. You know what it takes to get re-elected in this district?"

"Extortion?"

"Pork, boy. Every year, we send tax money to Washington. My job is to get our fair share of it back. Like the watershed project two years ago or bringing a photo development company to Morgan. To make sure we get what we're due, I have to lay the groundwork with things like local zoning and such. I need the town councils and county commissions."

"Shouldn't be problem. You own most of them."

"Your friend likes to stir up dirt. He interrupts and impedes the orderly completion of town business. He confuses the councilmen—"

"With facts?"

"He exposes them to information irrelevant to the purpose of the ordinance."

"He tells them what will happen when they implement those ordinances. Your precious watershed project displaced fifteen families. Four of them moved out of Bliss County."

"The price of progress, boy."

"Owen doesn't measure progress by your yardstick. I can't help you, Congressman. I don't think we see this issue from the same angle. If you don't mind, I need to get back to work."

He turned toward the gym, but Rennie grabbed him by the shirt sleeve and dragged him back around.

"I don't think you understand. I'm not asking this as a favor. Not for me. For Owen. He's near the head of the line for a beat-down. He's been on Sheriff Mattox's shitlist for years. Now that Larry Stilson is Chief Deputy... well, I don't have to tell you there's bad blood between Wheeler and Stilson. You know what a man wearing a badge and a gun can do in Bliss County, Jude?"

"What?"

"Any goddamn thing he pleases. I got a chopper waiting. Remember what I said. Tell Owen to get his head on right. You can spare your friend a ton of grief."

He gave a mock salute and retreated across the field toward the waiting helicopter. Jude tried to unscramble the meaning of Rennie's words, as thinly veiled a threat as he'd encountered.

The custodians stacked the chairs and wedged a hand truck beneath the lectern. The grandstands had emptied. A breeze whistled through the bare branches of the oaks and maples and poplars. It brought a pocket of cooler air that made Jude shiver.

He'd savored the moment when Tony Morven was offered a full scholarship to play football at LSU after winning the conference championship his senior year. Rennie's favorite, Ty Bickford, rode the pine for two years at a juco in South Carolina before dropping out to work for his uncle in Morgan. Jude might have gotten new uniforms for playing Bickford, but Tony had given him a championship trophy.

Before Tony headed off for LSU, Jude had sat him down in his office. He was a good-looking boy—tall, broad in the shoulder, with quick eyes and a winning smile. Smart, too, top ten percent of his class.

"You know I played in the NFL," Jude began.

"Yes, Coach. I saw the film."

"I reckon half the human race has seen that damned film," Jude said. "I can talk to you like that, because you're leaving high school and heading out to college. I suppose, like every college player, you think someday you'll lead your team onto the field at the Super Bowl."

"Gosh, Coach, I'm not even at college yet."

"I know. I just want you to understand the pressures that are going to be placed on you."

And he had explained, step by step, all the compromises Tony would be faced with over the coming years. He outlined how other people would try to control him.

Finally, he advised, "If I can tell you only one thing, it would be don't build your life around the game. Don't presume it will always be there to prop you up, because when it ends, it ends in a second, and you never know when it's coming. Build your life on something else. Find the thing you can't live without. I guarantee it won't be football."

Jude's heart broke when Tony Morven's car ran off a highway in his freshman year at college, flipped into a blackwater marsh, and landed on its roof, trapping the youth inside. He avoided thinking about the greasy muck rising as Tony beat against the thick glass windshield, believing he'd be saved until the instant the light blinked out behind his eyes.

Like the weather on this late winter day, Jude and Grace had run hot and cold for four years. For weeks, they would spend every night together, alternating between houses, and then—almost like flipping a switch—not at all for months. Twice a year, their erotic tanks ran dry, and they came together for a top-up. Eventually, sated, they slowly drifted apart. Months later, they would forget why they weren't seeing one another and, attracted by their mutual gravity, accrete like primordial dust. At that moment, they were on the outs, but prom season was on the way, and summer vacation, which meant another long trip somewhere together. Grace was due at his door any day. If she didn't show, Jude wouldn't force it.

Leaving the course of their affair to Grace allowed him to rationalize that he wasn't somehow cheating on Coral with her sister. He was completely aware of how creepy that might sound to others, but at least nobody could accuse him of pursuing Grace.

Then there was Owen, who was in greater trouble than Rennie imagined. When he and Chloe had married, Owen—already in his middle thirties—had told Jude he expected they would have a baby as soon as possible. Chloe, still in her late twenties, was chillier to the notion. A year had passed. Then two.

Almost four years after their wedding, Owen and Chloe remained childless. Owen tried to put a brave face on it, but the disappointment in his eyes was unmistakable. Beyond the tragedy of being unable to conceive and enjoy the experience of watching his children grow from childhood into maturity, there was an issue of inheritance. The farm had been in the hands of a Wheeler since before the Revolutionary War. Chloe had confessed to Grace during dinner at Jude's house that she knew she could have babies, because she'd traveled all the way to New York City in 1960 to get rid of one. The problem, she told Grace, did not lie with her.

Faced with the prospect of being the last Wheeler to own his land, Owen had thrown himself into a campaign to preserve as much of the Prosperity he'd known as he could. That meant becoming the fly in Rennie Poole's lemonade. The more Poole tried to make Prosperity a suburb of Parker County to the north, plowing under three-hundred-year-old farms to build tract houses, the harder Owen resisted.

Accustomed to a faster, brighter world, Chloe had told Grace she was stifled by the farm. She'd given it every honest effort but as the years passed a subtle barrier grew between her and Owen, a filmy distortion clouding their ability to see one another clearly.

Jude felt everything spinning out of control. He'd lived in Prosperity for over half his life, but some days he couldn't find it anywhere.

He pulled back the door separating the gym from the locker rooms and called, "Dad, I'm meeting Grace for lunch in a few minutes. I need to lock the office."

Nobody replied.

Curious, Jude walked the short hallway to his office door.

Hubert Pressley sat in Jude's office chair, an unopened bottle of Pepto on the desk in front of him. One arm hung limply over the back of the chair, as if he'd used it to prop himself up. His eyes stared blankly at the drawn Venetian blinds. His mouth hung open, his jaw slack. His head tilted slightly to one side. A rank, sour smell filled the room.

Jude dashed to his father's side. He palpated his wrist repeatedly, trying to find a pulse. He checked the carotid artery in Hubert's neck. He did it over and over, as if he'd done it wrong and only needed to change his technique to alter reality.

He stepped back, sat on the edge of his desk, rubbed his chin, and tried to make sense of the entire scene.

"Well. Fuck a duck," he said.

Chapter Thirty-Four

"**M**assive heart attack," Jude told Chloe as they hovered over a platter of cold cuts and cheese, making tiny sandwiches. "He thought he had indigestion. Doctor said his coronary arteries were almost completely blocked. Could have gone anytime."

Jude held the wake at his house. It was familiar ground, and he hadn't found an opportunity to go through his father's house and secure any valuables. Funerals, especially those of prominent men in a community, tended to draw from a wide swath of mourners, many of whom Jude hadn't met. He was more comfortable keeping an eye on them in a place he knew better than his father's home.

"I'm so sorry," Chloe said. "It must have been a huge shock."

"He started pounding on the weight when I was twelve, after Mom died. Got to a point he couldn't see any purpose in controlling it. Doctor told him he was diabetic a decade ago. He was sort of a time bomb. He took some pills, but he'd have been better off if he'd lost a hundred pounds."

Rennie sidled next to Jude.

"Can we talk?" the congressman asked.

Jude made his apologies to Chloe for the interruption. Rennie didn't bother. Jude led him down the hallway to his office. He'd installed a California claro walnut desk with a high-backed leather chair and matching side chairs. A glass case in the corner held a replica of the trophy presented to him the year Tony Morven led Prosperity to the conference championship, a picture of Tony in his Prosperity uniform next to it. Rennie crossed the room to the case and peered at the trophy and the picture.

"This is the colored boy who got killed," he said.

"Yes."

"I remember we discussed him a few years back. You decided Ty Bickford was a better quarterback."

"That's the way you recall it? What do you want, Rennie?"

"Don't get me wrong. This colored boy—"

"Tony Morven," Jude interrupted.

"What's that?"

"He wasn't *this colored boy*. He had a name. Tony Morven."

"Meant no offense, Coach. I realize you must have had some fondness for him. As I was saying, Tony was a fine player in his own right. He did his race proud."

"He did Prosperity proud. I have a house full of people outside the door, Congressman. If you have a point, would you get to it?"

"Of course. Your father… ah… that is… Hubert's sudden and grievous passing has had a profound impact on me. I don't know whether you ever appreciated the extent to which I depended upon him."

"I know you kept him on a short leash and fed him scraps. I know he took more midnight telephone calls from you than I can count on both hands and feet, and he was always out the door five minutes later. I know he considered you some sort of benevolent despot, without whom he'd never have achieved half as much. You were his favorite drug, Rennie. He couldn't get enough. In return, I think you regard his passing the way you'd mourn a devoted hound dog. Does anything I've said surprise you?"

Rennie placed both hands on the desktop. "I suspect your grief is influencing your words, so I will absorb them graciously. I wished to express my condolences to you personally, nothing more."

"I don't suppose you're at all interested in my father's bank accounts."

"Say again?"

"I met with Dad's attorney the day after he died. We went over his will. Seems it dated back to when Mom was still alive, before you completely polluted his life. He left everything to Mom. He never wrote another will. Since Mom predeceased him, everything goes to me."

"Everything," Rennie echoed.

"Everything," Jude repeated. "The attorney provided me with a list of bank accounts. All were in Dad's name. No corporate accounts. All personal. The deposit records are fascinating. Every month, on or about the first. All in round numbers—five hundred, a thousand. I'm no expert, Congressman, but if I were running a slush fund, I'd want to make it a little less obvious. Throw in a little loose change once in a while. But that's me. You're the Pro from Dover."

"I have no idea what you're talking about."

"It is an impressive amount of money."

"Yes," Rennie said. "I can imagine your surprise. You... you obviously have a lot on your mind. I won't take up too much of your time. I wanted to tell you how sad I was over your father's death."

"Thanks. I saw Sally Mosack bring in some fried chicken. You want to make sure you get some before you go."

Rennie walked toward the door. His hand made it as far as the knob. He glared at Jude. "The money. It isn't mine. I mean, it didn't come from me. There are people out there who expect a...well, a return on their investment."

"Give it to them. Take the loss. What you're selling doesn't cost you a penny."

"But... hat's..."

"Hundreds of thousands. Damned near a million. Think of it as a business loss. You take the hit and move on. I appreciate you admitting where it came from. I knew my dad was your personal cock socket, but I'd hate to think he was whoring for just *anyone* with a checkbook."

"Awful damned self-righteous, aren't you? Might want to pull the nails from your palms, Jude. You didn't earn them. How much money have you taken from the Prosperity High boosters?"

"Not a penny. They bought our new uniforms each of the last three years, because that's what boosters do. Didn't they tell you? Maybe you don't know your constituents as well as you think. While you're chewing on that one, consider something else. Why do you think my father never wrote another will, even though he knew he was tending your illicit fortune? He knew everything would go to me. Maybe he wanted it that way. After years of cleaning up your messes all across Bliss County, and getting treated like a lackey in the process, maybe he decided he'd get in one major fuck-you when he shuffled off into the hereafter. I think he wanted me to have the money, just to spite you. How about that, Mr. Congressman? The master manipulator got played by his fool. Dad spoofed all of us. He played the really long game. Maybe I'll take it into overtime. Might donate it to your Democratic challenger next election. Wouldn't that be a hoot? Hey, make sure you grab some of that chicken on the way out. Sally Mosack can fry the shit out of a chicken."

* * *

The mourners dwindled to Grace, Owen, and Chloe. Jude had been grateful when they tossed in and helped clear the accumulated dishes and flatware and trash. He located a couple of bottles of cabernet, and they sat on the screened porch.

"Rennie didn't look happy," Owen said. His voice was slurred.

"It's a funeral," Jude said. "Unhappy people get a pass today."

"What happens now?" Owen asked. "Do they hold a new election for the mayor's office?"

"Jesus, Owen," Chloe said. "Let the dirt settle first."

"It's a legitimate question," Jude said. "World keeps spinning. Art Tomkins is the mayor *pro tem*. From what I hear, he has his eyes on taking the job full-time."

"That would create an opening on the council," Owen observed.

"You should run," Jude told Owen. "How would you like that, Chloe? Wife of a town councilman?"

"I see him seldom enough now," Chloe said, quietly.

"Life of a farmer, babe," Owen said, patting her hand. "Work from cain't see to cain't see. It's an idea, you know. Rennie can't own every voter in Prosperity. There have to be hundreds of people who would like to see someone on the council who isn't in Rennie's pocket."

Jude emptied the bottom of a bottle into his glass. "Another couple of snorts, and you might decide to run against Rennie for Congress in November."

"Now, there's an idea!" Owen shouted.

Jude felt an urgency and excused himself. He stepped into the bedroom and used his private bath. He walked out and found Chloe sitting on his bed. She crossed the room to him. She stood only an inch or so away and peered up into his eyes.

"Don't encourage my husband."

"Pardon?"

"You don't know how things are on the Wheeler spread. I see my dentist as often as I see Owen's cock. Ask Grace. She knows everything. She's the only person I can talk to in this fuckin' town. I don't need Owen running for town council. If he loses, it'll break him. Don't feed his drunken fantasies. And if you were a real friend, you'd get him in a program. He won't listen to me."

"A program?"

"One of those twelve-step jobs. Your buddy has a real problem. He's shooting blanks. Most nights he can't even find his cannon. After he gets up to piss, the bathroom smells like a distillery. I'm not saying this to embarrass you. He doesn't need more complications in his life. Be a pal. Get him straight."

"Owen's on his own trip," Jude said. "He's never taken the first piece of advice I've offered."

"That's what I like about you, Slick. Your detachment is a constant. Thanks for the support. It means a lot. Maybe I married the wrong Trinity guy."

"Which time?"

"Both of them. Don't take it as a compliment. It's a reflection on my own weakness."

She threw her arms around his neck, pulled herself up, and planted her mouth on his. Her lips parted, and her tongue darted around his teeth. He could feel her breasts pressed against his chest, and he responded to her, even as he was compelled to push her away. She drew back and brushed at an errant hair across her forehead.

"Four years. I got tired of waiting. If it weren't for Grace, I'd think you were some kind of pansy." She cupped his stiff phallus in her palm. "Sweet. Nice to see I still have it. You'd never know it around my house. Might want to wipe off your mouth. You got lipstick smeared on it. Got any more cabernet?"

Chapter Thirty-Five

The first week of September, Owen Wheeler walked into the Voter Registration office in Morgan and declared his candidacy for Prosperity Town Council.

The day after registering for the election, he drove into Wolfville to the Feed and Seed. As soon as he walked through the door, the manager stepped from behind the counter.

"Sorry, Owen," he said. "Boss says your money's no good here anymore."

"Say that again?"

"Got a telephone call from Mr. Poole this morning. Said I wasn't to sell you any goods at all. I haven't heard Mr. Poole this angry since... well, ever. He called all the way from Washington. Told me to let you know it's no good driving to Mica Wells or Morgan, because they won't sell to you either. I'm sorry to turn away a dependable long-time customer, but orders are orders."

When he told Chloe about it over dinner, her face clouded. She didn't say another word until the dishes were finished. Owen settled on the couch, staring at *M*A*S*H* on the television. Chloe dropped onto the couch beside him. She turned off the set. He didn't look at her. He could feel her frustration from the other side of the sofa.

"You shouldn't have registered," she said. "You brought trouble on yourself."

"Someone has to take a stand. Rennie controls the Town Council, the Sheriff's Department, every farm supply store in Bliss County, and half the Bliss County Commission. He's like a despotic medieval earl. Someone has to row upstream for a change."

"Why does it have to be you?"

"Nobody else stepped up."

"He'll destroy you."

"He can try. He doesn't own the supply stores in Parker County."

"I'm not talking about the farm. He's going to try to destroy *you*. Personally. He's going to come at you with both barrels blazing. God knows, he has enough with the drinking alone. He knows things about me he could use. If he comes at you through me, I don't think I could stand it."

"If he does, I'll—"

"What? Beat him up? Challenge him to a duel? Kill him? You don't have much of an arsenal compared to his. He can hit at you from a dozen different angles. All you have is righteous indignation."

"I'm going for a walk," Owen grabbed his jacket.

"I'll come with you."

"Don't. My head feels like it's about to burst. I wish I could understand how you think. It's like you can't see the world beyond the end of your nose. Don't look at me like that. This shouldn't be news to you."

He returned an hour later but didn't go inside. In the still, crisp, fall night sky, the new moon revealed the filmy sweep of the Milky Way laid out like a wispy three-dimensional painting. The outside lights were extinguished. In the stand of trees separating the house from the Morgan Highway, he could hear animals scurrying through recently harvested fields.

He opened his fourth beer of the night.

* * *

Two days later, Owen needed a new fuel filter and fuel pump for the tractor, which was getting balky and slow to start. When he walked into the tractor supply store in Morgan, Ty Bickford stepped from behind the counter. The former high school quarterback had gone to suet since leaving his junior college to work for his uncle. He was paunchy and sallow. He wore a royal blue broadcloth shirt with sodden armpits and a yellow tie that made an inverted question mark as it rode over his protruding belly.

"Need a fuel filter and pump for a Massey-Ferguson," Owen said.

"Can't help you, Mr. Wheeler," Ty said.

"Don't have it in stock?"

"Naw. We got it. Just not for you. Uncle Wes said we weren't to trade with you anymore. He didn't say why, but there it is."

"Is Wes here?"

"Not today. Wouldn't do you any good to talk to him anyway. He was really clear about it. *We don't sell to Owen Wheeler,* he said. *No ifs, ands, or buts.*"

"Let me guess. He also said if I wanted parts, I could drive over to Parker County and buy them there."

"No, sir. He told me, and this is a quote, *'If Wheeler wants parts for his farm machines, he can go straight to Hell.'* I was surprised. Uncle Wes ain't the type to cuss. He's a church deacon, you know."

* * *

Halfway back to Prosperity, Owen saw flashing lights in his mirror and heard a quick *whoop* from a siren behind him. He pulled the truck over to the side of the road and waited, license and registration in hand, for the deputy to approach him. Larry Stilson stepped out and strode up the driver's side of the truck. He didn't ask for the papers. Instead, he leaned in, sniffed a couple of times, and looked Owen in the eye.

"Mr. Wheeler, have you been drinking today?"

"It's ten in the morning, Stilson," Owen said. "What do you think?"

"Sheriff's Department dispatch got a call from Ty Bickford at the tractor supply. Says you was over there making a ruckus, and they refused you service. Ty said he smelled alcohol on you."

Owen took a deep breath and blew it gently in Stilson's face.

"Do you smell alcohol?" he asked.

"I'm gonna ask you to step out of the truck."

"What the hell?"

"I need to conduct a field sobriety test."

"The hell you do. I suppose Rennie Poole called you from Washington, too."

"Okay," Stilson said. "Give me your keys and step back to the cruiser. In my estimation, you are currently impaired. I'm transporting you to the Sheriff's Department in Morgan for a blood test."

"You're shitting me!" Owen protested.

"Step back to the cruiser, Mr. Wheeler. I won't ask again."

"You haven't *asked* anything!"

The next thing he knew, he was on his knees, which had collapsed when Stilson slapped them with his riot stick. Owen grimaced as Stilson bent his arms around to cuff him behind his back.

"I'm delighted you chose the hard way." Stilson jerked Owen to his feet using the cuffs chain. "I really am."

Smiling, he crab-walked Owen to the squad car and dumped him in the back seat.

* * *

The blood test at the station in Morgan was clean. Owen asked for a ride back to his truck, which had been left by the side of the Morgan Highway. He was informed the Bliss County Sheriff's Department wasn't a taxi agency. He'd have to find his own way back. Owen demanded to talk with Sheriff Mattox.

"We've done this dance before, you know," Owen said after he was admitted to Mattox's office. "Broken taillights and muffler hangers. Now you're rousting me for drunk driving?"

"If you weren't such a notorious inebriate, you might not raise people's suspicions," Mattox said with a smirk.

"We both know what's going on. Rennie Poole's pissed because I'm running for the Prosperity Town Council. He's calling in favors to harass me until I drop out."

"If that's true, I sure wouldn't want to be in your shoes. If I were, I might consider it in everyone's best interest if I took myself out of the picture. I'm not giving advice here, you understand. Just saying how I'd handle a problem like yours. I'm busy, Wheeler. Unless you want to file a complaint against Deputy Stilson, we're finished."

* * *

Chloe didn't say anything until they were outside Morgan, driving to the truck.

"You're in over your head," she said, her voice brittle.

"I thought the scenery looked familiar," he joked.

She didn't smile. She dropped him at the truck and didn't wait for him to get in. The Fairlane tires chirped on the asphalt as she dropped the car into gear and jabbed the accelerator. He watched her disappear around the next bend. He could hear the throaty exhaust of the Fairlane for almost a minute.

Owen waited impatiently for Rennie's next run at him. It took two weeks. Anticipating a difficult harvest due to harsh summer weather and a hailstorm in August that flattened his soybean crop, he'd approached the farmers' bank in Morgan for a loan to help put in the winter vegetables. The loan officer, in August, had been open and friendly and all too willing to provide the money. In the third week of September, Owen received a form letter from the bank informing him the loan offer had been rescinded. No explanation. Without the loan, planting for winter would be difficult, but not impossible. Finances would be tight around the Wheeler household until the winter field produced. It didn't help that Owen was funneling cash into his campaign for the Town Council, a fact Chloe didn't hesitate to bring up when their discussions about money frequently overheated.

* * *

On election night in November, at Jude's house, they waited for the tallies to come in. Jude, Owen, and Chloe relaxed on the screened porch, a fire crackling in the stone hearth, and drank and talked about uncertain futures. Jude and Grace were in one of the troughs in their on-again-off-again affair, and she remained at home.

Around ten-thirty, the final results from the Prosperity elections were posted. Owen had lost his contest by six dozen votes—a virtual landslide in Prosperity.

"Well, shit," Owen said, as he watched the results. "It was a longshot anyway, right? In a town run by Rennie Poole, what else would you expect?"

He poured another shot of tequila and pounded it back.

"Might want to throttle back on the juice," Jude warned. "Tomorrow's a workday, regardless of the election."

"Does it matter?" Owen said, his voice wet and slurred. "By the time he's done, Rennie's gonna own my farm, and every other farm, and every goddamn house and television and car and tree and rock in this goddamn county."

"You're gonna blow a gasket. Why don't you hit the hot tub?" Jude said.

"Got no swimsuit."

"Do I give a damn? I've seen your scrawny dick a thousand times in locker rooms, and I'm sure Chloe would love the opportunity to get reacquainted with—" He stopped short. The liquor had blown out all his filters.

"Jude," Chloe said. The caution in her voice was palpable.

"What do you mean?" Owen demanded.

"I don't mean a thing, bud. Sorry I said it. It's the hooch."

"Gonna take a walk." Owen pushed the screen door so hard it banged against the porch frame. He staggered off into the woods past the gate and the *No Trespassing* sign toward The Ledge.

"Go with him," Chloe said.

"Shouldn't you?"

"Owen and I don't work that way anymore. He thinks most of what I say is a waste of breath. I think I made a mistake marrying him."

"I'm sorry," he said. "Still. It seems you should be the one to comfort him. He got kicked in the balls. You need to be there for him. Wasn't there something in your wedding vows about good times and bad?"

"We took those vows in the shadow of a hundred-foot neon clown in a Mexican sombrero, in a tourist trap amusement park that smelled like hot asphalt and fryer grease. It's a metaphor for the entire marriage. I told him not to run. I told *you* to tell him not to run. He ignored both of us. Fuck him."

Jude found Owen sitting on The Ledge, aimlessly chucking pebbles into pitch darkness. They plopped as they landed in the pool. Owen didn't turn around when Jude walked up to him.

"Suppose there really are mermaids in Six Mile Creek?" Owen asked.

Jude grabbed a pebble and tossed it into the dark. "I've spied a couple of unusually attractive salamanders."

"I never had a chance, did I?"

Jude sighed. "It's politics, man. Money and patronage rule. Ninety percent of this county owes Rennie one way or another. You went up alone against the Russian army. Gotta hand it to you, though. You flipped 'em off all the way down. You have a great future as the Baptist saint of futile crusades."

"What was I thinking?"

"You wanted to make a difference. Maybe you did. Maybe someone with a little more clout will see what you did and make a real run at Rennie and his machine. You don't always hit the nail with the first hammer blow."

Owen took a swig of vodka and handed the pint bottle to Jude.

"You should open a bar," Owen said. "You could retire on what I've tossed back tonight. What was that crack about Chloe?"

"Nothing, man. Forget it."

"Because I know I've been neglecting her. But I thought she got it. I thought everyone got it."

"You were doing a thing," Jude said. "Maybe a noble thing. Now you're not. Time to work on the situation under your own roof. My ass is freezing on this rock. Let's head back to the house."

* * *

Owen didn't stop drinking. By midnight, his slur turned into a low, raspy growl. His eyes were glassy slits. Jude suggested they crash in his spare bedroom, but Chloe insisted on pouring Owen into the car and driving him home. Jude helped her walk him out to the Fairlane.

As he watched the taillights shrink, Jude realized he was exhausted, all the way to his bones. He'd tried to keep pace with Owen, but after the first hour he could only put away one beer for every three his friend emptied. Owen's surrender to dissipation was depressing and painful. The drink had allowed Owen to believe the delusion of beating Rennie Poole's handpicked candidate. It had been a suicide mission from the first notion.

He cut the lights in the house, poured a glass of chilled white wine, rolled a tight doobie, threaded a Grateful Dead concert tape onto the reel-to-reel, dropped all his clothes on the screened porch floor, and slipped into the hot tub. The tubbing craze had caught on nationwide, and Jude had replaced the archaic wooden barrel tub with a sleek new fiberglass Jacuzzi, complete with body-molded seating. Alternating tokes and sips, he reveled in the night sounds from the woods and the creek beyond them. He punched the button for the water jets, which drowned out everything except the syncopated beat of Mickey Hart's drums, leaned his head back, and closed his eyes.

A body slipped over the edge of the tub and into the water. Startled, Jude raised his head and found Chloe on the other side, the ends of her ebony shag-cut locks dipped into the water which rose to the tops of her naked breasts.

"Should lock your front door, Slick," she said, languidly. "Never know what kind of reprobate might walk in."

"Where's Owen?"

"Passed out at home. Never even took off his clothes. I think he pissed his pants. Pass me that bomber and the lighter. And give me a sip of wine. I forgot to pour one before I crawled into the tub."

She pushed off from her side of the tub and floated across to him. Without a word, she stood, arching her breasts over his head. She drained the last two ounces from his glass in a single gulp, toked a couple of times, and settled on the same bench he was on. Her skin was smooth and wet, pressed against the right side of his body. She dipped her hand under the water.

"Wow. So that's what one feels like when it's happy," she said, grasping him. "I'd almost forgotten."

Jude never understood why he was so weak. The bottom line, he determined later, whenever he tried to see any trace of honor or integrity in his decisions, was he gave up the battle. He surrendered to his impulses and basest nature. On the worst night of Owen's life, he took his best friend's wife to bed and made her howl.

* * *

Owen woke an hour before daylight. His room smelled like a saloon urinal. His head alternately pounded and spun. He checked the den, thinking Chloe might have bunked on the sofa. The room was empty. So was the bedroom on the second floor. Her Fairlane was missing.

He couldn't recall how he'd gotten home. Had Jude driven him, or Chloe? He tried to pull together the fragments of the evening, but only found huge gaps. There was a snippet of him and Jude sitting on The Ledge, but he couldn't recall the substance of their talk. He knew he'd lost the election, and he blamed his intoxication on disappointment, but he couldn't remember much more about what had transpired since dinner the night before.

He grabbed his pickup keys and stumbled on the front door weather strip. He sprawled across the plank floor of the gallery, clumsily pushed himself back to his feet, and shambled down the steps to the gravel circle.

She's left me, he thought desperately. *She's had enough and taken off.*

He had to find her, apologize, try to make things right before it was too late. Without a clue where he was going, he stomped on the gas, did a one-eighty spin on the gravel, threw pebbles onto the front porch, and aimed for the narrow drive that careened through the trees to the Morgan Highway. The truck fishtailed as he made the turn deep in the trees. The rear bumper banged against an ancient white oak, tearing chunks of bark from the trunk.

He made it almost three-quarters of a mile before revolving lights flashed in his rearview mirror and a short burst from a siren signaled him to pull over. He parked the truck on the shoulder and jumped from the cab as Larry Stilson opened the cruiser door.

"Had a notion you might be out and about tonight," Stilson said, as he walked toward Owen. "I'd ask you to assume the position, Wheeler, but I think you'd fall over. Let's take a ride. There's a needle waiting for you in Morgan."

"Can't," Owen mumbled. "Chloe. Have to… find her." He wavered on his feet, shook his head, and started to turn back toward the truck cab.

"The only place you're going tonight is the drunk tank. C'mon, man. Don't make this any harder than it has to be."

Owen spun and took a slow, lazy swing at one of the heads in his beer goggles. Stilson easily sidestepped it. The momentum carried Owen halfway back around, tangled his legs, and he fell to the ground in a heap. Stilson helped him back to his feet, cuffed him, and stuffed him in the back of the cruiser. He turned off the truck, secured the keys in his pocket, and returned to the squad car as Owen lurched forward and heaved sour vomit down the front of his shirt.

Chapter Thirty-Six

Chloe woke before dawn, the pink glow of sunrise growing over the horizon. She looked at the clock. Six-twenty-five.

Then she realized it wasn't her clock. Memory swept in from the dark corners of her hung-over brain.

"Oh, shit," she mumbled. Her breath offended her.

The other side of the bed was empty. Over the roar in her ears, she could discern the gentle whisper of a shower behind the bathroom door. She padded across the hardwood floor, placed a hand on the bathroom doorknob, and debated what to do next.

The night before had been an act of desperation compounded by anger and resentment. She'd become a stranger in her husband's house, an ornament he appreciated in passing, but on which he never lingered. His heart had been appropriated by his vendetta against Rennie Poole, the alcohol he swilled like iced tea, and internal demons who danced on his soul in spiked boots and about whom he never dared to speak.

Owen had done worse than abandon her. He'd ignored her.

And Jude had made her feel so good, in a way Owen hadn't in months.

Marrying Owen had been a mistake. She wasn't intended for marriage—not the happy forever after kind of marriage she'd been indoctrinated to believe happened to good people. She hadn't been faithful to Billy by a long shot. She'd hoped moving to North Carolina with only the stuff she could fit in a Fairlane would mean changing her life and finding the contentment she'd sought since childhood.

Her marriage was a failed experiment. Her nature was her nature. She was

Chloe, unchanged, unreformed, and unreconstructed. She was immutable. The only constant in her life was chaos.

She opened the door, pulled back the curtain, and stepped inside the shower.

"Don't kiss me, darlin'. Dragon mouth," she said. "But parts of me are gonna need an extra scrubbing this morning."

* * *

Jude dashed about the kitchen. He had an eight-thirty class, but he also had to do something about Chloe.

Sleeping with her the night before had been bad enough. He could rationalize it, though, by invoking the influence of drink and weed and high emotions.

What he'd allowed in the shower was sheer indulgence, and another matter.

Grace was skilled and attentive and even, on occasion, surprisingly inventive between the sheets. Tossing on the mattress with Chloe, in comparison, had been like strapping into a Ferrari and pegging the speedometer on a curvy backwoods road. She gave him aches he'd forgotten he could have. Bedding Chloe was the decathlon of debauchery.

It wasn't as if he was exactly a rookie at infidelity. How many married women with gold bands stashed in their purses had picked him up in bars across the country during his football days? How many men had watched him play on television the next day, sublimely unaware that the women at their side still had Jude's little swimmers inside them? He hadn't lost sleep over those adulterous adventures. Whatever reasons those women had for picking him up was their trip. He was only hitching a ride on their private railroad to Hell.

Now, he'd cheated. His attachment to Owen predated Chloe by decades. He'd cuckolded his best friend and had no excuse other than his inability to resist his glands. And, even though their commitment to one another was as inconstant as the appearance of comets, he'd also cheated on Grace.

"He can't know," Jude said, without looking at Chloe, who sat on a barstool in the kitchen. "Ever."

Chloe swirled orange juice around the inside of her glass. She was dressed, after a fashion, in Jude's bathrobe. One mischievous nipple popped out as the robe gapped when she bent to pick up the glass.

"Don't feel like stopping," she purred.

"It's going to be hard enough to keep him from finding out about last night. I feel awful about what we've done already."

"I don't get that vibe at all. You sure weren't remorseful in the shower."

"It can't happen again. I have a class. You found your way in. I'm sure you can find it out. Just lock up when you leave. Here's some toast, and there's butter and jam. I'm really late."

* * *

Anvil-dark clouds lined the sky as Chloe drove the three miles from Jude's house to the farm. The wind whipped fallen autumn leaves across the asphalt, carpeting the road with golds and scarlets and orange. Chloe had presumed Owen would be sacked out on the bed, snoring off a hangover. As she drove up the winding gravel drive, she could see the field hands working a plot of cabbages in the distance. She didn't see Owen's truck.

The bed was tousled and empty. Gravel was strewn on the front porch, and she could see the valley of rocks in the parking circle where he'd cut a doughnut spinning the tires. Her chest tightened, the physical manifestation of all her fears. As incapacitated as he'd been the previous midnight, Owen couldn't possibly have been sober when he drove away. Her first impulse was to hop into the Fairlane and look for him. There were only three or four places he'd check, and she knew he hadn't gone to Jude's house—thankfully.

She was at the front door when she saw the blinking light on the answering machine next to the telephone in the kitchen. She pressed the play button on the recorder. Owen's tinny voice vibrated from the miniature speaker. It sounded thick and slow and slurry.

"Chloe? Where are you? Sweetie? Honey, I need your help. I'm at the jail in

Morgan. I got arrested. I was set up, Chloe. Stilson was waiting for me. I need you to come get me out... What?... But I need... Chloe, they tell me I have to get off the phone. The Morgan jail. Come as soon as you hear this."

The beep when the message ended was like a punctuation to their marriage.

* * *

Jude sat in his office chair, updating the attendance roster, when Chloe pushed open his door. He glanced up, and a dark cloud crossed his face.

"The fuck, Chloe! You can't be here!"

He yanked at the cord to close the blinds on the window opening out into the locker room.

"Owen's in jail."

"Say that again."

"There was a message on our machine. He woke up drunk and confused. He couldn't find me, so he took the truck. They got him right away. He says it was a setup. From what I know about Larry Stilson, I'm inclined to agree. I went to Morgan and faced down your sheriff. He's a real prick."

"You have no idea."

"He says they won't arraign Owen until tomorrow morning. They're charging him with assault, Jude. They say he took a swing at Stilson. I think this is Rennie twisting the knife."

"What's the point? Owen already lost the election."

"I think Rennie's definition of victory includes annihilating the enemy and salting the fields."

"I don't see it. He doesn't expend capital—money or political—unless there's a legitimate payoff. He'd already gotten what he wanted. He has something else up his sleeve."

"We can worry about Rennie later. I have the truck keys. It's sitting by the side of the Morgan Highway. I need you to ride out with me and drive it to the farm."

"I'm working."

"Hell, you can drive from one end of Prosperity to the other in five minutes. You need more than that to take a decent dump. You need to work on your priorities, Slick. Remember why Owen's in jail in the first place. Every drop in him came from the bar on your porch, and you and I were bumpin' uglies when he got popped."

* * *

Chloe paid Owen's bond in cash a half-hour after the arraignment hearing. She didn't say a word as she led him to the parking lot and helped him into the Fairlane. He stared out at the trees, still festooned in the scarlets and butter golds and ginger of North Carolina's delayed autumn. His breath fogged the glass. A tear fought its way from the corner of his eye and coursed down his cheek.

"Where were you?" he asked.

"I was angry. I took a drive."

"Long drive. I called you from the jail at six-thirty."

"Watched the sunrise. You really want to make this about *me*, Owen?"

He drew random shapes in the fogged glass.

"No," he said, quietly. "Of course not. I have to make changes. Huge chunks of the last year are lost to me."

"What are we going to do?"

"I'm thinking on it."

"While you do, think about how we're going to replace the bail money. We have cobwebs in our bank book."

At home, Chloe went directly to their bedroom to change clothes. As she pulled on a pair of jeans, she heard a popping sound in the kitchen, and her heart broke as she envisioned Owen starting in on his first beer of the day.

Then, she heard a second pop.

She found Owen standing over the sink, pouring beers into the drain.

"I've seen this movie," she said. "Don't think dumping your stash'll do it for you, lover. The brewery didn't burn down."

"I know," he said. He sounded like he was talking from the base of a well.

"It's a start."

"Yeah," she said. A smile formed at the corners of her mouth. She couldn't recall when she'd last felt it. "I guess it is."

She grabbed a can, popped the cap, and poured it into the sink.

* * *

Jude found Rennie Poole's Continental parked next to the garage when he returned home. The congressman sat in one of the chalk-white railback rocking chairs on the covered front porch.

"I suppose I should offer my congratulations," Jude said, as he walked by Rennie and opened the front door. "Heard you retained your seat Tuesday night."

"Never in doubt, but thank you, Jude. Most gracious of you."

"Been sitting in the cold long?"

"Long enough to turn my clappers into ice cubes."

"Maybe you'll catch pneumonia and die."

Rennie faced him. "Your father was a good man, and a great comfort to me. I wish I had a better relationship with you."

"We've had this conversation."

"Whatever passes between us can be hashed out later. I'm here about your pal, Owen."

Reluctantly, Jude led him into the house. All signs of Tuesday night's boozefest had been cleaned the evening before. The house smelled of cleaning spray and lemon wax. Jude pointed toward the sofa.

"Think I might get a drink?" Rennie asked.

"This isn't a bar. You came here uninvited. Remember when you didn't get a Christmas card from me? That wasn't an oversight. What about Owen?"

"Your friend is in a bad way, son."

"Never call me that again."

"Owen went hip-deep into debt to fund his campaign. Gonna be a bear to pay off. He might skate on the drunk driving charges, since—beyond all probability—it's his first offense. The assault thing, though, that's a toughie.

250

Minimum of a year in prison if he's convicted. Maybe more, unless his attorney can prove mitigation."

"Mitigation."

"You know, mental illness, psychological distress, impairment. The important thing to focus on is a minimum of one year. Maybe nine months on the county farm with good behavior. It's a sad thing. I don't have to tell you. You grew up in this town. You've seen farms go belly-up before."

"If you came to gloat—"

Rennie held up his hands. "Gloat? I came here to *help*. The election's over. Bygones, and all. You're like family to me, Jude. I watched you grow up. I feel an obligation. That extends to the people you care about. As a show of good faith, I've lifted the moratorium on selling to Owen at my stores. Same goes for the tractor supply in Morgan."

"Big of you."

"There's more. I want you to listen carefully. This whole business with Stilson? The assault? I can make it go away."

Jude walked into the kitchen and returned with two cans of beer. He handed one to Rennie and opened the other.

"Let's say I'm interested," Jude said.

"Please, son... Jude. What did you once call me? A benevolent despot? Maybe you weren't so far off. I do hope, after my passing, people will focus on the 'benevolent' part. I trade in favors, Jude. My family coat of arms is one hand washing another. Your friend needs help right now, badly. I'm offering it."

"Sheriff Mattox. You own him."

"Let's say I have a timeshare on his office. When he was a deputy, I showed him a faster path to get what he wanted. The sheriff has complete free will, like everyone else. Why worry about details? I am telling you I can make Owen's troubles go away. Do you really want to see the sausages made?"

"Depends on whether I have to eat them. What do you get out of it?"

Rennie set the beer can on a coaster on the coffee table and laced his fingers together.

"Your father and I had an arrangement. We were a team. Since his passing,

I discover all my day-to-day operations are impaired. I want to fix that."

Jude laughed and walked over to the front window. He looked at the overgrown fields that comprised the remainders of the Lincoln farm.

"You want the money," he said. "My father's slush fund accounts."

"Not precisely," Rennie said. "Sure, you could write me a few checks, but what do I do with them? You know the government requires any deposit greater than ten thousand dollars to be reported. The accounts you're talking about took years to build. The money had a specific purpose, only to be accessed in times of emergency."

"Like when some palm needs greasing. Wouldn't look right for the money to come from a congressman's bank account. My father was your bagman."

"Oh, Jude. He was so much more. He was my eyes and ears on the ground in Prosperity. He put out the fires. He was indispensable—much as I hope, someday, *you* will be."

"Dream on."

"Don't reject the idea prematurely. Think of those bank accounts as warehouses. You only need to go in from time to time, and take out a little here, a little there. Leave it in an envelope on your front porch. Someone will pick it up. Nothing could be simpler. In return, you take out as much as you need to pay Owen Wheeler's campaign debts. He can get a fresh start without owing half his future to the bank. Long as you don't get greedy, feel free to skim a little off the top for yourself. The money belongs to you, after all. I hear you've been squiring Arlo Pyle's daughter Grace around town. Might be fun to take her on a real vacation. Europe, maybe. When you think it over, I believe you'll see the potential in this offer."

"You're putting me in a box."

"It's lined with mink. Could be worse. You did this to yourself. If you hadn't fought me tooth and nail for years, we wouldn't be at this unfortunate juncture in our lives. If you only knew..." he stopped.

"What?" Jude asked.

Rennie settled back on the sofa. "I remember so many conversations with your father. He had such tremendous hopes for you—many of which you fulfilled. Sometimes, when you faltered, he came to me for advice and assistance. I helped him whenever I could because he was of such great help to me. One hand washes the other, right?"

"What do you mean, you *helped*?"

"Jude. Do you truly believe Coach McCandless suddenly took a mind to pay you a visit? You popped up in his head and he drove all the way from Virginia to check in on you?"

"As I recall, he told me he was in the area."

"Funny thing. I was in the area of Ryland College a week or so before he visited you. Entirely by chance. Visited the coach to pay my respects. We had a stimulating conversation."

"You're saying I owe my college scholarship to you."

"And, by extension, your pro career. But you're missing the point, boy. All your dad and I did was open the doors. You charged on through and made your own success. I didn't win your conference championship at Ryland, and I didn't win your high school coaching championship. *You* did that."

"I wouldn't have had the opportunity if you hadn't manipulated and orchestrated it."

A thousand images flashed through this mind. All the triumphs. All the tragedy. He saw the anger on Coral Pyle's face as he told her he was going to Ryland. He watched her stomp away on The Ledge because she didn't want to deal with his news, and he watched her die for the millionth time. He saw Ev Howard dancing at the end of a rope, because Jude was too frightened to speak and unwilling to throw away his new good fortune. His entire life had started over on the day Coral died. Nothing had been the same since.

"I don't expect thanks," Rennie said.

"You don't know. You have no idea what you did. You don't know how it affected everyone else."

"I don't understand."

"You should leave. I have a lot to think about."

"I suppose you do."

"And if I refuse your offer?"

"Nothing. Like I said, the money is yours. Of course, I'd have no reason to help Owen, but who really cares? You'd have your integrity, after all. Think it over. I know you'll come to the right decision. There are tremendous opportunities on the horizon. The governorship is available in four years. Think I might make a run at it. I want you to be a part of that. Any capacity you like, but I want you on board. You're an interesting guy, Jude. I'd rather have you with me than against me."

Chapter Thirty-Seven

Every several weeks, an anonymous message showed up on Jude's answering machine. An amount, and a date. The pickups were always during school days, while Jude was teaching. He never saw the exchange take place. He'd leave the envelope behind a planter in one corner of the front porch in the morning. When he arrived back home in the evening, it was gone.

As Rennie had promised, the assault charges against Owen were dropped. The DA accepted a plea deal on the drunken driving charge, reducing it to reckless driving. Owen paid a fine and walked out of the courtroom without a criminal record.

Getting his buddy out of trouble did nothing to salve Jude's aching conscience over the affair with Chloe. She possessed some sixth sense for his moments of weakness. They slept together three more times before Thanksgiving. After each occasion, he emotionally excoriated himself for allowing it to continue. Neither of them entertained even the slightest notion they were in love.

Weeks of sobriety had beaten Owen to a pulp. He'd suffered insomnia and night sweats and retching and the sensation his entire body had been rolled into a tight knot and was being consumed by fire ants. He lost fifteen pounds. When he could sleep, the dreams that hounded him were built from symbols and archetypal images rooted in the great terror of Revelations.

The physical symptoms of withdrawal abated, replaced by the lancing pangs of desire for a drink. Even for a man who had made his life under the grueling Carolina summer sun, his thirst was unlike any he'd ever imagined.

Sometimes Chloe was there to help. Sometimes she wasn't. Her nature was to avoid unpleasantness. He could tell she tried.

The week before Thanksgiving, three weeks after the arrest, he awoke on Saturday morning with a sudden, unanticipated sense of energy. He showered, shaved, dressed in freshly washed and pressed clothes, and set about making breakfast before Chloe woke. The smell lured her into the kitchen. She padded across the linoleum and stood behind him, her hands on his shoulders.

"Are you all right?" she asked.

He turned to her. The smile on his face was placid. "Better than I've been in months. Want to take my best girl to the movies tonight. What do you think?"

He kissed her, turned off the stove, picked her up, and carried her into the bedroom.

Later in the afternoon, he attended his first AA meeting. He was surprised to see Clyde Dillard sitting across from him. Their eyes met. They both cocked their heads to one side, and both sets of eyebrows rose in surprise. As unobtrusively as possible, Owen made his way around the circle and sat next to Clyde.

"When did you start coming to these things?" Clyde asked.

"My first meeting. I don't have a clue what I'm doing. How about you?"

"Almost a year. Pay attention. You'll figure it out."

In the end, Owen stood, and with the help of the other men sitting in the circle, he completed his first step—admitting he had a problem and was incapable of beating it alone. The other members encouraged him and told him they were there to support him through the process.

Invigorated, he took Chloe to the movies, and they went home and made love again before collapsing in a heap on the bed and falling into a deep sleep.

* * *

Tuesday night, after football practice, and as the last of the students' cars had left the darkened parking lot, Jude straightened the locker room and prepared to shut the gym for the night.

The heat in the building had been dysregulated all day—some malfunction or another. It would be fixed before the return to school after the Thanksgiving break, but the entire gymnasium wing had hovered in the middle-eighties since morning. Jude was hot and sticky and decided to hit the showers before heading home. He grabbed a crisp, clean towel from the rack outside the locker room and a fresh wafer of soap. He draped his clothes over a locker bench.

He lathered himself, feeling the stresses of the day fade as he stood under the steaming spray. Feminine arms encircled him, and a mouth pressed against the base of his neck. Soft, wet, naked skin slid along his back.

"Jesus," he said, without looking back. "We can't keep doing this. You aren't even supposed to be here."

"Well of course not," Grace said. "That's the fun of it. It's the boys' locker room, after all. If you like, we could get kinky and go play in the girls' shower."

Jude's pulse rocketed so quickly he was faint and queasy.

Tomorrow was the beginning of the Thanksgiving break, the point each year when, rather than face the trials of the holiday season alone, Jude and Grace had traditionally drifted back together for a few months. Wracked with guilt over his dalliance with Chloe Wheeler, he'd forgotten Grace was destined to swing in his direction any day.

He turned. Grace flattened herself against him. "You've been on my mind lately, Slugger. I've missed you. Got any ideas what I should do about that?"

"Dozens," he said, and bent to kiss her. Like her sister Coral, she was only an inch or so over five feet. He stood a foot and change taller, and she craned her neck back to meet his lips. She laid her head against his chest and kissed one of his nipples as he stroked her hair. *Surely*, he thought, *she must feel my heart jack-hammering inside my chest.*

He recognized an opportunity. Grace could provide the perfect foil with which to fend off Chloe. "I take it you got your dinner invitation for Thanksgiving?" he stammered.

"You mean the drawing you made around your hand on mimeograph paper, and stuck in my mailbox in the office? Yeah. I got it. Consider this my RSVP."

* * *

Driving by the school, Chloe recognized Jude's Willys alone in the parking lot. She remembered he had football practice on Mondays and Tuesdays, and reasoned he must be working late. She couldn't see Grace's car, parked in a separate lot behind the school.

She entered the gym through the front doors, one of which was still unlocked. Two short hallways shunted off the ends of the main lobby. Boys' lockers to the left, girls' to the right. She heard an echo of running water to the left, and hesitated.

The events of the last month had overwhelmed her. She wanted to say she had her husband back, but she'd never had *this* husband. Owen had been a heavy drinker from the moment they met. Their first frenzied coupling in his house arose during a binge. She'd never enjoyed him as a sober spouse.

Perhaps he was reveling in the afterglow of his newfound temperance. He woke each morning without a hangover for the first time in years. Despite a constant sadness in his eyes, the rest of his features seemed more youthful, his smile warmer. He was more attentive to her, which she loved. Stuffing a cork in the bottle had paradoxically unleashed some sexual genii in him. They had gone at it every night, to the point she found bruises on the inside of her thighs, and a constant heaviness at the nexus of her legs.

She couldn't be certain, because the sensation was so completely novel, but she thought she might be falling in love with her husband.

As she walked the short hallway toward the locker room, she tried to decide what to tell Jude. The affair had been a mistake. Perhaps it was all that needed to be said. He'd been there in her moment of irresistible need, there had been a confluence of anger and desire, and the result had been irredeemable infidelity.

She'd awakened that morning with a smile. Owen was already gone—had been for hours—but she swore she could still smell his scent on his pillow, and the aroma of their frantic lovemaking the night before lingered in the sheets. She'd stroked the mattress on his side of the bed and murmured, "Everything is different."

That was it. She'd tell Jude, *Everything is different.*

Her hand rested on the office door but froze when she heard a gasp to her left. Startled, she dropped back into the shadows.

Jude lay on his back on a locker bench, his legs splayed to either side. Grace straddled him. Her wet hair hung limply across her shoulders. Her pelvis sawed back and forth. Jude's hands caressed her hips as she moaned and shuddered on top of him.

Grace suddenly arched her back, cried out, and collapsed against his chest, her hips churning against him.

Chloe was satisfied. The affair had ended without a shot fired. She'd simply stop going to Jude. She'd do so without a twinge of guilt since she could plainly see he was well-tended. In a year or so, it would be a forgotten dalliance, a brief, intense period of insanity over which they might cluck and blush, but which otherwise had no profound impact on their lives.

Chloe removed her shoes and padded in sock feet to the lobby. She'd seen more than enough.

* * *

"My friends!" Jude said, clinking a fork against his glass. "Welcome to the one night of the year I'm willing to let most of you inside my house!"

Christmas Eve was a tradition at Jude's home. Rather than contribute to the pandemonium of Christmas Day by piling on one more social engagement, each Christmas Eve Jude invited some special friends to his house for dinner, an orgy of food and wine that started before dark and extended far into the night. Since the little ones needed to be in bed dreaming of sugarplums early, invitees tended to be his childless friends.

Jude had hired a chef from a local country club. The man had bustled around the kitchen since three that afternoon. He'd brought two servers to hustle the buffet carts. A bartender on time-and-a-half provided the drinks. There was nothing for Jude and Grace to do, once the process started, except relax and enjoy the party.

As the revelers mingled and grazed the buffet table, Grace, Chloe, and Owen sat on a glider chaise on the screened porch, basking in the warmth of the flaming hickory logs. Grace had a glass of crisp Riesling. Owen and Chloe drank iced tea. Jude distributed the drinks and sat by the hearth.

"Gotta say it," Jude told Owen. "You look better than I've seen you in years."

"It hasn't been easy. I appreciate the support I got from all of you while I was drying out."

"I don't know the etiquette here," Jude said. "I guess I should apologize for asking you to a party with liquor."

"Forget it," Owen said. "Just because I don't drink anymore doesn't mean they stopped making it. One of the things they help with at AA is learning to live in the real world. People drink there. I have to learn to cope."

"Nice of you to be so supportive," Grace told Chloe. "Sticking with iced tea yourself."

"Well…" Chloe looked at the floor.

"You're on the wagon, too?" Jude asked. "What is this, a party or a temperance meeting?"

Grace said, "Sweetie, I think Chloe's taken the pledge, but only for a few months."

"What?" Jude said.

"Wanna tell 'em?" Owen asked Chloe. She nodded shyly. "Seems all that drinking must have interfered with my swimmers. Now I've quit, they're a little friskier. Took four years of trying, but it looks like Chloe will be bringing along a little Wheeler sometime in August."

"Well!" Grace said. "Something to toast! Congratulations, you two!"

They all clinked glasses. As they took the celebratory sip, Jude glanced across the top of his glass at Chloe, catching her eye. He raised an eyebrow.

She shrugged her shoulders and looked away.

* * *

"If there is anything sillier than a first birthday party attended only by adults," Jude told Grace as they drove up the driveway to Owen and Chloe's house, "shoot me before telling me what it is."

"These are our friends," Grace said. "Be civil."

The birthday boy had come into the world on the hottest day of August 1973, screaming and fighting the entire way. He was a big baby, which probably was to be expected given Owen's height and wide build. When he was born, he had a full head of the most beautiful sable hair the nurses in attendance had ever seen on a baby. "Just like his mother!" one of them had said. Chloe had laughed along with them, hoping nobody could see the sliver of doubt in her eyes.

Not knowing whether it would be a boy or a girl, Owen and Chloe hadn't chosen a name prior to the birth. Now, they had to make a decision. Owen had jokingly suggested they give him three names—the first names of The Trinity—Owen Jude William Wheeler.

"And we could call him Jude!" he finished.

"No!" Chloe had replied, a shade too hastily and far too shrilly. She dialed it back and added, "That would be confusing, Sweetie. You could use some variation of it though. I wasn't close to my family growing up, and as you know I got out of town as quickly and as soon as I could, but I did have an uncle I felt close to. Uncle Judson. He lived in Biloxi, in a big white house, and he was always kind to me. We could name him after you and Uncle Judson. Owen Judson Wheeler."

"Judson seems like a big name for such a little bug," Owen had said.

"We can call him Judd. It's close to Jude, right?"

He had agreed, and she had kissed him, and they had talked for hours about their baby's future, as Chloe wished, more dearly than she had expected, that he had been born a little towhead.

A year later, Jude grumbled as he and Grace pulled into the large circle of crushed gravel in front of the Wheeler homestead. "Now that Owen's gone dry, we won't even be able to get a decent drink," he complained.

"You're not fooling me, Uncle Jude. Once we get there, nobody will be able to get Judd off your knee."

"He's a sweet kid," Jude agreed. "Did I tell you he started walking a couple of weeks ago?"

"Only ten or twelve times. You better tell me again, in case it didn't sink in."

As he had progressed in his recovery, Owen had been forced to re-examine his life and the errors he had made along the way. The steps in the program called for him to give himself over to a 'higher power', which he had interpreted as meaning he had to get right with God. Anxious to preserve the newfound stability in their marriage with the baby on the way, Chloe had encouraged him to pursue whatever means were necessary to stay clean and sober.

Owen had started going back to church. Every Sunday, even during harvest time, he sat right up front at the Primitive Baptist Church where he had been baptized almost forty years earlier. His was the loudest voice during the hymns, and he was the first to volunteer to do whatever the reverend required. With alcohol hopefully permanently banished from his life, Owen had discovered a new drug, and he attached himself to it in the way only an addictive personality can. In Jude's opinion, Owen had become the most boring and annoying of creatures, a reformed drunk.

They remained close, but Jude wanted no part of Owen's evangelistic leanings. He tolerated the cheap newsprint religious screeds Owen left lying around the house, because he adored Baby Judd and enjoyed seeing the boy every chance he got. When Owen asked if Jude would like to come to church with him, however, there was no room for equivocation.

"Not going to happen," Jude said, time and again. "I'm happy for you, dude. I really am. You're healthy and bright-eyed and happy again, and that makes me delighted. I just don't need it."

"Maybe you need it more than you know," Owen had ventured once, and for an instant, Jude had thought he saw an inkling of suspicion behind his friend's eyes, but he had never seen it again, and within a month it was mostly forgotten.

As Jude and Grace stepped out of the car, the front door opened, and Baby Judd stumbled out onto the front gallery, teetering with every step, a stream of drool running down his chin from the left side of his mouth. Chloe had dictated that he would not have his hair cut before his first birthday. Judd's coal-colored hair was thick and long, growing down past his ears, almost to the point that—had he been dressed in neutral clothes—it would have been difficult to tell whether he was a boy or a girl. He grinned when he spied Jude, and toddled over to him, grabbing him by the leg. Jude picked him up and made a grimacing face.

"Kid's getting too heavy to carry. I think I need a truss!"

Judd reached up and grabbed at the bill of Jude's Prosperity High School cap. Jude took it off and placed it on his putative nephew's head. The child immediately grabbed at it and held it out, examining it intensely, as if it might hold a deep, earthshaking secret.

Jude and Owen did the man-hug thing, and Chloe kissed Jude on the cheek and insisted that everyone come inside before they melted into pink puddles on the front porch floorboards. She took Judd, and they all went into the house, as Jude thought that—maybe—first birthday parties weren't so bad after all.

Chapter Thirty-Eight

Sunday Free had grown into a beautiful teenager. Her African-American father and South Korean mother had blended the best of their genes and bestowed them upon their daughter. Her skin was the color of dark apricots. Her almond eyes always looked inquisitive. Her full lips pursed underneath a sharp nose with flared nostrils. Her features were classic, perfectly symmetrical. As she acquired a woman's body, the boys noticed. Sunday Free knew she need never worry about being asked to a dance, or out to the movies on the weekend. She was the first name on the list for all the hottest teen parties in Prosperity. She could be picky regarding her beaus.

Hank Bowie checked off every box on her boyfriend wish list. Tall, with shaggy blond hair that fell around his face in ringlets when he sweated, his piercing blue eyes endowed him with the look of a raging teenage Viking. As Prosperity High's quarterback, starting pitcher, and first-string point guard, he was muscular, nimble, and strong.

And he was rich. His father, Lance Bowie, owned a chain of dollar stores stretching from Miami to Richmond. They had built a seven-thousand square foot house, an ill-informed rendering of a Tuscan villa, in the first upscale development in Bliss County. The front of the house described a gentle convex curve, which provided for a concave shape in the back that partially surrounded a swimming pool and sun terrace, lanai, and cabanas. The lanai wrapped around the stamped concrete pool deck. At the back of the yard, a stand of longleaf pines half an acre deep ensured complete and absolute privacy. It could be said with assurance that Hank Bowie had never lacked for any material comfort.

For the Prosperity High Homecoming Dance in 1976, Sunday wore a Halston knock-off chiffon halter dress in a milk-chocolate tone that complimented her complexion and revealed her shapely legs. She checked her sheer angel-sleeve shawl at the coatroom, leaving her shoulders and arms bare. Several students immediately gravitated in her direction.

Sunday found Hank Bowie sitting on the second row of the bleachers on one side of the floor, surrounded by team members. He wore his Prosperity High letter jacket, one of the most festooned in the school. His peroxide-blonde hair hung loosely over his shoulders. She could see his brilliant white smile from across the floor.

"Excuse me," she told her friends. "I need to talk with Hank."

Hank watched her as she approached. The smile on his face suggested he liked what he saw. "How ya doing, Sunday?" he asked. "Nice dress."

"Thanks. Congratulations on the game. You were on fire."

Almost immediately, the DJ spun up Gloria Gaynor's recording of *Never Can Say Goodbye*, and Hank hopped up from the bench. "Want to dance?"

He took her hand and led her out on the gym floor, where couples were already paired up and forming groups to do the latest dance craze, The Hustle. Like most club disco tracks, this one went on seemingly forever, as the teens—carefully observed by the rookie teachers—stepped and clapped and twirled themselves into a frenzy.

Afterward, Hank walked Sunday to the concession stand for a drink.

"I'm having a party at my place later." He handed her a Coke.

"Who's coming?"

"A few of the guys. A few of the girls. My folks are on a business trip, so we'll have the house to ourselves. Figure we'll raid the liquor cabinet, fire up a few doobies, and hit the heated pool. Sound like fun?"

"I don't have a bathing suit."

"Neither will anyone else."

She could feel heat rising in her face. "Oh."

"Wow. You're embarrassed. Look, it's fine if you don't want to come. Really."

She thought it over as they walked back into the gym.

"What time?" she asked.

"Now, if you want. School dances are lame. I give the guys the high sign, and we roll."

* * *

She rode with Hank in his new TR7 convertible, the wind whipping her hair and plastering her dress to her body like paint. Hank torched a joint with the cigarette lighter, took a long drag, and handed it across to Sunday. She'd smoked weed a few times, but still choked and coughed. By the time they pulled into Ravenwood, a warm glow seemed to spread outward from her chest. She believed Hank looked even more adorable than he had twenty minutes earlier.

The lanai was crowded. The temperatures in late October were cool, but not cold, and the pool was heated for year-round swimming. Hank opened a bar built into the wall of the lanai and tossed out cans of beer and poured shots for the partiers. Once the immediate demand for liquor and beer petered out, he found Sunday relaxing on a chaise with a can of Budweiser, and handed her a pill with the number *714* etched on its surface.

"You should try this," he said.

"What is it?"

"Took it from my mom. She'll never miss it. Her medicine cabinet's like a damned pharmacy. It's a Quaalude"

"What's a Quaalude?"

"It's cool. You get all floaty and shit. You should stop drinking, though. These pills don't mix well with alcohol."

She popped the pill into her mouth and washed it down with the last of the beer. She tossed the can into the trash and grabbed a bottle of Coke. Hank dragged another chaise next to her.

A few of the bolder students dumped their clothes in lounges and plunged into the pool. In her entire life, Sunday had seen three adult penises. In the last five minutes, she'd doubled the number.

266

Hank stood next to her. "Going for a dip. Coming?"

Before she could answer, he yanked his shirt over his head and dropped his pants to the concrete pool deck. Sunday stared at Hank's member as it dangled in front of her face. Her heart raced as she tried to memorize it. This was far more than she'd anticipated.

"Maybe in a bit," she said.

"Suit yourself." He trotted off and dove into the deep end. She watched as he disappeared under the water.

Within minutes, her arms and legs tingled, and her head was foggy, her mouth dry. As Hank had described, she felt a floating sensation, as if she were suspended underwater instead of lying on the chaise. The pool looked damned inviting.

She stood, undid the halter, and allowed her dress to drop to the concrete. She carefully draped it over the chair, followed by her underwear, before she joined the other revelers in the pool.

* * *

When she woke, Sunday had no idea where she was. She was naked, in pitch darkness, lying on a rough surface like over-starched towels. Her head and body ached. She couldn't hear any breathing except her own. She probed the darkness to find something solid, her heart banging nearly out of her chest. Her hand banged against a wall to her right and she jumped back with a gasp. She stood, slowly waving her arms in every direction, probing the blackness of the room. Stepping carefully, she eventually came to another wall and felt the molded wood of a door jamb. Next to the door, she found a light switch. The room flooded with light, and she squinted as her head roared in pain.

She was in one of the cabanas. She'd been lying on the bare cushions of a daybed set up in one corner. She couldn't find her clothes. Her stomach heaved when she saw half a dozen used condoms scattered on the floor. She vaguely recognized the heaviness in her pelvis, from her limited experience. *I must have had sex*, she thought. *But, with who? If only I could remember.*

She barely made it into the washroom before her stomach emptied. After washing her face and rinsing the sour bile from her mouth, she returned to the main room and tried to remember how she had gotten there. A rack of oversized towels stood next to the door. She wrapped herself in one of them and stepped outside.

The lights around the pool were extinguished, leaving the entire rear of the house shrouded in darkness, save for the shimmering liquid glow from the pool's underwater lights. The concrete deck was littered with beer cans, discarded clothes, and a few snoring students who risked hypothermia. The clock over the bar read four-forty-six. Her head roared, but her stomach had begun to still itself. She tried to bring back the previous hours.

She vaguely recalled skinny-dipping with a crowd of other students. Hank had swum over to her, as they treaded water in the deep end of the pool and had placed his arm around her torso under her arms to help support her. She had thrilled at the touch of his body. She remembered staring into his eyes for a long time as they bobbed in the water, their fellows frolicking around them, until he pulled her to him, and their mouths locked together. And then—

Nothing.

Everything else was blank.

She wandered back to the lanai. Her dress and underwear still lay neatly folded on the chaise. She dropped the towel and dressed quickly, shivering in the night chill. She had to find Hank, see if he could explain how she wound up in the cabana.

She found him in a bedroom on the second floor, sprawled on his back on the bed, his limp phallus hanging at an angle between his legs. Natalie Weiskoff, one of the varsity cheerleaders, a busty redhead, lay naked next to him on her stomach, her left leg draped over his thigh. Both snored softly. The aroma of sex lingered in the air. Sunday knelt at the side of the bed and tried to rouse Hank. He mumbled but didn't open his eyes. She shook harder. He swiped at her hand before rolling over toward Natalie. Within seconds, he was snoring again.

Sunday returned to the lanai. The woods surrounding the house were silent, the water in the pool flat and glassy. She poured a quarter glass of vodka. The night was entirely too real for her to face sober. She savored the oily warm sensation as it slid down her throat. She poured another and stumbled over to the chaise where she'd dropped her clothes the night before.

If only I could remember.

The alcohol flowed in her veins. Her muscles relaxed. Her breathing slowed. Somewhere in the back of her head, she remembered something Hank had said, but it was hazy and difficult to evoke the exact words. Something about the pills she'd taken. Something about... what? They didn't mix well with alcohol?

Sunday begged to differ. From what she could tell, alcohol and Quaaludes got along famously. She'd never felt as relaxed and unsinkable. In seconds, all her cares disappeared, as she stared at the sky and allowed her mind to float and drift and course among the stars.

One of the football players found her shortly after sunrise, floating face down in the pool, her chiffon dress billowing around her body like a milk chocolate cloud.

Chapter Thirty-Nine

Owen and Clyde met early on Saturday mornings at the hardware store to discuss their temptations, lapses, weak thoughts, and the constant threat of the addiction demon that rode on their shoulders like a taunting gargoyle.

Clyde tossed him a honeybun and a fried apple pie and slid a Cheerwine across the counter as Owen walked through the hardware store door. It was part of their ritual. This early on a Saturday morning, they were unlikely to be interrupted. The wail of an ambulance rose, peaked as it passed the store, and faded in the distance. A fire engine followed shortly.

"Someone's having a rotten morning," Clyde said. "You catch *The Rockford Files* last night? It was a good 'un."

"Yeah?"

"Rockford had this client, and...well, they...huh. Can't seem to recall most of it. I know it was a good 'un, though!"

"Are you sure you watched it? Maybe you're thinking about last week. You worry me, Clyde. You forget stuff a lot lately."

"My brain's dissolving. The doctors told me it's on account of pickling it for all those years. Looks like I'm gonna go out with a whimper, not a bang. Can't stop it now. It's not like I don't have time to prepare. Some poor suckers wake up one morning in bed fit as a fiddle and get laid out on a slab before sunset. I get to take the long road to the cemetery. Don't you worry about my memory. Sure, it's got holes in it, and there's a day coming when I'll take all my food through a tube and won't recognize myself in the mirror, but right now I remember most stuff like yesterday."

Owen finished the apple pie, washing it down with long swig of the soda. "Like your mermaids?"

"Who said anything about mermaids?"

"You did. Right after Jude moved into his house a few years back. He and I were by Six Mile Creek. You shouted at us to watch out for the mermaids."

"I did?"

"Sure as I'm stealing another one of your apple pies. There are no mermaids."

"The hell there ain't. I saw one, a long time ago. I went to the crick to fish for my supper, and I saw her. She was slim and blonde and entirely nekkid, floating and playing in a pool next to the big flat rock. I watched her for a few seconds, and she turned into a real girl, and climbed back up on the rock and got dressed and ran away."

"Where did her clothes come from?"

"Beats me. What difference does it make?"

"What you saw was some young girl skinny-dipping, Clyde. Probably scared the poor kid out of her skin. When was this?"

"A day or two before Ev Howard. Hell of a week, it was."

He unwrapped another apple pie and bit into it. Owen stared at him.

"Clyde?"

"Hmm?" Clyde said, chewing.

"Did you ever meet Coral Pyle?"

"Who?"

"Coral Pyle. The girl Ev Howard killed. Did you know her?"

"Can't say I did."

"She was slim and blonde. Was this a tall girl or a short girl you saw?"

"I think she was short, but I wouldn't swear to it. My eyes have never been all that strong."

"Coral Pyle was short."

"The girl I saw might have been Coral Pyle? What would she be doing skinny-dipping all alone on Six Mile Creek? In 1954?"

"People do crazy shit for no reason at all. Teenagers do crazier shit than anyone else. They found Coral's body wrapped around a bridge support where Six Mile Creek goes under the Old Village Road. There was a big storm the night before. The flat rock and the pool you're talking about are upstream from the bridge."

"I'm not following."

"What if Coral didn't die at the bridge? The floodwaters the night before might have swept her into the bridge pilings from somewhere upstream. Let's say Coral died upstream and was dragged to the bridge during the flooding in the storm."

"Yeah?"

"The only evidence against Ev Howard was the tackle box found at the bridge. If Ev raped and killed Coral upstream, and she was swept downstream during the storm, why would he leave his tackle box at the bridge? The pieces won't mesh."

"But, that would mean… oh…" Clyde looked at the fried pie in his hand, and he gulped. Slowly, he placed it on the countertop. He looked across the store, at the storage shelf with reel upon reel of rope. "I don't feel so good. Jesus, Owen. Did we swing the wrong boy?"

"Yeah," Owen said. "I think maybe we swung the wrong boy."

Chapter Forty

J ude heard about the drowning on Sunday when he received a call from Principal Black. At first, he wasn't certain why Black was calling him until Hank Bowie's name came up.

Jude tried to build a mental image of the events Friday night as Black provided what information was available. There had been drinking, and drugs, and sex. Details were sketchy.

"Sheriff Mattox wants to meet with you, me, and anyone else we can find who can shed some light on the party," Black said.

"Sure," Jude said. "I'll be there. Does Grace know yet? Sunday was one of her students."

"No. You think Grace should be in the meeting with Mattox?"

"I think she'd insist."

* * *

They used the large conference room at the high school. Principal Black, Jude, and Grace sat on one side of the table. Brian Mattox sat on the other, alone at first. Tom Black had Hank Bowie excused from class and sent to the office to meet with them.

A couple of minutes later, the office assistant opened the door.

"Hank isn't here," she said. "He didn't show up for homeroom this morning, and he wasn't in his first-period class."

"I was hoping to do this civilized," Mattox said. "Keep it informal. Guess I have to go find the Bowie boy now. If I slip cuffs on him, things are going to get messy. Tell me about the boy, Coach. What kind of kid is he?"

"He's a teenager," Jude said. "With all the lack of impulse control that comes with it. He's not lazy, but he isn't the most motivated player I've ever had either. He seems smart. Sometimes he's a little cocky."

"Is he a bully?"

"Not at all. He's a good kid. Kind of spoiled, but he has a solid head on his shoulders. When he grows up, he should be an okay guy."

"Does he have any history of sexual misbehavior?"

"We don't talk about those things. You think he's some kind of rapist? I don't know what people like that look like. Is there some identifying feature? Do they have a secret handshake?"

Mattox turned to Black. "I was under the impression he'd cooperate."

"He is," Black said. "Read between the lines."

"This Sunday Free girl. What about her?"

Grace had been plastered to the back of her seat, her arms crossed under her breasts, her displeasure with Mattox palpable. Now she leaned forward. "She was in my choir, and in the Girls' Ensemble. She sang lyric soprano. A sweet, sweet girl. Bright, too. Near the top of her class. She wanted to be a teacher."

The office assistant knocked and opened the door again.

"Mr. and Mrs. Free are here," she said. "They brought their preacher with them."

"Maybe it's a good thing young Bowie isn't here after all," Mattox said.

The assistant escorted three people into the room, two black men and an Asian woman. The Asian woman was slight and thin. The taller man wore a two-inch Afro that blended into full sideburns and a mustache. His eyes were intense as he tried to record everything in the room.

The other man was short and lean, close to thirty, with neatly cropped hair that revealed a pattern of balding around the side of his head that looked remarkably like the outline of a motorcycle chain. He took the initiative to make introductions.

"I'm Reverend Angeloe Teeter, of the Mount Zion Church in Morgan. This is Ronald Free and his wife, Soon."

"Please," Soon Free said. Her English, while heavily accented, was otherwise impeccable. "We would like some answers." She rifled through her purse for a handkerchief to stem the tears that had sprung at the corners of her eyes.

"Please allow us to convey our sincere condolences," Principal Black said. "So tragic."

"No," Angeloe Teeter argued. "This was criminal. Someone gave a seventeen-year-old girl drugs and provided her with alcohol. Someone—several people, based on the evidence—violated her sexually. A crime has been committed in Prosperity against a child of color. As a representative of the Afro-American community in Morgan, and an advocate for civil rights, I have a keen interest in seeing justice done."

The office assistant ushered in Hank Bowie and a man Jude didn't recognize. Ronald Free glared at Hank, who looked as if he'd rather be anywhere else. The two newcomers took seats at the table opposite the Frees. The man was stout, which made him appear shorter. He wore a neatly tailored three-piece wool suit, Italian shoes, and a pair of round gold wire-rimmed glasses.

"My name is Carl Capshaw," he said. "Most of you already know Hank Bowie."

Ronald Free said, "Mister... Capshaw? Where is Hank's father?"

"Mr. Bowie is detained in Baltimore, on business," Capshaw said, solemnly. "He wished me to convey his regrets. I apologize for his absence," Capshaw said, without elaborating.

"Excuse me," Jude said. "Mr. Capshaw, what is your relationship to Hank?" "You are—?"

"Jude Pressley. Hank's football coach."

"Mr. Pressley, did you know about the party last Friday night?"

"I presumed there would be one somewhere. There always is after the homecoming game. Nobody told me any specifics. I'm not sure what your role here is."

"I am a legal counsel to Mr. Bowie, and by extension to Hank. I am here to ensure his rights are not violated."

"*His* rights!" Ronald Free said, standing and slapping his palms flat on the table. Angeloe Teeter placed a hand on his shoulder, and Free glared at him. Without a word, staring into Free's eyes, Teeter was able to calm the man with only a nod and pat on his chest with his other hand. Free sat back down.

"I don't think you understand the gravity of our situation," Teeter said.

"Precisely why we're here," Capshaw said. "Mr. Bowie was specific in his instructions. He is extremely troubled by these circumstances. However, until evidence surfaces to the contrary, the fact Miss Free's injuries took place on his premises, at a time when he wasn't present, does not place him in a position of legal responsibility over and above the limits of his homeowner insurance liability."

"You're not making things better," Jude said.

"I agree," Teeter said. "It's a little early to talk about compensation. We're still trying to figure out exactly what happened."

"This is a sad occasion," Capshaw said. "I would like to add my own sincere sympathies. I'm a father myself. I can't imagine being in your shoes right now. However, given the information we have so far, I think we should face the strong probability that—as horrible as these events have been—they may all be the result of a tragic accident."

"I see," Sheriff Mattox said. "I take it you plan to advise your client to keep his silence for the time being."

"Hank is a seventeen-year-old boy. Teenagers don't make the best decisions. I'm here to see to it he doesn't unintentionally say anything that might cause him to appear responsible for something he never did."

"Perhaps he can tell us what someone *else* did," Mattox said. "For starters, I'd like a list of the students who attended the party last Friday."

Capshaw opened his briefcase and slid a sheet of paper across the table. "We anticipated your request. This is the list, as best as Hank can recall. People came and went over the course of the night, so he might have missed a few, but he is certain about these names. You see, Sheriff, we desire to be as helpful as we can."

"Hank," Mattox asked. "When was the last time you saw Sunday alive?"

"Around midnight. Maybe a little later. A lot of us were in the pool."

"How could she be in the pool?" Soon Free asked. "She didn't have a swimsuit."

"None of us did," Hank said before Capshaw could stop him.

"Oh, Jesus," Ronald Free said, as he covered his eyes with his hand.

Teeter grasped his arm and squeezed. "Strength," he said. Free kept his eyes covered.

"Okay," Mattox said. "What did you do after you last saw her on Friday night?"

"He went to bed," Capshaw replied, instantaneously.

"With Sunday Free?" Mattox asked.

"Gosh, no!" Hank replied. "I mean, I liked Sunday fine. I would have dated her, but I've been sort of seeing someone else for a while now."

"Whom Hank might or might not have slept with at the party is immaterial," Capshaw said. "Except to the extent that person may be needed to verify his story. However, if he did spend the night with another student, I can assure you the name is on the list."

"Did you, at any point, have sexual relations with Sunday Free?" Mattox asked.

"We kissed a couple of times in the pool, but that was it. I liked her a lot. Sunday was a terrific girl. I never would have done anything to hurt her." Tears formed at the corners of his eyes.

"Do you know who gave her the Quaaludes?" Mattox asked.

"I'm going to instruct Hank not to answer," Capshaw interrupted before Hank could respond. "We haven't established she obtained any drugs at the party."

"Do you know who had sex with Sunday Free?" Mattox asked.

"Again, I'm going to instruct Hank not to respond," Capshaw answered. "We've already established he last saw her in the swimming pool before any sexual activity took place. Any response he might make about events after that point would be speculation and hearsay."

"Doesn't seem like you want to let Hank say much of anything," Jude said.

"We want to get to the bottom of this as much as anyone in this room.

Otherwise, I would have told Hank not to come here all. We have established Hank did give Sunday a ride to the party but was unaware of any activity after he went upstairs from the pool. I might suggest your investigation take up at that point with the other youths listed on the paper. I'm sure some of them would have better information."

* * *

Jude walked Hank and Carl Capshaw to the parking lot.

"How will this situation affect Hank's football status?" Capshaw asked.

"Can't see how it will, at least for now," Jude said. Hank relaxed visibly at the news. "Maybe it was all a horrible accident. Nobody has accused Hank of anything illegal, and no charges have been filed. Principal Black is steamed, but he can't impose disciplinary action against Hank for something he did on his own time, off school grounds. As far as I can tell, there's no reason he can't play."

"That's good news," Capshaw said. "Right, Hank?"

"Hold up a minute," Jude said. "I wouldn't call this a win. Word's going to spread. Someone at Prosperity High knows the truth. Others will presume they know, and life might get hard for you, Hank."

"I can handle it."

"All right. Get to class. Right now, you're still starting Friday night. Flunk your Algebra test this week, and all bets are off."

Hank shook Capshaw's hand as the class change bell sounded, and he ran off toward the front entrance.

"Thanks for your help," Capshaw said, extending his hand. "Mr. Bowie is also grateful, as is Congressman Poole."

"Rennie? How's he figure in all this?"

"I work for the Congressman. I thought you knew."

Jude left the man's hand hanging in dead air.

"Nice meeting you," Jude said. "It's always nice to put a face on the enemy. Got a class."

He walked away, but spied Angeloe Teeter waving goodbye to the Frees as they drove off. Teeter stood next to a glistening orange Mustang fastback as Jude drew near him.

"Nice wheels," he said. Teeter looked up, and tensed, as if he expected Jude to take a swing at him.

"Yes," he said, waiting for more.

"That's mine," Jude said, pointing at the Willys parked several spaces away.

"Kind of an antique," Teeter said.

"It's seen a few summers. I rodded it in 1953, and had it restored about fifteen years later."

"You built this?"

"The first time. My girlfriend's father owns a shop here in town. They did the second restoration."

"I know about restorations," Teeter said, laying a hand on the roof of his Mustang. "I bought this with money I earned lugging fifty-pound bags of seed and manure and loam and peat moss at Poole's Feed and Seed in Morgan. I washed cars and mowed lawns and painted houses until I'd saved enough so no white man could refuse to sell it to me. I paid cash for it in the morning, and by evening I'd been accosted by a race-baiting cop, beaten to a pulp, shot in the leg, had three teeth ripped from my mouth, and my car had been turned into a battered public toilet. These scars on my head? A souvenir from some redneck kid who only saw a black face. This car sat behind my house, under a tarp, for four years as I got an education, and for two more while I was at seminary. When I got out, I had enough money saved to restore it. It looks showroom cherry now, right? That's what I want for my people. I want them to rise from the ashes of Jim Crow and take their rightful place at the table."

"Cool," Jude said. "You're welcome to a ride in my Willys, but it might disappoint. All it stands for is fun driving. Nice to meet you, Reverend. Let me know if you'd like to catch the football game this Friday night. I can get you passes."

* * *

Jude found Hank Bowie waiting outside his office.

"I'm sorry, Coach."

"About what?" Jude said, unlocking the door.

"All this trouble. Ever since Saturday morning, I can't eat or sleep or anything."

Unbidden, the horrible video of Coral Pyle's death played for the millionth time inside Jude's head. "Believe me, it would have been far worse if you had tried to hide it."

"I didn't tell everything. I gave Sunday the 'ludes. I got them from my mother's medicine cabinet. I only gave her one or two, and I told her not to drink if she took them, but—yeah. She got them from me."

Jude closed the office door. His face darkened as he stared down his quarterback.

"Why on earth would you tell me something like that?" he asked.

"It has to come out sometime. I didn't want you disappointed in me."

"You don't understand, damn it!" Jude said, perhaps a bit more angrily than he intended. Hank leaned back, his face clouding. "I'm a football coach, Hank. That's all. Nothing you tell me is confidential. If an attorney asks me in court whether you had some part in what happened to Sunday, I'll have to tell him everything you told me. You might as well have sworn to it on a stack of Bibles. You want my advice? Get ahead of it. Sheriff Mattox is still here, interviewing students in the conference room. Tell him exactly what you told me, especially the part where you told Sunday not to drink if she took the pills."

Hank's eyes wetted, and he brushed at his hair with one hand. He swatted at a tear that escaped and rolled across his cheek. "Mr. Capshaw told me not to talk to Sheriff Mattox. He said nothing good could come of it. I'm really confused."

"Capshaw's your lawyer?"

"I never met him before. He showed up at my door Sunday afternoon. Said my dad sent him."

"Capshaw told me he works for Congressman Poole."

"My dad donates a lot of money to Mr. Poole's campaigns."

"Hank, listen carefully. If Capshaw works for Poole, he isn't representing your interests. His first loyalty will be to the congressman. I suspect Poole is much more interested in preventing a scandal for your father. Your attorney is supposed to work for *you*."

"What are you saying?"

"You need a new lawyer. Someone whose only duty is to you."

Hank swiped at his face again. "Do you know any?"

"A couple. I can give you their names."

"Will you come with me?"

"I can't. Nobody can know we've had this conversation. If they know what you told me, I can be forced to testify to it in court."

"You could lie about it. Say I never told you nothing."

"I've told way too many lies in my life. I'm done lying. If they ask me, I'll tell the truth. You can't let anyone know we've spoken, at least until you have your own attorney."

Chapter Forty-One

Prosperity High had a public announcement boulder on the edge of the Morgan Highway. Nicknamed 'The Rawk' by the students, it had grown incrementally over the years under hundreds of layers of paint proclaiming birthdays, graduations, dances, upcoming plays, and frequent taunts directed toward visiting teams.

When Jude drove up to the school the next morning, The Rawk was painted flat black. In brilliant white letters were the words *Who Speaks for Sunday Free?*

When Jude reached the mailroom, Principal Black collared him. "Hank Bowie is missing. He left school around midday yesterday. He didn't show up for his afternoon classes. Was he at football practice?"

"We canceled," Jude said. "I decided it would be in poor taste to hold practice. I last saw Hank a little after lunch. He's really upset about Sunday."

"There's another matter," Mattox said as he walked up behind them. He pulled an envelope from his pocket. "One of your players, Tim Aiken, was passing one of these across the aisle in sixth period yesterday. When his teacher saw it, she checked his bookbag. Kid had a half dozen Polaroids in his satchel."

They were taken from different angles and different heights. Each picture centered on a nude Sunday Free, sprawled on a narrow cabana daybed, engaged in different sex acts with various boys, all shot from behind. Sunday's drug-slackened vapid features, her body glistening with sweat, and her blasted eyes staring into a void, unfocused and swiveling like a chameleon's, reminded Jude of something. Something tragic, distant. He shut his own eyes, vainly trying to destroy the mental image.

"I'm no expert," Mattox said, "but these pictures, in my opinion, depict a woman of color being subjected to sexual abuse by a gang of white youths."

"Why show me this?" Jude asked. He shuffled the photos into a pile and returned them to the envelope.

"Thought you might be laboring under the misconception your players are a bunch of choirboys."

"I know better. I played football here back in the day. We were as wild then as my kids are now. Teenagers are like that. If you thought showing me these pictures would humiliate me, Brian, you're shit out of luck."

"So, you condone the behavior at the party on Friday night?"

"Don't put words in my mouth. I know my boys as well as any coach, and I know their warts, too."

"If you know them so well," Mattox said. "Perhaps you can identify some of them from these pictures. We know one of them is Aiken, but he's keeping his trap shut about the whole thing."

"I already looked. I didn't see anyone recognizable."

"Come on, Coach. Your office has a picture window looking out on the locker room. I bet you've seen every boy on your team buck naked a dozen times. Take another look. This time try to keep your eyes off the girl."

Jude flushed and considered climbing across the table to disassemble the sheriff. His hands trembling in fury, he took the pictures out again. He looked over each one, carefully.

"Recognize anything?" Mattox asked.

"Maybe," Jude said. "This one might be Todd Engelman, the boy who found her in the pool. Another could be Aaron Craighead, but I wouldn't swear to it. The rest? I got nothing."

"It's a start," Mattox said. "Thanks, Coach. You will let me know if Hank Bowie contacts you?"

"For what it's worth, Hank didn't have any intention of harming Sunday, and he didn't know what was happening downstairs when these pictures were taken. He's torn apart by the entire affair."

"Okay," Mattox said. "Whatever. Thanks for the help."

Chapter Forty-Two

Rennie Poole, rocking in one of the chairs on Jude's front porch, affected a gentlemanly wave as Jude pulled himself from the Willys. "You ever gonna trade that piece of junk, boy?" Rennie said, the forced bonhomie in his voice almost convincing.

"Something I can do for you, Congressman?"

"It's a raw day. You could invite me in."

"You've seen the inside of my house for the last time. I've had a tough day. I like the air out here. It's brisk. Invigorating. Gets the blood flowing."

"Have it your way. Misplaced any quarterbacks lately?"

"You're here to tell me where I can find Hank Bowie?"

"Not at all. You've done enough damage, advising the boy to find his own attorney. Is there something wrong with Mr. Capshaw? Not Jewish enough?"

"He works for you. That's plenty against him. Where's Hank?"

"He's safe and sound. His father and I have seen to it. Hank won't be returning to Prosperity High. Thought I'd let you know, as a courtesy. By this time next week, Hank will be enrolled out of state."

"Pulling strings to get him into some fancy prep school?" Jude said.

"Not... precisely. Lance thinks his son might need a little starch in his spine. Spending the rest of his high school career in scratchy wool seemed the best option."

"Military school."

"Only the best, and it's outside the state borders."

"You didn't tell your pet sheriff?"

284

"I'll get around to it. 'Tween you, me, and the lamppost, I'm not entirely satisfied with the sheriff's performance of late. He's beginning to think independently. I may be forced to recruit someone to run against him next election."

"There's always Larry Stilson. Yank his leash and he'll follow you anywhere."

"Excellent suggestion. I was thinking along those same lines."

"Deposing Brian Mattox might not be a good idea. He got his job by keeping a big secret of yours. What's the statute of limitations on lynching in this state?"

"Brian knows to keep his mouth shut. I have plenty on him, too. That's not why I'm here. I need a favor. A contributor to my gubernatorial campaign has requested assistance, a pressing matter involving a state contract to let."

"You want some of the money."

"About fifty thousand. I'd suggest taking it from several different accounts. A couple thousand here, a couple there. Looks less suspicious."

"I've been your bagman for several years now. I know how it works."

"I never asked. How did your buddy Owen Wheeler like getting his debts paid off?" Rennie tossed it off innocuously.

"He was relieved. I didn't use any of your dirty money. I have my own, you know. Football paid nicely for the little work I put in. Told him I was making a campaign contribution, one time only, and with one condition."

"What's that?"

"Never run for office again."

"Taking care of your friend. I admire that. Owen is a fine man, especially now he's sobered up. Roots a mile deep in Prosperity soil. I like the boy. But he isn't cut out for politics. You act as if you detest me, but we both know better. I held you in my arms the first week you drew breath. I've been there every important moment of your life. You might even say I raised you as much as your mom and dad did. You know what they say?"

"What?"

"Fruit don't fall far, kid. Big things are coming, once I'm elected governor. There's a role for you, too. A big one. Can't talk about it yet, but by God,

285

you're gonna love it. There's one more matter. I need you to develop a sudden case of amnesia. When Hank Bowie came home yesterday, he was in a state. Told a fascinating story about a conversation he had with you. I need you to forget you ever had that conversation. It's bad enough this Free girl died in Lance's house. If it came out Hank gave the girl the drugs that contributed to her death—well, it would be incredibly unfortunate."

"You want me to lie."

"I want you to forget. Who among us remembers every snippet of every conversation we have in a day? Just say you can't recall exactly what he told you."

"I won't do it."

"I'm just an old country boy, but I believe you'll realize my way is best once you put your mind to it. There's too much to lose going the other way, don't you think?"

"No."

"You will. Trust me. Fifty thousand dollars. I'll send someone to pick up the money on Friday. Gotta run. Still have to grease some skids at Overton Military Academy. Now I think of it, you're right. The air out here *is* invigorating. See you on the flip side, *son*."

Chapter Forty-Three

Picketers formed in a huge oval in front of the school shortly after sunrise, marching in rhythm to a hymn directed by Angeloe Teeter in the center. He looked like the ringmaster in a circus horse act, rotating with the protesters as if swinging them on the end of strings. Most of them carried signs—*Who Speaks for Sunday Free?* and *Justice for Sunday!* and several blown-up copies of Sunday's high school photo. News trucks from Pooler and beyond had parked on the shoulder of the Morgan Highway. Their crews were setting up cameras, the on-air talent primping before they stepped in front of the lenses.

Jude watched from Principal Black's office. "Things are getting out of hand."

"Tell me about it," Black said. "Any word on Hank Bowie? Did he show up?"

"No," Jude said. "Think the sheriff's department's gonna run them off?"

"Public property," Black said. "As long as they don't disrupt the classes or traffic in and out of the parking lot, they can march 'til the cows come home."

"Rennie Poole is in town. Anything is possible. Has he contacted you?"

"He's coming out later this morning to meet with Reverend Teeter, try to find a reasonable solution to this mess."

* * *

Rennie milked his moment. He arrived again by helicopter, marched up to the protesters, waited politely for an opportunity to step inside their marching circle, and headed directly to Angeloe Teeter. He was sure to extend his hand, fully aware the news cameras were watching.

As he grasped Teeter's hand, he leaned in and whispered a few words. Teeter backed up a little, his face pensive. He turned to his flock, who fell silent at his gesture.

"The Congressman and I are going to have a discussion," Teeter announced.

He and Rennie left the circle and made their way to the school office. The circle of protesters resumed their marching and chanting. An hour later, Rennie and Teeter emerged. Neither smiled openly, in keeping with the gravity of the circumstances. Watching on the television in his office, Jude recognized Rennie's expression of controlled solemnity, a posture he'd practiced for years. Rennie's eyes, though, betrayed his triumph. He'd been successful in stemming the unrest, and he intended to suck every smidgen of sweet he could out of the moment.

The pair walked back up the hill, where the picketers marched and sang. Teeter stood before the waiting cameras, his clear, baritone voice carrying over the crowd.

"I have met with the Congressman. He is personally taking oversight of the investigation at the Sheriff's Department. I believe in my heart—now—we have the attention of people who can get us the answers we seek. We asked, *Who Speaks for Sunday Free?* I can tell you. *You* speak for Sunday Free. *You* speak for justice. *You* speak for the truth. Congressman Poole heard you. Now, Congressman Poole speaks for Sunday Free!"

The crowd applauded and collapsed around the preacher and the congressman. On the tiny television screen in his office, Jude could see Rennie's face clearly. He looked like a wolf who had landed a plump fawn, but constantly careful to keep his good side toward the cameras.

* * *

"A *what?*" Jude asked.

"A rally," Tom Black repeated. "Congressman Poole would like to use the school auditorium for a public gathering Monday night. He wants the mayor and the sheriff and Reverend Teeter to attend and speak to the crowd. He wants to—wait, it's in the letter here—he wants to reaffirm his commitment to civil rights and universal human dignity and help to bring the diverse communities in Bliss County closer together, so they can learn there is more connecting them than there is dividing them."

"I might puke," Jude said.

"He wants you to speak too."

"About what?"

"Surely you two have discussed this? Congressman Poole thinks you could make a decent politician someday. He mentioned putting you up for mayor. Follow in your father's footsteps."

Jude closed Black's office door.

"Between you and me," he said. "what did Rennie give you to make me football coach?"

Black shook his head and sighed. "I was ninety percent in your corner already. I agreed having a former pro as coach would give our program a boost. You probably would have gotten the job anyway."

"What made it a certainty?"

"Poole sweetened the pot. That's all I'll tell you. It's all you want to know, right? As a football coach, you are invaluable. What is it with you and Poole anyway? You snarl at each other like a couple of fighting dogs. I'd think it would be a real benefit to have a guy with his juice in your corner."

"Sure," Jude said. "It's a game-changer. I gotta boogie. Have to get to the banks before they close."

* * *

Grace spent Thursday night at Jude's house. Their on-again-off-again romance was in the distant past. Those days had ended the night Grace snuck up on Jude in the boys' shower. Jude and Grace had been constant companions for almost four years.

They lay on the bed, the sheets twisted about them, her blonde hair draped over his arm. She drew random shapes on his chest with her fingernail.

"What's in the bag downstairs?" she asked.

"Which bag?"

"The glossy, new-car-smelling, high-priced Corinthian fucking leather mailbag in the entrance hall. You know damned well which bag."

"Present for a friend. You got a mouth on you, Mrs. Corey."

"You'd know. It's been all over you."

She rolled on top of him. A half-hour later, they collapsed into the pillows again.

"Not bad for a couple of forty-somethings," he said, as he drew her inside his arms. Later, he said, "Why in hell would Rennie want me to speak at the rally? What do I know about race relations?"

"You corral an interracial gang of brutes with gallons of testosterone and auxiliary Y chromosomes every week, and you get them to work together to beat another gang of brutes. You're like the poster child for peacemaking."

"Yeah, but what do I talk about on Monday?"

"You're a jock. It's a low bar. Tell a joke, toss off a few sports metaphors, sing a verse of *Kumbaya*, and bring it home."

"Bring what home?"

"The bacon, baby. Make the women wet and the men jealous."

* * *

Shortly after lunch on Friday, the telephone rang in Jude's office. He'd been expecting the call.

"Jude? This is Congressman Poole." On the surface, Rennie's voice was crisp and businesslike. The undertone was pure worry.

"Something I can do for you, Rennie?"

"I received the package you left on the porch."

"You like the bag?"

"Yes," Rennie said, his voice concerned. "It's nice. The…the contents are… confusing."

"I'm sure you've seen seven hundred thousand dollars and change in one place before. Sorry it wasn't a nice round number, but I took some out to buy the bag."

"What does this mean, son?"

"I told you never to call me that. I'm just an old country boy, myself, but handing all the money over to you appears to sever our ties. The preacher over in Morgan, Angeloe Teeter? He seems like a nice kid. Did you know he used to work for you, loading bags of seed and manure in your warehouse?"

"It didn't come up."

"A real success story. Think I might have to take the reverend out to lunch sometime next week, tell him all about the man he's in bed with. Maybe put a bug in his ear, tell him you know who gave Sunday Free the quaaludes."

"You want to dump the gravel from your mouth?"

"We're finished. I handed over every last penny from my father's accounts. I closed them yesterday afternoon. Do what you want with it."

Poole's voice dropped to a hoarse whisper. "What in fuck's sake am I supposed to do with this much cash? You know how long it will take to deposit it in dribs and drabs to avoid reports to the feds?"

"Your problems are not automatically my problems. I just relieved myself of a five alarm headache."

"I don't mind saying, boy, this complicates matters. Could I convince you to reconsider your decision?"

"It's your money now. Maybe some of your mob buddies can launder it for you. Might get a quarter on the dollar, but it would be something. I'm busy, Congressman. Got a speech to write, but it's been real nice talking to you. See you on Monday, right?"

He dropped the receiver to the cradle before Rennie could answer.

* * *

At his campaign office in Morgan, Rennie slammed the phone receiver into its cradle three times.

"Damn that boy!" he shouted.

Sitting across from him, Deputy Stilson didn't look up from paring his nails with a pocketknife. "Coach giving you fits?"

"I tried," Rennie said. "God knows I tried. The boy is impervious to reason. Now he's put me in a real spot. What in fuck am I supposed to do with all that?" He gestured toward the fine leather bag in the corner, bulging with cash.

"I'll take it off your hands."

"You would, too. I suspect Coach Pressley has crossed the Rubicon. He may be irredeemable now."

"What are you suggesting?" Stilson asked.

"He knows too much. I thought I could keep him in line. I was mistaken. Drastic measures might be required. Tell me, Larry. Just how badly do you want to be sheriff in Bliss County?"

Chapter Forty-Four

Owen was overjoyed, not only to have a child, but to have a son to carry on the farm and the Wheeler name.

Chloe was another issue. Owen saw flashes of fear in her face, the kind you see in caged animals who have only recently comprehended the permanence of their captivity. Judd was the padlock on her marriage. With the baby, Chloe was stuck fast. Unless she wanted to ruin all their lives, she was strapped in for the entire ride. She sweated through dreams of being buried alive and had no need of Doctor Freud's expertise to explain them.

She lay in bed, trying to block out Judd's cries in the next room. A tickle in the back of her brain told her she was supposed to do something about him but, as hard as she willed it to rise, her body refused to obey.

Before Judd was born, Chloe believed she was falling in love with her husband.

This is love? she thought as Judd wailed in the next room. *What a cheat.*

Four years after Owen hopped on the temperance wagon, she realized she'd been infatuated. He'd shown her affection and caring and love, in a way he hadn't since their comic strip wedding in Dillon. He'd made her feel valued and desired. She'd lapped it up—until it started to fall apart again.

Once Judd arrived, it was her job to care for him. Every fucking minute. Every goddamned day. Her putative maternal instincts never seemed to kick in. She loved Judd, but she also resented having every detail of his care foisted on her. Owen was almost no help, as he hopped out of bed before sunrise and was out the door to the day's work on the farm. By the time he dragged himself back into the house, showered the sweat and the grime from his body, and ate his dinner, he was so wiped out he went straight to bed. She was cuckolded by a force she couldn't fight. The Wheeler land was intertwined with Owen's DNA long before Chloe was born.

Judd called out, "Mom-mee!", and the crying resumed.

Chloe tossed the covers aside and padded to the kitchen. She didn't bother to wrap her naked body in a robe. There was nobody to peep at her. She might as well be on a deserted island, thousands of miles from another human being. She pulled a bottle of vodka from under the sink in the kitchen, way back in the cabinet.

"He's got his fuckin' farm," she said, as she unscrewed the cap.

* * *

Saturday morning, Owen met with Clyde Dillard at the hardware in Prosperity.

If possible, Clyde had grown even more pear-shaped over the years. His sunken chest and narrow shoulders dropped like a ski slope to his wide, corpulent hips and rotund belly, as if someone had put clothes on a Hershey's Kiss. The hair on the top of his head had thinned to a few lonely strands which sprung directly up like wiry curled antennae. His glasses magnified his eyes into imposing owl-like orbs.

Satisfied that both of their recoveries were safe for another week, they had switched to gossip and small talk. During a lull in the conversation, a light seemed to come on behind Clyde's eyes.

"Oh, hell, what am I thinking? Been carrying this around for several days." He pulled an object from the pocket of his overalls. "You wanted to know about the mermaid out on Six Mile Creek?"

"Clyde, we settled that. There aren't any mermaids. Not in the ocean and not in Six Mile Creek. What you saw might have been Coral Pyle skinny-dipping."

"A couple of years later, I went back. Fishing, you know. I saw the sun reflect off this thing, wedged under a rock. Pretty, ain't it? I held on to it in case I ever got myself a girlfriend. Not much chance of that anymore, I reckon."

Owen examined the heart-shaped locket. Something about it spurred a memory so indistinct, so hazy, he couldn't grab it as it flitted about his head. He slipped a cracked fingernail between the locket halves and sprung them open. "Looks like a picture in here."

"Yeah. Couldn't make it out, though."

Owen's voice was suddenly solemn. "Bet you could if you gave it enough thought."

The picture in the locket had faded over the years, but there was enough of an outline—including a full head of black hair combed into a ducktail pompadour—that he could recognize it. He'd seen the same picture a dozen times over the years as he reminisced over his high school yearbook. He'd know the silhouette anywhere.

"Mind if I borrow this?" he asked.

"Take it," Clyde said. "Hell, I don't see any of them disco chicks dropping into my lap. You can have it. Make a nice present for your wife. What's her name again?"

* * *

Reverend Angeloe Teeter slid into the passenger seat of Jude's Willys hot rod.

"Smells like new," he said, over the rumble of the engine.

"Thought we'd air it out a little on the back roads. Bet you've had your Mustang over the limit once or twice."

"Me?" Teeter said. "Naw. I'm a straight arrow, man. Can't let the flock think I'm a big ol' scofflaw. Of course, you can do whatever you want. Punch it, Parnelli."

They headed out of town on a back highway toward South Carolina.

"You don't sound like many of the holy rollers I've come across in my life," Jude said.

"You're white. White religion arises from a position of privilege. It's polite and genteel. It's about preserving all the lovely perks you people have hoarded since—well, forever. The kind of faith we promote in the black community is more akin to what Joseph's descendants practiced in Egypt."

"Meaning?"

"They knew they were living in the bottom of the cesspool, but there was hope for better. White people go to church for congregation and confirmation. Colored people go to ward off desperation."

"I like what you do there. The rhyming."

"Part of the package. White people sow their wild oats all week, and on Sunday they pray for crop failure. Black people carry their church around inside them all week long. I remind them the better days are coming, if we're patient enough to wait and strong enough to fight. This rust bucket only goes up to eighty?"

Jude goosed the loud pedal, and the rear tires fishtailed. "It'll go faster. Didn't want to scare you."

"Can't scare me, Jasper. When I was a kid, I thought I might want to drive race cars. Dumb idea. I mean, whoever heard of a black race driver—at least, a winning one? I watched every race I could find on TV. My favorite driver was Billy Mosack."

"He and I played football together."

"No shit? Were you good friends?"

"We were close. He could be an asshole, but we always worked through it. Have a question. Maybe you can answer it."

"Shoot."

"I know who gave Sunday the Quaaludes."

After a long beat, Teeter said, "Haven't heard a question."

"I'm getting to it. I have to make a decision." He pulled the car into a vacant gas station and let it idle. "If I don't tell the police what I know, it'll get buried, and nobody will ever know why Sunday died."

"Following you so far."

"If I tell, I violate a trust."

"In the interest of a greater good."

"Jesus. You're what? Twenty-eight? What do you know about the greater good?"

Teeter fingered the halo of scars around his head. "Enough. What about the person who gave her the drugs? Why can't he come forward?"

"He's juggling bad advice from powerful people."

"To keep himself safe? You're sure that's bad advice?"

The image of Coral Pyle's face flashed in Jude's mind. "Yeah. I'm sure."

"Sounds like you have to change his mind."

"I can't get to him anymore. He's... relocated."

"Leaving you holding the snitch bag. Wouldn't want to be in your shoes, Whitey."

"I was hoping for advice."

"You want me to tell you what to do? My advice is you drive right back to Morgan and tell the sheriff everything you know."

"And violate a trust?" Jude asked.

"I don't give a damn about any trust some rich white kid has placed in you. If he squealed on himself, it's his problem. My interest is in my parishioners, one of whom recently went into the ground long before her time. I want justice for Sunday Free. So, yeah, I'd recommend ratting the kid out. On the other hand, I recognize your dilemma, and I hope I live a long life without facing one like it. I can't tell you what to do. I appreciate you telling me, but we'll keep it between us."

"I also want to warn you," Jude said. "The sit-down you had with Rennie Poole. I hope you didn't give away the farm."

"I didn't give away anything."

"I've known the man all my life. You can't trust him. Ever."

Teeter chuckled. "You think I *trusted* that cracker? I don't trust any white man, Coach. Not even you, and you've been civil to me."

"He's using you to—"

"And I'm using him. Times are changing. We're more than a hundred years past Reconstruction, and the black community is still scrambling for crumbs. My goal is to make us self-sustaining. Never gonna take the white man's second-hands again. We're taking our seat at the table, any way we have to."

* * *

Chloe had finally gotten Judd out of the crib and was feeding him in his booster seat at the kitchen table. Her vision was bleary, and her mouth felt like kitty litter. She'd pounded back five or six shots of vodka, impatient for the buzz and glow to kick in, and had overdone it. She was drunk, which put a cheerier aspect on the day but otherwise rendered her incapable of processing anything around her except her most important function—making it to sunset with Judd still on the breathing list.

Owen's truck pulled into the gravel circle in front of the house.

"Daddy's home," she said sourly. Judd spit a mouthful of peas onto the placemat.

The truck door slammed. Owen walked into the kitchen, went straight to the refrigerator without talking to Chloe or his son, and poured a glass of sweet tea. He sat at the table and stroked Judd's head, his eyes fixed on Chloe.

"You've been drinking," he said.

"So?"

"I found out something today. Something important. Something that might be terrible. I need to talk to you about Jude."

An icy cataract flowed down the inside of her chest. Her heart seemed to stop for an instant, and the room spun. If Owen was asking her about Jude, it could only mean one thing.

"It doesn't matter," she said, her words falling from her mouth into a slurry puddle in the air. "It lasted a month. That's it. You had practically turned your entire life over to a losing political crusade. You were so drunk you couldn't get a hard-on with a milking machine."

He blinked once or twice. "I don't—"

"You had stopped being a husband. I was desperate. He was available," she said. "And, like I said, it doesn't matter. I'm leaving you."

"What?"

"I'm going crazy on this fucking farm. Day in, day out, the same thing, over and over, forever. I don't want your money, and I don't want any settlement. As long as you didn't know about Jude, I could cope. Now, you know everything, I can't look you in the eye anymore. You can keep Judd. The only thing I want is out. You finish feeding him. I'm packing."

He appeared at the bedroom door several minutes later.

"I put Judd in his playpen. I'm confused. You? And Jude?"

"You want the details?" Chloe said, as she flung clothes onto the bed. "Want to know how he was in the sack?"

"I...don't..." He wasn't tracking. "When?"

"A long time ago. Before Judd was born. Before Jude and Grace became a permanent item. It's been over for years. I can see the hurt in your eyes, Owen. I'm sorry, but you knew who I was when you married me. Jude tried to warn you. *I* tried to warn you!"

She closed the suitcase and fastened the straps.

"Where are you going?" Owen asked.

"Wherever the road stops."

She carried the suitcase out the front door and dropped it into the trunk of the Fairlane. He followed her.

"You don't have to do this," he argued. "We can work things out. Counseling, maybe."

She turned to face him. Her cheeks were flushed and wet with tears. "I'd have to care. Don't be hard on Jude. I tried for years to land that dumb hunk of meat, and he fended me off every time. I caught him in a moment of weakness. We were drunk and stoned, and I wanted to hurt you as badly as you could hurt. All my fault, Owen. Put the blame on me. See you around, farm boy. It was fun."

She kissed his cheek and slid behind the wheel of the car. The engine rumbled to life, shaking the ground underneath Owen's feet. Without looking back, she peeled out on the gravel path through the woods to the Morgan Highway.

* * *

Jude dropped Angeloe Teeter off at his church in Morgan and pointed the

Willys toward Prosperity.

The young preacher impressed him. What he hadn't done was make Jude's decision any easier.

He turned onto the Morgan Highway and cleared the pipes with a sudden burst of acceleration that forced him back in the seat. The pressure soothed all the cracked and chipped bones in his back from his football days. It seemed all the sins of his youth, physical and moral, were catching up with him in middle age.

The land on either side of the highway was open pastureland and fields of corn stalks left over from harvest. They'd be plowed under in a week or so, to decompose and restore the earth. The smell of the harvest lingered in the air, a mixture of dust and decay and mold and rot, accented with smoke from a hundred trash fires in fields stretching from Morgan to Mica Wells. The perfume of autumn, a single happy fragment from Jude's childhood that triggered memories of hayrides, and trick-or-treats, and long Christmas vacations from school. Despite the mountain of worries heaped on his shoulders, Jude dared to allow a smile to creep onto his face.

He didn't see the battered Ford truck bearing down on him from behind.

* * *

Owen sat in the nursery, rocking Judd in an antique bentwood chair that had been in the family since before the Civil War. He hummed an old hymn softly, trying to comfort the boy, who snuffled and asked several times where Mommy had gone.

Owen tried to make sense of the waterfall of words that had cascaded from Chloe's mouth as she walked out of his life. The betrayal was horrible, but it paled in comparison with his other suspicions. As soon as he saw the weather-bleached photo inside the locket, the pieces fell together. Clyde Dillard had discovered the locket on the flat rock face, above the flood line, years after Coral's death. The picture inside the locket was undeniably Jude. Nobody else—except Clyde—knew about the rock on Six Mile Creek. Jude and Owen had discovered it when they were teenagers and had never told anyone else about it.

When all the parts meshed, the conclusion was obvious. Jude must have had something going with Coral and had shown her the secret sunning and swimming spot on the creek. She'd been there the day she died. She'd removed her necklace, for fear the picture might be ruined, and placed it in a safe niche in the rocks.

Then... what? How did she die? The extent of her injuries seemed to defy an accidental death.

"Oh, Jude," Owen whispered. "What in hell did you do?"

* * *

The blur of motion in the mirror caught Jude's attention an instant before the truck rammed into the rear of his car. He fishtailed, got out of the gas reflexively, and waited for the car to settle. The truck dropped back ten or fifteen yards. Jude could see a billet of pressure-treated two-by-ten bolted to the bumper as a battering ram.

"What in hell?" he said, just as the truck engine roared again, and the distance between them shrank. He stabbed at the accelerator, too late, and braced himself for the impact.

It sounded as if someone had dropped a piano on the roof. The Willys' rear tires lifted off the ground. The car lurched to one side, the nose pointed toward a cow pasture on the right side of the road. Jude turned in the direction of the slide, only to have the rear wheels dig into the asphalt and snap the car in a spin to the left. The momentum carried it off the road and into a drainage ditch, where the bumper gouged into clay and launched the car in a series of flips end-over-end across the brown stubble and cow patties in the field.

As he left the road, and before the world began to tumble, Jude caught the face of the man driving the truck. The face leered at him, the mouth twisted in a triumphant sneer. There was no mistaking the man's identity.

It was Larry Stilson.

Chapter Forty-Five

Jude woke in the hospital, wires poking in all directions from under his thin cotton gown. A persistent beep annoyed him. A swarthy male face framed by a dark beard loomed in from above.

"Mr. Pressley? I'm Doctor Patel. Can you hear me?" His voice was heavily accented, with a British lilt.

"Sure," Jude said. "Where am I?"

"Bliss Regional Hospital. You were in an automobile accident. There don't appear to be any fractures. Your head took a beating, though. From the ambulance report, your car traveled quite a distance after leaving the road and flipped several times. I'm surprised you aren't injured worse than you are."

"It's a pre-war Willys," Jude said. "They built them like tanks."

"A fortunate happenstance, though it is my understanding your car may be beyond repair. We have run a few tests. I'm waiting for the results. We should be able to release you tomorrow."

"Tomorrow?"

"A precaution. We'll keep you overnight for observation. Sometimes the consequences of a bump on the head take some time to manifest. Believe me, you don't want any post-concussion complications."

"I was a pro football player, Doc. I know about getting my bell rung."

"Then you will appreciate our caution. I'll be back later to check on you. If you need anything, you can buzz for the nurse. Is there anything I can get you right now?"

"A phone," Jude said. "And a telephone directory."

* * *

"You think this is a good idea?" Grace said the next day, as Jude lowered himself into the hot tub and settled into the body-molded seat. "Seems I read somewhere you should stay away from these things if you have a head injury."

"I got my noggin thumped," Jude said. "No worse than any hard hit I ever took on the field. The rest of my body feels like I went fifteen rounds with Muhammed Ali. The hot water takes the ache off."

She dropped her robe and climbed over the edge next to him. She handed him a glass of iced sweet tea, the strongest thing he was allowed to drink for the next week. He took a sip and allowed his head to roll backward into a cushion.

"Please don't come to the rally tomorrow," he said.

"Why on earth not?"

"I can't explain. I just don't want you there."

"Well, that's a fine thing. Biggest event in Prosperity since July fourth, and you tell me to stay away. You're scaring me, Jude."

"If it keeps you away, fine. If you have a shred of love for me, you'll skip the rally."

She pushed up from the seat and floated closer to him. She placed a hand on his chest. "I have a damned sight more than a shred of love, Coach. This has something to do with Rennie Poole?"

"Everything in this damned town has something to do with Rennie. This is mostly about me, though. Stay away?"

"Promise me. Take an oath on whatever it is you hold sacred you won't do anything stupid."

"Not a chance," Jude said. "Those days are over."

* * *

Jude was in his office in the gym, threading a tie around his collar, when Owen caught up with him on Monday, half an hour before the rally.

"Owen!" Jude said when his friend rounded the corner. There was something strange about Owen's face. It looked twisted, a tortured scowl.

"I have to talk to you," Owen said. "It's important."

"Absolutely. Right after the rally. You're going, right?"

"The whole damn town is going. I need to talk to you *now*."

"I'm sorry, bud. Don't have time. I have to meet with Principal Black before we go to the auditorium. I love you like a brother, man, but *tempus fugit*." He tapped his watch.

"Okay," Owen said, his features darkening. "After the rally. Have something for you until then."

Jude never saw the punch coming. It started somewhere around Morgan and moved at damned near the speed of light. There was a thunderclap in his head, a bright flash of light, and he was on his back, leaned up against his filing cabinet.

"That's for fucking my wife, you son of a bitch," Owen said, his voice barely containing his fury. "We have a dance date after the rally. You'd better be there."

* * *

Jude's sport jacket handily covered the splotch of blood on his shoulder. At least, after the wreck on Saturday, he had an excuse for the shiner emerging under his left eye.

What really bothered him was the sudden onset of dizziness that struck the instant he tried to stand from his office chair. Adding one concussion on top of another didn't necessarily result in additive injuries. Sometimes the increased severity was exponential. Through the haze and spins, he recognized one critical issue.

Owen knew about him and Chloe. There was only one way he could have found out. Chloe must have confessed.

One more debt to set right.

Bracing himself, he stood. Holding the wall for support, he made his way to the principal's office.

* * *

The auditorium at Prosperity High had been constructed three years earlier, another of Rennie Poole's pork barrel projects to bring tax money back to Prosperity. It had been designed to hold six hundred people in modern plush upholstered chairs. By the time Tom Black and Jude Pressley joined the rest of the party onstage, the house was almost full. Jude's dizziness subsided and was now mere light-headedness. The butterflies in his stomach were warring with one another and, from all indications, they were lobbing nukes.

A lectern sat in the middle of the stage, in front of five chairs. Rennie Poole, Principal Black, Sheriff Mattox, Reverend Teeter, and Jude were all scheduled to speak. Tom Black had asked Jude to introduce the congressman. Rennie and Teeter waited backstage with the sheriff. When he saw Jude, Rennie made a beeline toward him, his hand extended.

"Jude, my boy," he said, his voice expressing practiced solicitation. "I heard about your accident only this morning. Are you all right?"

"I'm fine," Jude said.

"Well, I'm grateful you're able to make it today. You never know, do you? You can be here one second, and—poof—gone the next. I'm just an old country boy, but it's an awe-inspiring thought."

"Yeah," Jude said. "Sometimes you never see it coming."

Jude scanned the crowd. Owen and Clyde Dillard sat in the front row, next to two men in dark suits. Owen glowered at him. Clyde looked sedated, but he usually did.

He didn't see Grace anywhere, and he forced himself to relax.

Tom Black finished his portion of the presentation. "To introduce our first speaker, the Honorable Congressman and candidate for governor of North Carolina, Prosperity's own Reynolds Poole, I am happy to bring to the podium our state championship-winning football coach, Jude Pressley."

The applause warmed Jude inside. One thing was certain. The community loved him. *If only they knew*, he thought, and immediately saw the irony in it. They would know, soon enough. He stepped, a little unsteadily, to the podium.

"I must apologize, should I stammer or lose my place. I had an automobile accident two days ago, and whatever stuffing I have in my punkin' head got disarranged."

The crowd chuckled, though some whispered back and forth, and a few had expressions of concern.

"Didn't help my looks, either," Jude said, pointing toward his bruised face.

"You had some to spare!" someone yelled from the back of the room, and the crowd laughed again. Jude checked Owen, in the front row, and saw his friend still scowling.

"I've been asked to introduce Congressman Reynolds Poole. You know, he's been going by that name for years, and I still can't wrap my tongue around it. For me, he'll always be Uncle Rennie."

The people applauded, some of them tenuously. Jude looked back at Rennie, who beamed.

"For as long as I can remember, he's been a fixture at our house. He and my father were business partners and political partners and just plain buddies for many years. A lot of plans were hatched under our roof. Many of you knew my father, and the close relationship he had with Mr. Poole. I can tell you, without reservation, my father, former Mayor Hubert Pressley, loved and revered the congressman."

Another wave of applause. Jude glanced back at Rennie, who whispered, "He was a wonderful man, your father," loudly enough for the news cameras to pick it up.

"Yep," Jude continued. "My father loved the congressman so much, and believed in him so thoroughly, he gladly ignored his own political and legal safety to help Rennie."

A hush fell over the crowd as they gazed at Jude quizzically. Jude checked Rennie and saw the same look.

Good, he thought.

"I bet I'm one of only two—no, maybe three people in this auditorium who know that, for years, my father, Hubert Pressley, operated a dozen slush fund bank accounts for Mr. Poole. I found out about them when

I inherited his estate. But, don't worry, my friends. Congressman Poole has stated on many occasions how he would like me to fill my late father's position at his side. Let me tell you, he makes one convincing argument, so I finally agreed. At the congressman's earnest insistence, I have continued the family tradition. I have administered Congressman Reynolds Poole's slush fund myself for years."

He pulled an envelope from his jacket pocket.

"I have all the records here. Also in this envelope is a picture of Chief Deputy Sheriff Larry Stilson picking up a money drop for Rennie from my front porch. I hired a private investigator in Parker County several weeks ago to conduct surveillance. He has completed an affidavit stating he watched the parcel from the moment I put the money in it until Deputy Stilson took it from my porch."

In the back of the auditorium, one of the doors banged open, and a figure lurched into the hallway outside.

"That would be Chief Deputy Stilson," Jude said, leaning over the microphone. He stole a quick glance backward and saw Rennie fidgeting in his seat. The audience laughed nervously. "He was also driving the truck that ran me off the road on Saturday, after I told Rennie I wouldn't be his bag man anymore. Officers are posted at all the exit doors in the school. He won't get out of the building."

Poole started to rise, looking to both sides, plotting a convenient escape. The wings of the auditorium both revealed men in dark suits, watching him intently. He retook his seat. His face was green under the hot bright auditorium lights. He leaned forward and stared at the floor.

"When I awoke in the hospital, I realized there was only one way to explain my wreck. I had refused to obey him, and the information I knew could hurt him, so my Uncle Rennie decided to kill me."

The crowd burst into agitated chatter. Jude held his hands up to silence them. They grew quiet again, laser-focused on Jude Pressley.

"I placed a few telephone calls. The two gentlemen in the front row are Agent Tilghman of the Federal Elections Commission, and Agent Wise of the Treasury Department. They're here to have a conversation with

Congressman Poole after the ceremonies. Their friends from the FBI are waiting in the wings to escort him."

As the audience erupted again, Jude turned to Rennie, who glared at him through red eyes.

"Nowhere to run, Rennie," Jude said. "You're strapped in for the whole ride."

He turned back to the microphone.

"But, we're not here today to talk about politics. We'll have plenty of time over the next several weeks to discuss Congressman Poole's finances. We're here today to recognize the congressman's efforts with Reverend Angeloe Teeter to quell the recent disturbances in Prosperity over the unfortunate and untimely death of Sunday Free. Both Mr. Poole and Reverend Teeter deserve our thanks and our congratulations. I have spent time with Reverend Teeter. We've had some intriguing and stimulating conversations, and I know him to be a thoughtful, peaceful, caring, decent, devoted servant to his community."

"Please," Teeter said from his seat, holding up his hands. "Just stop there. I have enough problems!"

The laughter subsided in a few seconds, and Jude continued.

"It really was an accomplishment. They took a situation that was out of control, and they spread oil on the waters. I was impressed at Congressman Poole's efforts to bring racial harmony to Prosperity High School. I was especially stunned, because I've known Uncle Rennie all my life, even back when he was Grand Dragon of the local Ku Klux Klan."

The hall erupted. Jude waited for them to turn their attention back to the stage.

"Rennie's dedication to race relations warms my heart. It proves people really can change. This is not the same man who organized and carried out a lynching in Prosperity only two decades ago!"

It took almost two minutes for the audience to quiet. Jude looked at Owen Wheeler. Both he and Clyde Dillard stared back at him, dumbfounded.

"I was there. The unfortunate young man was named Everett Howard. Some of you remember when Arlo Pyle's daughter Coral died. Her body was found under the Old Village Road Bridge over Six Mile Creek. Nobody was ever charged, because Ev Howard was located the night Coral's body was discovered. Two of my friends and I found him. We thought we were taking him to the sheriff in Morgan, but Rennie had other plans. He and his fellow Klansmen decided to exact their own form of justice. They drove Everett Howard to an isolated pasture and strung him up on a black walnut tree."

Owen tried to catch Jude's attention. He shook his head and mouthed 'No'.

"Arlo Pyle had fired him for stealing money. Everyone jumped to the conclusion he raped and killed Coral as revenge for being fired. That was why he died in a lonely field, struggling at the end of a rope, as Rennie Poole and his buddies hooted and howled and drank and celebrated."

"You can't prove it!" Rennie shouted, jumping from his seat. Angeloe Teeter grabbed his jacket and dragged him back to the chair.

"Don't have to," Jude said. "This isn't about you, Rennie. I've lived with this shame for almost a quarter-century. I can't live with it anymore. Everett Howard didn't kill Coral Pyle. I know this for a fact because... I was with her when she died."

A stream of news people scurried down the aisles and parked themselves at the base of the stage. Five cameras pointed up at Jude and clicked away incessantly, as the room reverberated with talk.

"Coral and I had been dating," Jude said over the noise. The amplifiers boomed with the confession. "We were teenagers—dumb, crazy, not much more than hormones in sneakers. We had a secret affair. I...*we* made love the afternoon she died, on a large open rock on Six Mile Creek, about a half-mile upstream from the bridge. I had been offered a football scholarship to Ryland University—a scholarship arranged by Rennie Poole, I later learned—and I hadn't told her. She was angry and ran off toward the water. She... she slipped, and fell, and hit her head. She was dead before I reached her."

Where it had been raucous seconds earlier, now the room was dead silent, drinking in Jude's revelation.

"I was horrified," Jude said, a sob breaking up the words. Tears began to stream down his cheeks. "I thought, as soon as people knew I had been sleeping with Coral, I'd catch the blame for her death. I'd lose the scholarship, the chance to play football again, an education, everything. It sounds strange now, but I was a teenager. I didn't know how to cope. I... I am ashamed to admit it, but I left Coral by the side of the creek. The next night, I watched my father and Rennie Poole hang Ev Howard for a crime I knew he hadn't committed, and I said nothing. I was more interested in protecting myself. I have no other excuse. I was frightened, and I was weak, and I did a terrible, terrible thing. I have had to live with this horrible secret for over two decades. No more secrets. No more." He grasped the sides of the lectern and looked toward the floor in shame.

"I'll have you in court for slander!" Poole shouted, standing again.

"The hell you will!" someone shouted in the crowd. Jude turned and saw Clyde Dillard stand from his front-row seat. The cameras swung in his direction.

"I was there, too," Clyde said to the audience. "Jude's father, Hubert Pressley, held a gun to my head and forced me to fetch rope from my hardware store. He made me watch as they strung that boy up. I saw every second of it. I'll swear to it on a stack of Bibles!"

"You're nothing but a drunk and a fool!" Rennie shouted. "Who'll believe you?"

"I still have the rope," Clyde said to him, ignoring the cameras. "I went back, after everyone left. I cut Ev Howard down, and I buried him. It was the only decent thing to do. I couldn't go to the sheriff. Hubert Pressley held a gun on me and swore he'd kill me if I told anyone. I saved the rope. It's at my house."

He looked directly into the cameras clustered around him and smoothed back the ten or twelve unruly strands of hair poking from his scalp.

"I can show the authorities where Ev Howard is buried."

Flashbulbs popped and reporters pelted Clyde Dillard with questions until someone on the front row yelled, "Look!" and pointed toward the stage.

CHAPTER FORTY-FIVE

Jude had collapsed at the podium and was writhing in convulsions on the floor.

Chapter Forty-Six

The last time anyone could remember a sophomore quarterback at Prosperity High School was when some guy named Jude Pressley did it in 1951, nearly four decades earlier. A plaque commemorating his accomplishments still hung in the trophy case outside the cafeteria. He'd played so long before the current Prosperity High students in 1989 were born, it was regarded as an ancient relic. Some students laughed at the picture next to the plaque, of seventeen-year-old Jude in his old-time uniform, his raven mop shaven into a flat-top, the bangs waxed into a dam of hair.

Prosperity High football was nothing to laugh at, Owen thought, as he sat in the bleachers and watched the 1989 team practice. It was a ritual handed from generation to generation in this town.

He'd handed it to his son, Judd. The boy was sixteen years old, a sophomore, and Prosperity's starting quarterback. He'd grown tall and strong, weather-tempered in the heat of the Carolina summers on the farm, muscles bursting from exertion in the fields behind the house his great-grandfather built in 1921. His dark hair and blue eyes and handsome features—so like his mother's—made him one of the most popular boys in school. He'd done Owen proud through the years.

Judd Wheeler took a snap, dropped back five paces, and launched a frozen rope twenty yards directly into the numbers of his best friend, Sean Burch. Burch turned, stiff-armed a safety who tried to bring him to ground, and sprinted toward the goalposts.

When Chloe had walked out of their lives, thirteen years earlier, Owen was lost. He couldn't imagine how he might tend his farm and be the primary caregiver for his toddler son. He'd managed. Friends had helped. With time he learned how to juggle the roles of both father and mother.

Owen couldn't count the times Chloe had promised to visit Judd and failed to show. On one especially pathetic occasion, Judd—only five years old—had waited in a lawn chair where the driveway met the Morgan Highway, all day long, in scorching heat, because Chloe had told him she'd take him out for lunch and a movie and some ice cream. Long after sunset, after trying to comfort the boy, and patiently listening to Judd's tearful exhortations that he hated his mother for abandoning him, and after his son fell into a fitful sleep, the tracks of tears still visible on his face, Owen had come within seconds of running out to find a bottle of Jack Daniels and a tall wide glass.

In times past, in moments of weakness, he'd always been able to call his sponsor, Clyde Dillard. By 1978, Clyde was gone. The years of hard drinking finally caught up with him. There was a fancy hyphenated medical name for the condition, but it boiled down to the fact that Clyde had pickled his brain beyond repair. Over the course of only a year or so, he slipped deeper and deeper into dementia. His last word, spoken six months before he finally succumbed, was, "*Mermaid.*"

He'd been famous for a while, after leading the state police to the grave where he'd buried Ev Howard in 1954. The fallout from Jude Pressley's public confession and Clyde's corroborating testimony was quick, brutal, and widespread.

A week after Larry Stilson admitted to working directly for Rennie Poole, and attempting to kill Jude Pressley, Sheriff Mattox resigned from office. Some people said he did it to absolve his sense of shame for turning a blind eye on the night Ev Howard was hanged. Others thought he quit as part of an immunity deal to testify against Rennie Poole.

Years of chicanery and conniving finally caught up with Congressman Poole. He was charged with money laundering, obstruction of justice, and a few dozen FEC violations. His attorneys soaked him for every penny he had but were only able to plead him down to a couple of counts of campaign violations, obstruction, and the biggie—civil rights violations. The final nail in the coffin was when young Hank Bowie appeared in court, took complete responsibility for providing the drugs that contributed to Sunday's demise, and detailed how Rennie had instructed him directly not to discuss his role in the death of Sunday Free—obvious obstruction of justice. His testimony made Rennie's conviction a slam dunk.

The state added a charge of murder, which eventually was reduced to manslaughter, the sentence to run consecutively after he was released from federal prison—a point in time Rennie was unlikely to ever see. A little over two years after the Nixon scandals, the courts were unsympathetic toward dirty politicians. Rennie was sentenced to twenty years with no possibility of parole. He'd tried to get into the Club Fed at Allenwood Penitentiary in Pennsylvania, where the inmates played tennis and painted and golfed their way through their sentences, but the judge would have none of it. He did real time in a real federal prison, where he remained in 1989.

Somewhere along the way, Rennie contracted a virus nobody had heard of in 1976, and it had eaten away at him. Every couple of years, the local paper would run a puff piece about its favorite incarcerated politician. The most recent article had portrayed the formerly muscular and robust man as haggard and balding, his body a star map of lesions, pockmarks of Kaposi's sarcoma ravaging his face. He was dying by degrees, a convenient target for any contagion making the rounds. He spent every day in his cell praying to pass quickly and painlessly and—Lord willing—as soon as possible.

Hank Bowie never was charged with any crime, nor were any of the youths who violated Sunday Free at the party. The District Attorney in Morgan who declined to prosecute them went down in defeat in the next election, largely due to a huge contingent of Bliss County's black population, organized by Reverend Angeloe Teeter, who voted him out. Hank quit football, to his father's consternation, and went to college on an academic scholarship, where he studied—of all things—pharmacy.

Owen hadn't heard from Jude Pressley since 1977. After the clot of blood pressing on his brain was evacuated, and after he provided state's evidence in Rennie Poole's trial, Jude simply vanished. Some people suggested he'd moved away, wracked by shame, to a distant reclusive life. Some imagined the remnants of Rennie's machine had caught him and finished the job Larry Stilson had started. Some thought Jude had gone into the witness protection program and was living under a new identity somewhere far away.

Owen didn't know. He tried not to think about it. He also tried not to think about how hard he'd hit Jude minutes before the rally, and how he'd nearly killed his dearest childhood friend.

When Arlo Pyle learned he'd actively participated in the murder of an innocent man, he sold the garage, retreated from life, and spent the next year staring at the television and drinking.

Jude's admission he'd been in an affair with Coral troubled Grace deeply. She resigned her position at the high school at the end of the next semester, citing distress and depression, and devoted herself to caring for Arlo until June 1977, on the twenty-third anniversary of the lynching. That night, Arlo drove to a secluded clearing in rural Prosperity, in the middle of which stood a gnarled ancient black walnut tree, and he hung himself from the stoutest branch, the same one on which Ev Howard died.

After Arlo killed himself, Grace also disappeared. The hopeless romantics among Prosperity's gossips maintained that—no longer responsible for her father—she'd finally joined Jude in exile, and they were living together somewhere, finally happy.

Owen hoped they were right.

Owen Wheeler was fifty-four years old. He'd kept his promise never to run for political office again. He'd become a deacon at the church, and there was talk he might be made treasurer when the calendar ticked over into the 1990s. The decades of outdoor life had bleached the sand from his hair, leaving only silver and gray. Liver spots battled for real estate on his face. The skin on his arms was like tanned rawhide. It had been thirty-five years since he and his high school buddies had huddled in a truck and tearfully watched Rennie and his Klan mob murder Ev Howard. The dreams still tortured him, but they were fewer and farther between. Jude had sacrificed himself on the altar of justice and had taken complete responsibility for Ev Howard's sorry fate on his own shoulders so artfully, nobody knew about

Owen's involvement. In his last public act—his parting gift to Owen—Jude shielded his best friend from taint and disgrace.

Owen mused on how many times he had been protected from his worst instincts. The MPs in Saigon, who prevented him from killing Thanh. Jude keeping his name a secret. There had to be a purpose in his life that had not yet been fulfilled.

Owen watched Judd on the field, and he knew what his purpose was. He had known for years. Jude had left behind one final parting gift.

Judd, so tall and strong and dark, took a snap and faded back. Almost instinctively, he sensed an encroaching tackle on his blind side, juked to his right, spun, danced around to buy time, and hurled the ball deep into the end zone where Sean Burch waited. In a real game, it would have been an easy six points.

Owen had seen the move before. It described something genetic, a gift of dexterity and nimble footwork and instinct that couldn't be taught. It was inborn, a talent that had eluded Owen entirely and consigned him to pounding the line as a running back. Watching Judd command the field took Owen back almost four decades when he'd watched Jude Pressley bop and boogie his way around the pocket, evade tackles, and grin on the way to his thirteen school records. Owen recognized in his son the same energy and remarkable field presence and he knew, beyond doubt, that Judd hadn't inherited his dark features and size and talent entirely from his mother.

"Damn you, Jude," Owen whispered for the thousandth time, even as he acknowledged the debt to his best friend that could never be repaid. Nobody would ever know. Regardless of the blood that flowed in his veins, Judd would forever be Owen's boy.

Thunderheads gathered in the August sky to the west. Owen watched hazy streaks of rain fall on fields a dozen miles away and calculated the direction and speed of the storm. He offered a prayer for the sustenance the rain would shortly bring to his farm. In the end, after all the loss and death and lies and corruption and revelations, the fertile land that had been in the Wheeler family since before the American Revolution was the only thing he and his beloved son could truly call their own.

That was enough. It would do.

About the Author

Richard Helms is a retired college professor and forensic psychologist. He has been nominated eight times for the SMFS Derringer Award, winning it twice; seven times for the Private Eye Writers of America Shamus Award, with a win in 2021; twice for the ITW Thriller Award, with one win; four times for the Killer Nashville Silver Falchion Award with one win: and once for the Mystery Readers International Macavity Award. He is a frequent contributor to *Ellery Queen's Mystery Magazine*, along with other periodicals and short story anthologies. His story "See Humble and Die" was included in Houghton-Mifflin-Harcourt's *Best American Mystery Stories 2020. A Kind and Savage Place* is his twenty-second novel. He would like to acknowledge the contributions of developmental editor Derek McFadden in the production of this manuscript. Mr. Helms is a former member of the Board of Directors of Mystery Writers of America, and the former president of the Southeast Regional Chapter of MWA. When not writing, Mr. Helms enjoys travel, gourmet cooking, simracing, rooting for his beloved Carolina Tar Heels and Carolina Panthers, and playing with his grandsons. Richard Helms and his wife Elaine live in Charlotte, North Carolina.

https://www.richardhelms.net

https://twitter.com/RickHelmsAuthor

www.ingramcontent.com/pod-product-compliance
Lightning Source LLC
Chambersburg PA
CBHW050523110726
47899CB00005B/1566